TAKING THE DRAWING-ROOM THROUGH CUSTOMS

SELECTED STORIES (1972-2002)

Acknowledgements are due to editors of the following where some of the stories in the earlier collections first appeared: *Ambit, BBC Radio 4, Bim* (Barbados), *The Caribbean Writer* (St. Croix), *Kunapipi* (Denmark), *London Magazine, New Writing 2* (The British Council/Vintage), *Oasis, Paris Transcontinental, The Trinidad & Tobago Review, Wasafiri, Worldview* (USA), *Writing Ulster.*

Place of publication or date of composition are appended to the stories in the 'Uncollected' section.

Grateful thanks to Trevor Coope whose practical editing of the text constituted part of his Literary Editing degree project at Sheffield Hallam University (2001-02).

TAKING THE DRAWING-ROOM THROUGH CUSTOMS

SELECTED STORIES (1972-2002)

E.A. MARKHAM

Dear Michael
I hope you like [illegible]
here. All the best
Archie
23/10/02

PEEPAL TREE

First published in Great Britain in 2002
Peepal Tree Press
17 King's Avenue
Leeds LS6 1QS
England

ISBN 1 900715 69 4

CONTENTS

1: New and Uncollected

2: from *Ten Stories* (1992)

1: NEW AND UNCOLLECTED

A SHORT HISTORY OF EMPLOYMENT IN BRITAIN (A STORY)

i

It was the first day at the factory, but the word factory was not used. And these places, really, were not factories: they made ladies' belts, they made hand-bags, they made assorted buttons and buckles in leather and suede; and often no one place made all of these things. They were situated here and there in upstairs rooms, two rooms, three rooms, in Great Portland Street, and the side streets around. All over that part of London, in fact, including Soho. Pewter had worked in one in Baker Street, further away; though that was more factory-like, being on the ground floor, and employing more people than the others: that one hinted at those places in the East End, around Aldgate and Old Street where you had rows and rows of women lined up behind their machines, half-drunk cups of tea here and there; women singing along to the radio, *Workers' Playtime,* or laughing with the comic relief, Ken Dodd and that woman who was big then – late '50s-early '60s – Gladys Morgan, with a Welsh accent. Pewter didn't mind at all coming back here in the holidays; everybody knew he was a student. But, that wouldn't be the same for his mother.

How to dress for the job: she wasn't going to church, she was going to work in a workshop where they made ladies' belts and buckles and buttons in leather and suede and material, meaning cloth. She would make him late, but Pewter had planned for that. As they started out from Ladbroke Grove to Great Portland Street his mother's flowered dress, hat and handbag gave Pewter the sensation of setting out for church. But Pewter didn't really mind that. He was secretly proud that his mother hadn't succumbed to the utility-type uniform, grey on grey on grey that characterised, in his mind, the factory-worker.

On the way there, luckily, they didn't need to change trains, six stops: so if it worked out, she shouldn't have problems doing the journey on her own. Pewter reiterated the dos and don'ts in this type of set up.

In the belt-place, everyone would be friendly but not always in a way she would understand. They already knew all about her, her place in society at home, her big house in Coderington, her other splendid house in town where the headmaster lived, her servants; though they probably didn't believe it all, so no need to go on about it again in case people thought she was boasting; and remember, the people she would be working with were not ashamed to be working-class. Also, a couple of them smoked, and that would be unpleasant, and sometimes they did it in the loo; but you couldn't really tell people what to do in their own place. And in any case they didn't overdo the smoking at Spencer's because with glue and stuff like that all around – inflammable stuff – they were a little bit careful. His solution for the tea was not to have sugar. Remember, this was England and they were always making tea and coffee; so when they made the tea just take it without sugar. Because the jar with the sugar was usually left open with its top off; and what with the dust from the belts and the place, generally, settling on the top of the jar, she wouldn't want to have the sugar. Best not to offend them and point it out, just drink her tea without the sugar. What else? She could have his *Manchester Guardian* to read during the tea-break, and the lunch-hour:

much better than to have taken the Bible into the workplace and draw attention to yourself, etc.

As they got off the train at Great Portland Street Pewter's mother reminded him that she didn't like drinking tea without sugar.

He would be working at the other branch of Spencer's, Rathbone Mews, off Charlotte Street, and a bit of a walk from Great Portland Street; but he wanted to see her settled in and to buy her some sandwiches at the little café opposite the hospital; tomorrow, she could bring her prepared chicken, as promised: Pewter's mother would have preferred something hot for lunch – a taste that Pewter inherited – but *she* reassured him that they weren't at home now, and they had to make sacrifices.

ii

She answered to Christine though she would have preferred to be called Mrs. Stapleton. Obviously, she wasn't stupid, she didn't expect them to call her Miss Christine, those days were over. They wanted to know if she could sew the belts; she said yes. Was she a machinist? Well, she wasn't going to say yes to that in case that was a new word for seamstress. A seamstress was someone you employed at home to make your dresses, like Edith, or the boys' clothes, like Croggins, though as a man you called him a tailor. So no, she wasn't like Edith or Croggins, so she wasn't a machinist. But she could sew the belts, particularly after this man whom she didn't trust, in a brown coat, showed her how to sew the edge of the belt. And after that the woman, who brought her a cup of tea and put sugar in it, showed her, again, how to sew the edge of the belt. She didn't want to criticise the way they were doing things, but she didn't understand why they weren't using the right colour thread

– they called it cotton, she must remember that, though cotton was cloth, as far as she was concerned, not thread – anyway, they were using the wrong colour thread to sew the belts.

And then half-way through the morning they took her off that and put her on sticking the little bits of suede and leather onto the metal frame to make the buckle. It was a hard job because you needed piano-playing fingers for that, and the whole bench got sticky and everything stuck to everything, and to your fingers; and even when you got the thing to stick exactly to the frame, then everything was covered with glue which was difficult to rub off, particularly on the suede; and sometimes it was just easier to take the whole thing off and start all over again. Except, here was this man again, in the brown coat, telling her she didn't have piano-playing fingers, as if he knew that she had never learnt, really, to play the piano, even though she had had lessons; and she had to tell him that she had left a nearly brand-new piano at home in her house in Coderington, and Teacher Kitty came over twice a week to dust it in her absence. Then it was the older man, the partner, who came over from the bench where he was cutting out the leather into shapes for belts, came over and said that suede was expensive and she was wasting it; and they couldn't afford to throw away so much suede: she just didn't like the way he said that. But then of course you couldn't answer them back because they didn't know where you came from and thought you didn't know any better.

When she went to the wash-basin next door to the loo she was shocked at the smell coming from the loo; and she wondered why they didn't have someone to clean the place: was it safe to drink the cup of tea the woman made her, sugar or no sugar, because the water came from this very pipe – they might call it a new name, they might try to confuse you and call it a tap, but what she knew was that the water for her tea came from this very pipe – with the smell coming next door from the loo? She didn't have to follow Pewter in everything and drink the tea; he might be living his own life now in some far-away part of Wales, at university, but Pewter wasn't above some of this English nastiness; and no one was going to make her indulge in nastiness just to please some people, particularly the likes of that man in the brown coat.

After the buckles they put her on another job, which she believed was to test her eyesight; and then soon it was lunch-time. If she hadn't arranged for Pewter to come after five o'clock so they could go home together, she would have gone home then, because the way they put her on three different jobs in the morning meant they just weren't happy with anything she did; and she just wasn't happy about the way she was being treated.

'All right, Mrs Stapleton?'

Ah, so they knew her name.

'All right?'

That was the boss, the youngish one, Spencer, not the older one who had told her that suede was expensive. He came out of his little box-room, in his white coat, came over to her bench eating his sandwich; and his hands weren't clean: she was certain he hadn't washed them before taking out his sandwich; but he wasn't her family, she wasn't responsible for him. At least he had the manners to address her by her name.

Yes, she was all right.

'Yes, thank you. I'm all right.'

'You haven't done this job before, I think.'

'Oh no. I don't do this type of work. I never work for people.'

'Thing is, do you think you will like it here?'

'You have to do something; you can't just not do something.'

'You're not used to this, though.'

'No, I have people to... We all have to try.'

Then they talked a bit about where she came from and what she was used to; and he took her into his confidence and admitted that he, too, was a refugee, though from another part of Europe. (Pewter had already told her that Mr. Spencer was a fifteen-year-old boy when he had had to leave his place because of persecution.) So she had to tell him that *she* wasn't a refugee, she came here of her own free will; she could have gone to Canada or America where she had family; but she thought England was best for the children, for their education. And they talked about Pewter and his education.

That's when the man suggested that after lunch she have a go at putting some eyelets into the belts, using the eyeletting machine.

She thanked him, of course, because she knew her manners: they were determined that she would never settle into any one job.

iii

The boredom of it: how did anybody get through a day like today. When they spoke to her she still missed half of what they said, what with the radio going and one of the machines making a noise, though that machine wasn't used too much. They liked to make out it was her hearing that was the problem; and when she spoke it was her accent. Well, she had perfect hearing, as everybody knew, and her accent was one that people praised, including parson Ryan from Ireland, who said it sounded a bit like his own. The entire family were known to speak the best English not just in Coderington, but in town. Even the servants in the house spoke good English when they had to. And better than some of the language she heard on the streets here, or in the shops. That man who had come to the house to fix the geyser, the plumber, had made a point of telling her how well she spoke English; and here you had people, two of them not even English, coming from somewhere where they weren't wanted, telling her there was something wrong with her hearing or with her accent. But she didn't come here to have a row; she just wouldn't talk to them when she didn't have to. She would concentrate to last out till just after five.

When Pewter came – half an hour early – he sensed immediately that something was wrong. These were OK people, he'd worked with them for about a year before his GCEs, and then during the summer break last year and the year before. He liked to think his relationship with the partners transcended a master-worker one. He had always been able to have an intelligent conversation, a joke, with both of them; and that extended to a visit to the theatre. Last Christmas, Spencer decided to take everybody to see *My Fair Lady* – including Pewter who wasn't even working at the belt-factory, but at the Post Office; and over dinner at the Strand Palace Hotel, he remembered having a very satisfying discussion of the original Shaw play. So, all in all, he didn't think they would insult his mother. They tried to pull rank, of course: what was the point of going to university to read novels or even poetry when every educated person did that in his spare time. So Pewter had to stress his interest in, say, Chaucer, his growing familiarity with Anglo-Saxon, to put some distance between himself and his ex-employers. He was in luck, anyway, because his second subject was Philosophy; and that impressed the partners more. They tried to catch him out with questions on cosmology and astronomy. Or, at the other end of the scale, on how to resolve ethical dilemmas – should Hitler's mother have strangled him at birth, sort of thing. He had always hinted that discussions on literature and, if not exactly on philosophy, at least theology were part of his environment at home, his grandmother's house, therefore his mother's home: with that background they couldn't possibly make vulgar assumptions about his mother.

So, what was wrong: where was his mother?

They didn't know, but her bag was here, her handbag was here and her sandwiches remained uneaten.

What happened? If her bag was here, she couldn't have gone home; she wouldn't have had money for the fare.

The old man was at his table cutting into a skin of leather with a Stanley knife, and the woman went off to start sweeping up. Spencer motioned Pewter to the dustbin, took out a pile of belts, in material, and displayed them, the eyelets looking wrong to him, but that wasn't Pewter's concern.

What did his mother say? Before she left: did she say where she was going?

Apparently, she had just walked out, saying nothing.

Pewter took the handbag, started to say something to Spencer, but shrugged and left the workshop.

Outside Pewter turned right and at the corner of Mortimer Street, turned right again, along the front of the hospital (might as well keep going) across Berners Street and up to Tottenham Court Road. Now what? Back again on the other side of the road. It was his fault that his mother had got into this; others in the house didn't want her to humiliate herself in this way, working in what was, not to put too fine a point on it, a factory. He had said that this was better than being alone in the house all day: what he privately felt was that it was important for someone barely into middle age, to get out and learn a skill, any skill rather than vegetate and brood over what was lost, what was left behind. He would be blamed for this. But he tried not to panic. And then he saw her.

As he turned back, left, into Great Portland Street there

she was approaching him from the other end, her hat on.

What's the matter, where had she been?

Was it after five? He had said he'd be there after five, so she had tried to get back by five; she'd been for a walk. Now they could go home.

But they couldn't just go home without saying something to Spencer.

All right; if he liked.

He knew this mood of his mother's; it was a quiet intransigence, like a mask coming down over the face; but what upset him was that she had clearly been crying. He had witnessed this maybe only two or three times in his life, once at his grandmother's funeral in St. Anne's, at the graveside. And then on the boat, the row-boat in Barville harbour to take them to the ship to England. Pewter couldn't deal with his mother crying so he had convinced himself on the row-boat, that it was fear of water that did it. The boat was lying so low in the water, so over-loaded, that the edge was only two or three inches above the sea, and he, too, feared they might drown right there in the harbour, before getting on the boat for England. She hadn't cried, as far as he remembered, on the three-week voyage – only being endlessly sick – so he preferred to think that the crying had been brought on by a fear of small boats. But this was different.

When they came in, Spencer approached in his unbuttoned white coat, and seemed anxious to say something but Pewter's mother walked straight past and went to the loo, while both men stood awkwardly, trying not to accuse each other. Spencer went again to the pile of belts on the eyeletting counter, gave up and retreated into his little cubby-hole office.

Pewter went over to take a look at what had obviously caused the problem: his eyes fell on the mushroom eyelets, which didn't seem right; but mushroom was notoriously difficult because there were so many shades and they were all mixed up in the boxes, and you had to be experienced to get the right balance of shade along the five eyelets. They shouldn't have put his mother on this so soon.

'It stink in there, eh?' Pewter's mother said, emerging from the loo, and, seeing the bundle of belts, she went to the eyeletting counter.

Inside the little cubby-hole, Spencer was on the phone; you could hear him as the walls didn't go all the way up to the ceiling. Pewter sort of understood this way of pretending that everything was normal. But the voice that his mother heard coming from the cubicle was the one that had abused her earlier, the man in the white coat standing over her at the eyeletting counter not listening as she explained that the machine had been stiff to operate with the foot-pedal, and needed oiling to stop the squeaking. And the man in the brown coat had oiled the machine, but not put enough oil on. He had left the oil-can on the counter, so she had oiled the machine again. She couldn't help it that a little bit of oil had got onto the belts. But he didn't want to hear reason, and he called her useless. No one had ever called her useless in her life; and even if this man wasn't English but came from wherever he came from he was a big man now and should have some manners; he should be taught manners.

The other woman, having swept up the workshop, was distracting Pewter on the other side of the room, explaining something. At which point Pewter's mother came over to join them. She had the bundle of belts, and held up one for special inspection. Pewter didn't like the look on her face.

'Can you see any oil on this belt?' she demanded.

(*Moving Worlds*, No. 1, 2001)

THE GOOD-LOOKING GUY WITH THE GLASS

Why you all get taken in by this Harriet?

We weren't taken in by Harriet, we just liked her style. Not that there was anything flashy about Harriet, that's the point; her style was sparse, minimal, which suggested, if anything, the general move away from clutter, from refugeeness: *Not that we're accusing anyone we know of being a refugee.* And since she had only one sister, and that didn't suggest a childhood surrounded by chaos and noise, kids screaming all over the place, competing for the parents' attention, Harriet's style wasn't that easy to explain. *Her parents' attention?*

- What parents? My sister asked.

- OK. The mother. For the mother's attention. (For the father, like a father, was often away from home.)

But Harriet was usually quick to point out that the father didn't spend any more time away from home than other fathers did; only in this case the dad organised it in, well... in blocks of time, whereas even now, here in these countries too, the father managed to disguise being out of the house most of the hours of daylight, leaving for work and coming home from work at the start or the end of the day. Even at weekends he avoided time with the family, by heading for the pub or betting shop. Or hi-jacking the sitting-room for the worship of football, to be indulged by others in the house who didn't believe in that religion. It was almost better, as in the old days, to see the lord and master prostrate on his back at Sunday worship, in the street outside, gazing up into the mysteries of the motor-car.

Not that she was defending the dad in pointing out these things; it was her sister, who hadn't come to England, who was in the habit of defending the dad; Harriet herself was quite relaxed about friends who had a different view about these things; she didn't need to show people evidence of her life.

And whereas I could see the advantages of growing up in a household where there was no Big Daddy to boss you about, and hog the bathroom just when you needed it, and be served the best pieces of meat at table, and have the right to beat up your mother – not that this happened to us as my father wasn't at home either; but it happened to some of my friends, and it happened in the newspapers and on television – I still felt that Harriet went a little far, in her flat one night, when she pointed to something that had captured the attention of one of her guests, and revealed that the 'good-looking guy with the glass', was her father. And that, yes, he could serve as a sort of role-model for others less fortunate. The fellow was stuck up on the mantle-piece, in a small frame, and looked suspicious.

To start with he seemed a bit young for her dad. Or, perhaps, a bit more groomed than you would have imagined. *So her fastidiousness was inherited!* Though, one had to be careful: the dad on view was the pretty-boy type that was easy to brand as irresponsible; he had neatly-combed and parted hair, and the bottom row of teeth showed through the smile, all in good order. Other things came through to alert you to something posed – that general air of ease and leisure and relaxation that the picture suggested. The soft, white shirt was expensive, one sleeve loosely folded to the elbow revealing a chain, a loose bracelet, well down on the arm, nearer elbow than wrist, casually right; and the hand held a glass of white wine.

That was not the picture of any old dad we knew. Dads were stiffer than that, the way they held themselves. Even when their bodies were loose, they were still stiffer than that – particularly in those early photos taken away from home. Usually, dads wore some sort of uniform; an army uniform, or a uniform with a dog collar. Those of the distant past, who went to places like Aruba and Curaçao to work in the oil refineries, or to America to places like Detroit to build motorcars – all looked as if they were in uniform, posing beside huge bits of machinery or factory architecture. There was even a famous photo of Pascoe's uncle standing in some hush hush place in front of an aeroplane that he and his mates had built.

But this picture of Harriet's dad was different; it exuded relaxation and a lack of tension that you had to call class: *Why was the chain on the man's arm so neat and unflashy? Why was the drink in the glass white wine? Why was the white wine in such a long-stemmed glass?* Why did it all fit so neatly Harriet's dream of an understated flat?

My sister, who wasn't a particular friend of Harriet's, pointed out that that was not the picture of a man who cared for his family. That picture was one of *personal* preening and *solo* well-being: for a man to strike that sort of pose abroad, it meant only one thing, that he wasn't missing the family; that he was having a good time, thank you very much, away from all that mess and responsibility of women and children – a good time shared with others who may well have been cut out of this picture for a purpose. This picture was clearly a *detail* sent back to placate those left behind. Or worse.

There were rougher types from the islands, that we all knew, whose photos caused us less of a problem. These crude fellows from the country would all make sure they ended up living in the capital city abroad, as if that conferred a sort of legitimacy. One of those fellows – to come back to Harriet's picture – would have taken a little bit of the gold from the chain on his arm and put it into his mouth; he would have got someone to coat his teeth with it. Just one tooth, perhaps. To show style. And of course the drink, the drink in the hand would not be white wine.

That night in question, when the guests had gone, Harriet resolved to write to the dad: 'I am very well and happy'. That's how she would start the letter.

In Canada, Harriet's dad was thinking about Harriet. He loved her, of course; and knew she would do well in her studies: she had taken after him; she would not throw away her advantages. Though the mother spoilt her, the child would survive that, and sometimes it was no bad thing to err on the lenient side, particularly when the environment in which you found yourself was one where no one knew your value. So the girl was headstrong and wanted to go her own way: that must cost her some. She had every right to expect credit for the *style* she maintained, scorning all that climate of *accommodation* around her. A dad would be right for her now.

And yes; at a certain time in life, a man must choose to be responsible. A man was not whole, not complete without the family around him: family scattered all over the place made no sense any more. That made sense only if it was done to some strategic purpose. But there were no countries in the world named after him; there was nothing, even playfully stupid, named after him. So present policy wasn't working. If his family had branched out he could hardly lay claim now to being that steady *tree* people talked about. Unless he started grafting those branches back onto the old trunk. But then again, he could leave things as they were.

His life wasn't that bad; his life was pretty good. Nothing was in crisis. And where would she be, exactly; his missing limb? How was she to be addressed now she was no longer a child and in need? What name would she be accustomed to answering to?

Some years later, in a restaurant in Stoke Newington Harriet was thinking how unfair it was of a couple of her friends to question the account of the break-in at her flat: the entire world had gone into police-mode thinking that evidence had to 'add up', that reports of an incident had to be consistent. Then she looked up from her vegetarian fajitas and saw him. There was no mistaking this time. Nor would she miss her moment. She reached for the handbag and snapped it open. There was no haste. She clutched the cold handle of something she hoped wouldn't let her down.

(*Enter Text*, 2.1, 2002)

PASCOE & CO.

Part One

i

I quite liked Jenny, and found her refreshingly forthright, as they say, on the occasions I met her; but then I didn't have to live with her. When Pascoe referred to her as 'doctrinaire' and 'a Christian fundamentalist', I recognised that as the privilege of a partner, a husband who might even be patronising me a little, in betraying a confidence he wouldn't risk with someone closer. So I was careful – in public, at any rate – not to take sides. Anyway, Jenny's character isn't the issue here. Though I have to admit that what crosses my mind is that image you get when reading those old Russian novels, you know, strangers sharing a carriage from the country to Moscow. Or from Moscow to Petersburg. Then the literary trek, meandering the history back, each member connected to family, clan, like retracing the tributary of a river, till you end up with floodwater the like of which only a continent (or a Tolstoy) can produce. Well, I'm not going to use Jenny to speculate on her first meeting with Pascoe and then track back through their first marriages to families on opposite sides of some divide or other, brought (by destiny) together. It's just that when you finally agree that you're not the centre of the universe, the stories you tell can't all be centred on yourself; and Jenny seemed a good enough lead in. But what I'm recording here is essentially three men getting together to watch a cricket match, without their wives and partners. (The third man was Eric, and I have to say, for what it's worth, that his wife was a beautiful woman.)

The point about Jenny was that Pascoe rang last night pretending to call it off. Though that was bluff: he just wanted me to know that in order to come up here to go on to Manchester he had to stand up to, slap down, face down – whatever it is they did in their house – the fundamentalist objection to a man having his day out with the boys. Naturally he was coming, and would stay over, in case West Indies didn't contrive to lose the Test in one day, as you never knew what new trick the boys would pull this time. You know, Pewter, he said, Men of our age had to be 'authors of ourselves' and assert our right to do our thing, even though it wasn't so much our thing any more, and, true, we had lost the war, and the battles leading up to the war, but why was that a bad position to be in, from which to negotiate. (At least he didn't say: '...to negotiate the terms of the surrender.') No, Pascoe hadn't lost it.

Oh, we talked about the vulgarity of the times, the banality of our masters; and for a minute or two applied our minds to sorting out a few of the so-called crisis spots that seemed to be confusing other people, places like Northern Ireland and the Middle East. And Saddam and Marathon. Drugs barons in the Caribbean (though why call these fellows barons, why abuse language) and paedophiles named and shamed by the *News of the World* and having their look-a-likes beaten up and their houses torn apart. All that. Though, maybe talking of Saddam and Marathon might be confusing for some; so maybe it was better to fall into line with the old history books and refer instead to *Darius* and Marathon. But what the hell – give the people the vote. At some point I remembered to ask Pascoe if his son, Franklyn, who was an actor, had graduated to playing the lead in *Coriolanus* yet; and Pascoe said, careful, that was a low-grade, working-class kind of question; to be expected of someone working in one of these new-fangled universities; so I apologised for letting the side down; and then we got serious and turned the conversation back to cricket. As Pascoe said, it's not as if we were proposing to go and spend time in some whorehouse in Manchester. Or in a pub or betting-shop.

The mention of the betting-shop was deliberate because that was a sore point between him and Jenny. But it was just Pascoe's signal to me, not so much that he was toughing it out – after all Jenny wasn't the sort of woman who would really make a fuss about her husband going up to Manchester to watch West Indies play cricket, because she, too, wanted them to win – but that he wasn't sliding into retirement and domestic armchair cosiness.

The betting thing might be worth another mention: Pascoe had irritated Jenny by talking her out of putting a one-pound bet on the National Lottery one Saturday. Jenny wasn't a gambler, but occasionally had the urge, which Pascoe interpreted as being almost religious and bad for your health. So he had talked some rationality into her, using arguments first of psychology, then of probability and finally of philosophy. The result: he deprived her of between £160,000 and £225,000 depending on how her four numbers would have affected the shareout. Jenny could be consoled for losing out on the money she hadn't earned; she might even have been slightly relieved when she reminded herself of the religious arguments against gambling and money-lending and Christ in the Temple, and all that sort of thing. What she couldn't forgive that fool of a husband for, that jackarse who thought he was so clever and who still had some whore in wherever-it-was running rings round him – what made her mad was his way of talking down to her as if she was some bitch he'd just picked up off the back streets of Sweden, or worse. And he was doing it on purpose; he was only doing it because he still wanted to patronise black people.

I was visiting them in Torquay some time after the lottery event, and this was the scene; it still clearly rankled.

Pascoe was lighter-skinned than Jenny, and he refused to rise to the bait.

But Jenny was not mollified: 'If you're a black woman you get it every which way,' she said. 'You're put on this earth for punishment. And the ones punishing you are them that have you trapped and cornered in the house.'

Pascoe made a silent signal to me to say something, so I put my arm round Jenny and after a few grunts and noises, risked a blackwoman joke.

She sucked her teeth and freed herself, but it worked. And after a pause she said, in a voice that wasn't at all hostile: 'What you know 'bout black woman? What any of all you know about black woman?' And her shrug out of my arm hadn't been that unfriendly; and that was the signal that all was going to be OK.

Last night Pascoe was saying on the phone that the wife was accusing him of being in love with another woman, and did the fancy woman know that he had false teeth he had to take out in the night?

False teeth?

That's the sort of foolishness you have to put up with in this damned house. But, fortunately, as you know, Pewter, I'm not a violent man.

So what's this about?

Oh, some woman on the television. Rubbish.

(Oh, so it wasn't serious.)

So, who's this fancy woman on the television?

Oh, some programme, late night programme.

Ah.

No, man, none of that foolishness. Woman come on and

talk a lot of sense, one of those talk programmes, discussion programme. With some religious arse going on about God. Woman talk a lot of sense. Intelligent. Looking good, too.

Ah.

Then Pascoe switched subject, and asked if it was safe to come up to Sheffield ('I ain't have inoculation and thing, y'know.') because he remembered that I'd come down with food-poisoning because of something I ate or drank in Sheffield; and had the city got it together to import a fridge yet, which was where normal people kept their food, before it went off and poisoned you.

So I warned him that on no account should he risk setting foot in Sheffield, because though we had a fridge now, we hadn't got used to it; so he should just fly straight to Manchester if they had an airfield in his part of the world from which to fly.

You'd have thought she'd ease up on this kind of foolishness, by now, he said, returning to the wife. (So maybe there was something in it.)

There's a woman on the television I quite fancy myself, I said.

And is only because she's a blonde woman, that's all it is.

Ah.

And why should a woman be blamed and harassed because she's a blonde woman?

ii

Pascoe was the first one of us, really, from St. Caesare, to set out to find his roots, and the light-skinned boy with a Cornish name, *just* missed landing in Cornwall, and ended up over the border into Devon. Not that he accomplished *that* easily; it took him a couple of decades and several attempts at navigation, with diversions first to the middle of

Wales and then to Scandinavia, where he still had a wife and daughter living. I, for my sins, followed him to Wales, in the early '60s, that was.

Our families weren't close, particularly. To us Pascoe was just the son, really, who would inherit the shop on Constitution & Liberty which said *D.O. Pascoe & Son, Ltd.* In reality, the first *Son* was Pascoe's father, who went off to fight Hitler and all that. Of course *my* father also fought Hitler and must have got closer than Pascoe's father, because my father never came back. Anyway, they said the reason Pascoe *père* returned from the war more Cornish than British was that too many black *black* people from the islands were now claiming extra *Britishness* on top of being British anyway because of the colonial thing, *Britishness* on account of themselves having defeated Hitler. (It was only some foolish people in England, after the war, who thought that Hitler was still alive.) Well, no wonder light-skinned fellows like Pascoe were beginning to find it a little crowded – all this Britishness around them.

So by the time I went to Grammar School over in Montserrat with young Pascoe, he was a *Cornish* nationalist, and planning to go back to his root. No one on the island at that time was talking of going back to Africa. And we'd never even *heard* the word *negritude.* And then I came to England and lost touch a bit. But I'm sure everyone who knows me has heard this story. So maybe now I think of it, I'll give Eric a ring, because he's coming up for the match, too, coming up from London. Eric generally puts me in a better frame of mind than Pascoe, even though they both gave me a hard time. But it was less stressful with Eric. Eric's wife gave me a hard time and that kept Eric slightly on the defensive. Eric's wife was a ridiculously good-looking woman, Persian; and when a woman like that thinks you're a really bad influence on her husband, well, as the book says, she's practically on her way to making love to you.

Eric was serious *also,* because he had a daughter who was a scientist and hence capable of blowing up the world. We'd offered the child half a dozen Caribbean islands to experiment with, and when St. Caesare went up in flames about five years ago, three or four of us sent a card to Cambridge congratulating her, and urging her not to lose nerve now: we volunteered to leave town in a year's time and hang out in some far-away sleepy place in Northern Canada or Patagonia so she could have her wide choice of land to erupt for her finals. The beautiful Maryam (her mother) called us *young,* when she heard of the card. I didn't think the remark significant, particularly; but when Eric elaborated – with some relish – and said that his wife had referred to me as genetically modified, you couldn't help reading between the lines: a beautiful woman, a heavy metaphor. Dangerous-sounding. Nice.

So what did Eric and I talk about? (Eric's daughter was living in Manchester doing research in chemistry, the sort of thing we didn't understand when we had it explained to us; so Eric would be coming up anyway, for the match.) What did we talk about? Oh, yes, the cricket. But then, what's there to say about cricket that we hadn't said? If we were young men we'd start supporting the opposition. But too late now to play the bad guy. And what with the world collapsing and students no longer interested in reading *Kalidasha* or Ortega y Gassett, or wanting to know how you interpreted old Clovis's Salic law to ensure that women inherited the kingdom of France – Ah, faced with that sort of thing, that sort of resistance to learning, what was left to do but save yourself, your few friends and the special people whom you could co-opt into your family.

What did we talk about? Oh, we talked a bit about how the West Indian fast bowlers could exploit their *names* to psyche out the opposition. Curtley Ambrose had done the trick as Curtley; but if he should suddenly come back at Manchester, not as old Curtley, but – using his middle names – as 'Elconn' and 'Lynwall', he was bound to confuse the English boys who, Atherton apart and maybe Hussain, wouldn't have had too rigorous an education. Except that our team probably wasn't much better prepared, mentally.

And, you know, I said to Eric, or he said to me: Say what you like about fellows like old Pascoe, they weren't the worst to have come out to bat for you, in a manner of speaking.

iii

Pascoe didn't win the Island Scholarship, even with special coaching. I'm not making a point about this, we all had special coaching, and I certainly wouldn't have won it, had I been on the island at the time. Scholarship boys (and the odd girl) usually went to Oxford, Cambridge and London (London *University,* not the new places in London that have set themselves up as universities). Either that or to Trinity College in Ireland, if you wanted to do medicine. So where was this Cornish nationalist to go? There was a little university at Exeter, which was, it seemed, the nearest university to Cornwall. (Exeter was in Devon, another county – wasn't that where Walter Raleigh came from? Never mind.) Exeter didn't have the ring of Oxford or Cambridge or London. Or Trinity College, Dublin. So. So Pascoe, *Son.* Or Pascoe *fils*, decided to be bold *and cross the border into Wales* – (Fluellen country. Owen Glendower) and ended up at Lampeter. I lived in London and had never heard of it. When I consulted Mrs Yetten, my English mistress who had a little beard, and who was giving me a hard time over Jane Austen because I'd written a rather sharp piece on *Emma,* Yetten said, Yes, there was a college at Lampeter, but they taught mainly Theology, and turned out young men for the priesthood: the idea of Pascoe as a priest reading the psalms backwards had some appeal. In my first year at the university I did some sketches for the review with a Pascoe-figure rendering bits of Paul's Letter to the Ephesians in a rough form of nation language, and put it in for the *Eisteddfod,* and won third prize. He ended up, did Pascoe, with a degree in Philosophy & Cornish, the Cornish bit specially designed for him. *Ah. The days.* Now (with whatever it was they taught in Cornish, and his Plato and Wittgenstein and Kant) he was ready to take over the shop in St. Caesare, ahead of his big sister, Rosie.

★

Pascoe came up on the Wednesday. Eric was going straight to Manchester where we'd meet him outside the gate to STAND C on the Thursday morning: I didn't want to risk putting the tickets in the post.

Over dinner in the Chinese restaurant where I took most of my guests who visited, Pascoe and I talked about not so much old times, as *other* times.

Old times would be about the wife, or the wife before the wife or the business of not going back to be the *Son* of *D.O. Pascoe & Son, Ltd.* Dining out with someone else and talking about Pascoe, that would have been OK; but you couldn't expect Pascoe to find his own story funny.

For even in the old days the *& Son* thing had bothered him, maybe not in St. Caesare days, but in Lampeter days. The wiping out of the big sister was one thing we discussed in, when? '62, or some such time, which is part of our claim to be feminists out there before the feminists. And we used to say to the girls, the women: It's because we men had been out there burning our bras for years, that our breasts have now taken the hint and contracted.

Anyway, apart from big sister, Rosie, to wipe out the

other sisters – all the possible sisters: *Kant, yes?* – was a pretty fundamental thing to contemplate when you were at university reading a certain type of philosophy. But there were other things that must have started to get to Pascoe by that time and he tested them on me – I was in my first year working through *The Republic* and Aristotle and struggling with Anglo-Saxon, so I was up for *debate.* What if Pascoe wasn't the only son? Well, he was and he wasn't. It was true that where the business in St. Caesare was concerned he was the only *Son,* in terms of inheritance; but where the father was inclined there was known to be one, maybe two other sons, though they didn't live in Barville, and they didn't use the family name. So Pascoe came right out with it and said: he didn't mind them re-branding the name of the shop. Either *D.O. Pascoe & Sons, Ltd.* Or better still, *D.O. Pascoe & Daughters,* to redress the gender thing. Now that was a pretty radical thing for a boy like Pascoe to be saying in nineteen sixty-two or three. So I've always had a lot of time for Pascoe.

What we talked about in the Chinese restaurant wasn't that stuff, but these crazy American dads, the Sports Czars, domestic equivalents of, you name them, those fellows in history who leave the place a wreck and make tragedy seem possible to write about. We were talking about the dad behind the tennis-playing Williams sisters. And the extraordinary dad behind soon-to-be-billionaire Tiger Woods. And this other strange *strange* man who was Ronald Reagan's favourite black man, forget his name now, Principal of an inner-city school on the West coast, who was sending all these daughters and nieces to the Sydney Olympics: was this frightening; was this totalitarian Plato in action, or was this just something *big,* bigger than our little inheritance of St. Caesare gave us the means to comprehend! *Should we all have been born in America and have done with it.*

Though it was on my mind I was careful not to mention

Coriolanus again, though I'd seen Franklyn in the play a few years back, at that little theatre in Kentish Town. I forget his stage name, vaguely Russian sounding; I should have looked it up before this meeting; that put me on the defensive, slightly. I recall young Pascoe, looking vaguely dark, playing one of the Volscians, the SECOND VOLSCIAN, I seem to remember – that, after playing a ROMAN CITIZEN and looking suitably Italian. I took careful note, because I was expected to be an ally, quoted by the dad when, later, Pascoe and Jenny argued about it. For my sins I'd been in the theatre, semi-professionally, since the late '60s, and had written about it; and of course, my present job kept me more or less interested. So people expected me to be informed.

What do you say in defence: that you were glad the boy was playing a Volscian and *also* a Roman, a sort of political balancing act which, these being two minor parts, shifted the discussion from his stature as an *actor* to the *politics* of which side – Roman or Volscian – he'd made seem more credibly human. I noted that at least in this production the Volscians were rather better dressed than the Romans. Though the Roman Citizens seemed to speak the verse a little more clearly (Racism: *Even our lad seemed to enunciate a little bit more clearly as a Roman.* Or was it in the writing, the easier-to-say arrangement of vowel and consonant in the Roman parts?) These are things that Pascoe would insist on discussing. Or he might want to keep it general: in the spirit of Third World solidarity, sort of thing, would you want your lad to aspire to playing Aufidius rather than Coriolanus. Not even because the Roman fellow was an out-and-out fascist with little capacity for reflection – *Odd that, in Shakespeare* – and was vengeful, and suspect in the way he feared his mother and ignored his wife – though pride and hatred of the people are natural enough – no, but that a man with roots in the Third World couldn't possibly support a Roman against a

Volscian. *Though Aufidius was a bastard. Duplicitous. Anancyman.* Not easy. *God, Shakespeare was a bastard.*

So, in the restaurant, I wasn't going to draw attention back to all that, and to the likelihood that young Pascoe hadn't graduated to playing either Aufidius or Coriolanus. Or to the fact that the book on Shakespeare I was working on at that time – my self-imposed creative therapy project of Shakespeare invisibilising all those wives, not just Coriolanus's but the sad woman married to Antony, forget her name, in the other Roman play, Octavia – never got finished. *Too close to home, too damn close to home.* One for the archives. So instead, Pascoe and I talked about the fathers of the Williams sisters. And the father of Tiger Woods, rich and young and 24 years old, women throwing themselves under his buggy.

They doing that?

Who knows, who cares?

And we talked about that weird man with the girls going to the Sydney Olympics. *All black men we'd have to face down on some dusty Main Street if this was the American West and we had our time over again. Or when the true history reveals that we really did defeat old Slobadan Columbus on Day One of the encounter.*

Only the damn journalists lied about it.

And the damn Indians pretended to be us.

So how's Kiri doing, I asked, the name suddenly coming to me. I still remember his *Coriolanus.*

He's moved on now, man. Into children's theatre and puppetry, and that sort of thing.

Brilliant. Brilliant. Less macho.

Maybe I should have been one of those scientific daddies, boy. Kicking the child's arse, kicking his arse all the way to stardom and riches.

Part Two

i

'The little shit got away. *Shit.*'

'Sarwan.'

'What's that?'

'Sarwan. Think Sarwan. Young Sarwan. The hope of West Indies cricket. Well, if not the hope. At least saved the day. Might yet save the day.'

'That's different; that's something different. Whether the outcome of a cricket match can save the day is an interesting point.'

'He made a good 17. Seventeen good runs. Not out. You never know. With Adams still in...'

'Let me just go and ring up Jenny and say: We've had a run in with two of your friends; young boys dressed up like policeman. They've taken down our names, which means things are looking up: they can read. Can write, anyway. We escaped a night in the cells segregated, I'm sure you'll approve, from womankind. We.' Then a thought animated Pascoe. 'Actually, it would be quite good to ring up Jenny and give her some satisfaction.'

'Only, of course, she'd blame me. Jenny.'

'That's all right; I'm relaxed about that; you ain't have to live with Jenny. Though that fucker on the train got off scot free.'

We were oppressed by the incident on the train. I, too, thought the conductor had got off lightly. Pascoe and I had been made to look foolish.

'Even Eric got off lightly.'

Unfair, but who was into fairness. Eric hadn't come back on the train with us. After play we had all taken the tram back into Manchester. To Piccadilly, where Eric's daughter was meeting us; and the plan was to have a drink or a meal or something; and, in the end the decision was to defer it till tomorrow; so Eric stayed behind with his daughter and Pascoe and I decided to head back to Sheffield immediately, to try and catch *Today at the Test* at maybe half-past eight. We'd eat in Sheffield.

We'd just got back and, of course, missed *Today at the Test,* which we would have missed anyway, as it turned out to have been on at half-past seven.

'So, shall we eat?' I asked him. I was host now, not only on my patch but in my flat. I had bought a bottle of wine at Piccadilly station. For no particular reason, really, as there was lots of wine in the flat, but we had seventeen minutes to wait for the train, scanned the book-shop and found nothing we wanted to buy, and I supposed that's why I grabbed a bottle of wine, rationalising that the flat contained mainly white wine and at least this was red.

So now I poured us from the bottle of red, and felt it was my turn to make an attempt to recover the old buoyancy.

'How about chicken? I asked.

The groan that issued from Pascoe was precisely what I'd hoped for. We'd had two chicken dinners today and hadn't quite recovered from either; and what with the business on the train and the position West Indies were in – that made us begin to be uncertain, depressed, even, about certain things, not least whether these reunions were a good thing. Why not more chicken.

Pascoe sipped his wine and looked round the sitting-room he'd shown some admiration for last night.

'So, boy, you still living like a student?'

Last night he was admiring my private library, making reference to Borges and Lowell. (Apparently, Elizabeth Hardwick, a wife of Robert Lowell's, had written somewhere of the challenge of moving 7,000 books when you moved house.) Tonight, I was the student.

And at that point I could relate more to what Pascoe had

hinted at earlier, about Eric getting off lightly; Eric had missed out on the humiliation on the train; the only humiliation he had had today was the way West Indies had played, and that was something you had to pretend to rise above, particularly when you were with your daughter; so much so that when we left them in Manchester, Eric was innocently telling his daughter about our earlier encounter with the chicken-sellers.

So here were we in Sheffield trying to deal with a real problem – Pascoe hadn't phoned his wife, I had no one, really, to phone – and Eric was no doubt over in Manchester, without a care in the world, talking about how our decision at lunch-time to be patriotic and go for the West Indian chicken outside the ground was frustrated because the chicken wasn't ready: the Chippery was ready, the Traditional Carvery was serving. Steak & Sausage. Ultimate Burger. Greasy-fried. Everything was ready at one-o'clock, but the West Indian chicken – four slow-moving people, one man slow-cleaning the barbeque – *cleaning it at one-o'clock prior to lighting. And miraculously expecting to have the meal ready at one-o'clock* – And a fat boy behind the counter eating... All that.

Eric would be recounting to his daughter what we had been saying at the time, about the West Indian genius to miss the boat at business, that it was the conjunction of West Indianness and Englishness that did that; that if these same people – slow-moving while everyone else was making money, and the fat boy inside eating – if these same people had landed up in New York or California – or Lagos or Melbourne, *their West Indian chicken would be ready to catch the lunch-time custom.* (Of course it got worse: as the West Indian cricketers more or less disowned us by their performance, *I tell you, can you blame Coriolanus banishing the Romans in return!* so we had seriously to find a new name for these cricketers. Nevertheless, we decided we had to be loyal to *something*

West Indian, and wait for the chicken. The wait got us soaked; got us to the pub and back, *and at half-past three to be greeted, at £5.00 a go, to chicken and rice and a plastic fork* (Never mind the plastic fork, we could live with a plastic fork, these weren't normal times; you even occasionally got a plastic fork at work: *but could you imagine Pascoe's mother, Eric's mother, my mother* serving up this foolishness with a plastic fork *particularly at a time when West Indies were losing to England after barely an hour's play?* The signals the West Indies food tent were sending out were that (a), their own chicken-constituency would materialise whenever the chicken was ready, and they didn't need new custom. Or (b), that they weren't the sort of people who sold chicken at cricket matches and they were deliberately being inefficient to prove the point – though that class statement didn't square with the fat boy eating behind the counter before the food was ready – definitely not a class act. Or (c), that they were depressed by the state of the match, and the rhythm of their work reflected that – so we would have to wait until tomorrow, to see if West Indian fortunes improved, and see if that affected the delivery of chicken-dinners. So the decision had been to give them the benefit of the doubt for the *concept* of the thing, not for the execution. Definitely not for the *execution;* for after all that the chicken was burnt on the outside, raw on the inside; and the rice was under-cooked.)

That, Pascoe and I were sure, having our quiet glass of wine in the flat in Sheffield, was the sort of mishap about the day that Eric was regaling his daughter with, at this very minute.

So yes, we felt cheated. And more or less abandoned by Eric.

And I *would* do some proper chicken to rescue us first from the lump of greasy whatsit, then from the West Indian burnt on the outside, raw on the inside travesty at Old Trafford.

In the kitchen I started preparing the chicken and boiling

water for the rice. In the room with the books I refilled our glasses, opened another bottle. I started running a hot bath because the dampness soaked up during the day was beginning to get to me; and I invited Pascoe to phone home if he felt like it, while I had my bath.

ii

'Smells good.' That was Pascoe; he was in a better mood, he was referring to my chicken, which was nearly ready. I had had my bath and was feeling a lot less stiff and, well, threatened. (I recalled the story of Descartes getting on with his work, living in perfectly happy seclusion in Holland, tempted out to Stockholm by Queen Christina: the man promptly gets wet, gets pneumonia, and dies at the age of 54.)

'I was thinking of Descartes,' I said. 'Fellows like Descartes and Shakespeare. Imagine giving them the years we have on them: how would they have dealt with tonight? On the train.'

Pascoe threw out a few names of people who had died young.

I added a few more.

Artists. Musicians. All sorts. Then Pascoe returned to the question.

'Those fellows...' he said. He sipped his wine. 'The women might say something else. The women might say something interesting. But them fellows. They ain't want hassle. They take one look at this provincial pantomime. And they chuppes and say. "I glad I dead." And they turn over and go back to sleep, man.'

It was good that Jenny hadn't given him a hard time on the phone; I had heard him on the phone as I was having my bath – he was on for a long time, and that was reassuring.

'Everything all right?' I said. 'At home?'

'Ah. I must pay you for that...'

'Come on, Pascoe, don't be...'

'No, man I... I think it's a call I should pay for.'

'Pascoe...'

'I made a call to Norway...'

'Ah.' But that wasn't judgemental. 'So, why should you pay for it?'

'Not guilt. Don't give me that shit.'

'Let me go look at the chicken, man.'

'Wait, man, wait.'

'Pascoe, I...'

'You thought I was phoning in one direction. Part of the deal...'

I shrugged: it was obvious.

'...Phoning in another direction, so to speak. Not part of the deal. Not that it was particularly deliberate. I'm not going behind anyone's back. No, that's a lie, I am. What I mean to say is: I'm not seeking the opportunity to go behind anyone's back. There's a difference between going behind your back, and *seeking the opportunity* to go behind your back.'

So which one of us was being the student now?

'OK.' I said.

'So if there is an element of deceit. *If.* Then it's you who have been deceived, not Jenny.'

'Why don't you ring Jenny as well, rather than...'

'Pewter, I despair of you. Your house is full of books. Your name is Stapleton. You've lived with a woman whom I can only call a princess. And you expect me now to pick up the phone, phone home and humiliate Jenny *by talking to her after I've just talked to my first wife?* A woman Jenny thinks I'm still carrying on with.'

'Oh, your *wife.*' I was dissembling. 'I was thinking maybe it was your daughter.'

'You fellows, you know, are sentimental. You fellows who don't have daughters, are very sentimental about daughters. *I* am sentimental about a woman who shared my life for fifteen years and has suffered for it. That's a woman who knows what the front line is. Lived it here. Lived it in London, and lived in, believe me in supposedly colour-blind Norway. And people actually say to me: to communicate with this woman is to do something underhand!'

I wasn't a stand-in for Jenny: I wasn't going to get into this. The years of sitting up all night generating argument had proved exciting as a student. The same method twenty, thirty, forty years later had proved disastrous, and exhausting. I would see to dinner.

The chicken was good, the rice was good, the wine flowed.

'Persian rice.'

'Of course.'

And both Pascoe and I felt relaxed enough now to discuss the cricket. Not so much the cricket but our response to, or – as Pascoe would have it – our responsibilities concerning the cricket. Pascoe had said at some point late in the day, when Stewart was taking the West Indies bowlers apart, that to save not ourselves but *them,* the players, from further humiliation we should change their name from, y'know, West Indies, to something less sensitive, something more like Kosovo or Wyoming.

'I like Wyoming.'

'You know, one of those nothing sorts of states.'

'I once met a woman from Wyoming.'

'Yes?...I expect, everything was in the right place?'

'Well...Two eyes, y'know. Walked forwards rather than backwards.'

'Well, if there're enough people like that in Wyoming, maybe we should give them independence.'

'Ah. Doesn't work like that.'

'You're right, not enough oil and cocaine.'

So we talked about how Wyoming had got on today at Old

Trafford, and it was much easier to bear the humiliation.

Later, over a cognac, we agreed that we would look up Wyoming in the dictionary:

> **Wyoming**. A state in the NW United states, 97,914 square miles, capital, Cheyenne, entered the Union, July 10th 1890; nickname, Equality State.

'"Cheyenne," eh?'

'"Cheyenne." Philadelphia, incidentally, means "City of Brotherly Love".'

'Nice one.' (George dubbya Bush's Republican convention was being held at Philadelphia.) 'Two things here,' Pascoe said. 'Incidentally, good cognac.'

'Not bad.'

'Ah, life is not, y'know… the worst thing that can happen to a man. But, as I was saying: two things. Where would we have been, say, in 1890, when the cricketers entered the Union.'

'Good point. Eric's the historian.'

'See what I mean. Eric's given up history. Abandoned us to history and has moved on to bigger things, no doubt, sitting down in Greater Manchester discussing the problems of genetic mapping of the cholera bug – and the big social history issues of the day, like naming and shaming the paedophiles, and bringing out the crowds of lynching housewives and babies.'

(The paedophile reference brought back, maybe the only minor triumph of the evening; but we weren't going to get into that now.)

So, abandoned by Eric, we were on our own, with our cognac. And our ignorance of history.

'So, if Wyoming, why not St. Caesare? Your family, my family must have been negotiating something with somebody in 1890. How come they missed out? 97,000 square miles. 97,900. Nearly 98,000. Little bit bigger than Guyana. More than twice the size of Cuba. I was reading something by a Cuban the other day: made the case for Cuba not being big enough to be a country. So Cubans will forever over-achieve and be under-valued. Producing science that others will *tief*. And lots and lots of black boxers and runners that people like to see box and run. Wyoming. Twenty times the size of Jamaica. Actually, you know, the Wyoming team should have some history lessons kicked into their backsides at break time.'

In the middle of the night, the flushing of the loo woke me, and I realised I'd fallen asleep over my book with the lights on.

Pascoe came in.

'You awake? I saw your lights on.'

'I'm awake now.'

'Do you think Illingworth was in that Stand today?'

'O, God, Pascoe, give me a break.'

'Because if I see that man, I have to kill him, too.'

Now it was my turn to go to the loo. Coming out I rang up the time; it was gone three o'clock. Pascoe was back in the sitting-room; I turned on the kettle in the kitchen and joined him. The television was on.

'What's on?'

'Oh, not the porn the wives dream about.'

But it seemed of interest, so I watched a bit while the kettle was boiling. Pascoe brought me up to date.

'Rapist,' he said. 'Upstairs in the loo.'

It was an American film. East-coast? West-coast? Three women. Three young women sharing. Attractive.

'There's a blizzard,' Pascoe explained. 'Snow, anyway. Three women sharing the house; one pregnant; only just, nothing showing. In the middle of this snow or whatever –

Oh, yes, it's night time. Young man calls and asks if their plumbing has gone wrong or something, because he's a plumber. Great plot line, eh? Naturally, they're suspicious and won't let him in. The fellow's slightly fat. But one of the women – there's always one – one of the women says to the others, Hi, remember the loo needs fixing. She doesn't say "loo"; she says whatever Americans say when they mean "loo". The loo needs fixing. So she runs out in the snow…' *So, it's obviously East coast.* '…one of them does, and calls the potential rapist back, who's parked some little way off. Another clue. And then she goes up to show him the loo, and he bolts the door from the inside and rapes her.'

'What, this one?'

'No.'

One woman now goes up to check on the rapist in the bathroom where the women, having tied him up, have dragged him from the loo. He's freed himself: *who makes these films; why can't three women tie up one man?* He now confronts the lone woman. He's arrogant and cool, saying, 'Let me go, we'll say nothing more about it; just let me go.' And *her* body-language is saying No. (She does the I-go-to-the-gym routine, and all the karate-type posture; but the fellow doesn't take her seriously.) And attacks her. Two, three times. Overpowered, but she kicks out. Combination of kicking him in the crotch, and kicking out, and getting him in the face and head, is beginning to work. But the man won't be defeated, is coming back for more, lunging. And each time he lurches, she kicks him in the head.

Yes.

Again. And she kicks him in the head.

Yes.

And yet the man comes.

Yes. Kick the shit out of him.

And she does.

And again and again the rapist keeps coming.

'Kick the shit out of him.'

'Yes, kick the shit out of him.' My voice is competing with Pascoe's.

And he's lifeless. They try to revive him. We hope it's too late.

'Well then.'

Silently, we drink a little cognac. No toast.

In the film it's next morning. The girls contact the authorities. The man is stretchered out. The girls fall out amongst themselves. But that's necessary to the story; they'll be OK.

I say goodnight to Pascoe, and return to bed. Forgetting to make the tea.

Part Three

i

So this is what happened on the train from Manchester.

We were in reasonably good spirits despite everything. After all, you've got to pretend that a game of cricket was just a game of cricket and not the real politics. Who wants to talk anymore about colonial hangovers... no political unity... the proximity of America. No landmass. No continuous landmass: *Our scientists should be making land, filling in sea.* Losing the fight against international criminals and drugs dealers doesn't help, the brightest and the best now staying behind to go into crime. Maybe we should just accept it, accept that the abysmal showing of the team was a reflection of our true condition, the years preceding merely flattering to deceive.

What was surprising, though, having left Eric and his

daughter (who wouldn't want to be written into this story, she's not a loser but a scientist helping to decide what the rest of us will end up eating) – what was surprising was to find so many people on the train to Sheffield. It called itself an Express but it was only a two-carriage job, which should still be able to do it in fifty minutes or so and get us there for *Today at the Test,* if it had been on at half-past eight rather than half-past seven.

In retrospect, it was perhaps good not having a seat because we'd discussed the state of the match enough, and it was better just to forget it all and concentrate on my book. I was reading – reading around, really – a book on philosophy, a decision prompted, I knew, by Pascoe's visit: there was still something of the old competition between us. Unlike me, (and Eric for that matter) he had never succumbed to the academy and had worked for local authorities and that sort of thing, in no very elevated position. That he had never attempted to write anything on his subject perversely allowed him to pull rank. ('I'm not one of your literary fellows, I ain't know anything about literature', and then come out with the theory that the way his son Franklyn played the crowd scene to prevent Coriolanus being made consul, showed that he still kept his 'character' as the SECOND CITIZEN who understood irony – his *body-language* showing resistance to being subsumed in the Shakespearean *crowd.)* So before renewing contact with Pascoe, I tended to demonstrate that I, too, was in touch with the old texts. Pathetic, we knew, but true.

We were in that section of the train between the carriages and it was so packed that, though it was possible somehow to reach for your book in the bag, there was no space or proper angle to read in comfort. The newspaper I'd already read during the delay for rain, and I didn't want to take it out now just to check on the time of *Today at the Test.* I'd read the match programme, exhaustively, and discussed it; so –

making a little statement – I settled for correcting a review I was writing. (It was due in, it was late; and why should Pennine Express deprive me of the means to work?) When I looked across at Pascoe he was squashed near the door reading the cricket programme, holding it over the heads of the people next to him.

The usual stir signalled the conductor on his way; it brought you back to considering what was happening. First of all it was so hard to squeeze through the bodies that the loo was inaccessible. It seemed so odd that the conductor would add to the pressure.

But what was suddenly noticeable was that we weren't moving. We had been stationary for some time and it had just occurred to me that there had been no announcement, and – the irritating thought – we were in danger of missing *Today at the Test* when we got to Sheffield. The conductor was still a little way off and I reminded myself to ask about the reason for the hold-up, when he got to me. I gestured and mouthed to Pascoe that we would miss *Today at the Test.* He took it in, then seemed to shrug, non-committal.

'Any reason for the hold-up?' I asked, when the conductor came.

'Can I see your tickets, please?'

'Do you know why we've stopped?'

He said something, which I didn't catch, the words disappearing into his little beard; and then spoke very clearly: 'Can I see your ticket, please?'

'Yes; hang on, hang on.'

'The man has asked a question. Simple question.' That was Pascoe, five or six people away, turning all attention to him now, including the conductor's. 'I think we'd all like to have an answer to the question. As a customer…' He turned round and surveyed the crush. 'We might look like an old-fashioned crowd. Or even cargo. But humour us, no, man; you're wearing a jacket of authority. You safe.'

The conductor's lips twitched, rather thin lips, but he ignored Pascoe and turned back to me; by which time other passengers were trying to make up their minds whether to associate themselves with us; one or two were proffering tickets.

'Can I see your ticket, Sir?' That was to me.

So he thought I was the weak link. The *Sir,* coming out of the thin mouth, bristled with something that wasn't pleasant. *Little man, big threat.* People around were pretending not to notice, but delay on my part wouldn't leave Pascoe exposed. Not delay, I'm not talking delay, would the fellow understand *finesse*. I hadn't made any attempt to get out my ticket. But at the same time I hadn't made a decision not to show it. Pascoe would think me wimpish if I didn't carry this off with a modicum of wit. Eric would have been useful here, he would have defused this with an apt historical reference whose context would please some and whose *tone* would reassure others that they were in on the joke – *Ah, he deserved a beautiful wife and a daughter who was a scientist, did Eric.* And yet we were stuck here in the middle of, wherever, without apology, without explanation, and a man in a crumpled jacket pulling rank.

'I wonder if you've got a Complaints Form?' I asked politely.

'And one for me too, please,' said Pascoe, not bothering to look up from his programme.

'You're not going to be silly about this...'

'Aye, aye. Man using language on you, boy.' Pascoe wasn't helping; the slight sense of possibility, evident in other passengers earlier, open to a bit of light relief, was beginning to ebb, to gel into something negative; we were on our own. Also, I didn't appreciate being called silly.'

'I'd like a Complaints Form,' I said, hoping to convey finality.

'You'll get that at the station. But unless I see your ticket,

I must ask you to leave the train.' He saw me glance outside in the dark – we'd left Stockport ages ago – the middle of nowhere; and added, 'At the next station.' And he started reciting the Law and the sub-Clause of the Law that I was breaking by travelling without evidence of a valid ticket; and he turned his back on me and continued to inspect tickets. Everyone but Pascoe showed their tickets and he moved on, without hassling Pascoe.

On the back of one of my review pages I wrote a note for Pascoe. SHEFFIELD. NEXT STATION. WE GET OFF ANYWAY. And handed it over.

Pascoe read it to himself, nodded, and said aloud:

'Then we shall be conversing with the buttock of the night, eh? And not with another awful Manchester of a morning.'

This was done for my benefit; I forced my shoulders to heave. It didn't matter now because we had lost the rest of the crowd.

And yet I wouldn't disown Pascoe. Pascoe was, in cricketing terms, an 'in your face' sort of bowler; and my own tendency to go the other way, to avoid confrontation, was, though my friends called it prudent, less honourable. Or, not to be so precious about it, it yielded territory to the opposition, it made people think they could occupy your space, squash you, stamp on you, abuse you with impunity: you became a soft target, you ended up colluding in your own harassment: *Pascoe had broken a thug's nose somewhere in Norway, when he had spat at his wife and child.* I had allowed my partner to be abused on a train in Yorkshire, trying to keep it calm. Horror stories started flooding my mind of what was happening to people who could be identified as 'other'. From Dublin to Marseilles to Berlin. Never mind further East. *(Had these people heard of – where was it today – Mahlow?)*

The surprise was when the train stopped.

It wasn't our station; it wasn't Sheffield, it was a little station before Sheffield and the police were waiting for us on the platform. One, a young boy, rather short for a policeman, boarded, while the other one remained on the platform.

'All right?' the policeman asked me; he was blonde and fresh-faced, and weighed down by *equipment,* a truncheon, maybe and a walkey-talkey, things branching from his waist as if he were a miniature gunslinger. The conductor stood just behind him, ratfaced. I made an effort not to dehumanise him.

Was I causing an affray on the train?

No, I don't think so.

Then to Pascoe. Was he causing an affray on the train?

Pascoe said he understood the question; but was confused. Because he used to think that an 'affray' was a Surinamese dance. And, as one could see, his dancing days were over. Then he admitted that this was a joke. It had all come about, he confessed, because of a case of mistaken identity. When he had seen the conductor coming towards him, his face triggered a sort of recognition; he thought he recognised him as one of the paedophiles named and shamed in the *News of the World* last Sunday. And as a man with a daughter, his first instinct was to be vigilant. But he was prepared to accept that he had made a mistake: case of mistaken identity. It was a terrible thing. He had to support his wife over this, though he, himself, wasn't keen on crowd justice.

Did he want to spend a night in the cells?

No, officer, he did not; he was of a nervous disposition.

It was against the law to use bad language in a public place; did we know that?

Pascoe said he didn't remember using bad language in a public place. He may have called me by my name, Eric, which was a four-letter word in anybody's language. And now he thought of it he could understand how it might seem threatening to people who were maybe tired and oppressed by the railway-barons.

Eric. I'd acquired a beautiful wife and a daughter who was a scientist.

Could he see out tickets?

Certainly. We showed out tickets.

The policeman asked the conductor to verify that our tickets were valid; and he did so. And his face did look a bit ratlike.

If we assured him there'd be no more trouble on the train, he would permit us to continue the journey. Did we have somewhere to stay in Sheffield?

I told him I lived in Sheffield and that my friend was visiting.

He wanted no more hassling of the conductor on the train.

Pascoe started to say that it was the other way round; *we* were the ones who had been hassled.

At this point a young woman came forward. She wasn't criticising us for making a stand, she said, but this had gone on a long time; we were holding up the train which was already late; some people had children to see to at home; what we were doing was really selfish.

I apologised to her. I hadn't thought of that.

You see, Pascoe said to the policeman, nodding approvingly to the young woman. We don't all lose our ability to be SECOND CITIZEN even though we're forced to play the crowd.

The policeman started to go for Pascoe but changed his mind, and turned to me:

'Eric, right?'

'That's right.'

'Now, we're getting somewhere.' Then he said: 'Eric. You'll be a sensible boy and get your friend home without further trouble.'

I could hear Maryam saying this to me in different circumstances.

Yes, darling.

I assured the policeman that I would.

*

Next morning before we headed for Manchester, we decided not to make sandwiches but to wait until we got to Manchester, and go into town to a delicatessen, or maybe to the food store at *M & S* or some such place.

Before leaving, Pascoe decided to ring home. He told Jenny he didn't ring last night because he didn't want to disturb her and her fancy man. Also, he had had to rescue me from a beating by the police, because at my age I was still living like a student and taking the fight to the enemy, forgetting I was no longer a black youth.

Of the cricket, Oh, well: *Ars longa vita brevis.* And there was still a little life left to live.

(2000)

WHATSERNAME AND LA CONTESSA

i

I was stunned. I stopped in mid-chew, as if I'd bitten on a hard thing in the middle of the cake; or – for me – on something unpleasantly soft, like a currant or a raisin. And then I forced myself to continue, to chew on what my mother had said, that she hadn't had a holiday in over thirty years.

My first impulse was to deny it, not because it wasn't true, but because it seemed such an odd thing to say; it seemed so much the sentiment of someone at the far edge of privation, the sort of thing that, in another context, would make me want to protest, to defend the victim. And yet it wasn't like that. (Had she been working all these years? – an ungenerous thought.) It was true, yes, that she hadn't been back home, but that was largely of her doing; she had never, to my knowledge, expressed a wish to go back to see what things were like. She hadn't left the country, hadn't left London, even, in all these years: would a view of Manchester, of Milan have eased the sense of... being in the wrong place? Of being constrained? The English took their sorrows to the seaside, to Blackpool, to Benidorm: these were, we like to think, the small dreams rejected by the family. Some of our own people from the Caribbean went back to show off – new clothes, new accents, foreign partners – their new status. And why not? But we had decided not to play that game. It had taken decades to recoup our original position, getting back to roughly where we had been when we left the island. Now, we had to prove more before going back. This was obvious; it was one of the reasons my mother never expressed the wish to go back.

I was beginning to be able to cope with the accusation; I praised the cake.

I was on my mother's territory, in her room. I had learnt, over the years, that coming here was to submit myself to a process of cross-examination, at the end of which I would always leave, pleading guilty. She had observed earlier in the evening, apropos a news item on television, that the Governor of Hong Kong was only three years older than me, and had children old enough to be at university. I apologised, routinely, for not having children. I apologised, more feelingly, for not having got myself installed as Governor of Hong Kong, and thus restoring to the mother of the Governor a role commensurate with her inner status – that of keeping an eye on the morality and hygiene of the Colony, and spending her afternoons, in summer dresses, opening new supermarkets and banks. This had amused her enough to call me ignorant. Maybe this would be regarded as a large enough input by me so that I wouldn't have to read to her or to write a letter on her behalf before leaving. (I used to stumble over her Bible when asked to read from that text; so reading-matter would be from the book I happened to be carrying, and I took care, usually, when I boarded the train for Upton Park to walk with something unsuitable.)

But this imposed a penalty. It was important to demonstrate that I was among the privileged who were informed, to show that my store of random knowledge was as great at least as those people who appeared on television quiz shows, 'for they don't have your education'. The reason I didn't do all that, we would agree, was that I'd passed it up for something better, more dignified.

So there was a good chance that I would end up regaling her with, say, a list of rivers and towns in Yugoslavia – or anything browsed before the journey. I would then talk a bit about the country in question, making something of a joke of it, enough to bring on the dubious look, which made her girlish, and the reprimand for talking nonsense. This would be a successful 'reading'. I could then make an early exit, for nights in London were deemed to be dangerous, and I travelled by train, and lived a long way away. My guilt, on leaving, would be for a niece, who would be left with the chore of writing a letter for her grandmother, who had a touch of rheumatism or arthritis in her fingers.

I had thought, over the years, of taking her abroad somewhere, maybe to those places in Germany and France where I sometimes worked. I had spent many years trying to pacify little patches of territory in this or that country, and friends had sometimes been recruited for these acts of exploration. Pioneering work. That done – so the theory goes – the family would start travelling in style: a version of my mother, summery and gloved, cutting the ribbons to a Manhattan-style structure in Kowloon, declaring it open. More probably, I saw myself picking her up at Nice airport and driving west into the mountains, careful to take it slowly as she didn't like speed, to her new holiday home.

It seems too raw talking this way about your mother, so I tend to draw back sometimes, or to pull a little veil over it to protect us both; that's when I end up calling her La Contessa. I call her La Contessa because over thirty years ago, weeks before we left the Caribbean, someone had painted a portrait of her and had called it 'La Contessa'. We had never seen the finished painting and knew nothing of its whereabouts; but I fancy the image that the painter trapped was close to the image of herself that both La Contessa and I preserved. We now allowed the thirty years to pass only when it suited us. (I had dreamt of her the other night learning to drive the car, and she had reacted in a way which disturbed and embarrassed me – an old memory: it was the memory of her on the horse at home, Ruby. Ruby's docility was legendary; so when the painter, the man who was to dub her La Contessa, suggested that she sit on the horse for the portrait, it seemed fitting. The queens of England and those sorts of people were said to have their portraits painted sitting on a horse. And we'd also have a record of another aspect of the house; for the horse would soon be given away, and without the horse, the 'groom', who had been part of the house, would revert to being a labourer. As we might not be able to re-create the real thing in England, play it safe with the portrait. So my mother was got on to the horse, not without difficulty, for Ruby stood high, even against the front steps, and my mother's dress was newly ironed and not to be creased. Also, the groom and the painter had to be careful where they put their hands as they lifted her on. Eventually, she was sitting in the saddle and Ruby, not knowing what this was about, took a leisurely step forward, then another… and a third: was the portrait laughing? My mother's screams seemed so out of proportion to the danger that for a moment no one knew what to do. In the end she was hustled down, somewhat indelicately. My punishment was to have witnessed this. Much later, I was to discover that she had regarded such unseemly behaviour on horseback as an acknowledgement of sexuality, as a display, in public, of a wanton nature. I resolved to find a way, one day, to talk to her about this.)

But not yet. Maybe we could collude on something less risky, like joining the Open University and studying something where we wouldn't stand out among the pensioners from Bridlington and the rapists serving life at places like Albany on the Isle of Wight. Or, maybe I'd just take her on holiday.

But the family had priorities. We had, without articulating it, accepted that *holiday* was in some sense the reverse of *work,* a reward for work or relief from work; and we bought the notion that *work* had something to do with paid employment and little to do with whatever it was that La Contessa did – with her being in the house, etc. With such things informing our thinking, it was easy to see how a holiday for her seemed less pressing than other things we hadn't acted on. For holidays, themselves, had been deferred even by those who had 'earned' them, those who endured the attritions of the workplace, an environment which, if not always hostile, was demeaning. It was there where people pretended not to understand your accent, where they expected your face to be stretched into a permanent smile, where they thought any claim to a history before your arrival in this country was a boast. These 'workers' stored up their holidays, like interest in the bank, until it could be drawn on by children – nephews, nieces – who would need to take their bearings outside this strange world, the better to survive it.

I've become a bit obsessed with this matter because of my life-style, because I was the member of the family who travelled, and was therefore associated with 'holidays'. I'd been to four of the five continents, and I *had* taken people with me on some of these expeditions: so why not La Contessa?

Of course, many of my forays abroad weren't, in fact, holidays. Once, in the mid-1970s, I went to Germany to baby-sit a dog. A holiday. I'd taught in Germany, had friends there, so the opportunity to go back to baby-sit the dog – and to look around the Language Schools at the same time for work – was seen as a holiday. Can you imagine La Contessa sauntering down the Hohestrasse in Köln followed by a dog? Then what? Nip into the *Journal* for a drink, a Kolsch – Kolsch for me, hot chocolate for Mutti? Or maybe passing the hour sitting at one of the little tables in the square outside the Dom, the Cathedral, watching tourists snapping the monstrosity, snapping themselves – so many Japanese set in Gothic? She'd be introduced to the Language School crowd, exchanging Inlingua and Unilingua and Berlitz horror stories, speculating on the German sense of humour.

Possible. But I could go one better than that; I had a plan.

ii

Here is La Contessa looking down from that magnificent *palazzo* on the south side of the Piazza Signoria – the one with the clock tower. Ah, we are in Florence. There are people of a humble fourteenth-century aspect looking out from the lower floors.

'*Cui flavam religas coman*?' I pull out from somewhere to put myself in the mood, though I no longer know what it means. From the raked stand, I point out to my companions all the women in our family – grandmother, mother, sister, nieces – up there at the windows of the *palazzo,* in costume, fifth level up at least, looking down on the square, on the event.

'What event?' Whatsername would ask me later. (Whatsername, like La Contessa, needs her anonymity.)

'The Great Match. Not cricket, unfortunately. Football.'

'Football!'

Then I would have to explain the occasion. 'The family are looking down on a sixteenth-century event. Seats erected all round the square. The pitch sanded; sanded in the sense of tons of sand poured on to the square, and raked. A beautiful Tuscan summer evening. Today the two teams are the Greens and the Blues. But we don't know that yet, because the dignitaries are marching out, ruffed and plumed, in formation, dozens of them filling the piazza. Then comes the acrobatic stuff, all that business with flags and formation. They're never quite professional here: a few of them drop the flag...'

'These are the players?'

'The players have to wait their turn. The ceremonial takes a long time; the family upstairs are in no hurry. This part of the ceremony takes about an hour, while the grand folk look down from their windows, tossing the odd flower down. And the players come on...'

'Ah!'

'The referee has a sword and ceremonial hat.'

'Sixteenth century, you say?'

'Sixteenth century. Linesmen dressed like figures out of Piero della Francesca. OK. OK. Sometimes they step back a century or so. La Contessa sniffs at a flower and tosses it down, carelessly...'

'I can see her doing that.'

'Tosses a flower down... No one kicks the ball, of course. Very rarely, anyway. Each player fixes his opponent in a half-nelson and pins him to the floor...'

'Filth. Filth. Are they all men?'

'...Men and boys. And the few remaining standing try to get the ball to the opposite goal. Of course, there are five men in each goal.'

'You're making this up.'

'*Five* men in goal. There are about twenty-five players a side. This is sixteenth-century football.'

'Maybe men were terribly small in those days, and not well-fed. That's why you needed five in goal.'

'... But the goal is the width of the piazza. When someone scores, the cannon goes off.'

'I knew there would be violence.'

She is mocking my report of Florentine football, Whatsername is; but I vow to take La Contessa to this annual spectacle; next year would be her coming out. I'd witnessed it with friends, it was just right. After the match, rival supporters fought each other with arias from some sixteenth-century opera, and then they fought with tourists like twentieth-century people. There was no way that La Contessa could get out of coming to Florence to attend the Match next year.

iii

Next year she was in hospital and then she had died. How to deal with recriminations that everyone was too polite to make? Who will charge you with complicity? For already things have begun to unravel. One train journey, at least, has lost its shape, the story ended before we've got to the end. Look, you say. *Look,* you scream: how can it end when there are pages and pages to go! Pages and pages. You can't accept it, how good, how lucky that you're not armed. Planning to do this or that seems silly, tasteless. I had come prepared to read to you...something unusual, yes – a list of horses running at Epsom (for we both loathe horse-racing; it would have been funny. Or would it have reminded you of Ruby?). The 2 o'clock at Epsom had names like Sno Serenade and Dr Zeva and Cantus Firmus and All Shook Up: *All Shook Up, I'm In Luv.* Elvis... No one to giggle disapprovingly, no one to be girlish, at seventy-six: *All Shook Up, I'm In Luv.* Elvis... I'm building a house in Montauroux, north of Cannes. There, you could rest. Forty minutes from Nice airport. There you would rest and tell us where we went wrong. Then the next day, or the day after, whenever... a leisurely ride to Tuscany, plenty of time to choose your costume for the *palazzo,* then to your balcony, a flower in your hand, drifting down to the American tourists below. We're in Hong Kong, I'd say: reassure the people. Once, during our talks, she had asked about the bats that had lived in our old house in Coderington. The house had long been abandoned; a ruin: where had the bats taken refuge – with no large houses, no attics left in the village? I didn't know. I had promised her an answer. Now there was no… pressure to find out what had become of the bats. I could go through life now, not having to find answers to such questions. But I had prepared myself for this: I would have said that bats were the only mammals with the full power of flight. And then; and then to bring on the frown, the giggle, the charge of ignorance, I would have mouthed *Plectotus Auritus;* I would have clowned *Vespertilion Ide*… She knew bats slept upside-down. So it's enough now to think that bats are creatures that sleep upside-down. Something shared. Foolishly, I turn on her television to see if it works. There's someone wearing an arm-band, a whole football team: who are they to wear arm-bands? I turn off the box. I'm growing coarse. Whatsername had tried to prevent this, and I had defied her. Now, I must return and be contrite.

Whatsername had helped, had got me to the point where I could broach a subject of emotional risk with La Contessa, and I had found the opening, and had ducked it. It was before the hospital and I'd popped in to say goodbye, I'd be away for a few weeks; and we ended up watching cricket together. It was early in the summer, not warm. The understanding was that we'd watch the cricket till time for the Australian soap opera, and then switch channels. Though I was preparing to leave before then. But it seemed mildly appropriate, turning from one Australian *play* to another. That led me into a joke and then a sort of commentary on Australia, parts of which I'd toured: should I happen to settle there, would she come and visit? We'd call in on the Governor of Hong Kong on the way. Her image of Australia was uncomplimentary, so I tried to disabuse her, to talk of the beauty of the Sydney harbourfront, of the Blue Mountains – nothing like that in London. But her objection to Australia was its *distance.* Foiled again – and by someone who hadn't left London in all these years. But at that moment, something occurred on the television, which damned Australia.

It was a bowler whose modern haircut had already puzzled La Contessa but she had been persuaded to give him the benefit of the doubt. But the fellow didn't help himself. Walking back to his mark, facing us in close-up, this big man with the strange hair-style brought the shiny, red ball to his lips, looked at it, and then licked it copiously. Even I couldn't defend him after that. I had to agree that he was 'nasty', and volunteered for good measure the information that poisonous chemicals had been sprayed on the ground in its preparation. But this was a detail. The image that stuck was of a man, so uncontrollable, so lascivious that he couldn't resist licking the red ball *in public*: was this man's country the sort of place I wanted to settle in? Had I taken leave of my senses? Didn't I know there were strange diseases going round?

It was I who changed the subject. I had been accused by Whatsername of avoiding, of invisibilising La Contessa – all the La Contessas of this world; in effect, of denying them their holidays. These women had been uprooted, sometimes in early middle-age, separated, divorced; forced in one way or other to exchange the jurisdiction of husbands for that of sons, no better than husbands, but more puritanical. Forced in this way to live out their lives in a denial of sexuality. I was likened to a gaoler pretending to be an ally. I think now of the Australian licking the red ball. I think of La Contessa on Ruby preparing to have her portrait painted. And I think, yes; this room has been lived in.

(*New Writing*, No. 5, 1996, British Council/Vintage)

It was a fear so deep that she struggled not to let it surface; and yet it overpowered her, and broke out in moods, crankiness: why didn't he marry?

When the children were younger, and had to adjust to growing up in a new country, she thought that might help him to outgrow the ways of his father – though he looked so much like him. She hoped he would advance the family, not in the ways he was always planning, which would just bring failure and loneliness, but in ordinary, sensible things: he could advance the family in his choice of bride, he could advance the family by having letters after his name.

Dark thoughts were to be kept away. His friends were boys from school, from College: now men. That was only natural. They were well-brought-up boys who would know that at another time, in another country, she wouldn't be in the kitchen, she would be the one to demand service; she would be the one to be served. Yet, she couldn't help praying that she was wrong about him: it was better to think of other things.

And there were the girls, his friends; they frightened her. They seemed so alien for a son. Recently, one had appeared with a bracelet on her ankle: how could a son have moved so far to be friends with a woman who wore a bracelet on her ankle? And he'd been to that other place, whatever, where they walked around naked; women, practically naked: you didn't come back the same from all that. Now, he had grey hairs. Silly to worry, though. No man was so evil that he wouldn't find a woman to look after him. The more evil the man, it seemed, the better the woman that looked after him: what was she saying; she mustn't ... say that. She didn't want him to be any more evil than other people; though she was relieved that he wasn't all good.

And yet, and yet, Whatsername came and went. And here was a sinful thought: where was the child to record the event? But maybe she shouldn't wish for that. And Whatsername, the last time she saw her, was getting to the age where childbearing would be difficult, dangerous: what would the boy grow old with?

'How's Whatsername?' she asked as casually as she could, when he had come back from that place a few months ago.

'She's OK.'

She wanted to know, she wanted to know the truth; men never told you the truth. She had given one of them, one of the girls, a nightgown. It was too big for her, a slim girl, but she said she would wear it as it was: had she filled out to fit it? Not having seen her in many years, the mother thought she'd better not ask; these days she was inclined to get the names wrong, and that made him tense; so it was better just to call her Whatsername. Then no one would jump down her throat.

'You don't see her?'

'Been away, you know.'

She thought they were talking of the same person.

'You going see her?'

'Of course.'

That 'of course' was a giveaway. The boy would never be a liar, despite his other accomplishments, and that reassured her; that would protect the woman, Whatsername, or whoever. She had expected him on his birthday, but he was on the other side of the world, then. And Whatsername was somewhere else again; what had he done on his birthday; surely, she could ask him that?

'You spend your birthday alone!' Not quite a question, he didn't have to answer it. And the set of his mouth – the father again – and the settling in the chair seemed to confirm that he wasn't going to answer it truthfully; and then he answered it.

'We spoke on the 'phone.'

'To Whatsername?'

'Um.'

'From over there. From all that way…?'

'Well, that's what the 'phone's for.'

'You get through?'

'No problem.'

And she couldn't stop herself laughing a little. She stopped herself asking about the nightgown, just in time, because she knew he was talking about the one with the bracelet round her ankle. 'No problem,' he said, and she felt something shift, something fall suddenly within her: if it had been 'no problem' getting through, why couldn't he have made another call to those who didn't even know where he was, but wished him safe wherever he was. But she didn't ask, and he wasn't looking her in the eye.

★

He was thinking of that call, how he had spent hours calculating the time difference and getting it wrong. Before midnight – still on the right day – he had gone out in the government car, the Hi-Lux open-back – although you weren't supposed to use it after work. Of course, he could have arranged to use his friends' telephone, the Danish-Welsh couple who lived three houses away, all part of the 'compound'. They wouldn't have minded the late hour. But he decided to drive to the office instead and make the call from there. It wasn't just the lateness of the hour that made him decide that. This was one of those calls not hard to justify, and yet you felt slightly foolish having to explain, whatever the company: it smacked of school-boys, college-chums playing games; those people who keep in touch, who have a reunion once a year, or every ten years, something like that. Like in a film. That's why he decided not to make the call in front of others: he couldn't be sure that what was funny in front of friends at this end, would also be fun at the other end. This once-a-year call didn't need an audience.

And there *had* been problems getting through: he hadn't missed this call in...many years; he wasn't about to miss it now. He got back into his government vehicle – always a bit self-conscious driving this yellow status-symbol at night – and turned into the main road and kept going. He was thinking: Yes, better not put yourself in a position of having to explain why *you* called on your birthday, *she* on hers. The other way round was no good, told you nothing about the other except that he had, she had elementary good manners, or an average memory. *This* way ensured that *you* were thinking of the other even though you might be surrounded by others, physically closer to you. That was an intimacy not to be shared. Attention switched back to the road. Once on the road, there was nowhere to go but follow it, so he put his foot down and prayed he wouldn't have an accident. An hour along and he was half-way to the next Province, no point turning back. Macbeth, and all that. He checked his petrol, panic flaring and quickly subsiding; and he felt lucky. There were no radios in these cars and that was good. Clear mind; empty. The night. But had to concentrate on the road. Foolish to die on this road on your birthday: who'd 'phone Whatsername, then? And family nearer home: had he written to his mother? Must have done. How would she cope with outliving a son? He felt reckless, wanted to take his hands off the wheel, but steadied himself and tried to concentrate: how would she cope with death in the family on this road in a country she probably didn't believe existed?

As he approached the next Province he had to decide what to do. People didn't much mind being got up in the middle of the night – for the expat, this was 'pioneering' country. So he decided to call on an acquaintance and pretend that, something or other, a bridge, say, was out on the road: safer to turn back than risk having to sit in the car all night. He accepted the offer of bed and insisted on paying for the long-distance telephone call.

The reason there was no one in at her end was that it was an awkward time over there, either mid-morning or mid-afternoon, he couldn't think. He 'phoned again before breakfast. No answer. The wrong day? Had he missed it? How could he have missed it? Then he found himself dialling another number, another country. Yes, right, here Whatsername was up, having dinner with friends: how lovely of him to ring! And yes. Yes, she remembered his birthday. What's more, they would right this minute drink a toast to him. Right there over the 'phone. And as he waited for it all to happen, he began to calculate how much the call would cost.

'And when you goin' to see her?' the mother asked.

'Eh?... Oh, you know.'

'You going see her soon?'

'Yes.'

'You not getting any younger.'

'Oh, I don't know.'

'None of us getting any younger... You have to see her soon.'

He had to give her something.

'She asked about you, you know.'

'Yes?' she laughed. 'I don't believe so.'

'Oh yes. No question.'

'I don't believe she even remember me.'

'Oh, she asks about you all the time.'

'You tell her I going down? You must tell her…'

'You're not going down. Come on.'

'Going right down. But, is life.'

'And she's still got the nightgown.'

A flash of panic.

'You remember, your nightgown?'

Panic subdued: 'I don't believe that.' She was laughing now. 'It must be old now. She take it in?'

And they talked for a bit, like old friends, about Whatsername.

(*Paris Transcontinental*, No. 12, 1995)

FEMME D'INTERIEUR

And he brought it all back with that phrase, *femme d'intérieur*, that we had toyed with and even constructed something of a shadow life around over the years till, well – till we began to grow old. But there he was, Christopher, up in the pulpit in the old family church in Grasse, intoning in his mid-Atlantic voice that my mother had been, among other things, a *femme d'intérieur*. Perhaps it wasn't that that made one suspicious, more, it was Christopher's use of the older name for the village, Grasse, though it was never really French, rather than St. Anne's, which was what everyone called it: he was not just emphasising his own status as expatriate, but ours.

We were all there, back in St. Caesare for the funeral, most of us from England, a couple from France and quite a few, including Christopher, who gave the eulogy, from North America – an international gathering befitting *le Ministère des Affaires étrangères* (my patch) rather than a humble *femme d'intérieur*. And the more Christopher eulogised – his memories so far back in the past, his emphases, slightly odd to those of us who knew her better – the more he began to drain away the excess of grief to the point where limbs stopped quivering, the coffin in front of us began to seem an object, detached, floating in its own space, sanitised now as something on television, till I realised that the nails digging into my palm now constituted not a brace for the body threatening to sag, but a rising sense of exasperation with Christopher, up there in the pulpit – one of the two lower pulpits, on the left; maybe it was a lectern – for taking away our grief. I thought: maybe that's what these things are about; the man is performing a necessary function. So I let go, and let it pass over me.

We had all lived together in London, in the same building in Maida Vale, the top end of Sutherland Avenue, back in 1956. It was a double flat shared by us, the family – brother, sister, mother – and two of the Hastings' boys toying even then with the idea of going to America, where they had family, or to Canada. My sister and I were reluctantly at school, and my brother worked in a job that was felt to be beneath the family. We won the battle for Sunday mornings against my mother's pleas to go to church. She accepted defeat not with the bad grace of St. Caesare but with the resignation of London. Things like this made us begin to love London.

Not that we were allowed to lie in on a Sunday. My brother would go out early and get the newspapers – four or five of them – and we would spread them out before breakfast, and continue afterwards, and listen to the sounds coming up from below – Nat King Cole or Perry Como or Dave King – courtesy of Frank's new radiogram. Frank was Christopher's brother; they lived in the flat downstairs with their aunt, Miss Cassady, a large woman from Antigua. Frank and Christopher were into cricket and used to come up to invite us to the match of the day. They played either for the London Transport team or some other company which fielded a majority of West Indians. Sometimes the match was nearby, like Holland Park, or Scrubbs Lane, where they had a prison, but often we had to go all the way to places like Osterley, on the way to London airport, to games that always embarrassed me, because West Indians were expected to do well in these encounters, and I usually failed. My only recourse was to take my book of Latin verbs or something of that sort, and pretend only to be half-engaged in the match. My brother, of course, was a better player, so he didn't have these problems.

If the boys from downstairs didn't disturb our Sunday morning, Miss Cassady did: she looked larger in her dressing-gown than in normal dress, with her short hair in curlers; and came up, usually, to complain and to boast to my mother. On one occasion it was to relate that she couldn't use her own sink because one of her boys had brought home this woman, just a child, really, a little girl, Irish, you know; and this child was down there washing his shirts, and his brother's shirts, at the sink, in cold water, on a Sunday morning.

My mother verified that shirts were all right, though not underwear, to be washed in the sink. (I remember thinking that my grandmother would have given a different answer; it would have bothered her that this was taking place on a *Sunday* morning, and again I began to appreciate being in what they called a godless country.) But the two women went on to agree that times had changed (it was at this point – it always happened in these conversations – that my mother indicated that I shouldn't listen to what was being said; and Miss Cassady winkingly overruled her). What they were saying was that the situation downstairs wasn't entirely out of control, because at least the girl hadn't spent the night. Miss Cassady was always goading us, my brother and me, to own up to things similar to those her 'mannish' boys downstairs had accomplished, and we disliked her massively, so when Christopher first dubbed her *une femme d'intérieur*, we echoed it. Yes, we were from St. Caesare, we all had enough French to know it meant house-wife, but somehow, applied to the large woman in curlers – and she always had a pleasant expression, a smile – it conjured up armies and secret police who didn't speak English, and knocks at the door in the middle of the night, etc. When, later, Christopher transferred the title to my mother, I naturally wished him harm, and plotted strange punishments for him, his brother and his aunt (and maybe even, for Antigua). Could we gain comfort in the fact that the types of racial incidents that they got involved in seemed marginally more humiliating than those that we got involved in? At any rate, there was relief when the boys finally headed for America, to escape Harold Macmillan's call-up, and Miss Cassady, improbably, got married and moved to Wolverhampton.

And here was Christopher, thirty years later, using that phrase from the pulpit, from the lectern. But much had happened since 1956. (Ghana's independence in '57, for one thing; but that's not what we're about here.) The family had gradually transformed itself into a government, or maybe it was a sort of shadow government in the waiting, an Opposition. My brother was (Shadow) Minister of Finance, because of his property dealings. (Minister of Housing was too lowly, Minister of the Environment didn't exist until later, and Chancellor of the Exchequer was too comic-sounding, too much like putting on a suit, which didn't fit courtesy of the sort of fellow who owned this position in Macmillan's government.) My sister could have been the scientific advisor to the government as she was good at Botany; or she could have been Minister of Health, as she was training to be a nurse; but in the end we made her Minister of Education and Culture, as her French was better than ours. And, of course, over the years, the various in-laws and partners had been admitted to government. Two things, though, didn't change. My mother never became Prime Minister – we left the post vacant as being too demeaning as, among other things, you'd be forced to shake hands with too many people whom you didn't like. And I somehow managed to hang on to my portfolio as Foreign Secretary. (My appointment, in the late '50s, when the first of my

GCEs came through, and it turned out to be History, was, of course, lucky, and I knew I had to justify the position, to grow into the job. Adding Ancient History and Economic History to my armoury obviously helped, but the real test was the level of my performance, on the job, as it were, engaging and out-debating those whom other governments ranged against me. Most of my opponents are now forgotten, but those early encounters with, say, John Forster Dulles (America) and Andrei Gromyko (Russia) were bruising and shocked the family – (though those with Chou En Lai (China), effectively my opposite number, even though he was labelled 'Premier', were more civilised). The present crowd still keep me busy. I calculate in the job, I've had to visit some 34 countries – some of them many times – and I wondered if Christopher, from the little pulpit, would go on to assess my effectiveness, as my mother had often done, challenging me to make the world a better place, in our time. And then I snapped back to the present and noted that it was my mother, not I, who had died.

He was telling a tale I'd heard before, of my mother's generosity, feeding the multitude, students not only from the island; and he made the usual point that St. Caesarians make – the one about our not being as French as Guadeloupe and Martinique on the one hand, or as English as Montserrat and Antigua on the other – of our being more independent-minded, our being less prone to the Mother Country syndrome than others, etc. I was hoping for something – I don't know what, but something – different: why couldn't I concentrate?

I needed something to peg my mind down. In happier circumstances it would be cricket, picking the West Indies team: I was a better selector than player, but now this smacked of bad taste. I was thinking – some form of defence? – in spite of the failure of so many treaties that I'd negotiated for the family, where were we now? Had anything *taken*?... Hard to know how much time passed as this notion slipped away from me, slipped away and returned; maybe seconds later... but I seized on the image of Granny; *that* still held firm, *that* was being looked after. *Granny* wasn't, of course, my mother's mother, long dead, and buried in the plot next to... No, this was the Granny that Lee and I had adopted, the woman from – was it India or the Philippines? – and it was costing us, I think, £8 a month. Except, now that Lee and I had parted company, I'd lost track of Granny – though I thought of her from time to time – and it seemed so pedantic to split the standing order to correspond to our new status of non-couple, non-coupling... Must contact Lee the moment I get back to London, to say I hadn't forgotten Granny; that was something we still had in common; we couldn't replicate our fracture in the world: enough, up there from the small pulpit, the man was talking, preaching, talking. And he was still telling us things we knew, though I didn't mind it now, even though the hand was still shaking...

... and soon I'll have to get up there, in the pulpit, and talk. In school, we used to know how to counter the nerves, used to find ways of driving little piles to steady us when lack of knowledge threatened balance. In Latin it was easy. In Geography – this was in London, of course; you could get away with anything – in the Geography class, we learnt the names of rivers as a back-up: TYNE WEAR TEES SWALE... starting from the top, from the Scottish border working down, clockwise: TYNE WEAR TEES SWALE... leaving out anything that was too awkward to pronounce: it wasn't intended to confuse the teacher, just to broaden the agenda, to give yourself time, space to settle; to ground yourself. Later, at another level, the German Chancellors did the trick: ADENAUER ERHARD KIESINGER BRANDT SCHMIDT and the present fellow – KOHL. That sort of anchor was needed now (had I left out any of the Germans? KIESINGER was usually the one; you always had to explain that you weren't referring to the American superstar in the ill-fitting suit whose extraordinarily bloody career the world went out of its way to reward); none of this stops the damned hand shaking. (The hand shook to some purpose in '57 when we celebrated with Ghana. A man on the platform at Great Portland Street Station, an African, came over and offered his hand. A warm evening, summery, though it was only Spring. March 6th. That was three years before the glut. All of Africa, it seemed, negotiated into freedom, my busiest year, 1960. From Cameroon to Nigeria... Chad, Congo, Gabon. The Central African Empire. (Republic now) Mali, Niger and Togo. And that wasn't the half of it. There was Zaire, June 30th. Upper Volta, August 5th. Mauritania, Senegal and Somalia. Ah.)

But this isn't a time for shop. No cricket. No foreign policy. I started running through the titles of Charles Wesley's hymns, but that was too strenuous. How about football? Going through the table to keep you here, pegged down. Couldn't cope with the emotionalism surrounding the English League. A foreign one, then. French: MARSEILLE AUXERRE MONACO... That's it. MARSEILLE AUXERRE MONACO... MONTPELLIER – (Montpellier rings a bell; I had promised to take her to Montpellier. But that was another... declaration of intent. Sorry. Sorry. And I may have left out a couple of those 1960 countries in Africa, gaining independence. Not done to ignore a country's independence... Ivory Coast. That's it. And Madagascar, June 26th. That's better). MARSEILLE AUXERRE MONACO MONTPELLIER CAEN (which I could never pronounce to French satisfaction) CAEN CAEN CAEN NANTES METZ (visited the Cathedral there with Lee, a cold day, drizzly. Must contact Lee about the granny...) MARSEILLE AUXERRE MONACO MONTPELLIER CAEN CAEN... NANTES METZ LILLE (home of Maurois,

Mitterrand's first Prime Minister, good man. Old-fashioned Socialist)... LILLE LYONS (of Raymond Barre, fat, fat man) BREST BORDEAUX etc. – these games are too tiring – with the southerners bringing up the rear: CANNES TOULOUSE NICE etc. And a few others. To miss out a team isn't as important as missing out a country: which country had I consigned to benign neglect recently? Guatemala. What had I done about Guatemala?... I was being asked to come up to the pulpit to read a text. Sorry, Guatemala.

Afterwards – I couldn't bear the sound of earth on the lid of the coffin; even if it was on television it upset me, but this time I was determined not to shut it out – it was a relief to join in the singing; the cemetery so rich in plant-life, the older headstones gently askew, large trees sheltering our family plot, and the singing so lovely in its tentative, somewhat ragged way, nice, not put on, not too knowing, no one trying to appropriate; though the people did, in truth, look as if they were in costume – was that what living was? – the styles either too plush for the faces or too young for the bodies; just tailored for the wrong bodies. As I sang, I purged myself from the confusion which had ensnared my earlier attempt in the pulpit, having to read out those verses about God's goodness, those verses from *Hebrews*, verses that everyone in the congregation seemed to know by heart, and I, reading, had to struggle to keep up: in the end I had stopped resisting, stopped trying to see my original speech under the *Hebrews* text, and went with the congregation; and now I was singing.

It was the second time in a week that I had had to put my prepared speech aside – my Report. First, at the hospital in London when I had arrived too late. I had been delayed, trying to get it right, to eschew the easy plea of grapes. I would, at this grave time in our lives, Madam, report in a way befitting to someone who has for so long led our government: it would be my final State-of-the-world speech. Two days before I had been frustrated; I arrived and found you holding audience with someone not privy to our secrets; and you signalled that I should put it on hold, so we talked about other things – you couldn't deny others access to the hospital. I, wink, wink, reassured you then – knowing that we know our codes – that, yes, we had taken in the cassava-mill from the front lawn, and put it away in the servants' room, thirty years ago, before we left the house; and we had tidied up that era, and felt no guilt leaving a mess, having left no mess behind back in 1956. ('56 was Nasser's year, too, remember!)

Now, I must resign without a speech. I had thought of slipping something in, that only you and I would appreciate; in my thanks to the *femme d'intérieur*, ma'am, who had, like a magician, produced goods out of thin air, but never disguised that a house, with essential members absent, would lead to bad government: a house of twelve rooms, supported by houses on neighbouring islands, always resisted being squashed into the shape of a flat in Sutherland Avenue, in 1956. Later experiments – Ah, but I have no audience now for this. You have halved my belief in things I wished to pursue – those things picked up in travels seemed not quite local colour – the New Guinea clan doing its dance, its chant to prevent us falling off the edge of the world; elsewhere, people who might have enlarged our island, this time in Colombia, the Kogi, the Mama Kogi fasting nine days and nights to restore space to the world and harmony to this house. And should I question all this now? ...Should it not work out, you had said, and should we fall, like others, into the disrepair of Englishness, then bury me elsewhere. I had come too late to the hospital to report on that decision; and that day, I did bring grapes.

(1989)

SAFE HOUSE FOR PHILPOT

Pewter Stapleton

If the letter was confusing, the tape was more so, and I seem to have spent the entire weekend reading myself into a tangle. OK, Castine was still on the island. The island was now recognised by CNN; no one could doubt its existence any longer. Furthermore – and the tape made the claim seem credible, there were lots of voices, many of them French – at one time there had been as many as 1,500 people on the island of St. Caesare, evacuees from Montserrat, courtesy of the French air force. The French had also dropped tents and rations for 1,500 people for three days. But they changed their mind in mid-operation and re-evacuated to Guadeloupe and Antigua. They left rations and 600 tents on the island, now in possession of Castine. With Castine was the Commander seeking asylum, which, in my name, Castine had granted. We were to address all correspondence to *The* Castine. Barville Post Office. St. Caesare. West Indies.

I couldn't be bothered to work it out; another of Horace's jokes; Horace not taking his tablets; Horace feeling neglected by those of us abroad getting on with our own lives. I was in the middle of editing a book of plays and I wanted to make use of the Easter break – no teaching, no students – and was determined not to be sidetracked, despite the flattery. Castine was a literary invention of mine, oh, over two decades ago; but as my projected literary career stubbornly failed to take off, Castine wasn't exactly a household name. So I quietly accepted the compliment and tried to get on with my editing.

It was odd, though; that the volcano should bring into existence an island that I'd more or less created. And in the right place. Uncanny. Though I could live with that; because the island might not have been *exactly* in the place where I had put it: what seemed to have moved the argument on was Horace's claim of having given the Commander asylum. Horace had slipped into his role of Governor, of Priest, *the* Castine. The Commander was a sort of reproach to me that I dreamt about; relieved I hadn't had to encounter him in recent years. Earlier, he had grown used to my support, and when I tried to distance myself he accused me of something unpleasant. You had to remind yourself not to be fazed by this, for the man was a bigamist, a member of the Kreuger gang and a murderer: you could withstand the charge of moral cowardice coming from Commander Philpot. But Horace couldn't have known much of this. So, they were on the island, my island, a madman and a murderer. Or have I got it wrong again?

On with the editing.

The History

I remember years and years ago having a conversation with a friend, a historian from Montserrat; he had written a 'History' of Montserrat, including all the usual stuff about Columbus naming it on his second voyage in 1493, naming it without landing because his Arawak guides told him the island was uninhabited. (Though he also didn't land on Antigua and other islands that he had named on that trip.) We had several conversations on this subject.

A hundred and sixty years after that Columbus afterthought, the Irish stumbled on the same uninhabited island of Montserrat, which bore traces of habitation everywhere. When I pressed my historian friend for an answer to the vanishing population – documented information which he didn't challenge – he reminded me that these were hurricane islands, earthquake islands, but that without studying the archaeological evidence, and maybe taking on board the anthropology of the Mesoamerican people, he couldn't speculate. Well, these weren't my disciplines, so I was prepared to speculate.

I'm speculating now: It's 1492, early in the year, before the arrival of you know who; the region is pre-Isabella, pre-Ferdinand. So, this is *not* Guanahani, this is St. Caesare, hot and guilty, fresh up from the sea, wisps of smoke – not yet named, of course. The Great Man comes by a year later (what the world calls his Second Voyage) and *misses* it because he comes up on the wrong side, the Montserratian side from Dominica going north. The guides didn't tell him the twin island had cooled down enough for patches of vegetation to appear, a place possible for their friends to camp out, as the priests had divined that Montserrat was due to blow in three days. Though it was a bright morning, the Italian took the cloud of smoke hanging above Montserrat as mist, and diverted himself by naming Antigua to the east and Redonda straight ahead as he sailed on.

So there you have it. Taking risks the historian couldn't, I had the new island still barren enough in the mid-1660s to deter the Irish dissidents, expelled from St. Kitts by Governor Warner: they gave the unnamed mountain wide berth (granting it a few choice Cromwellian epithets) and settled on neighbouring Montserrat, unaccountably still uninhabited. Then the French got into the act, came by and named it. 1660s. A Cartesian joke, probably, calling it Caesar's island; a place from which to keep watch on the English (and

Portuguese and Spanish and Dutch and anyone else they could think of); a smugglers' nest and a place later proposed, and rejected, for an Emperor's exile.

After centuries of colonial neglect it became my island in 1972 when, in Sweden, I needed to attend a conference, a UN-sponsored conference on the sea, and my advisers said that being ambassador of somewhere obscure would help: what are uninhabited islands for (with the Arawaks long gone) but to have you represent them in calm and grown-up places like Stockholm?

Our Horace/Our Castine

In the seventies Horace had briefly held a post with an international agency in Europe and this, despite everything, made us inclined to give him the benefit of the doubt. But that was a memory more or less erased now. The letter was redirected from my London address to Sheffield and got here the day before Good Friday.

The St. Caesare postmark made me suspect more than a joke because just over a fortnight ago my sister had rung from London to say that she'd received a package for me. From St. Caesare. It was obviously from Horace, playing the fool. And – she was a wicked wit, my sister – she congratulated me on having secured my own island at last, complete with Post Office. She wanted to know if I had sent out the stamp machine to Horace: so when were we all going to go and settle down on my estate, sort of thing. But after the knockabout she revealed her real concern for the people of Montserrat where the volcano was threatening, yet again, to blow: how could they bear it? We had family there, too, who were old and sick; no one knew where they were camping out: you couldn't contact anyone who had been evacuated, and they didn't think of getting a message to you.

Then there was this funny report by CNN that there were people on St. Caesare! I had told her to hang on to the parcel because I would try to get down to London over Easter. But after getting Horace's letter I rang and asked her to put the parcel in the post.

It didn't help; it clearly was a joke, but that didn't help. There was no stamp as such on either letter or package (which turned out to be a tape) but a franking machine had been used: why did it cost the same amount to send both letter and package overseas? And why was it in French francs, as it would have been in my version of the island? The letter said that Castine was in post, that things were calm, that his little Latin and less Greek had grown rusty so he had stopped labelling the island vegetation, and would pick up that aspect of things when I arrived to help out. Meanwhile, he would continue to secure the family lands. That was the letter. If there was too little information in the letter there was too much on the tape.

There were lots of voices on the tape, voices in French as well as those that were St. Caesarian or Montserratian, following Horace's self-conscious 'The isle is full of noises' introduction. People sounded tired and subdued rather than panicky. They told stories of endurance and rescue, breaking off to send messages to friends and family that they were alive and OK. Apparently, a couple of people had been drowned and a few injured but on the whole everything was OK, though with the ash and sludge everywhere, even if homes survived intact, everything would be spoilt. God was good, good in mysterious ways. There was universal praise for the French who had kept them warm and dry and had supplied food, as well as mounting the rescue effort. One or two even sent prayers and blessings to me and my family (my mother, now dead); clearly thinking that I had had something to do with it.

When I checked with my sister again she said it was CNN

who had told the people they were on St. Caesare; and when you're tired and traumatised you'd believe anything. She thought maybe they had taken the evacuees to nearby Redonda and realising there was nothing there, had then moved them on to Guadeloupe and Antigua.

So how did she account for Horace thinking he was on St. Caesare? And the St. Caesare postmark?

Oh, Horace was a sad case. And didn't I hear the latest? The British were sending out infected beef to the islands as part of their aid effort, so Horace was clearly the first one to come down with the mad cow disease. But it wasn't right, it wasn't right for old and sick people to be moved around like baggage, one day here, another day there, not even knowing what island you were on.

I called various people who, like my sister, had Sky-TV, and tried to piece together the information. No one could make much sense of it, though the feeling was that the French were putting energy into the operation to claw back some credit, their public stock after the nuclear tests in the South Pacific and their dodgy operations in Africa and the Middle East needing some sort of lift. That's why they had dropped all those tents on an uninhabited island in the Eastern Caribbean.

But there's no doubt they had established a massive refugee camp on the island. The BBC, apparently, had confirmed this, but not the name of the island – though the BBC had continued to tarnish its reputation for accuracy by repeatedly referring to the Dominican Republic instead of Dominica as the place where the British Government, under Saudi pressure, had wished to send Saudi dissident Muhammad al-Masari into exile. *The Guardian* had, in the same issue, referred to Montserrat as a British colony (true) and as a Spanish island (false) and to St. Caesare as a nearby French dependency. Both the *Financial Times* and the *Spectator* mentioned evacuees having been taken to St. Caesare.

Because I'd been busy with my editing I hadn't been watching the news or reading the papers much, so I hadn't come across any other reports.

But the Montserratians had been taken off St. Caesare. Horace's figures had been confirmed: 1,500 people had been involved; 600 tents had been dropped with rations for three days. When they were re-evacuated after only a day the tents and rations were left behind. And it seems that the Castine and the Commander were now the only inhabitants of the island.

There was a mischievous message on Horace's tape that the Commander sent his best to me, and said he'd never doubted that I'd deliver. (Philpot getting in a low blow.)

The Castine

Framingham. Nr Boston. USA. Dr Ruth Krim looks at the time and sighs; it'll be too late now to do anything. What's the point in having a night off if you can't even get it together to go to a movie? Is she growing pathetic in her old age? A woman past forty living like a student? But without the car, going into Boston is out of the question. But it was right right right to go back to school even if it meant you didn't have a life, though if it meant debts you didn't even want to think about and being holed up here, still, in Framingham... She doesn't have anything against the Portuguese, it's just Framingham; not that she wants to go back to Boston, to Brookline – way out of reach now, anyway: maybe she'd take up that offer to share an apartment in Weston – a bit far out but maybe safer; security, security. Something flares inside her that life has to revolve round *is it safe, is it safe?* As if she's some Nazi criminal in a Dustin Hoffman film. Ah, well, she's too tired to go out anyway; and too depressed. Workdepressed. Lifedepressed. Come on, girl, pop something into the microwave and *eat;* pretend to have a normal life. See if there's a video worth watching.

Why is it that turkey no longer tasted of anything? Or is it Framingham? Or having a TV dinner on your own? With the prospect of years of the same coming up? She doesn't want to think about work. Lucky to have a job, they say, but she doesn't ever want to go near burns victims ever again. Or stroke victims. Victims don't cheer you up. She needs a personal comedian, that's what she needs. Maybe she's just more tired than she thinks, for when she turns on the video and sees some foreign army doing heroics on an offshore island and hears the name St. Caesare, she panics and thinks things must be getting to her.

Sheffield

Twenty-four years ago I invented the character Castine. I was travelling in Sweden with my partner, Ruth. Ruth Krim. We'd had a bad experience on the outskirts of Stockholm and were more or less rescued by a couple in the Tampax business. Olga and Matz were a Danish-Swedish mother and son whom we contacted, and they set us up in a flat in the middle of Stockholm free of charge. They were only friends of a friend whom we'd met in London at a poetry-reading venue, so their generosity was appreciated. They adopted us partly for their own mildly voyeuristic reasons (which we didn't mind, particularly) but also because of our 'spirit': they claimed the outsider's privilege to be bored by Swedish Volvo dullness and lack of imagination. They found us small jobs giving poetry readings in the Old Town; and we also gave the odd performance to the American draft-dodgers (there were reputed to be 40,000 of them in the city) when we could. The Tampax daddy had been an airline pilot (and his wife flew planes as a hobby) but he also ran a small business making herbal tea; and we were initiated into that, a messy job but well-paid, and convenient because the herbs and berries for the brew were kept in the basement of the building.

Largely to live up to their expectations Ruth and I decided to gatecrash the UN Conference of the Sea being held in Stockholm. It was Olga who had casually remarked that if we were writers of imagination and short of money we might consider it an adventure to turn up at the conference and bluff our way in as official delegates. After all, there were people from all over the South Pacific, from islands no one had ever heard of, so it shouldn't be difficult. It was, in a way, inviting us to sing for our supper. So within two or three days I had transformed myself into Castine, 'native' representative of St. Caesare (what today we'd call 'First Nation' representative) in the Eastern Caribbean, with Dr Ruth Krim, anthropologist and linguist, the beautiful American, as my official interpreter.

Framingham

Ruth is impatient, excited; she's on the phone, enunciating to show this is long distance.

'The little creep,' she says, not unkindly. 'So where's he got to now, he still in Manchester?... I expect he's married with lots of kids. Oh. Let me just get a piece of paper. I guess Sheffield's the place where you get all that steel, uh?'

She's writing down the telephone number and maintaining the conversation.

'OK, OK; I'm good; I guess... And is 0114 the code for Manchester, sorry, Sheffield? Right...'

She listens for a bit, then. 'Oh, I suppose it's just going back to school and sort of losing touch and. So how're you folks doing over there?... Well, thanks for the number, say hello to everyone, I don't know if you're in touch with people like Simon and Gunda. OK. Well... Oh, one last thing before I sign off. *Don't,* I mean, on any account, eat British beef, that's official.'

She kills the tone and immediately starts dialling; stops.

'The little creep.' She puts down the receiver but continues talking to herself in a normal voice. '*I* took the risks, you creep. I was the one to do the last-minute dash to Oslo to sort out the language. He just had to dress up and be colourful. And teaching in Sheffield certainly beats fucking Framingham any day.'

This time she does dial.

Philpot

I knew Philpot before he was the Commander and that makes me sentimental: we are dangerous, sentimental people; we sacrifice the individual to save humanity. Rubbish. And we say rubbish when you tell us this. Rubbish. That, they tell me, is my problem. OK, so I can safely stop worrying about failing eyesight and of dreaming about my hygienist in other circumstances, her mouth open instead of mine: I can treat nagging thoughts about unpaid bills and debts and overwork and lack of fame and being raped by a man and editing a book nobody's going to read – I can treat all of these to a local anaesthetic: these things are nothing compared to my problem which is sentimentality.

But Philpot is an important part of my life. He belongs to that going-with-the-ideas strand of my life. Whether that's unfinished business or abandoned business, I leave to others to tease out. I don't want to be bothered now by Philpot; I don't have energy for Philpot, I want to get back to my editing; there'll be serious questions there, enough, and we can call them aesthetic ones; then we'll come up roses.

OK, I give up. Philpot: *This here island's too small for the both of us.* Philpot and I came over on the same boat in 1956. Setting out from Montserrat. Of course I was a schoolboy and he a man deep into his twenties. We seemed to be about the only two people on the three-week voyage who didn't get sick. So we strutted a bit, the young scholar and the man of the world who had done the usual things: labouring on Government Works projects all over the island – building the new grammar school, the hospital in Plymouth, the new jetty after the '54 storms. Here were we setting out on conquest; I would be the General, he the troops. I would command, as the ancients did, in Latin and Greek; Philpot would be the new boys, the Russians and Americans *combined.* 'Watch this hand,' he'd say, holding up an arm: 'I coming for you, women of every shape and size in London, England. Feel this muscle. This is man who cut cane, work cotton ginnery, grind cassava; you ever see Englishman with muscle like this?' On the boat, we sealed the pact with Italian wine, which, after the second day or so, we were the only two 'tourists' in a position to drink.

True, we more or less parted company in England. He went to live somewhere near Finsbury Park and we settled in Maida Vale, and 'England' intervened, really. Then I remember that strange winter of '62-'63 when I was holed up in Wales, at Lampeter; and if my memory serves me right the first man through that Russian landscape was Philpot. He had come to Wales to ask my advice considering I was a scholar and that my subject was philosophy. The problem? Maureen, the woman he lived with, was about to have a baby and Philpot wanted me to look through my books, my Plato and Aristotle and the logic of things Greek, to come up with a suitable name for it.

This created a difficulty; apart from other things, I hadn't actually got to Aristotle yet, apart from background stuff like Russell's *A History of Western Philosophy,* and I suspect Aristotle may have been the one most likely to name babies. But we had a go; can't let the troops down. I remember taking down a book from my shelves: Voltaire's *Philosophical Dictionary.* So, starting at the start, how about Abraham? Or was that too tame. Though Abraham was a Big Daddy of a name in several cultures. Asia Minor. Arabia. And it must have been Voltaire who suggested the international possibilities for Philpot's child – Thoth (Egyptian), Zoroaster (Persian), Hercules (Greek), Odin (Swedish), etc.

Nothing there. But we had time; the baby wasn't due in weeks. After Sunday lunch, at which Philpot pronounced himself satisfied with the Latin grace which went well with the gown, we thought of being up-to-date and robust, something German, perhaps. But Philpot thought that would threaten the English, reminding them of the bomb-sites all over London, and they would probably kill the child as a war criminal to prevent it, when it grew up, moving into the middle classes where it belonged.

So it was back to the classics for a name that would fit. There'd been a programme on television on the Shah of Iran's 'White Revolution', and that gave us Cyrus and Darius and Xerxes. But you couldn't assume the child would be a boy so I had a look – seeing we were in Wales – at the *Mabinogion* to see if some Welsh Queen would come through. But Philpot objected. We should stick to boys' names. Even if I came up with something girlie from the *Mabinogion,* the book was too hard to pronounce and a man shouldn't make a fool of himself by not being able to pronounce the source of his child's name. Furthermore, he liked a good, strong name that would suit either boy or girl. When the child was born, a girl, we called her Nigel.

Philpot came back to Lampeter, down the old A40, to see my play the following year, and to apologise for allowing himself to be overruled by the women who had made him change Nigel's name for something girlie. The child, he felt now, would always be ordinary. But we had a good time after the play, talking philosophy, chopping logic.

Murders start out as things innocent as words. Philpot at the supermarket in some northern town he's not used to, explaining why he has to take action against the assistant who refused to wrap his cheese. Philpot on his coach deep in the country, middle England. Behind him, schoolboy beating up schoolgirl; everyone on the coach relaxed about it; Philpot pulls up, threatens to shoot the boy dead, to, well, just take him out unless he got his shit together. But the passengers take exception to the language of the coach driver, for this is middle England not America; and the driver shrugs and drives on. *Again,* Philpot on the phone asking about his telephone bill. The account is closed, the voice at the other end says. The account is not closed, Philpot says, I've got it in front of me. The account is closed, the girl says, using one of those voices you want to push back down her not-really-expensive throat. Can you put me on to the Manager, Philpot says. Why, she says. What d'you mean, why, I want someone who knows what he's talking about. *I* know what I'm talking about, she says. No, you don't. Don't talk to me in that tone of voice, she says. Don't *you* talk to me in that tone of voice; I'm the customer. What tone of voice, she says. *That* tone of voice, that *illiterate* tone of voice, despite the accent. You're the one that's illiterate, she says, and hangs up. So, a man can't win with language; so a man will have to *act.* A man will have to accept that this is America; he might have to poison the entire water system to get redress for that voice.

This is nothing; this is old Philpot.

I suppose I detected a change in the late seventies when we came back from abroad, from Germany, with Ruth deciding to go back to America, a lowish point for us; and I have a memory of Philpot turning up in uniform. He had lost a battle at school over his daughter. Not *that* daughter, another daughter; another family. One daughter had been deprived of her name and now this; he would not let his children subside into becoming anonymous 'black youth'. There was a war on. First they divert you; they divert you into the foolishness of getting rid of one of your families: why? Did he beat his women? He did not. He used to, but for a long time now he did not. Doris Day's husband beat Doris Day; Philpot did not beat his women. The law should come down on the husband of Doris Day and give Philpot a break. In the days when he beat women he thought he was the scum of the earth, though he acted otherwise. And all the other wife-beaters knew they were scum. Now it's different. Evidence is that there is no grand lady, no queen or princess that hasn't felt the back of some man's hand. Or worse. So don't talk to him, doing his best to keep two families going. So here we were again, the soldier and the scholar. Of course there were those who said you had to be both, soldier *and* scholar, though that's unreasonable to expect. He'd met a fellow who claimed to be both, but the man was a fraud. Though he did write a good essay on the necessity for fraudulence; had I come across it?

There were things going on in my life which made me not entirely receptive to Philpot so all I could say was no, I hadn't come across the essay, though it reminded me vaguely of Machiavelli.

No, that wasn't it; the man's name was Kreuger.

Good name, we both agreed.

Founding Persons

'Is that Sheffield?'

'Yes, this is Sheffield.'

'Come on, Pewter, what're you doing in Sheffield, is it the middle of the night in Sheffield or something?'

'No, it's just...you know, it's just...Sheffield, I know that voice, let me guess.'

'I hope you're not thinking of Hillary Rodham Clinton, you sound very British.'

'Ah, gets to you, gets to you. Incidentally, if anyone asks, Hillary and I are just good friends. So, Ruth, fancy hearing from you. I mean, good, good to hear from you.'

'You get my card?'

'Your card? No, I... Oh, your card! I got a card about two years ago, three years ago...'

'So you got my card.'

'... saying you were going back to school.'

'You never answered my card, creep.'

'There was no address on your card.'

'There was, too.'

'There wasn't. Otherwise...'

'Well, the address is a closely guarded secret. National security, and all that. So what's going on on our island?'

'Oh, you've heard about that. Weird.'

'I reckon if we've still got our island then everyone's got it wrong. For years they've been getting it wrong. You know what that means? It means that old McGovern must have beaten Tricky Dick way back in '72 and that Eleanor must be out there on our island hanging out, waiting to be taken out to dinner. Remember Eleanor?'

'I remember Eleanor.'

'Remember how Eleanor complained that George was so depressed after the defeat that he wouldn't even take her out to dinner!'

'Well, Nixon won, so he got the chance to take Eleanor out. So how're you, Ruth; have you graduated? Is it Doctor Krim?'

'We won't talk about that; I'll send you my graduation photograph, if you give me your...Sheffield address.'

So we talked about St. Caesare, with Ruth reminding me

it was her island too, bringing each other up to date, though that didn't get us far; so we hung up while there was still a lot to say, giving us the excuse to ring back.

An hour later Ruth rang back. What was I doing?

I was actually in the middle of reading Ionesco's *The Killer*; so I said, nothing much, just reading the paper, doing a bit of editing. Ruth was thinking of old friends: was I in touch with Simon and Gunda?

No, I hadn't seen them in years.

What of Josh and Ginette?

Yes, but they're in France.

Do they live in France now?

No, but, you know.

And how're they doing?

Oh, you know.

And who else was there? Simon and Jo.

Yes, yes. Of course I don't get down to London that often. Well, I do but, you know, I don't stay over that often. And Simon and Jo have got their own place now.

What of Hanz and Karen?

Oh, I'm not in touch with Germany.

OK, who do we know in England? The Leanings in Manchester, are they still alive?

Wouldn't have thought so; they were, what, fifty-six, when we knew them, sort of late seventies. Mid to late seventies; and she had angina and was in and out of hospital. Though *he* wasn't ill, no, he must be around somewhere, though probably not in Higher Openshaw.

Ruth liked the Leanings.

Yes. Maybe I'll... Yes.

And talking of Sweden. Any news of Matz and Olga?

We must contact Matz and Olga. Because St. Caesare is their island, too. Olga was sixty, which means. No, she's only mid-eighties. Now about Matz, we're not so sure.

So who else was there?

Oh… How about, let's see… Kate and Hernandez?

Who are Kate and Hernandez?

No one, I just made them up.

I see your jokes haven't improved; your jokes will be banned on the island.

Philpot

He pointedly didn't blame me for the break-up of his marriage, his marriages. Philpot had one family in Finsbury Park and another in Scotland (in Paisley), which was convenient during the years he was a long-distance coach driver. He wished to maintain both families openly, as aristocrats do, and asked me to advise, from my reading, on how best to present the situation to the simple-minded and the morally timid. I had failed to do this, so first one then the other of his marriages had collapsed, leaving his children with more than unsatisfactory names.

Then one day he materialised to say that a friend had killed a man in order to teach others a lesson. This friend from St. Vincent, a postman, had killed a man. (I noted his tact in suggesting that the 'friend' was from 'another island'.) Anyway, this was the situation.

A postman?

Yes, a postman.

So, this man was a postman and he had a sense that there was something funny about one particular house where he delivered the mail. It was clear that the woman of the house was being knocked about. Nothing as obvious as black eyes and that kind of thing. Once, when he heard whimpering inside he went round the side and looked through the window and saw her bent double easing herself up from the lino on to a chair. But some things aren't your business; you're not paid to mind other people's business in this country. And he put it out of his mind. Time passes; you have to attend to your own life. So with the Vincentian. But then he gives up his job as a postman because of the weather and takes on a job as a school caretaker, and then has to give that up because of the violence. He tries to get his old job back at the Post Office but is out of luck because the technology has changed. (Even the Post Office has changed its name.) So, to cut a long story short, he gets out the old uniform and becomes a postman again for the day.

He seeks out his old patch just to see how things are getting along. (Will they recognise him or is he just another anonymous threat?) He knocks on a familiar door with a mock-registered letter and a prepared story – you know, wrong number, wrong name, something like that. There's no answer so he goes round the side, and what he sees is not pretty to report. But the same man and woman, torturer and tortured, are demonstrating that nothing has happened in the world since he last passed this way. The neighbours, the police, God and Allah are asleep. Even the woman's stamina doesn't know when to say 'enough'; she can't be expecting rescue, she doesn't even look that much worse than before. And the man is calm, a perfumed man, in his element, smiling; he invites the postman in, prepared to have a little chat, not bothered about the concentration camp in his kitchen. So the Vincentian does a bit of sign language as if he's an idiot, smiles, and withdraws, not for him to intrude on the people's thing. But that night he comes back with a friend, and they persuade the torturer to go for a drive to a place you don't need to know about, and they let him understand that this thing won't be quick.

The Vincentian was a follower of a thinker who called himself Kreuger, though we suspected that wasn't his real name; and this was the phase of preventive action; and this was a service that more and more bruised and battered women were beginning to call on.

Horace

I never quite understood the term 'Ur-Shakespeare'; but I fancy this is Horace's phrase. Not for him Gonzalo's *The Tempest* speech; he would admit traffic; he would be magistrate, etc. On his island, 'letters', in both senses of the term, would be known. He would take care of management of the family lands, castigate idleness and not necessarily insist that island women be pure. And he would make himself spiritually responsible for the Commander.

The last time I saw Horace was after the 1989 hurricane, hurricane Hugo. I'd flown out to the islands as part of the relief effort; and we landed on Montserrat and waited for the smugglers to get us to St. Caesare. Horace's sister Margot, who was a government official, was expected to meet us there, but she was engaged elsewhere, and instead we were met by a little group headed by Horace. He looked like a priest down on his luck, but what I'd taken to be a dog-collar was just the top of a white T-shirt underneath the rest of the costume. The rains had continued after the hurricane and even such clothing as was saved was impossible to get dry, so Horace was taking advantage of the general dress spree before the Red Cross hand-outs imposed the more conventional look of have-nots.

Scorning to dwell on his own predicament, he made gentle fun, I seem to remember, of my greying hair. Even then he presented himself as Margot's representative: Horace was your perpetual stand-in. He was irritating, he embarrassed us, he looked after our interests in ways we wouldn't have sanctioned even if we knew what he was doing. (He had escaped to France once, via Guadeloupe, and through exploiting friends and family, managed to erect a couple of benches in the Alpes Maritimes to a great-aunt of ours who had apparently died a heroine.) You could be angry with Horace, but it was an effort.

Maybe he was the right Governor for the island.

Founding Persons

'So you're not married with children and...'

'Afraid not.'

'... making the world more crowded.'

'Nah. And what of you?'

'Oh, men are... difficult propositions.'

This was getting awkward, so we talked about St. Caesare. 'Can you remember your Castine speech?' Ruth asked. (It was early evening and I was trying to calculate the right sort of tone to adopt for America in the middle of the afternoon.)

'Course not, that was twenty years ago. Twenty-five.'

'Uuyeewang moro wiinong iikanabairong. Got that?'

'Ridiculous.'

'Remember what it means?'

'Oh. I'm sure it's something like: ME BIG CHIEF. ME DRINKY MORE COCONUT WATER THAN LITTLE CHIEF.'

'Yes dear, very funny. "Upon everybody bestow that which is good." Got that? Remember that? Though I hope you're not still talking in translation.'

'I think you're making it up. You know I just thought of a use for our island. We could rent it to the BBC for all those people they send to desert islands. It'll be groaning with Bibles and Shakespeare, but think of all that music, we could sell some of the classical stuff and keep the Dylan and the jazz.'

'That sounds a bit stressful.'

'We can always get rid of the Bible.'

'Yes, dear, but what do we do about your jokes.'

'Talking about jokes, I heard a good one by Norman Mailer.'

'Oh no.'

'No, really. He's in this downtown restaurant. *Elaine's.* Manhattan.'

'That fool.'

'He's having dinner, and this English reporter comes up with her microphone, because, you know, *Elaine's* is the place to be if you're a writer or… And she says. "Are you Norman Mailer?" And he says, "Yes, I'm Norman Mailer," surprised that anyone should recognise him and… And quick as a flash he says: "I'm getting to be so old I live in Massachusetts. Er."'

'Fool.'

'It sounded better first time round. So we won't have any Mailer jokes; what else?' (I was thinking we should have Andrea, the hygienist at my dentist's, but I wasn't going to own up to that.)

'It'd be nice to have everyone come to visit, maybe once a year. But you know what I'd really like?'

'What's that?'

'A really good drug store. Stacks and stacks of stuff, never running out. And maybe a reflexologist.'

'A reflexologist! Someone mucking about with your feet!'

'I knew you wouldn't be ready for the island.'

And we talked about being ready for the island, the most comprehensively stocked desert island with Shakespeare, Bibles and luxuries, and above all, music. Add to that – a large, benign animal that was not a carnivore. (We took it for granted that among the luxuries was a strawberries-and-cream plant (strawberries-and-no-fat-cream plant) and a statue of Muhammad Ali.) There'd be no place, repeat no place for Bob Dole after the *débâcle* of '96. But, talking politics, a luxury could include the voice of Irish President Mary Robinson, acceptable to both parties, like soft Irish rain, warm and health-giving; also a pastrami sandwich place like the one on the corner of Arlington and the main street, though Framingham must never be mentioned. Instead of Framingham, the second town or main village should be called McGovern (or maybe even Dakota – not quite Omaha – but maybe something like Sioux Falls, though not Badlands). Or just call it McGovern. Or George 'n Eleanor. And what else? Definitely no bicycles on a mountainous island (a reference to Ruth's difficulty in riding a bicycle in flat Stockholm in 1972); certainly no pressure to ride bicycles. Granted. And the luxury of luxuries: a troupe of players as in Shakespeare, better still in Jonson, dwarfs and mountebanks, fat men with high-pitched voices and women who could play Lear; and they would, of course, do Molière and Chekhov and Soyinka and improving speeches from Emerson.

Don't shoot, don't shoot, this isn't a plague of locusts; these are tuneless songbirds migrating from the English countryside. Wrong again, I'm bleeding something other than blood, and my eyes are open: that's what comes when you go to bed thinking of a woman visiting campus with her baby; or thinking of Ruth creating a language; thinking of the hygienist; thinking of Audrey, the cleaner, ten years your senior, while reading a few pages of Henderson the Rain King. *Glidingly, the woman with the baby comes across a big tree sawn off at the root: the flesh-like wound causes her to turn the baby's head away. The experiment with the cleaner, ten years your senior, hasn't worked, doesn't buy credit, doesn't serve to extend your life: her cheerfulness relentlessly closes the ten-year gap between you; she recommends having all your teeth out, and a seaside holiday. The next cleaner must be ten years on the other side of you. A moral issue? Ruth is over forty now, who's to blame for that? Framingham? Time to count sheep.*

It's raining, the tents have an eerie feel; I miss them, though I know they're there. I'm dashing from tent to tent of this ghost city and bump into Professeur Croissant, an old teacher from the past, long dead: he looks the same as he always did, maybe that's why I know he's dead. Without surprise he points out the burial-ground (ah, he changes into the Commander, but never mind): he points to the place where Horace, in his robes, is reburying a member of the family, disturbed by the earthquake in the village. When I realise that other members of the family, long dead, are piled up waiting reburial, I wake in panic, in relief. And reach for the book.

Strangely familiar, while I'm trying to figure out where the landmines which were definitely in the dream, fitted in. Strangely familiar because I'd picked up the wrong book, the Ionesco, which I'd just finished reading; not really finding a justification for murder; though the Architect and Berenger seem dated, childhood figures, 'Their Radiant City', a seventies title, a book long-read. It's true, isn't it, that both Mill and Kant justified capital punishment. And there was some clown on the radio recently going on about suttee. Good thing for women of eighteen, bereaved. I'm thinking that I would provide Philpot a safe house in Europe, live up to expectations, come through, accept my historical responsibility.

I'm reading Bellow, but reading doesn't distract you, except to make you vaguely superior to the bulk of England asleep and vulnerable. Matz and Olga's basement in Stockholm would do, then he could make the herbal tea, be useful. Or bring him to Manchester, Higher Openshaw: rewrite the Leanings into history. Though again, Germany at the moment seems tempting before it settles down to order. (Which is more dangerous, civil order or disorder? Discuss.) Billet him on our old friends, the Moogs, out in Buckfost. Herr and Frau Moog, one son and one daughter – bright child, the daughter ('I want to do my homework, I want to help to make Germany strong again'). Or maybe we should ease up on Philpot, take him across the river to Ebertplatz, our old stamping-ground, Aquinostrasse, where Ruth and I had problems with the Turks, and with the Köln police, seriously big and cigar-smoking (or that may have been the taxi-driver, the night in question). Whatever. The Commander is a man with cane-cutting skills, a follower of Kreuger.

It's too late to ring Ruth. (On the island it would be useful to have one of those fellows from *Gardener's Question Time,* with his Latin, to help Horace out with the plants, the one with the accent which doesn't grate too much: a castaway would have left Pliny's *Natural History.*) Bellow promises too many pages. Tomorrow, I'll ring my sister and ask if it's true that the volcano has disturbed the family burial-ground.

Once, a long time ago, Philpot asked me a question which I thought might be philosophical; it had to do with the nature of *time.* Precisely: *Where does time come from?* I thought I'd work on this, a chance to shine. But he quickly put me right. He was into being domestic, doing the cooking, and noticed that *thyme* had disappeared from the shelves round his way, even in the supermarket: what was going on there? What Third-World thyme-growing country was being torched to impair his cooking? As a scholar, I should know. I might put my mind to that now (for you can't, seriously, justify editing at this hour of the morning); and really, Saul Bellow is such an odd name for a man, don't you think?

(*New Writing*, No. 6, 1997, British Council/Vintage)

...though she was looking good, plump, the one that bore my name; and now maybe we should be talking about the normal things, the gym, exercises, salads, the decision of whether to go for looking good in clothes, which used not to be my preference, rather than in bed, with breasts no longer sagging from loss of weight. All that was over, all that was past for us; though she was, indeed, on the plump side.

All was pleasant today; we read the newspaper together, read out bits to each other, like old friends, recalled funny things that had happened on the television. Chitchat always had a price. Chitchat was welcome as a prelude to something, and if it seemed to be heading no nearer to that thing, then impatience would give way to argument, to anger on her part, protestations and denials on mine; finally hysteria – which had led to this. But that was the old life. Those were times past. Now, like old friends, I could visit her, we could read the newspaper, tell jokes, be calm.

She had been watching the boxing on television. I was told this by an attendant with a smirk of satisfaction, as I was waiting to see her: she, who was so much not into violence, not into male things – people hitting each other in the face, hitting each other anywhere – had flicked the receiver, flicked from this to that, from comedy where people seemed to be laughing a lot, to a talking-heads programme of men in suits, and a woman among them, in a suit, to the News, to the boxing; and she settled on the boxing, and sat quietly and watched it for a while, before getting bored and wandering off. And that, I was told, was the extent of her progress; she was ready in fact, to return home. Progress could now continue at home.

Violence had been the thing that had brought her here. She had suffered it at the hands of lovers, though she seemed not, when I first met her, entirely obsessed by it. Naturally, it was there in the background (as a man you learnt to be sensitive to that, to the fact that it was a reality for women) and when she referred to it, it was with a slight self-consciousness, which you knew to be part of her protection. Yet her 'I know you would never hit me,' was as unsettling then as it is now. I hadn't hit her and, in fact, I didn't think I would ever hit her. I wore my professional 'Man-Against-Beating-Up-Women' badge so *openly* it embarrassed my friends. I was shrill against the batterer, demanding almost Biblical punishments for his kind, and of course, the cynic in me wondered whether I was protesting too much.

For I had come close to violence when she had irritated me, when she goaded me into doing something (again) this way instead of that way, her way instead of my way, when she objected to the way I said Good night, to the way I greeted her (the degree of passion in the welcome), to the way I said Goodbye on a railway platform; she objected to the language I used when I wrote, to my habit of writing post-cards instead of letters (love-talk on post-cards?); she objected to what seemed a lack of desire, a lack here, another lack there, to my not giving her what she needed. She objected to my protestations that I was giving her these things; and of course she objected to being put in the position of being needy, demanding, neurotic. She objected to my voice, to the tenor of my voice, the level pitch, the suggestion of control whatever the situation, to the hint of power contained in this (the suppressed violence?) and naturally to the way it undermined the partner, the lover, the other, making her powerless, desperate, foolish. It was that voice, protesting its love, a voice without warmth, that had driven her over the edge.

'They say I'm ready to come home,' she said, smiling. I knew that smile, I knew how easily it could change, knew how the even spread of the lips could suddenly break up. I thought back to that last night together, when I had to hide the kitchen knives, to accompany her to the balcony as she smoked, to stop her wandering out of the flat in the middle of the night. By then she had lost – and not for the first time – the power (another power?) of speech. Lovingness brought it back; the way she smiled at the word darling, 'Darling', which melted me to the point of loving. Soon, she had no need to write things down but could talk, like someone new to speech, then like a foreigner, then more like herself. Every little noise, though – the wind rattling the window – made her jump, recoil. My gesture, putting an arm round her shoulder, made her recoil. I urged her from the stiff, crouched position, fingers clenched in a sign ancient or secret, something I couldn't read. My gesture to make her more comfortable on the bed, to put my arm round her shoulder – caused her to start, or to recoil, or to stiffen, fear in her eyes.

The first words when they came were about the 'terror', and she pointed to her head. She said something about the film in her head. She pronounced it terror. Caressing her head, stroking her hair, I reassured her that I would protect her: so, what was she afraid of now?

She was afraid of men who beat women. (She didn't actually say 'women'; her sentences were incomplete.)

I reassured her that they were beasts, that I would protect her from them, from all men who beat women; that I would never beat her. Remember?

Yes. No. Her voice was back but there were things she couldn't say. Her sentences didn't peter out, but ended on something like a knot, on a word that wouldn't come. I played the guessing game, generally getting the wrong word, but thinking it helpful to keep it going.

Yes, she knew I wouldn't beat her. She was frightened of me.

Yes. Yes. I would protect her against people who frightened her.

I frightened her.

Yes. Yes. In that case, I would protect her against me. Like this, like this. Now, she wasn't frightened, was she?

My voice, my calmness, *my lack of hostility* frightened her. That was how men were, sitting on the edge of the bed, before they hit the woman: such men didn't do it when they were out of control, they did it when they were calm. Like me. (It was better to be out of control when you hit a woman; then you might break down and ask forgiveness; that showed you cared; it gave the woman the satisfaction, the power of knowing that you cared. In the end she gave up: though I agreed, it was clear that she had given up.) She tried to put some space, on the bed, between us.

So I told her she was right, and I could hear the new tone creeping into my voice till it was almost jolly, jokey; I told her that tomorrow I would chase her across the park, chase her round and round, and watch her embarrassment as, braless, she tried to cope with this and yet stay ahead of me. This brought back the smile of 'darling'. I told her, my voice keeping pace with the occasion, that when caught, when captured, she'd be claimed and loved, right there and then, in the park, in the open, in the presence of passers-by raw with jealousy; and then – you couldn't over-do these things – when we got home we would play our own private game where I would describe every inch of her body, inch by inch, and tell her what it suggested, tell her how it spoke to me in all her accents, all her voices, from lewdness to song; and we would imagine the epics of verse emanating from the upper knee, the shelves of novels from this mole (there there, *here)* too near the armpit. And this operation, this task, this adventure, greater than pirates sailing to the New World, vaster than Moonmen to the stars – this adventure would take days, weeks, more than one lifetime, and like the House of Royalty, like Dynasties of the past, would be bequeathed, the describing of her a gift to my successors, passed down the generations, inch by inch. This was the prize that the world would fight for.

Smilingly, she hoped they wouldn't fight.

And then I was relieved when it was all over, and I could go back to my normal voice, my normal thoughts, my life. And here I am again, jolted out of that normality.

'They say I'm ready to come home,' she said, smiling. How carefully chosen were the words, 'come home'. She was good at putting me on the spot: was she unaware that time had passed? In my home was someone else who now shared my life. And here was someone to be accommodated; her children had left home, the house had been rented, to protect her, so there would be money. She was half-packed as if home was only a drive away. She was always bright: was she enjoying a joke at our expense?

I made sure that my voice wasn't cold or over-controlled; that would also guard against the risk of solemnity. So what could we talk about? The surroundings, the trees, the birds – she was romantic but not sentimental. I reminded her (a private joke) of the awful noise that most birds made, in their thin, penny-whistle way, little better than barking; only the lack of volume saved them from being dogs. We should all go out and march against the poets who promoted this notion that birdsong was beautiful.

And she laughed at that.

Birdsong was a violence against nature.

The dropping of the word 'violence' in the conversation was deliberate: a test. Her face clouded with uncertainty.

She had seen on television animals in ill-fitting harness, with untreated wounds; that was in some other country; that was cruel.

I took this to be a signal to me that she was controlling her personal fear of violence, and could object to it in the normal way, without being unhinged: was that why she had watched the boxing on television?

But then she could always watch the boxing on television; even more the wrestling. What frightened her there were the talking heads at *Question Time,* politicians in quiet voices battering one another. Could she now watch *Today in Parliament* or tonight's newscaster being immune to the *News?* Could she survive coming home?

Then she said, in apology:

'Sorry, darling. Sorry I put you through all this.'

I protested that she hadn't.

'It must have been hell for you.' And before I could deny it. 'I'll watch my words. I won't make demands. I realise you need your space, too, to function... But only if you want to,' she added, guardedly, catching perhaps something of my panic. She had no sense that time had passed.

'It was awful what I put you through that night.' She was pursuing this with a deliberateness somewhat alien to her, I think, so it must have been part of her determination to show that she was better, that she was able to face the past, that she was ready to come home. And she deliberately brought us back to a scene that she had avoided in the past, a scene where we had been trying to heal ourselves, inventing games. She had been sitting on the bed, fingers clenched, hunched, staring ahead, starting at the slightest noise, gesture. She hadn't yet lost her speech. And she proposed the game to make me see what I had been doing to her. The theme was, as it had been for a long time, the imbalance in the relationship.

'I give you...' she had said, and waited for *me* to repeat it.

'I give you...'

'Softness... Warmth... Love. Loving...'

'... I give you...softness, warmth, loving. Yes, yes yes, I agree, and...'

She indicated I shouldn't embellish, just repeat, so I waited for her to continue.

'You give me...razorblades; you cut out my tongue; you wall me up.'

I had to think about that. Eventually, I admitted. 'I can't say that. You give me love, yes. Yes yes, lots of love; but let's not...'

And with a slight shrug she accepted that that game, too, wouldn't work. And now, all this time later, she was apologising for having put me through that – and other games.

'That's all right,' I said, knowing there was no way of saying this without conveying something suspect. 'Let's not think about all that.'

'Do you love me?' she asked suddenly.

'Yes, yes, of course. And...'

It was too late to take it back.

And then we were making, as in the old days, plans for a life together. The more I got into it, the more I wondered how to get out of it. I knew other men in this situation who had miscalculated, and the result was the kitchen-knife, the razorblade in the bathroom, a leap from the balcony. I was thinking that I hadn't let this happen in the past and I wouldn't let it happen now. So we talked through it, and I countered her fears and hesitations with reassurance, always remembering to put some energy, some passion, some colour into my voice so that it was the opposite of cold. And I accompanied her in this way through the rest of her packing, which didn't take long: she had always been tidy, she had never spread herself; and I compensated for the fact that she was nervous, her hand shaking a little; and she turned her face away when I attempted to kiss her.

And then we started out on the journey home. In my home there was a partner awaiting my return. In hers – her children gone – there were tenants.

(*Planet*, No. 102, 1994)

AARHUS, DENMARK

i

Will the country run out of money and starve its universities and force the libraries to junk their books? From what he knew of the history of Denmark, dull, low-lying and able to absorb invasion without permanent harm, his books would be safe at Aarhus. The collection would be substantial enough to effect the sort of critical mass to have an impact, to make visitors aware that this section of library, this corner of Denmark belonged to Pewter Stapleton. The name Stapleton was sufficiently un-Danish for them to pause and, out of curiosity, pick something off the shelf. (Though, later, someone would make a case for Stapleton and Jorgensen being related, separated mainly by a trick of phonetics.) So, back to the library: sitting at a nearby table, books piled high, would be the necessary prop – pin a good Danish name on her – Anna – pretty but not uncomfortably so, glasses, working on her thesis. (Remember that Gavin Ewart poem where the aging poet fantasises about his becoming a thesis?) So this Anna looks up, not really distracted (thinking) but curious about the visitors: what book does the visitor go for? They are not Danish, this lot: foreign visitors to the library. People interested in the Commonwealth thing, no doubt; lots of Australian books here, lots of Australian interest. Anna wonders if the books should be segregated in this way, creating a Commonwealth ghetto. She might make this point in her study. She recalls

Stapleton writing about being type-cast. Her supervisor had been non-committal about her Stapleton project, and had in the end remarked that Stapleton seemed a hidden sort of poet; and Anna had liked that. Well, she did and she didn't: 'hidden' was a code word for 'unknown' or 'minor'. But, on the other hand if someone was hidden and you were the means to make him known, *to make him visible,* wouldn't that be marvellous? Ja. And of course, 'poet' would be used in its wide sense of writer, including fiction and drama. If she pulled it off, they might even acknowledge that she had an English sense of humour, a way with irony – like Brandes had. So, she's working on a thought, the pen lightly tapping her lips, then she makes a note in the notebook. She is left-handed.

Pewter would have preferred an offer for his library from an institution in this country; better still, not his library but for his *papers,* his archives. That would have shown some appreciation for him as a writer rather than as an assiduous collector of books: it was as if he were a second-hand bookseller going out of business. His friend Carrington's *papers* were being collected down at Canterbury; he knew a couple of people, of no great renown, being lovingly catalogued, their old theatre programmes and unpublishable poems and stories, no less, up at Hull – Larkin's old place. Now, Hull would have been convenient, an ideal place for the archives, a short train-ride from Sheffield: then he could get rid of his old notebooks (those he still nervously wanted to hang on to with their jottings and fragments) in an accessible place, just in case. You wouldn't want to have to get on a plane every time you had the urge to see whether these few lines made on a building-site in France in 1972, or that note scribbled at the dress-rehearsal in St. Croix, were things that suddenly seemed relevant. Though that wouldn't help you if the collection were in the Caribbean. Except you'd have there a sense of the thing coming home, of *something* coming home – even if that home wasn't quite St. Caesare. But that option wasn't on offer.

That was the problem, perhaps, with St. Caesare. When your land disappears in a cloud of volcanic ash it seems churlish, sitting pretty elsewhere, to bang on about the imminent loss of your books. He had promised to organise the delivery of books to St. Caesare. Everyone thought it a good idea, of course; but in a way that organising an exhibition of St. Caesarian arts and crafts in Birmingham was a good idea. To make money. Pewter had attended an exhibition of St. Caesarian arts and crafts in Birmingham a couple of years ago, and it did make money for the volcano relief. It made money because singers and poets were invited to perform, and food was provided. There was a charge at the door, and the event was well-attended. Pewter tried not to be cynical as he acknowledged to himself that the few people left in St. Caesare would be more impressed if he had sold his library to the highest bidder – Aarhus weren't offering that much – and then just sent them on the cash.

One image from his last visit to the island stayed with him. He wasn't now talking disaster-stuff, the buried capital, the two-thirds of the island fenced off as 'unsafe zone'. (How do you cope with that, two-thirds of the island fenced off as unsafe zone: how do you adjust to the remainder of 'island' as living-space? Ah, but then he'd said all that, drawn his comparisons with old Beirut and present-day Chechnya.) What he was thinking about now was the visit he had paid to, ah, the Professeur, CJ Harris, his old schoolmaster, St. Caesare's grand old man of letters. CJ was eighty-nine years old, resplendent in his private room in the Home, wearing trendy socks.

What Pewter couldn't get over was the bareness of the room, not like a writer's room. A writer without his books seemed, well, like a man stripped naked. Pewter recalled talk of the blind Borges in Argentina knowing where exactly on the shelf his favourite books were and, when visitors came, would take one down and quote from it – *read* from it. That was the *style* of the blind writer. And CJ Harris didn't seem to be blind. So the visitor had to make sense of this, this act of renunciation: if St. Caesarians had had a reputation for being puritanical, this would maybe make a sort of sense. But had they? No one actually knew what kind of people St. Caesarians were, and already they were being dispersed by hurricane and volcano. Into refugeedom. Refugeehood. The Nearly People. Pewter's family library had vanished in an earlier trick of migration. He felt he owed it to something, someone to restore the *presence* of a family library on the island. Call it a sense of symmetry, nothing more.

ii

Why collect Stapleton?

Well, it seems as if all the obvious people were spoken for, the people who had been to Aarhus in its heyday when Anna Rutherford (the Australian Director not the researcher) and her Commonwealth Studies programme ruled the roost. Those sort-after papers had all gone to expensive places in America. And other 'names' wanted to do the Nationalist thing and help build up archives at home. A couple of very distinguished Caribbean writers with long association with Aarhus couldn't be approached because they were now into their eighties, and it seemed gross and predatory to hover like crows over their assets. Even Andrew Salkey's magnificent library in London was problematic, because Andrew had a widow and children; and really, the books were part of the family's shared furniture.

More, shared memory. So Pewter Stapleton was in luck: he had no one to mourn his books. (Though he did write a letter to the people at Aarhus reminding them that he had no sudden terminal illness he was aware of, that he hadn't retired from the university and wasn't in the process of moving house – so willingness to get rid of part of his private library shouldn't be seen as an act of desperation. Later, to a friend who had given up on him, Pewter presented this as a way of uncluttering his life, as she had demanded.)

Pewter didn't have to make a difficult decision in parcelling up his literary estate. More simply, he didn't have to think very hard what books to send to CJ Harris in St. Caesare and what to reserve for Aarhus; for Aarhus had specified the *West Indian* collection. No opportunity, then, to surprise them with the range of his internationalism; he'd just have to stun them with the depth of his Caribbean holding. (Would Anna in the library, surveying the Caribbean Collection – Caribbean authors writing about Caribbean characters, Caribbean critics writing about Caribbean authors, Anthologies which included work by Caribbean authors – would she still be able to write about him as someone transcending type-casting?)

Pewter recalled being in Malaysia earlier that year, and running into a private collection in the university library. He had gone out to give a few lectures at the National University, part British Council, part National University at Bangi, and when he visited the library he ran into 'The Muhammad Haji Salleh Collection'. He had no idea who the benefactor was and soon gave up trying to form an image of the fellow as an *individual,* from his choice of reading. Interesting, perhaps, that there were none of the heavy theological or Islamic tomes you might have expected, but a range of titles from Giradoux to Gide (the Autobiography – *Si Le Grain Ne Meurt)* gave you the feeling of being manipulated. Here was the stuff that would be in everybody's library – Joyce,

Sartre, Chekhov. Boll's *Group Portrait With Lady,* Bellow's *Mr Sammler's Planet.* Gunter Grass. Behan. John Osborne. Brecht. Conrad. Interestingly, considering the location, *Nostromo,* not *Lord Jim.*

Pewter was puzzled by the collection. The selection presented here from what he imagined Muhammad Haji Salleh's real library to be, told you little about the man except that he was determined to present himself as cosmopolitan: I-might-be-living-in-the-sticks-but-I'm-in-touch-with-the-metropolis sort of thing – an old-fashioned sentiment these days. MHS did have an interest in theatre – lots of volumes from Sophocles to Beckett. But the overwhelming impression was of the Hemingway, the Marquez, etc. that stared out at you, somewhat tiredly now, from your own shelves. Recalling this Pewter felt that maybe a bit of good old-fashioned type-casting wouldn't come amiss. A young woman in Germany had translated a couple of his poems into German for his *Festschrift* last year, and in her note she said that one of the things that interested her in Pewter was that he seemed to have left *ethnic* concerns behind. (Anna, in Aarhus, would certainly have read that.) But then you're only 'ethnic' if you're put in a foreign context. So what would he have to do now to *creolise* Denmark?

iii: *A History of Denmark*

We start with the Rise and Fall (c. 850-1814) of the Kingdom's fortunes (which already gives it a longer recorded history than St. Caesare. So far so good). Then there's the rivalry between Denmark and Sweden, *boring, boring,* till we get to Frederick III having the nobility's leaders exiled (see 'Siege of Copenhagen, 1660 and aftermath, culminating in the rise of the absolute monarchy'). All this, and various transformations leading up to the Second World War.

The Frederick III thing might be interesting (the seventeenth century used to be Pewter's area). He could imagine a little scene in his grandmother's drawing-room in Coderington, with one of Frederick III's exiled nobles, debating the problem with CJ Harris and Mr. Ryan, the clergyman: they'd be served tea – coconut juice and iced lemonade and coconut tart and home-made ice-cream – by Mady, who would have a Danish name; and before evening service (which CJ, an atheist, wouldn't be attending) they would have hammered out an agreement, part of which would have the grandmother inheriting an estate in Denmark for her grandchildren.

As he got more interested in the history of Denmark, Pewter became conscious that The Faeroe Islands, Greenland and The Danish West Indies, gave him a lever to treat Denmark as any other colonial power past its prime and not just a harmless little country between Germany and Sweden struggling to keep its head above water. He would demand more for his books.

Even with the literature, there seemed more than he'd bargained for: not being interested in children's authors, he had assumed that Karen Blixen was the one to beat. (And maybe Kierkegaard, if you wanted to pursue things to the fringe of philosophy.) Hemingway had thought Blixen was the big cheese, but Ngugi begged to differ, pointing out the lady's propriatorial attitude towards Kenya, in her book *Out of Africa,* and her infanticising of the Africans. The film version certainly confirms Ngugi's reading of this. There was this other fellow, the critic; but who reads that stuff now. And the Hamlet play, of course, would be reassigned to Englit rather than Danelit.

But the book Pewter was reading said there'd been a Golden Age with the arrival in Denmark of the romantic philosophy of Schelling (nineteenth century) with, not just the fellow who wrote the stories but names new to Pewter.

Grundtvig, he liked the sound of. And the pronunciation of Hauc. But he'd give a miss to the fellow, Ingeman, who was said to have written historical novels in the style of Walter Scott.

So, is the *presence* of all this enough to turn him into an 'ethnic'?

Updating the scene in his grandmother's dining-room in Coderington, Pewter decided to have his characters focus on events in England, early in the century, 1606 maybe, when Christian IV visits his brother-in-law, James, newish to the English throne. CJ, the historian, and Mr. Ryan, the clergyman, show themselves remarkably well-informed of the hunting and feasting and drinking indulged by James and his brother-in-law, etc.

Simultaneously, there's a private scene in the grandmother's bedroom, over the breadroom, where a miserable but resigned Queen Ann (sister to Christian, wife to James) is saying that, all in all, she was no more unhappy than other women; and that liberation wouldn't come for some time.

Grandmother herself is saying that things here are pretty hard without real male support. Problems every which way. The old man Effingham (excuse the Spanish) doesn't seem to be able to bring in the fishing anymore, people in the village are talking, calling him names. Where to look, eh, for better service: the island's small, small. And apart from everything, the young boy she'd come to rely on, young Cecil, forceripe like the rest of the clan, was now demanding a piece of her land for services rendered: was it all worth the hassle?

Anyway, enough of girltalk: maybe they should join the men in the drawing-room, to stop them getting into mischief.

With the Aarhus thing in mind, Pewter brought forward the dispatch of books to CJ Harris, in St. Caesare. Though CJ had, of course, translated Molière and done other things for the stage thirty years ago, that wasn't why the selection of books to him was mainly drama. Pewter recalled very precisely his state of mind in selecting those books for the old man. Books, indeed, to furnish his room.

Pewter had started with his earliest shelves – earliest in terms of his collecting books as a schoolboy in London; and they happened to be mainly drama, plays, as theatre was his first real interest. This wasn't an ego thing to show off his library, but at the same time you had to put together a collection worthy of being *noticed,* worthy of respect for CJ Harris as a leading literary figure who had had all his own books buried under sand, under ash. A collection of three to four hundred books seemed appropriate. So he started at the top shelf of his stacks of plays. *First shelf, thirty-nine books.* Mainly Elizabethan and Jacobean, with a bit of Restoration thrown in, including critical stuff – Tillyard and LC Knights and that sort of thing going back to the dark ages when he was a student.

So that's thirty-nine books. *Next shelf.* More than thiry-nine here, more individual volumes (the first thirty-nine included, as well as the complete Shakespeare, a two-volumed Ben Jonson as well as Beaumont & Fletcher and selected Middleton and Farquhar). So, *Second shelf, Sixty-four volumes.* Everything. No method. From Dryden (the fine, original Mermaid series – won't do so well in the heat and grit of St. Caesare) to the volume of Soviet plays by Andreyeff – the stuff one used to read then! (Volumes acquired at Foyles's secondhand department on the fourth floor, late-'50s, early-'60s) plus all the usual suspects – Aristophanes, Anouilh (in French), Osborne, Ionesco,

Stoppard. Ah, well, Pewter never did claim to be original in these matters: how would George Chapman, say, go down these days: would anyone in England be putting on *Westward Ho* now? Then send him to St. Caesare. Also Seneca. No one here wants him. Pewter had run into some Italian scholars who had never heard of Ugo Betti, so maybe Pewter's enthusiasm for *The Queen and the Rebels* (seen one wet Saturday afternoon in the '60s at a nearly-empty theatre in Watford) was misplaced, to be appreciated now only by an eighty-nine-year old *savant* in St. Caesare. So, what have we? *Sixty-four books and thirty-nine, that's nine and four = thirteen; one and six, seven and three = ten, that's one hundred and thirteen.* That's two shelves. And some good stuff here, Plato, *The Last Days of Socrates,* etc. *Shelf three.* A big one. Lots of books piled up on top of books. Deep shelf. Bond. Pinter. Soyinka. Arden. Also Pirandello and some Americans. But Dario Fo was there. (Long before the Nobel.) And the younger Americans: August Wilson. Wendy Wasserstein. *So what's that now? Ninety and a hundred and something. Hundred and thirteen. That's two hundred and three.* Another two shelves of drama. Big books. *Seventy-five in all. So that's two hundred and seventy-eight.* Enough. A lot of these are collections, which must bring it up to between three hundred and four hundred pieces for or about theatre. This lot included a volume of *World Drama* (Dover Press), which contained *twenty-six unabridged plays* from Aeschylus and the *Sakoontala* to Sheridan (this was volume one). This was enough for a man of eighty-nine to furnish his room with: this would help the visitor to know what it is to be St. Caesarian; this would provide a glimpse into the St. Caesarian mind.

There was a bit of theatre criticism thrown in. Ken Tynan. A *Paris Review* volume on contemporary French theatre, John Elsom, etc.

Easy now, to send the rival 'Caribbean collection' off to Aarhus.

V

The pedants have to be abused and Anna has to be amused. And as well as the West Indian collection for the library, Pewter has slipped in a box of archives, carefully selected pointers to his own work: there are odds and ends stretching back over five decades, letters from literary people, all designed to be of value to the browser of a lively curiosity, and to the research student with her glasses and ambition to succeed. Buried in the box is an early story, unpublished, but with a Shepherds Bush address, which would put it some time in the late 1960s-early 1970s. Here, the Danish-St. Caesare literary dance is more or less taken for granted. It is called 'A Coderington Childhood'.

A Coderington Childhood

I must give my family their Danish names, now that the habit seems to be spreading. I am in the British Museum in London, in the Reading Room. In the North Library, in fact, falling asleep over a minor seventeenth-century play. Now concentrate. Our author has confused his Allwit with his Witall, and the result is social satire of a kind, which shows people living in the Interregnum-Restoration were not entirely unlike ourselves...

Again, that image from St. Caesare floats back. I'm a child looking through the railings of the verandah at Caroline washing clothes in the stone trough below. (Caroline will later join her cousins in Denmark, in Silkeborg.) I'm recalling other things seen from this verandah, looking down on the ritual of the cassava being ground on the front lawn, old Barefoot Blueteeth from the village, rhythmically working the pole with one foot - left foot firm on the board on the lawn; right foot pedalling, up and down on the pole, rhythmically, while he feeds the cassava, peeled and washed, into the throat of the mill, onto the spinning wheel which eats your fingers if you're not careful. Blueteeth, the expert, suddenly strikes the boy looking down from the verandah, as an athlete: much later, he would refer to that flash of realisation as a Tolstoy moment - one of the images from which we date contemporary St. Caesare literature. Grandfather Christian, though dead, is to be imagined looking down on this scene.

In the drawing-room - not the same day but these images collide - Professeur Croissant and Mr. Ryan, the clergyman, are having one of their usual debates - today over issues for St. Caesare thrown up by the sayings of Grundtvig and Kierkegaard. Maria Frederica (or it might be Maria Sophie today) comes in with iced-lemonade and coconut juice, coconut tart and home-made ice-cream.

My sister and I are growing delinquent at our unchanging names. My brothers, Erik and Soren have unluckily ended up in England. Those long boat-trips are a lottery.

This sad story covers six pages.

(2000)

BALHAM'S DUKAKIS VOTE

Pewter Stapleton was back home with friends – an old girlfriend, Lee, and some of her friends. It was almost like old times, out for a curry in Fortune Green. It was usually a toss-up between Crouch End and Fortune Green, but Crouch End still had personal associations for Pewter and Lee, best avoided, with him thinking, given a chance, he'd play it differently now. He was back from teaching in Germany, but that was stale news, this wasn't the sort of crowd where you sat around talking about your experiences abroad, unless, perhaps it was further abroad – if you were back from Thailand, say, having refused to pillage the pagoda; or, on the other side of the world, having stood firm and left something Aztecy in its rightful place – then you were listened to with interest. So Pewter opted for a story nearer home, about running into an old friend, Balham, in a bookshop in Camden Town, and how Balham had dared him to go on a street demonstration this Saturday.

Demonstration about what?

'Oh, you know Balham. Government policy. Government lack of policy.'

As they waited for drinks Pewter started filling them in on Balham. Balham had done this and that, the ultimate self-promoter: he had read Sociology at university and that sort of thing, read a bit of History back in the '60s; published pamphlets. But, more interestingly, he had just been to America and voted in their Primaries, voted for Dukakis rather than Jesse Jackson. Balham was British – Jamaican-British – and lived in London, and had no Green Card.

There was interest, certainly, at table, in Balham's story; but then it was time to order, and Pewter caught himself going on a little too long about Balham, bringing back the sensation of boring the company, of talking to himself, something he occasionally caught himself doing in the street.

Not that it was a worry, just something to watch. Everyone knew the feeling: someone ahead of you would turn round, and walk on for a bit, and then unobtrusively cross the road. (Maybe they used to do that years ago, older women, as Balham insists, but then they were making a statement about the group, the clan.) This morning in Crouch End, Pewter had been standing at the lights, waiting to cross. The lights changed, the green man flashed and suddenly this quiet fellow on the other side let out an explosive, chicken-like sound, then proceeded to cross over in the normal way. The man, middle-aged and somewhat squashed, acknowledged Pewter like a kindred spirit, and went on his way. Give it ten years, Pewter had thought. Less.

In the restaurant they discussed the menu, Lee's hand pointing at something they might order, and the hand inevitably set Pewter prickling, recalling an image of the same hand pointing upwards at dinner (she'd taken it out of the sling) because they couldn't stop the bleeding, and how unfazed she had been; and, in the end, they were almost beginning to make themselves believe it was an omen, the drawing of blood sealing something between them that would be there in later years to look back on, to be grateful for, a cementing that would hold, in spite of everything.

Well, it was already later.

So, after they'd sorted out orders for biriani and tandoori and extra vegetable and nan bread – and was it more wine or lager? – the table turned to stories about children and school, and the quirks of aging, and the aliens that ex-partners had become – then someone remembered that Pewter had been telling a story about Balham who had been to America and had voted for Dukakis instead of Jesse Jackson. Pewter, saying the story was too long to tell, tried to nudge a signal from Lee, as he vowed not to fall into bad habits of hogging the lime-light, but Lee seemed relaxed, and the feeling was that he should tell the story, and leave out the boring bits.

So he ran through the business of Balham getting an Apex flight to New York, then a quick train down to Washington, DC, where he voted in the Democratic Primary. That was earlier in the year. Now, Balham was planning to go back in November – American democracy was an expensive thing – back in November to vote in the Presidential election. In the Primaries he had voted for Dukakis and not Jesse Jackson as he didn't want his non-American vote to taint Jackson's legitimacy. Now, in November, he would vote for the Republican Bush to make the point of the illegality of the American political system.

At the table, everyone had a view on this, and before people got carried away, Pewter reminded them that he, too, had had a chance to vote in the American elections – and this time from as far away as New Guinea! But that was a mistake. He noted the flicker in Lee's expression; he was falling into the old habit, cashing in, appropriating someone else's few minutes of glory. Anyway, it was clear, round the table, that whereas Balham's exploits in America had seemed vaguely daring, Pewter's Papua New Guinea reference merely served to make him seem exotic. And everyone round the table was used to the exotic.

* * *

The next day, a Friday, Pewter met Balham in the middle of town, at a bar near Leicester Square tube. It was Balham's choice, as Pewter had said to him the other day he was hunting down a couple of books that he hadn't been able to find in the Camden Town bookshops. Balham had automatically assumed the next stop would be the Charing Cross Road and Foyles. For Pewter, Foyles suggested an earlier time, student days when you went up the rickety lift to the fourth floor to scan the second-hand section: that froze Balham a little further in the past, vaguely comforting to Pewter. With Balham you tried either to demonstrate your street credibility or to do what Pewter now saw as his smarter option – to emphasise his ignorance of what was going on in England while he'd been away on the continent. But Balham, too, had European connections – an ex-wife from student days, who was French – so Pewter concentrated his talk on Germany.

Balham wanted to know about the beautiful Lee; and Pewter was pleasantly non-committal on the subject. All right, then, how about Pewter's sister, Avril, whom Pewter was on his way to visit, in the East End: was her husband still working nights?

It was unnerving the things people remembered about you, though as Stewart was into catering it was a good bet he'd be working nights. Pewter returned the compliment by asking about Balham's ex-wife, about his daughter.

The daughter was visiting from France. Pewter missed some of what Balham was saying as he was trying to remember the girl's name and to think how old she would be. Old enough, because tomorrow she'd be joining the march, carrying a banner for a black man murdered in England. The name of the man didn't register with Pewter, and Balham, pleased, said it was all right; he wasn't the only ignorant person in England. Pewter cited teaching in Germany as excuse. Balham said Pewter couldn't have been *that* long in Germany as our man had been murdered some time ago, by the State. 1820, to be precise. But while Pewter bought time in Germany with *die Fräulein* – and why not, why not, that was part of the struggle, too – Balham's daughter would carry a banner for the murdered brother. They would go past the Old Bailey, of course, where it had all happened. The Old Bailey may have changed its name but it was still the same old Newgate Gaol. Balham, of course, would be on the march, with a few thousand others – tens of thousands, who knows? – just to remind people who needed reminding of the tolerance of those who didn't forget and didn't forgive.

It was like conceding defeat when Pewter allowed Balham to accompany him to the East End to his sister's.

ii

Avril is thinking: here are the uncles come to visit, her daughter's uncles, Maggie's uncles. They are as removed as her own uncles; they puzzle her. It doesn't matter that one of them today is a substitute. Maggie, spoilt as always, refers to them as Greeks bearing gifts. Only, the uncle hasn't brought what Avril has asked for. But here they are playing their role, impressing the child. Soon, one of them is telling a story they know, with Maggie playing her part of genuinely wanting to hear it again: did he really vote in the American elections when he was in New Guinea? And did he vote for President Reagan? This gives Pewter the opportunity to explain that though this had really happened, the choice hadn't been between the actor and the undertaker, which was how Mondale was known. It had simply been a massive vote of confidence in the man from Texas, Lyndon Bains Johnson. LBJ. Pewter explains that this is a legacy from the Vietnam war when a detachment of US troops either deserted or were diverted to New Guinea – to New Britain, one of the islands that helped to make up Papua New Guinea – and had made themselves useful to the rulers. Ever since, in every US Presidential election, West New Britain has voted and returned a solid majority for LBJ. Officials there have names like Air Force One and White House East Room; and each time he is elected, Johnson sends a representative to make the acceptance speech, and the man is always introduced as Thirty-Sixth President.

Avril is conscious that the other uncle is matching the story with one of his own, determined to impress the child. Avril has been brought flowers and is still looking for a vase, vaguely puzzled that this isn't what she has asked Pewter to bring for her, but he makes no reference to his mistake. Somehow she has difficulty keeping calm. The two men have altered something of the balance of the house. First, the flowers, nice but suspicious, then the subtle alliance with Maggie who is now upstairs playing her music too loudly. Now the tall one – she can't really be expected to call him Balham, but she can't remember what he used to be called – wants to know if he can smoke. Well, he can't smoke: good manners can't be a one-sided thing; host and guest must co-operate. They always put her in this position, the uncles. She's trying to put down the little rills of irritation, put them down to the fact that she's had a hard day at work and doesn't have the energy for these man-woman games. Suddenly, she can't take the noise coming from Maggie's room: *Maggie, turn that thing down. Now! Leave her be. She doesn't overdo it, unless there are guests. Or if her father is sleeping, knowing he has to work odd hours.* Avril is thinking: they're so intact, these men. Not growing old like other people. As if they're just grafting deafness and blindness onto the same old child bodies, like students you remembered, going grey.

She maintains the conversation, about Stewart, about catering, until the new uncle begins to make her feel foolish, guilty about not going on the march tomorrow; and though she finds a vase and puts the flowers in a prominent place, she must still be subjected to a history lesson, without which, she clearly wouldn't deserve to be on the march tomorrow. She thinks vaguely of being born in one country and living your life in another. Or of having a partner who works nights. But these are not the reasons to take to the streets. Something she is about to ask the uncles slips out of her head, like those newspaper games Maggie and her father used to play, little picture puzzles where you have to find the ball, cunningly disguised; a child's game, a man's game. She demands quiet upstairs and gets it, and ashamed, invents dinner as an excuse.

For she has to prepare two dinners: Maggie being vegetarian. Not a strain in a catering household, though she worries she might be indulging the child – even in something good for her: imagine wanting to go and sleep rough one night, in the middle of London, to show solidarity for the homeless. As if Maggie was already a Member of Parliament.

The uncles decide, despite Avril's strenuous protests, to contribute something to dinner.

* * *

Pewter and Balham nipped out to do some shopping that wasn't required; Pewter was guilty that he had forgotten to bring whatever it was that Avril had asked for, and though it wasn't food, he thought the gesture of mushrooms might help. So they came back with a bottle of wine and some mushrooms.

Pewter thought of Lee, years ago when they had first met, and she had decided to cook a meal. Naturally, he popped round the corner for the wine, and when he got back there was blood all over the white-topped kitchen surface. She had cut her hand on the melon, that soft space between the thumb and the first finger; and at the hospital when they couldn't stop the bleeding, they sent her home with her arm in a sling, the hand pointing upwards. Naturally, Pewter had blamed himself then and he blamed himself now; and he thought – and he thinks – nothing short of perpetual devotion would suffice. And that's why he panicked on his way back from the shops with Balham, convinced his sister had had an accident preparing Maggie's courgettes.

At dinner, Balham mentioned Louise Day Hicks. They didn't know about Louise Day Hicks and her squeaky, high-pitched voice? It was impossible to understand the Civil Rights battles of the '60s, in the US, without reference to Louise Day Hicks and her Boston's School Committee. Well then, he'd tell them about Louise Day Hicks.

They live whole sections of their life in blocks, these uncles, Avril is thinking. Uninterrupted by children. All that time gained not having to punish your body, not having to keep that little bit in reserve in case someone else needs it. They live 150 years in Russia, these uncles, surviving on yoghurt.

Now, it's the German uncle's turn to entertain his niece, making difficult jokes about foreigners and the English language, and about the English and the English language. Maggie, of course, responds to this; she, too, has out-of-the-way knowledge: And did they know that the *Cat & Fiddle* derived from Catherine of Aragon and that *Elephant & Castle* was a corruption of the Infanta of Castile? The men like this sort of *play* and talk to the child about Spain for a bit, and Maggie leaves the table in a good mood, and the washing-up undone.

Later that night Pewter phones Avril to apologise for having brought Balham (and reminds her of his name before he was Balham), and apologises for having forgotten to bring along what Avril had asked for. And, of course, Avril dismisses it as unimportant but senses, nevertheless, that Pewter isn't talking to her as he normally does; he is too guarded, what he is saying sounds prepared; he must have thought she was someone else.

And they say that's what happens to men, their memory, their enthusiasms grow a bit... she can't think of the word. *Sporadic,* is the word she thinks of later. That's why they throw her off-key, unless she is prepared. A husband working now at nights, now in the day, throws you off-key. The other brother sometimes comes to visit without phoning. Like the surprise uncle today whom, already, she can hardly tell from the others. Avril has a brief horror of them living on through all those Russian years, and is, of course, immediately guilty. They're so clever – one, apparently, voted in the American elections – and she can't remember why.

(*Planet*, No. 107, 1995)

PREACHERMAN

i

It was a Sunday like today and, for a few seconds I thought I might have an opportunity to quiz the Preacherman on his famous sermon. But of course we hesitated; how could you recognize a man 40 years on – and here of all places. Though we *were* in Italy, and that was a trigger. I was staying with friends near Orvieto, in Umbria, and had broken free of them today, having a quiet lunch, in the square. And the man disappearing out of the square might not have been Preacherman – though he did have a beard, now white. He'd retired now, clearly (Grandchildren? Did they speak English? I could imagine an Alessandra waiting back at the flat: what did she look like?). I tried to recall his play of wit in that 1956 sermon – Sermon on the Mount, Sermon on the Plain, whatever. And the talking-point of the day, his mispronunciation of St. Lucia. A decade later, when I emerged from the railway station in Venice – Stazione St. Lucia – I was tempted to relocate Preacherman in the canal city. (He did, after all, travel on an Italian boat in '56.) But you couldn't really see him as a gondolier, and even I, feeling a little bit of rheumatism in my hand, didn't want to consign the fellow to a life on water. Better to place him here in Orvieto, one of the minibus drivers doing the precipice-run. Pensioned-off now, making his way to one of those hot, walk-up flats above the little square behind the Piazza del Populo where we had dinner last night – one of those windows curiously unlit at night: what does he say to Alessandra when he gets home? *Just went past a poor bastard on the Piazzo Duomo, eating alone, tucking into his tagliatelle. Had the smug look of a tourist who'd just taken in his bit of culture, just seen the Luca Signorelli frescoes in the Duomo, bought the postcards. Had to nod, hadn't I, know how it is. Put me in mind of someone from home catching his arse in England. Should have invited him back for a drink, I suppose; but who can be bothered.*

And in the square, as my *secondo platt* arrived I was thinking: would the fellow have kept pace with my memory of him; would he be settling down now to, well, Leopardi, during his siesta?

ii

That Sunday in '56 was another matter. We were full of expectation and apprehension; expectation because we were leaving the island in six weeks, and as we'd been ready for months and months the time was dragging. Apprehension because, well, because of lots of things: there was no new Minister at the Methodist church in Coderington since Parson McPherson had retired and gone back to Scotland, and his replacement had, we just learnt, gone down with food poisoning, and had to be put off the boat in Barbados. We didn't want to read too much into things, but once you admitted bad luck you began to feel not just unlucky but threatened: for instance, by the boat stuck in Plymouth harbour over in Montserrat. What to make of a huge boat, an ocean liner bound for England, having engine trouble even before it set out. There were hundreds of people on board from down the islands: how could they now trust this ship to make the three-week crossing to Genoa or wherever? And what was worse, this was the ship that would be coming back for us in six weeks' time. The feeling in the house, that if we were going to England we should really be going on an English boat, grew. But we tried not to talk about it much in case it brought on bad luck.

What distracted everyone was the decision to allow the passengers – banana workers from St. Lucia and St. Vincent, cane-cutters from Barbados, all sorts – to come ashore on Montserrat and St. Caesare; they were all over-dressed in the sorts of clothes they didn't normally wear, and we were uneasy that when our time came for England we wouldn't be able to distinguish ourselves from them.

Then news came through that, as the ship was still incapacitated, and as it was Sunday, the ship's chaplain would come over to Coderington, to our church, and preach the sermon.

Even my mother perked up at that, because she was unhappy at the prospect of being sent off by Reverend Philpot, who was stricken in Barbados. Mr. Philpot had worked in Africa and elsewhere; and there was a feeling of resentment in the village at being asked to take on Africa's leftovers. St. Caesare might be a backwater, but people who treated us as an afterthought must be made to think again, and that applied to the Church, as to anyone else. Of course, the poor man couldn't be blamed for having served in Africa before coming to us, so whatever happened we had to conduct ourselves with dignity. (My brother, who was the bright one, said that if the Reverend had learnt some serious obeah in Africa, then that was good news; he could pass on some of the secrets to us so that we'd be able to juk the English when we got to England; but my mother told him not to be ignorant.)

My mother's general nervousness transmitted itself to us in all sorts of little ways, radiating through the house – down to the business of the ironing of our clothes. When my grandmother had been around to object, we couldn't do the ironing on a Sunday. Of course we did it, Nellie did it; but it had to be done surreptitiously. The breadroom, where the ironing took place, was underneath my grandmother's room, and Nellie had to be careful, bringing down the flat iron gently on the cloth so as not to make a noise. When my grandmother died these restraints were abandoned. But today my mother invoked the old rule of the house that there should be no ironing on Sunday: whatever small creases were left in our suits had to be endured and brazened out. As to her dress, the dress wasn't the important thing when you set out for church: *was this my mother talking?* But we knew she was distracted and anxious at what would await her in England; she didn't, though, stop me polishing the family shoes on the verandah that morning.

At the bottom of the hill on our way to church we ran into Professeur Croissant. Professeur Croissant was a heathen who shouldn't have been allowed to teach in the church school because he didn't believe in God. There was that, and the fact that he sometimes came to school with canejuice on his breath: either way he shouldn't be allowed to teach people's children.

He made a joke of our being dressed up and going to see God. My mother would normally remind him that the Stapleton family dressed like this every day of the week, except when the children were in their school uniform; and that we weren't like some people who lived behind God's back in some ghaut, who wore whatever they wore during the week and had only one dress-suit to their name, something they had to put on not only for church but for weddings and funerals and whatnot; christenings. But today she didn't take him on.

The Professeur, as usual, apologised for his joke, in his own way, and told us if we happened to run into God, ask him to make the island a little bit bigger, so that an honest man could fart on it without his neighbours hearing and badmouthing him; because he was sure that that was why fastidious people like us were scurrying off to England where people didn't fart in public.

My mother was calm through this little scene (Hurry on, England) and managed to wait until he was out of earshot before calling the Professeur a fool and a jackarse: she should have ordered the car to drive us down, away from all this; but everyone said that you had to start preparing for hardship in England; we would have the car for the return journey up the hill, in the sun; we had to be resilient.

iii

No one had seen a parson with a beard before; and no one reckoned that he would be black – not black in the sense that Rev. Philpot, who had spent years and years in Africa, might be black, but black in the sense that we were black. (Why would an Italian ship have a black chaplain?)

And his voice wasn't even preacherly in the way you would expect: he stood there behind the lectern and talked to us of the Sermon on the Mount (Matthew, something or other) and of the Sermon on the Plain, which was somewhere in Luke. There was a bit of confusion here because most people in the congregation misunderstood 'Plain' and thought he was talking of travelling by air, pulling rank, so to speak, when everyone else travelled by boat. And that made it difficult for him to get a fair hearing. And then, on top of everything else, he mispronounced St. Lucia.

We'd had a visiting clergyman mispronounce Deuteronomy, but how can you mispronounce St. Lucia and be from these parts: he certainly didn't have an Italian accent. Afterwards, my brother was cut short when trying to explain just how radical the sermon had been. My mother was annoyed because the man had treated us like Africans – she seemed to be confusing Preacherman with the clergyman, stricken, down in Barbados; she resented the way he had talked to us about England, saying that we had been brainwashed, that *they* had been preparing us the wrong way to go abroad, maybe even to go to the wrong places. We had already put on, he said, the hand-me-down cloth of Europe and had no stomach to face our own nakedness. And here there had been a little eruption in the church, led by Miss May from Windy Hill, who shouted out in the middle of the sermon, that she hadn't come into God's house to hear any nastiness, any foolishness about *naked*; that no one in their life had ever seen *her* naked, and he had better wash out his mouth. My mother wouldn't have shouted, of course, but she permitted herself a suppressed giggle.

And in truth the fellow was being impertinent: did he think we were from some canefield or plantation, making an arse of himself not even being able to pronounce St. Lucia! The Preacherman with the beard had ended by saying that we were not dangerous enough to travel to foreign parts.

Then he and his friends hurried back to the boat in Barville harbour; the Italians had managed to repair the engine, and they set sail by nightfall. The debate, as you would imagine, was whether the ship's parson was a clergyman in truth; and if he was from these parts, why had he so totally misjudged the congregation?

Professeur Croissant, who wasn't at the church, said a man who deliberately mispronounced St. Lucia, then corrected himself, had a certain sort of credibility, because he was paying attention to the right sort of detail; he had much more difficulty with the sort of fellow who got up in the pulpit and was sure of his Beatitudes and his Doxology. (*Jackarse.*)

The boat sailed before we could establish much more about Preacherman; there were those who felt he was legit, with his fresh interpretation of the Beatitudes, etc; others claimed that his political message was bogus. Over the next few years, in England, we tried to check up on passengers on that trip which had preceded ours, but no one could recall a Preacherman, black or white: the man was brazen, but he had imagination.

My brother insisted that the way to read the sermon was this: we should go to Canada or America – those of us who were going to those places – and refuse to live where they wanted us to live and refuse to do the jobs they offered us: when they invited us to pick cotton and cut cane we should retaliate by demonstrating knowledge of the American and French Revolutions, and about the agricultural revolutions of the Gracchi brothers in Ancient Rome – that, and by being able to point out the Gulf of Carpenteria near Australia on the Atlas. We should demand to be treated with respect. If that wasn't enough there were boys here who could translate Thucydides *unseen*, when they put their minds to it: what this meant was that when we got to England we should request an audience with the Prime Minister, Mr Eden, who would of course be impressed and recommend a meeting with the Queen, who had been told lies about us. My mother, impressed, called all this 'ignorance'.

iv

Everyone, of course, had a theory about Preacherman: he was a poor boy from this or that island; or from some country area, who inevitably vanished without trace in England. (And for good reason, because – think back to that incident in '56: the boat had docked in Barbados before coming to us. Among the few passengers from England to be put off on the islands, while the migrants were picked up for the return journey, were Reverend Philpot and his wife: wasn't it odd that they came down with food poisoning and had to be put off in Barbados; was it true that his gown and dog-collar and Bible had been stolen?)

Some had it that the fellow jumped ship at the Canary Islands, or Genoa or Barcelona, all the stations on the way to England. People still occasionally talk about the beard, the mispronunciation of St. Lucia.

And I've just seen him, of course, here in Orvieto, disappearing in the direction of the Piazza del Populo, going home to his Alessandra. Nice.

(*The Caribbean Writer*, Vol. 113, 1999)

ARM BAND

i

He barely hesitated. Pewter phoned Eric convinced that it was he who had phoned. Stupid to have missed it but he had been in the next room and... he wasn't in the mood for anyone making reference to his being hard of hearing. Eric answered immediately and Pewter made the comment about being hard of hearing, an attempt to restore a sort of normality to the situation. But it wasn't Eric who had rung.

'Where to start?' Pewter asked, knowing there was no good place to start. 'These boys. Can't be drugs. Or the boots not fitting. Though watching King run up to bowl what can you say? And the bowling isn't the worst of it. Nobody's paying them to lose, because there's no point in betting on a foregone conclusion.' And then Pewter asked, not entirely rhetorically, if those fellows felt they could escape physical harm in Leeds tonight, as some people whom they'd humiliated might not have a sense of humour.

Earlier in the week Eric and Pewter had talked of possibly going to the ground on the Saturday, depending on the state of the match. It wasn't a problem for Pewter, coming from Sheffield, only 30 miles down the road; but Eric had to come up from London and they'd had a bad experience when they had teamed up for the Old Trafford match a couple of weeks ago. On balance, Pewter was happy enough to watch this one on television.

But about today: 'They should make them bear the cost of the refunds. All the refunds. For the three days lost.'

'Three and a bit.' Eric was a stickler for detail.

'Three and a bit... Walsh, Ambrose and this boy, excepted. Sarwan.'

'Yes, they seem to be the only three...'

'Put their homes up for auction... Cars, whatever.'

Eric said he'd been talking to someone who said that the boys' wives should be forced, publicly, to leave them. Wives and girlfriends.

Sure, they should bring back the old Chinese treatment. Public humiliation. As advertised during the Cultural Revolution.

Eric said, thinking of someone they both knew: Imagine giving up your well-earned holiday in Florida for this. He was referring to 'Arm Band'.

'And missing out on the £300 suits.'

Arm Band at Leeds would be given to less clowning than the Arm Band of Old Trafford.

'Well, he predicted it wouldn't get any better.'

They had met Arm Band queuing for his West Indian chicken outside the ground during one of the mid-afternoon breaks for rain. He was in a somewhat fractious but essentially genial mood, pontificating.

'I am not a rich man,' he was saying to the dispirited few, waiting for chicken. 'Not a rich man; do I look like a rich man?'

He didn't look like a rich man, and Pewter was about to tell him that he looked very much like a rich man in disguise, when he noticed the fellow's arm band. So, naturally, Pewter and Eric became a bit solicitous, putting things, if you like, into perspective. Eric, acknowledging the man's sleeve, said that the cricketers didn't have that sort of excuse.

'I could have played tourist,' Arm Band said, 'like some of them fellas here in this country. Save up and buy the £300 suit and go back home like saggar-boy, pretend I ain't catching my arse in this place.'

He had an audience round the chicken tent, discretely egging him on.

'I not pretending I catching my arse more than any other black bitch in this place catching arse; I not playing that game.'

Pewter and Eric were among those quietly assuring him that they, y'know, knew where he was coming from.

Nevertheless he'd had enough of this pappyshow; this foolishness, because humiliation wasn't his middle name. He repeated it.

Humiliation was not his middle name.

No, Sir.

They must be think that Humiliation was his middle name, but humiliation was not his middle name. (It wasn't appropriate, it was a little late now to speculate on his name.) And then in an aside that showed he wasn't just a local presence, but a genuine supporter, he said: 'I was at Lords on the Saturday.'

'Ah.' *The* Saturday: that was when West Indies were bowled out for *54*. Say no more, Master, say no more.

Now this. (It didn't have to be spelt out.)

Mention of the Lords thing concentrated minds; this was beyond clowning. But then the enemy had already seen you naked, as it were, and were still aroused at the sight. Eric eventually struck the right tone of banality: it might be better tomorrow, you never know, the boys might inexplicably get their act together, that even at this late stage – despite what happened in Pakistan, despite what happened in South Africa, despite what happened in New Zealand, *even they* couldn't be so lacking in, in what? – *even they* couldn't be so lacking as to go on playing the fool in this way.

Arm Band wasn't having any of it: 'Maybe you know something that I don't know.' He was enunciating very precisely now, a little too theatrical for a man in mourning, sharpening a sort of fuzziness about him, the arm band looking more and more like decoration: a brand – a *name* for himself

'Maybe you know something that I don't know. Maybe you have inside information. And if I wrong, I don't be wrong and strong. But until I know better, I goin' keep wearing this.' He gestured, without surprise to Pewter now, at the arm band. The black band was, indeed, for the death of West Indies cricket.

The point he went on to make was that it was costing him the same amount of money to follow these jackarses round the Test grounds of England as it would have cost to put on *style* and live it up in some foreign country. Or to go home for two-three weeks and play the big shot.

That was at Old Trafford a week and a half ago. And now, whatever the boys on the field got up to, they were not going to give either Pewter or Eric a heart attack. Eric and Pewter would not give them that sort of satisfaction. So the two talked on the phone, calmly, as if nothing had happened, as if there was, if you like, some rationality left in the world: they put up this or that excuse, knocked it down, knocked down others. Returned to what had been said before: No, it wasn't arrogance that made the team lose because their body-language told you different. No, it wasn't a question of throwing matches like the South Africans did because if anybody was going to buy West Indies, it would be to induce them to *win* the odd match, not to lose them all. Edgbaston being the fluke, West Indies should just save themselves further humiliation by not pretending to play cricket at this level. West Indies should be forced to stop competing at Test level, as the Australians had more or less done to New Zealand, whenever.

ii

In Paris, Eugene Stapleton, Pewter's elder brother, was making his way to his cousin, Beverley's place. Yes, he could have done it the easy way, got a taxi and maybe taken Jennifer with him, but Jennifer had had enough for the day, and Eugene wanted, just once, to do it the other way, his brother's way, difficult. It seems the way of the writer was, deliberately, to seek out hardship, and then turn it to your advantage. For his brother had had his false starts, and was shameless about owning up to them in public. In print.

So, having dropped off Jennifer at the hotel, Eugene took the metro: one stop to the Odeon, change to M10 and out to Javel. No problem. With Jennifer in tow they would probably have given up somewhere along the line where they had to change and taken a taxi, because Jennifer had suffered a bit, standing so long in the queue at Versailles; and it was hot today. Eugene imagined his brother doing this journey, taking out his note-book from time to time and jotting down things that came to mind, or caught his eye (like those Africans at the entrance this morning, selling post-cards, three men with little multicoloured umbrellas fitted onto their heads, like carnival head-gear. Embarrassing to have to whip out your note-book whenever a thought struck; but maybe you got used to it. If you started young enough you'd get used to it; if you were a child of the '60s, and all that). Eugene very quickly discouraged a strand of thought that he knew would lead to bitterness. He was on holiday: he was missing out on the cricket in England, deliberately, as an act of faith. By absenting himself he would give the boys space to prove him wrong. Eugene was unlucky and would miss out on the victory; but he was prepared to do that for the team. *Doing* Paris for the duration of the Test, would be a credible sort of cover. As he turned into rue Sebastian Mercier, Eugene felt mildly virtuous, both for himself and for the team's imagined performance at Headingley.

'So what's this business we hear about Clinton and Ra... Ra, what's his name, Ra...?'

'Oh, Alanbrooke, the opposition leader?' Beverley was asking about events in St. Caesare since the volcano.

'Yes. D'you know this guy?'

'Yes, we know him. I know his elder brothers. And big sister. I think this one went to school with Pewter, and then came over here young. To England.'

'So what's the Clinton connection?'

Eugene went on to explain that it had nothing to do with Clinton, the man, the President, but was the name of the new town, capital, going up in post-volcano St. Caesare.

They chatted about that and about events at home through the first course of dinner. Beverley wanted to be brought up to date with all the news, the gossip, but Eugene, who found the fortunes of the real Alanbrooke more interesting – history was his passion now, in retirement – enlightened her of the man's exploits in the last war. Later, on the way home, he slipped back into wondering whether he had hit the right note today, with writing up the post-cards.

From time to time, more so lately, he had been mistaken for his brother, the writer. He wished his brother well, naturally; and yet there was a feeling – what was it – of slight wrongness. Maybe of something not entirely dignified to be confused with your younger brother; he couldn't brush aside the sense that people were slightly disappointed that he was the wrong brother. The way he explained it to himself was that the whole thing had grown slightly one-sided. He had no urge to compete, of course, and his brother did lots of foolish things he wouldn't himself undertake – even though some of them seemed to rebound to Pewter's advantage. To go into situations likely to be embarrassing, knowingly, with an eye to writing about them, now that was something else. Though maybe he was being unfair to Pewter: the writing about them maybe was a consequence, not the aim. Nevertheless, that story about the Nazi on a French autoroute... Pewter hitching with a blonde woman in France. Being picked up and then put off on the autoroute by a Nazi, late at night: *was that worth a short story?* At points like this, Eugene couldn't see the family resemblance. But what was he thinking about, anyway? Yes, postcards.

He wrote the one to Mr Browne in French; that would cheer up the old boy, his old school-master who had taught French at the grammar school in Montserrat, now exiled in Barbados. He sent one to some friends, his brother's friends, really, in the south of France. It had seemed right to write in French. Two or three times over the last few days he had been forced to act as translator, at this or that gallery or public monument. But when it came to it today he wrote his brother's card in English.

On the way back to the hotel Eugene realised that he had been all at sea, really, in trying to explain the phenomenon of Ra Alanbrooke to Beverley. Ah, well, who understood those clowns? What he was still pursuing, at some subterranean level, was the post-card to his brother in England.

He wrote in English because he felt that he had already invaded his brother's territory a couple of times that day, and to write in French – he suspected his French was better than Pewter's – would be to be making some sort of statement that was unworthy of another member of the family.

A long time ago, without regret, he conceded the literary field to his brother; and all sorts of little pointers had confirmed this to be the right decision. Whenever they met, Eugene usually came away with another prickle of conformation that one brother's writing would remain locked in the head while the other's would be displayed on the page. Eugene recalled recently discussing something fairly trivial with Pewter. Goods displayed in an up-market shop-window, the cost of various items which they both thought inessential.

Afterwards, Pewter had said, casually, that the price tag on this or that article told you something or other. And suddenly they weren't just talking the price of goods: when Pewter said price tag, Eugene immediately *saw* again the object referred to, distinct from other objects in the shop window. It was the little word *tag* that had swung it for Pewter on this occasion: Eugene himself wouldn't have bothered with that extra word; but *tag* made something that had grown fuzzy suddenly *there.* Or was it as simple as that?

So rather than striking out on a new career – too late now – he helped his brother. Earlier today when he and Jennifer were in the queue at Versailles, with the Chinese and Japanese and all sorts – Italians, Spanish, a family wearing Venezuelan T-shirts, the woman not looking good in hers – as they inched forward in the sun he had had a thought. (There were French people, too, of course, in the queue. Jennifer had joined some of the Chinese/Japanese in the shade, sitting on the low wall at the side while one member of the party queued – though, of course Jennifer didn't sit with them, she stood, a little apart.) As he was standing there in the queue he saw a man coming out of the palace on crutches, and he thought of his brother.

★

In Sheffield Pewter thought he heard the phone ring; he had fallen asleep in his clothes; it was late.

But it couldn't have been the phone; it was his mother's voice, and he hadn't lifted the receiver. His mother didn't speak to him often now, not like the first few years after she had died.

'Sugarcake pattacake baker's man. Boy, I can't even remember who I am.'

'I'm sorry?'

'And fiddling & piddling & what they call it, I don't know.'

The voice was still familiar.

'As they say: Time waits for no man. NICE 2 – CRETEUIL 0.'

He turned on the radio, and yet…

'A stitch in time… A bitch called Chaim. Gordon Bennett.'

There we go; it must be something he ate.

'Getting your arse kicked. Big man like you, big men like you. Getting your arse kicked by England: I just can't believe you're still out there getting your arse kicked by England.'

It was late, too late to phone anyone, to hear another voice.

A couple of days later Eric phoned Pewter, unable to let it rest: of all the solutions for West Indian cricket the St. Caesare off-shore plan seemed interesting.

Pewter hadn't heard of the St. Caesare plan, and it was possible that Eric, being from Guyana, was pulling the small-islander's leg – usually referring to his 'home' as an offshore island.

'So what's this plan, then?'

'Practice facilities for the team in St. Caesare.'

A joke: St. Caesare didn't have any flat land, not since the volcano; certainly, there was nowhere to lay down a cricket pitch. Nor in neighbouring Montserrat, either.

'Ra Alanbrooke's offering them their pick of the volcano zone, the "Exclusion Zone" for practice, day or night, lit by the, y'know… burning discharge. "To build up character".'

Pewter had an image of all those black athletes in America, in the news; middle-class girls, taken to the ghetto to practice their tennis and 800 metres – shooting in the streets all around – to improve their concentration.

'So, your friend Ra's offering the volcano environment to sort out the mentally tough from the handicapped.'

Pewter liked people with imagination.

'I always said Ra Alanbrooke would come good, eventually.'

*

Eugene, back in England, phoned his brother.

Pewter thanked him for the card from Paris. So how was Paris?

Paris was smoky.

Pewter vaguely filed that away as a 'writerly' observation. As – he had to acknowledge – had been the conceit on the postcard from his brother: the notion of a man, severely-crippled, hobbling into Versailles, being carried through rooms tacky with seventeenth-eighteenth-century drapes and surfaces of gilt and gold-leaf and mirrors, so overpowering that you suffered something transcendental and came out *healed* by the power of art – an aesthetic alternative to Lourdes. The idea appealed to Pewter: he could see new possibilities for the National Gallery, the Tate Modern – all that.

So Pewter thanked him for the card. And told him how lucky he was to have been out of the country during the debacle at Leeds. And on top of everything, those worthless fellows were responsible for his mother's dramatic change of idiom. But he didn't say that to his brother. Then Eugene said he was bored with talking about the cricket.

So they talked about Paris.

And they talked about St. Caesare: did Pewter think that Ra Alanbrooke understood irony? His military references seemed a bit obvious.

But Eugene put it down to volcano trauma. You confused yourself sometimes when you tried to be clever about history: otherwise you ended up pretending to be Chief of the Imperial General Staff when what you were was an unshaved idiot in a dirty jungle uniform called Wingate.

Ah, this was going to be a different sort of call from what Pewter might have expected. He had been nursing a slightly cloudy thought about needing to remember the boundaries of the old East and West Germany before reunification; and on top of that, an even lighter thought of where one might locate Eastphalia, granted that Westphalia was the Bonn-Koln area; but he quickly shook that out of his head and pulled up a chair and sat down to the telephone seminar by his brother on Churchill's generals; soon to discover which *bits* of Churchill's generals Ra Alanbrooke might have chosen if he were to get the *narrative* of the post-volcano leadership in St. Caesare right. Wavell was a man of scholarship, a somewhat reluctant fighting man facing, usually, unfavourable odds; Slim, the ironmonger's son from Birmingham made good – Burma, and all that – could be exploited to good effect. A rehabilitated Percival seen from the perspective of contemporary Malaysian and Singapore history could be an alternative way of rewriting British history. Of course the arrogant, racist Monty would have to be cut down to size, etc.

At some point Eugene stopped and apologised for going on because he knew how busy Pewter was. But, incidentally, did Pewter know that Slim had ended up as President of the MCC?

No, Pewter didn't know that.

Sometime in the '60s.

No, that was really interesting.

And had Pewter come across Slim's *Defeat into Victory?*

No, Pewter hadn't. He would certainly, y'know, get it out of the library.

Well, of course, Wavell was the real intellectual. Cambridge, and all that. And – just a thought – even when we had four great fast bowlers in the '70s and '80s, we weren't bowling out sides for 54 and 61. Now England has good fast bowlers but not great fast bowlers. So when we were bowled out for 54 and 61, what did that say about West Indies?

Pewter had no answer to that, and shortly afterwards the brothers signed off, each feeling slightly virtuous.

And now Pewter came back to the story he had been struggling to write since the first day of the Test. He knew that there was a story there somewhere, but it was eluding him. Initially he had thought of building it round that fellow at Old Trafford, whatshisname, Arm Band. But Arm Band no longer seemed so interesting now the mood had gone flat; so, instead, he thought he might write something about his brother, Eugene. Suitably disguised, of course.

(*Trinidad & Tobago Review*, Vol. 23, 2001)

JUMBIEMAN

I was on my way out when he phoned, my brother, to ask if I had heard that Jumbieman's daughter had died; and I hadn't, so he told me about her, and then the conversation turned to the father, who had had to flee the island; and we had an argument about that. I felt a little bit ashamed getting so steamed up about these things, living so far back in the past, after years and years in this country, still arguing about what made us proud, ashamed, about growing up in St. Caesare. Certainly, to my mind, people like Jumbieman had made the picture of childhood that little bit less grey.

Jumbieman had to escape to Montserrat in order to live down his reputation, and had set up in business there: a bakery. But he was still a sort of legend to us boys growing up in Coderington. We all tried to emulate him, one way or other, sometimes with tragic results, as with my cousin, Princeton, who died one night coming back from Barville on Maas Archie's bus. He had tried to do his 'Jumbieman' by leaping off the vehicle as it was labouring up the *Soeur Pelée;* and hit his head on a stone or a nail or something and died instantly: that was the year before he was to go over to Montserrat to Grammar School, so he must have been ten at the time – we were all about ten at the time, and had been turned down for the French School together, and were trying to prove something from that. That was when they ran Jumbieman out of the village, till he had to go over to Montserrat, to open up his first bakery. But then, when his reputation caught up with him in Montserrat, he had to come over to England, to Britain, where he settled down in

Wales, in a little university town called Lampeter, where he continued baking bread, for the students. There were no St. Caesarians in Lampeter, and the one Montserratian who went to the College decided not to give him away. At the end of his life, when Jumbieman staged his final trick, it was in the summer holidays and most of the students were down.

His original skill was walking through wire. Just as a magician does foolish tricks like sawing women in half on the stage, and a conjurer produces white rabbits out of his hat, people expected Jumbieman to make a habit of walking through wire, do it as a profession, to become an entertainer. But Jumbieman had played no trick when he walked through the wire; he had not walked under it or over it, but *through* it, and he neither broke it, nor did the wire break him; and he had done it in the presence of witnesses who had excellent eyesight and were sober. One of the witnesses was my great uncle George, himself a man who had travelled, who had been to Cuba and Haiti and to some other place, either Curaçao or Panama. Uncle George swore to his dying day, as did the other witness, a boy from Look Out who used to keep goats, and whose name slips my mind at the moment – they swore that Jumbieman walked right through unhindered while the other two were held back by the wire, which was at least waist high. And remember, this was good strong purpose-built wire that everyone was putting up to mark out their boundaries, all round the Plain, when it was rumoured that the French government was going to buy up the land, or lease it, and turn St. Caesare into the bread-basket of the islands, as part of their war effort.

Jumbieman's trick was hotly debated. Some had tried to explain it away by reference to other incidents, like the time when it rained on old Mr. Hastings's banana plantation, but stopped short of his neighbour's further up the hill. Though on the far side of the island, behind Look Out, this was still in the general direction of Jumbieman's earlier triumph – so maybe there *was* something funny about the East. Concerning old Mr. Hastings, there had been a drought and everything was suffering, crops dying and, just when it was needed, Mr. Hastings got rain. It rained on his land, right up to the edge of his banana plantation and didn't even sprinkle on the other side of the fence where crops were dying. It had to be obeah – just as Jumbieman had worked obeah with the wire. Not so, said Professeur Croissant.

Professeur Croissant was a man of the twentieth century, and our teacher. When it rains, he said – use your head, man – it doesn't rain on the whole world at the same time. We, in the 1950s, were a long way from The Flood, assuming The Flood ever happened. Well then, it stands to reason that if when it rains, it doesn't rain on the whole world at the same time, it has to stop raining somewhere. (Someone at school had had the courage to ask and the Professeur was explaining clearly: he was a man who didn't believe in God, so his opinions were both dangerous and sacred to us. The adults were always challenging him: the Catholic priest, my grandmother...so he was our ally. Or, perhaps I should say, *we* were his allies.) And Professeur Croissant, who was an historian who believed in Science, said: since it didn't rain everywhere at once, the rain therefore had to end somewhere. Now, mathematically, in some place, at some time, the rain was bound to stop at the edge of someone's land; and why not at someone's land in St. Caesare, and why shouldn't that someone be old Mr. Hastings!

This was a revelation to us boys, because it was the first time we accepted that if something interesting was to happen in the world, it was possible that it might happen right here in St. Caesare. That's why I always thought of Professeur Croissant as one of the great figures of St. Caesare, in spite of his drinking, and the foolish things he sometimes said. My brother and I tended to fight about this, too.

But nothing eclipsed Jumbieman in our minds, because

when you came down to it, there was an essential difference between walking through wire and having the rain stop at the edge of your land. For although old Mr. Hastings's experience was no doubt impressive, it had to be seen as essentially passive, whereas that of Jumbieman, well, that was *active.*

I was on my way to see Lee, the woman in my life, and was in the process of trying to build up a relationship with Mark, her son by a previous marriage. And both Lee and I agreed that I should try to kindle in the boy some sense of the magic of a life beyond England, a life before England. He had, himself, done a fair bit of travelling, so my stories about wandering about Europe weren't especially interesting to him, but he did show greater tolerance when I talked about the great people of St. Caesare, people of my grandmother's generation, who had had big dreams, who had overcome enormous odds, and who were, in a sense, let down by their own children and more particularly, by people of my own generation. Not that I was doing the old Golden Age number. I didn't believe in that: not really. Last night, for instance, I had told him about Kmark; Kmark of Senegal who was not, of course, from Senegal; and how the name had come about – something I won't go into here. (Kmark was almost his namesake.)

Now, Kmark was rich, but that wasn't what made him interesting. Kmark came from nowhere, as they say, and ended up somewhere. The only two things we knew for certain about Kmark were that he had secured a Bank Loan of £80,0000, and that he was into doors. *Doors.* If Kmark had had £80,000 in the bank, that would be nothing. Unusual, perhaps, but no big thing. That he had got the NatWest Bank to lend him 80,000 *was* a big thing. What further intrigued us was that he wasn't into the usual things: show-business, or selling sportswear, or running a grocery or a cornershop. Or a chain of mini-cabs; he was into doors. No one quite knew what he did with doors, whether he was on his own or with partners, or who he would leave his doors' fortune to as he had no children, no wife (though his mother was living; women in the family were said to be long-lived). How do you measure Kmark against Jumbieman? My brother and I disagreed on this.

So little was known about his life – a man of our age: no wife, no children. A friend had pointed out, a woman from St. Caesare, gloating somewhat, that the sad thing about Kmark was that with all those doors there was no daughter at college to brighten up her accent and slip in, 'Daddy's into doors,' when her friends admitted that their daddies were 'into paint' or 'into nails,' etc. (Mark and I had a long chat about a possible father of whom you could be proud: 'Daddy's into coffins.' Or 'Daddy's into wigs.' But we drew the line at the daddy into clamping cars, or into telling fortunes on the television. Bright lad, Mark, a credit to his mother.)

And Mark's mother, too, had been intrigued by the man from Senegal who was not from Senegal. She claimed, from my description, that the man had the whiff of the sexual tease. So now I had to begin to read his 'The doors are warped, man, warped' differently. Kmark was not an artist, he dealt with real doors which often had to be *rehung* because they were out of alignment, and sometimes as you opened them the bottom scraped along the tiles (not floor, note, but *tiles:* a sexual thrill?). Sometimes Kmark's doors had shrunk (Oh dear) this way, that way (though *wood* was so tactile, don't you think? The *grains* were so alive with risk: doors had to be sanded (brute), replaced (beast), lifted (sexist), lowered (sadist) etc.). And we wrestled with the thought, all the way to the top of the stairs, that for Kmark, there was no daughter at College to say: 'Daddy's into doors.' Later, I was invited to inspect Lee's magnificent, mounted and framed, picture of 25 Tuscan doors, photographed in good light.

Tonight, it would be Jumbieman. Jumbieman was not ahead of his time; to say that would be discourteous to St. Caesarians. But he was misunderstood. He was misunderstood even by those who had tried to emulate him, boys like my cousin, Horace, whose complicated plan to have a fixed link between all the islands from St. Caesare to Cuba in the north, and again from St. Caesare to the Guyanas in the south, anchoring us to the continent so that we wouldn't bob about, landed him in the care of a psychiatrist – and did damage to Jumbieman's reputation. As, of course, had the death of Princeton, jumping off Maas Archie's bus in that Jumbieman dare, that time when we were young.

But there was the other side to this. There was the integrity of the man, a man who had never attempted to repeat that early trick, as he was not a magician, he was not a performer: walking *through* wire wasn't something you practiced. He, himself, had refused to talk about it. It was left to his dwindling band of allies, like Professeur Croissant, to put you straight. If everything is right – I could still hear the Professeur saying it – if all the forces accidentally come together, and are in harmony, and you happen to be there; and, without thinking about it you find the wire in front of you and you happen to step forward, it is entirely possible that you might walk through unimpeded. But don't expect to do it twice; this isn't a trick, this is something natural. And for this, says the Professeur, the poor man is sent into exile: let's have a drink to keep our sanity.

So far so good. What I wanted to talk to Mark about tonight was Jumbieman's last twenty minutes of life, his last twenty minutes in Lampeter. His death was documented in the usual way, by adults with good eyesight. And then he chose to come back to life for a further twenty minutes: what do you do with those twenty minutes? Change your Will? Think up a *bon mot*? This was Jumbieman, remember, who earlier in life had walked through the wire. And there, in Lampeter, at the end, he chose to come back, not as the baker from St. Caesare who had a grown-up daughter in Leeds (the woman of whose death my brother had informed me earlier). No, Jumbieman chose to come back, not even as a man, but as a Persian Lady: 'Daddy's into becoming a Persian Lady.'

Now, this was something very strange for the people of Lampeter to digest. They had never seen a man die and come back as a Persian Lady, and in the confusion that ensued, eyewitnesses tended to contradict one another. In residence at the near-empty College – it being summer – were some archaeologists on one of their digs, but they distrusted so recent a corpse, and declined to revise the genealogy of the Celts. But tell me, tell me, this Persian Lady: was she pretty? Did she speak Farsi? Welsh? But was she *really* pretty? 'Daddy's into being really pretty.' All this would no doubt give life to the debate back on St. Caesare. There were those who said our magic, transported, would never work. Mark would be taken with all this. He would love the pointlessness of dying and coming back to life for a further twenty minutes. As for Mark's mother, well, last night's Tuscan doors had been a success; and I fancy that the story of Jumbieman, coming back to life as a Persian Lady, would at least lead us to Khayyam some rhymes upstairs together.

(*Planet*, No. 89, 1991)

I remember the panic when she visited the second time, as I was still being blamed for the disaster of the first visit, having missed it by being away at university. For, it was said, there'd been no one in the house to play her at her own game, to talk to her in French, etc.; she had insisted on slipping into that language, even to her dog, Zimi, who had had the temerity to lick my mother's hand. And how did she get the dog through customs when there was so much talk of their clamping down on people – unless that was another example of the English preferring animals to their children, particularly if the children were black. We were the poor cousins now, having landed in England on the wrong side of the channel; the tables had been turned. On Madeleine's second visit I happened to be present – that was in the mid-'70s – and it hadn't, in my opinion, gone too badly, though the family blamed me again, this time for colluding with the visitor's little stratagems to humiliate us all. Me, a man with a degree: how could I have failed to counter the woman's deviousness? But at least she didn't bring her dog that time; we were spared Zimi.

Today, I bought the wine and predicted all would be well. We would be intellectually adult and talk of the world economy and the pollution of the planet and that sort of thing, to show that our horizons hadn't been narrowed by living in England; we would talk about human rights and prisoners of conscience, the lot, to show where we really were. But these weren't the immediate concerns in the house: the quality of the wine had to be debated, we must resist the tendency to over-compensate.

The family had had a jolt to its confidence, wine-wise, some years back, and we were still on guard. This derived from a somewhat obscure incident, in the late '50s, when a fellow-countryman happened to drop in on us, in Ladbroke Grove. Not that people coming unannounced was particularly unusual at the time, but this fellow had brought a little party with him, two women and a man, none of whom was a friend of the family. Anyway, they stayed to dinner and a good time was had by all; but afterwards, one of the guests, a woman, was heard to complain that my mother's Cyprus sherry had given her a headache, as she had a low tolerance for any wine drink that wasn't French French. (St. Caesarians from a British-French outpost, tended to parody the snobberies played out by the principals.) So, after that, when I was about and there were guests, I got to choose the wine. As I'd long ceased to live in the family homes – and was often out of the country – this wasn't onerous.

But back to this afternoon: the conversation was familiar, little changed over the years. We were at my sister's place in Upton Park, where my mother now lived, awaiting my brother and his wife; and the talk was again about what to call people whom we'd known by one name but who, with the elevation of travel, had acquired another. Mady, in question, had clearly objected to the liberties we had taken with her name, and had decided to punish us for it.

'So call her Madeleine!'

My mother said it made life complicated to have to remember all these new names, two names for each person, but we had to move with the times. And if we forgot occasionally and called people by the old familiar name they should understand, for after all, it was *they* who were forcing us into this feat of memory: *we* hadn't put pressure on anyone by calling ourselves something new.

Though you had to admit, our case wasn't desperate. Pewter... well, Pewter and Avril and Eugene might not be

English-English (not like my mother's own 'Christine Stapleton', something out of the Shires) but you could live with the jokes they engendered. Not the same, was it, for Bobo? If you were called Bobo, you wouldn't want people all over England to be calling you Bobo. We weren't Americans who didn't seem to have any pride in what they were called – all those unpronouncable mouthfuls from Eastern Europe. That's why Bobo now called himself Charles Rupert. And he wasn't from Bugby Hole, either, but from some more neutral-sounding place, a place fit for a Charles Rupert to have been young in.

My mother found all this mildly funny, Bobo answering to Charles Rupert. What she didn't find so amusing was the effect the change of name tended to have on people like that. Bobo used to be a neighbour, a man who laboured a bit for my grandmother in Coderington, and who used to show due respect to the daughter of the house, calling her, as they all did back then, 'Miss Christine'. But now with the change of name and country, he had joined the others in referring to her as 'Mother' – and he a man not much younger than she, never mind the fact that he was no relation. It was no laughing matter that she had come to this.

Though Mady, calling my mother, 'Mother', last time, was different. Mady was, in effect, family.

The response to this didn't need to be spelt out.

Mady had grown up in our house in Coderington as an auxiliary member of the family, and you never know how this sort of thing was going to work out when people found themselves in a foreign setting. Some had accepted that we all now faced a new challenge, a common enemy, so to speak, whether in England or in France, and that it was necessary to line up on the same side against that enemy. But others – and Mady was, apparently, among them – didn't see it like that: Mady's subservient position on the island had rankled; a servant was a servant however unabused physically. And to see the people who had lorded it over her treated with casual contempt by every Tom, Dick & Henri encountering a black face, seemed like further humiliation heaped upon herself.

During dinner last time, she had talked of her younger sister, Dominique, who was a delicate child, who had been brought up differently from the rest and was now, for her pains, being taken off to the South Seas to become a Princess. Our response to this had clearly disappointed Madeleine. Dominique, she insisted, demanded to be treated like a precious form of life, even the temperature in the room where she sat had to be just right. This room, for instance, where we were now, wouldn't do for her sister. It was all right for us, of course; we had learnt to rough it, even those of us who had been privileged in St. Caesare; we had grown out of the habit of being delicate. Even Dominique's diet had to be watched – and not from overweight! You couldn't serve her chicken or pigmeat or anything coarse like that. And for this, Madeleine took the blame. It was she who had told her sister what her own life had been in St. Caesare, in Coderington; how, sometimes, when there was a chicken to be killed for Sunday lunch, she was the one called upon to chase it barefoot round and round the yard, having to watch your step where it was rocky, and again to be careful to avoid stepping in mess, not getting chicken-mess between your toes, a feeling you couldn't describe to those who'd never experienced it. That was enough to put Dominique off, you didn't have to labour the point about wringing the chicken's neck and watching it, headless, flap and scratch about the yard. The child was put off eating meat for life.

So what did Princesses eat?

Everybody knew what Princesses ate. But for us, Madeleine reassured my mother, for those of us hardened to these things, we could eat our chicken with a good conscience. Anyway, she supposed that these chickens, in these countries, were killed by mechanical means, so in a way that spread the load, it was like the whole country wringing one little neck, that way you could hardly feel it.

We had tried to broaden the discussion into the usual one about living in France as opposed to living in England. When we met with Montserratians and Jamaicans the talk was about those living in North America, but with St. Caesarians, the comparison was with France. (Mady had, indeed, got a brother, Felix, in America. Felix used to help out my grandmother baking on a Saturday, and we sometimes fell into the habit of speculating that if we'd been from Eastern Europe, say, boys like Felix, within a couple of years of getting to the US, would have used their tenuous connection with baking – cutting wood and lighting the outside oven – to end up opening a string of pâtisseries in New York or Boston, and providing the financial base to go into right-wing politics.) But here we were, being told that one of our own was about to go off to the South Seas, to become a Princess. It seemed churlish not to want to find out more about Dominique's prospects.

'So where would she be going, exactly. I mean, she'd be Princess of what country?'

'The A & A.'

That sounded like an Art Gallery to me; or maybe a ship, a fleet of liners. I must have looked suitably blank.

'Amis et Amants. Didn't you ever take them in on your travels?' she asked.

'Well, I'm certainly planning to visit New Caledonia and...' I didn't want to be discourteous about her sister who was going to be the Princess – even though I knew this was a sort of dig at my mother who herself had been called a Princess on St. Caesare. Avril, my sister, also took it as a put down of her, and of M. her daughter at school who aspired, perhaps, to college, not to her own Court. But one wanted to be sociable. I said to Madeleine:

'I'll certainly try to take in your sister's island.'

'Dominique will make you welcome; she's kind.' And with that, she gave my mother and my sister a look of undiluted triumph.

I was relieved when my mother changed the subject and asked about Mady's mother, back in St. Caesare, whether her bad leg was getting any better, whether she was still able to get about. Mady answered in a distracted way, bringing in references to holidays in Italy and visiting churches and turning down marriage proposals in that country, and something to do with the psychology of driving on the right side of the road rather than the left, and much more that I didn't attempt to follow. Before she left she tried on my sister's bracelet, and said it was very much like her own, the one that had been lost in the crossing. That was the last meeting.

My brother phoned to say he'd be late, as Jennifer wasn't home from work yet and they hadn't sorted out the children. And he took the opportunity to ask if we could remember if anything of Mady's had gone down with the *Titanic.*

Why bring that up again; we didn't know, we couldn't remember, we didn't think so. *The Titanic* was our name for my mother's great trunk, which had been lost on the voyage from St. Caesare to England in 1956. And in it had gone down all our valuables. My mother still got very angry when we referred to her trunk as having been lost as she knew without a shadow of doubt that it had been stolen. She had pointed out to us – to my sister and me accompanying her – during that first week of the three-week journey, that one of the cabin crew had been eyeing her trunk suspiciously. Of course, she was being naive; she and my sister were sharing a cabin with four other women, and this was an Italian boat. The word was that Italians were worse even, where women were concerned, than the French. It was only the English who sometimes let race prejudice get the better of their sex. So though I was anxious at the thought of the young Italian hanging round the cabin (my cabin was on another deck, with the men) I didn't think he was after the famous trunk. The compromise was, agreed to with great reluctance by my mother, to hand the trunk in to the Purser for safe keeping; he made special provision for it, as it was larger than other objects of value that he had been given. My mother immediately pronounced the trunk stolen, and took to her cabin for the remaining two weeks of the voyage.

And she was right. With the loss of the trunk, revealed two weeks later, with the Purser's unnerving calm, and with the danger of missing the train connection at Genoa, we had to reconcile ourselves to not being able to draw comfort from the famous silver spoon which was relied on to bring us luck in the new country. We disagreed now, thirty years later, on the contents of the trunk. But some things were indisputable: the silver spoon, its misshapenness adding to our belief in its potency. It had my mother's old wedding-dress and shoes: you couldn't give away such things to someone in the village, who would probably wear them to the market, or to the roadside stand-pipe to draw water. There were the family photos, the only ones of grandfather that we had; pictures of the properties, of the house in Coderington and the shop in Barville, and the garage (which had been turned into a little house for Mr Skerrit), and the two town houses in Montserrat. Plus all the documentation of ownership. There were grandfather's letters and a few copies of my mother's magazines from her school in Antigua – not forgetting those mementoes of Martinique. (She had attended the '46 celebrations, and was a sort of celebrity. Guadeloupe and Guyane also celebrated at the same time their being made *départements* of France, but my mother was taken by her cousin, who was in politics, to prestigious Martinique, as recognition of her contribution to the war. She was a widow. Our father, who had been fighting in Europe, had failed to return at the end of the war, and you had to wear black even though you continued to hope that he was taken prisoner somewhere, and would still turn up: it took a long time before we came to accept that the Tomb of the Unknown Soldier, so beloved of politicians, was in reality part of our own family burial plot. Anyway, mementoes from that trip went down with the *Titanic*.) Not forgetting our china. We'd brought the best crockery with us because we thought that would influence people here as to our status at home, and we didn't want to risk that status in less secure luggage. What else? The family jewellery (modest, but each bit telling its own story) and mother's inscribed Bible. She brought another Bible – as we all did – an ordinary one, for day-to-day use on the boat.

My brother hadn't been with us, he had come on ahead and was helping to organise things at the English end; and he'd always had a tendency to distance himself from events on the boat. So he was asking now, over the phone, if we were absolutely sure that nothing of Mady's had perished in the *Titanic*. He had heard rumours that the Lady in France was claiming the opposite to be the case.

My mother was indignant, as always, at being thought to mix her own things with Mady's, Mady being a servant; and we had to remind her that it was nearly forty years since Mady was a servant, that her name was now Madeleine, that she had a sister who had gone off to be a Princess, and that she spoke better French than we did. (From being fairly neutral about her I was now developing quite a soft spot for Mady, because it was through her, checking up on whereabout her sister might be in the South Seas, that I became familiar with that whole area of Melanesia/Micronesia, to the point that I was beginning to see myself as something of a Social Anthropologist.)

My mother likened the loss of the trunk to the blacksmith breaking her wedding ring after it had got too tight and he had tried to get it off her finger. Everyone knew that if you broke a wedding-ring, that spelt a lifetime of bad luck; and the fellow had done it on purpose, and from that moment she had started her life-time of bad luck.

And here we had to go into the old routine, summoning to our aid people who were starving in the world, who were refugees, who were brutalised by their own governments, etc. – all of whom were worse off than someone who'd merely lost a trunk of valuables (we didn't mention the other loss, in war)... and who was now being upstaged by a non-servant whose sister was a Princess in the South Seas. As always, my mother accepted the argument much too readily, making us feel mean, for she had already worked this out for herself and we didn't want to think of her being reduced by England. At times like this, we just wished that the sun would come out again, with her young again, dressed in a summer frock, on a Sunday outing – being driven back home to Coderington. She'd be sitting in the front seat of the old Vauxhall next to the driver, who today would be washed and not smelling of drink; and without protest she would walk the last few yards up to the front lawn where the car couldn't make it, and pause and survey the calmness of everything, the mountains in the distance and the sea to the East so still and obedient under the gaze of the sun. And she would start up the wide front steps to the verandah, and flop down on a chair fanning herself. She would call to Mady for a glass of water, and Mady wouldn't answer until, perhaps, the third call, and would bring the water in a glass covered with a saucer; and Miss Christine would ask the child if the glass was clean, and Mady would say in a neutral voice, 'Yes Ma'am, the glass clean'. And the Lady of the house, having already taken a sip would say, casually, 'You sure it clean?' And Mady would say, 'Miss Christine, I wash the glass twice.'

'Then it wasn't clean first time.'

'Miss Christine, the glass clean.'

'Child, you getting too rude, you know. You getting altogether too rude for my liking. With all the problems in this life, I have to put up with you as well.'

And Mady, knowing she was dismissed, would walk rudely down the steps keeping her thoughts to herself. (You couldn't blame her now, if she decided to let us know what was on her mind.)

'She not married yet?' my mother asked of Madeleine, knowing the answer. We reminded her – we were all growing coarse – that if your younger sister had married a Prince, you would have to hold out for a King – *at least!* My mother had a theory that people who didn't get married were perverse and should be censured for lack of trying, a charge she had brought, over the years, against me.

Of Mady, we confirmed that there was a shortage of Kings in the world. 'She not trying,' my mother said.

Madeleine came to dinner and reverted to being Mady, warm and charming in a way that surprised us. She brought my mother a present of a cake, which she had made herself, all the way from Paris, and the customs had been kind to her, which was a good omen. This *bonhomie* threatened a little my agenda for the evening, though I was delighted at the tone of events. I was always accused of being too-easily taken in, but the fact that Mady wasn't crowing about her sister on some islands in the vicinity of Hawaii, the names of which I couldn't remember, made me go to the kitchen to reassure my sister that things were going to be all right. Also, I wanted to be in the kitchen, just to indicate to Mady that in our households, that sort of work was shared; though all I was doing was opening the wine.

'What's she saying in there?' Avril wanted to know.

'They're talking about making cakes; ingredients.'

'Showing off, as usual.' But her mind wasn't on it. She

had mixed feelings about M. her daughter, who, with some of her college friends, was proposing to sleep in the park tonight to help dramatise the plight of the homeless in our society, and although Avril approved, she was uneasy.

'Did Eugene say he was going to ring again? Or just come?'

'Oh, he isn't going to be here for ages. Jenny isn't even home yet.'

'Well, you better go and keep the company entertained.'

I couldn't deny I was prepared for this. Over the last few years I'd become quite *au fait* with outposts like Espiritu Santo and Malekula. For most St. Caesarians, the Pacific meant New Caledonia and New Hebrides (New Caledonia because some of the French officials on St. Caesare had served over there, etc. and the French government occasionally sent parties of politicians from St. Caesare to New Hebrides to study how their constitution worked in practice as, like them, we were a political condominium.) So, obviously, I wanted to have more to show for my study of the region than an airmail letter from a PO Box in Vila. But it was still irritating that I couldn't remember the names of those islands that young Dominique was Princess of. My sister, with characteristic common sense, simply said the islands didn't exist.

I thought, if you were to ask an Indonesian, say, about two of his or her outlying 3,000 – or, was it 30,000? – islands, you probably wouldn't get the response that they didn't exist. So even though I couldn't find the V & A or P & O, whatever, on the map, I continued to scan the waters around Australia and New Zealand and New Guinea. I'd investigated and rejected Tahiti and the Hawaiian islands. Fiji was tempting, but too familiar. As was Guam, which had a long history of entering the Miss World contest – and they'd never, to my knowledge, run a Princess. Western Samoa, Cook, Gilbert & Marshall Islands – all had the wrong initials. (Of course

Bikini was on the Marshall Islands where America had tested the Hydrogen bomb. There were some who said we were inheriting the earth after it had been polluted by others. So true. But you couldn't put a Caribbean Princess on Bikini for all that.) I was accustomed to getting nowhere in my 'research'. So I soon gave this up and rejoined the two women in the sitting-room, who were still discussing the cake.

'It's good for me, too, Miss Christine. Keep my hand in. In case I go home again, I don't want to be an invalid and have to rely on people.'

'You not going home!'

'Who knows? Who knows what life have in store?'

'What of your life in Paris?'

'What life? Sometimes I think we were all better off back there in Coderington. People used to help one another. Now I find that I fraid. I walk down the street and I'm afraid.'

My mother, too, was afraid, and didn't venture out; and they both warmed to the theme of not having been afraid at 'home'. Mady was saying that she was sick, sick, sick of Europe, sick of disrespect, sick of the young people, particularly our own young people who laughed at you when you tried to dream of better things; but you couldn't blame them because all they knew was Europe who had never taught them to respect themselves. But she told them, she went out there and told them that some of us knew what living was, that there were some of us, right here, who had been the highest in the land and knew what living was; and she told them about this family, the Stapleton family, across the water, in England.

Of course, she was too generous; we were struggling... struggling...

Africa for a brief moment, had threatened to do something for us, and then what? The media soon put a stop to that. All you saw now of Africa, all you saw on the television, all you read in the newspapers was of war, famine, women reduced to objects of pity, women and their children, by the men and the multinationals and the men behind those too terrible to contemplate: what did that do for anyone, except make the racists feel good? I agreed with her that the reporting of Africa was selective.

So she had to tell them about another life, about the Stapleton household in Coderington, the twelve rooms.

We reminded her that the house was no longer standing.

'It's still a sign of pride.'

But my mother, loving it, said we had to be humble.

'Since when we have to be humble, Miss Christine? Once a Princess always a Princess is what I say. Exile can't change that. You know you only have to lift a little finger and everybody on the island go come running.'

While my mother was denying this, I couldn't decide whether it was safe to ask about Dominique. A car pulled up outside and Avril said it was Stewart, so she started ushering us towards the dining-room, without waiting for my brother, and the conversation switched to news of Avril and Stewart. And M. – M.'s plan to save the homeless.

When we were seated I asked: 'So how did Dominique get on over…where was it, again?'

'Oh, Do came back, you know. Women are made to suffer.'

That's all she said. And as I was about to check on the names of the islands again, my mother interrupted:

'Why don't you pour the guest some wine?' and she looked at me, somewhat crossly, I thought.

(*Ambit*, No. 127, 1992)

Seminar on the Frank Worrell Roundabout, Barbados

She's not going to admit her name just yet. Maybe she'd get cold feet again and just pretend to be somebody else; and crawl away at the end of it all, furious with herself. When is she going to break through this terror? Her name is more likely than not to come up during the proceedings. And she's going to be accused of, well – she doesn't want to think of it. And she would go away without having the courage to come out. She's thinking of a poet called Stapleton, and how that time in Wellingborough he dealt with his other identities, particularly the one who was a woman, can t remember her name – Betty? Sally? – God, the simplest things absolutely refuse to stick.

Anyway, here's this fellow, a bit self-satisfied, hinting at his importance in the university, but interesting nevertheless, white hair and beard – all these Black men with white hair and beards! Glasses, too: as if made up to look like it! The degree show at the art college comes to mind: Black men. White hair. Glasses. Now Go Forth and read the *News at Ten* sort of thing. Though that one doesn't have a beard. Ah, but you're drifting, the woman tells herself, your mind's wandering. So now concentrate, concentrate; where was she?

Oh yes. Stapleton at Wellingborough that night: she *(come on, girl, be serious, the name is Eye See Eye, it's on your book, it's been reprinted)*, Eye See Eye, remembers someone in the audience asking Stapleton about his persona who is a woman. One of those names you hear from time to time and never doubt it's a woman. A book of poems under her name. Written by this man. A White woman written by this Black man. The only problem was that feminist magazines had printed some of the work. That was in the seventies. Looking back from the nineties, all that seemed fussy, precious. The nineties were more open; you could play it straight, not that Eye See Eye agreed it was that easy. And how did Stapleton deal with this, how did he get out of that one?

But the taxi driver is talking to her; she must have said something out loud: she's got to pull herself together, she's in no state to head up the hill to the university: better go round the roundabout one more time.

They were on the Frank Worrell roundabout and the taxi-driver wanted to turn off and head up the hill to the university, to Cave Hill. And she was on the point of telling him to take the next turn-off and head right back to the hotel so she could lock herself in her room till it was time to head home to Wellingborough. Because, really, she couldn't face those people up there, the experts, the writers, international figures, household names, who must see her as an upstart; and unwelcome. Unless she came in really heavy as *Eye See Eye: So bwoy, how yu doin', you arwright?* And maybe she could be carrying a copy of Kamau Brathwaite's *Barabajan Poems* to deflect attention. (Got to get the stress just right): *Barabajan.* BaraBAJAN. *Bajan.*

'Yes, of course, I'm Bajan.' That was the taxi-driver.

And Eye See Eye is covered in confusion because she had been talking aloud and the taxi-driver is now answering her and asking if she's ready to turn off the roundabout. Or what her intentions are. She had a momentary urge to shock him and say her intentions were to get laid early and often, but who knows if he has a sense of humour? So she just directs him to go round the roundabout one more time, if he didn't mind. And he says, 'That's your privilege.' She doesn't quite like the way he says that. Patronising. She'd have him know that in England she is written up as a West Indian writer, whatever her colour, and she can buss bad word with the rest of them: is not only Agard and company who caan mash up language. And she could push up she face and chuppes if any of them man give she grief. But she didn't want to pull rank and get too heavy with the taxi-driver, so she just ignored his tone. (*You talking to me?*) For even coming back at him would be something too intimate. In the end she just said, in her most neutral voice, 'Thank you; thank you very much.' No edge. Just the calmness of the voice to tell the bitch who in charge. And for the first time on the journey, Eye See Eye has a little smile on her face.

And it works, you know, the taxi-driver is apologising for breaking into her thoughts, and she is conscious that, sitting in the back seat of the car, maybe the relationship between her and the driver isn't as equal as it might be; so the edge in his voice probably came from that sense of uneasiness. But maybe he wasn't thinking any of those things because here he is making a little joke, a joke about having to make a pit-stop. When she understood what he was saying she bent forward, and looked at the petrol gauge and saw that he was very far from being out of petrol, so he was still at it. And, very calmly, she said she'd pay for the extra petrol.

It's not petrol he wants, he wants to go to the loo, and there's a petrol station just along the road next to the supermarket where she bought a heavy cake yesterday and a newspaper for the local colour. There was a loo in there. She quite appreciated his delicacy about the loo, and to be honest she too could do with a visit, so she said, 'Yes, why not.' Good idea, she isn't in a hurry.

So they turned off and drove a few yards along the road and pulled in at the petrol station next to the supermarket. And she went to the loo. When she came out the taxi-driver was eating a cake and drinking something from a bottle, and he asked if she wanted something to eat. She wasn't sure whether he was offering her some of what he was already eating or inviting her to buy something from the supermarket. So she said, 'No, thanks', and that seemed to put him out, because here was she, ready to continue the journey, and the driver was caught out eating, and she, the passenger, had to wait. Maybe that's why his tone changed. It was as if he felt the need to atone. And he explained his joke about the pit-stop.

Apparently, on one of the islands, in St. Caesare, a small island in the Leewards, they had a famous roundabout race, a race built on the idea of the roundabout. As most races are, come to think of it – apart from those hundred yards, hundred metres sorts of sprints. Anyway, this race was a motor race. Up in St. Caesare. And they say it's now spread to Beef Island as well. And Barbardos was the one to thank for it. Apparently, on those little islands, the sense of lacking hinterland was even more acute than in Barbados, and the idea of the roundabout came about after all sorts of studies of how to relieve *pressure* on the people, giving them a sense of not being hemmed in, giving them a sense of possibilities – a roundabout with lots of signs pointing to places where they could turn off. At the famous St. Caesare roundabout just outside Barville, the capital, you could turn off to places like Coderington and Windy Hill and the *Soufriere,* which of course blew up some time back. And you could turn off even to Montserrat, which was the next little island. Or you could just go into the capital, Barville. That was roundabout *one,* an idea that created even greater space for the people of St. Caesare, because who's to know that there isn't a roundabout *two* and a roundabout *seven* and a roundabout *twenty-nine?* And this whole idea of a roundabout to solve your problems of space was pioneered right here in Barbados, who had adopted this way of honouring its distinguished citizens without having to take up too much space. Worrell and Walcott were accommodated here on the Cane Gardens highway. Weekes and Sobers were further down the ABC highway on the way to the Grantley Adams airport. Nita Barrow…

Eye See Eye was taken by this idea of the roundabout to solve your space problem and thought what a clever way to relieve the pressure on you of feeling trapped in a small space. She couldn't help it, she had to take out her notebook; there was a poem here. There was a sequence of poems here. Now it was the turn of the driver to wait on her.

Eye See Eye felt better for that little briefing and note-taking session at the petrol station. She felt a bit closer to the taxi-driver as a result. Maybe he was the sort of person who might even attend the conference. She could see him now, sitting at the back of the room and saying nothing for a couple of sessions and then stunning everyone at the end of the day with a reference to some obscure Shakespeare play or with a really intimate knowledge of the early novels of Edgar Mittelholtzer and Austin Clarke and Earl Lovelace; so that the prominent writers and scholars and professors would suddenly have to take note and be guarded in their response. *This taxi-driver man will do.*

'So what do you think of Kamau's interview with Nathaniel Mackey?' she asks him.

'Oh, the *conVERSations…*' He thought about this for a while and then motioned that he was going to put the empty bottle in the bin outside. Then he wiped his mouth with the back of his hand even though the mouth was already clean, for he had wiped it with a napkin, but she noted the gesture. Then he signalled that she should follow him back to the car.

Should she sit in the back, as before? That film, whatever it was called, *Miss Daisy something something* with the white woman in the back of the car and the black driver doing his Hollywood thing, made her want to sit in the front. But what if he didn't want her to sit in front? *Driving Miss Daisy.* What if sitting in front gave him the wrong idea? So in the end she decided to get back into the back seat of the car and let him take the initiative. When they got back to the Frank Worrell Roundabout he seemed to hesitate a little, and instead of turning off to Cave Hill, he decided to go round the roundabout one more time. She liked that.

Third time round he started to talk. She was missing out, you know. On all the hugging and kissing and shaking hands and clapping one another on the back. (*Eye See Eye had a momentary image of Roman senators in the Capitol, and daggers...*) These conferences were little United Nations meetings, you know, folk down from Canada and the US and England. And in from the region. Guyana. Belize. Bahamas. All that. Breaking ice. Pulling rank. Liming. She was missing out on the easy entry for those who got there early. By leaving it late she was walking right into the spotlight. *She would be noticed.* She couldn't play shy then, or people would think she was standoffish. She playing fresh. And another thing – she would miss out on the security of sitting through those early papers which let you pick up the codes and tone of the thing – you know, the sort of reference being made about Kamau and Walcott this year. And whether that boy who took on Lamming at the Warwick conference last year was going to have anyone argue his case about tourism being a good thing for the islands. Or again, Naipaul: was his name still good to guarantee a little ripple of laughter and scorn in the audience? And so on. And she was missing out, during the tea-break and lunch hour, on a little bit of networking. It was a political thing, making out with people you really hate. (Of course, during your paper, you have to look up and see who's who in the audience, and make mention of them, like royalty.) Anyway, the way she was going, by the time she got there, all the invitations to future conferences would have been passed out.

Eye See Eye, in the back of the taxi, had stopped taking notes; clearly this man thought she was a novice: did he know he was talking to someone who only last year got an Eastern Arts Association grant for her poems and had invitations for readings galore but declined out of sensitivity to her black sisters and brothers. Anyway, back to the present.

(*Back to the present:* she thought that was a quaint little phrase, but no time to take it further now...) She was looking over the conference programme, determined to show the driver who was in charge here, who was on top, sort of thing. *Caribbean Voices: Early Years of Caribbean Writing in Britain.* All about Swanzy and Collymore. Swanzy in London, Collymore in Barbados. Famous BBC radio programme, forties, fifties, coming out of London. Gave space to all those people – Lamming, Naipaul, Salkey, Walcott, Mittelholtzer, etc. – the guys still beating us in we backside to this day. She had a mentor in England (no name mentioned) who had been encouraging her to get rid of the quotation marks from *Caribbean Voices,* opening it out, man, to the wider Caribbean, and not only to include those who live overseas and claim heritage, but to Caribbean people by adoption – Bob Shacochis from America, Stewart Brown from Birmingham. *Eye See Eye* from Wellingborough. She wanted to ask him if he's heard of Eye See Eye. But instead she asked about Kamau's interview with Nathaniel Mackey.

'The man's liming, man; liming.'

'Oh.'

'What them fellow call, them fellow down in Trinidad, call Semilime, man. Liming.'

OK, she could take it. And had he heard of Eye See Eye?

'They run the place, man; all the islands.'

'*Eye See Eye*. Not CIA.'

But he started telling her about the CIA. Eye See Eye sighed; you couldn't compete. And she wasn't focusing on the thing at hand. She remembered the way in which that fellow, the poet, had justified his female persona that night in Wellingborough. That gave her courage, so she sat back in the seat, closed her eyes and tried to keep cool, emptying her mind as the taxi-driver droned on about *Bim* and Colly and John Wickham, who apparently was alive but a bit shaky. And again, *Bim,* and the other magazines in the region, *Kyk-over-all* in Guyana and Edna Manley's *Focus* in Jamaica. That and more: nationalism and its effect on the literature. Paternalism from the centre. Then he was talking of the race to push the start of West Indian literature to a place further back in time than the last speaker placed it. From *Bim* to the twenties in Trinidad with Albert Gomes and CLR James and those boys round the *Beacon;* and from there further back to the newspaper stuff at the end of the last century; and of course from there, back to Africa; and beyond Africa to America before Columbus; and then to Noah and the Ark and finally to Eve, who was a West Indian woman come out of the water to find Walcott there again ready to give she language.

'Man, put wey you truncheon, le'me rest.' But she didn't say it. She was thinking of an Andrew Salkey image she might use if she ever got to the conference. There were two she had jotted down. His 'high-rise bottom', describing Caribbean woman; she wondered if the driver found it sensuous, but she didn't dare ask. The other image was the one describing the scattered nature of the West Indian family as a 'sea-split marriage'. Maybe that one was safer, if more tame; and she felt strong enough now to interrupt her tutor and order him to head for the university.

They drove into the campus. So far so good. They found the venue. No problem there, it was easy to find because there were important-looking people relaxing outside with drinks and nibbles, as if the drinks and nibbles were beneath them.

The writers. The scholars. The professors. Was she dressed right for this? The women looked so cool in the heat. Was her skin conspiring against her: was she, lacking in pigment, *deprived* in this setting? That man. A professor, clearly: how could he keep that line, down to the shoes, crisp and soft, not flabby soft, but soft. And he must be fifty if he's a day. Sixty. Body of a young boy. Even the shirt was cool. Classical and cool. How did his wife let him venture into a place dangerous as this?

And here was he coming forward to shake her hand; it was her knees that needed attention. And her stomach was rumbling, and she needed the loo. Her name was *...ackee & salt fish & rice 'n' peas & friedfish & flying fish & fish... And plantain & banana and ... and breadfruit and breadnut and mango. And guava and passion fruit... And de Lisser & Mittelholtzer. Just another Mittelholtzer, please. No glass. God, you didn't tell me it was going to be this hard.* And she is half-wondering how she is going to pay off the taxi. And she's missing Wellingborough, missing Wellingborough. And the professor-writer before her has white hair and a white beard. And she can't believe what she hearing because before he shakes her hand and hugs her up and kisses her on both cheeks, he calling her by name, Eye See Eye.

(*The Devil*, Issue 4, 1999)

RESISTANCE

I have hundreds of pounds in my pocket. I'm walking round Ladbroke Grove with hundreds of pounds in my pocket; it's not late, but it's evening and so much sterling in my pocket must be a problem. It's raining, I'm not wearing a coat, the cash must be safer in the pocket of a man not protecting himself from the wet: would passers-by fall for this? I fancy I hear a German phrase hurled from across the street, but no, it's nothing; the few people around are apologetic, as if explaining away the obviousness of spring rain, the odd burst of speech on the street lighter-sounding than German, as if to make you secure. I walk along the main road, deliberately go past Cambridge Gardens where – the things you remember – the man in question once lectured me on the Diaries of Richard Crossman: I was impressed by the hard-back volumes on his shelf. I walk, not thinking, to the corner of Chesterton and Goldbourne, turn right into Goldbourne as if programmed to return to a time when the century rather than *you* were in the fifties, an age, improbably, of possibility. Just off the top of this road, to the right, is the family estate, shrunk to a house, without land, no longer in the family. I'm standing before the house, which looks deserted: is it worth the bundle in my pocket? It would have to come down, this house, buttressed in the old days by a racist on one side and a school on the other; both racist and school seem to have been relocated, their premises mocking redevelopment. Rain on my face seems right. I'm thinking vaguely of the shop on Goldbourne which sold good cakes and my optician's at the top of the road and the girl who was the daughter of someone we never saw; and of St. Charles's hospital on the other side of Ladbroke Grove where I visited with grapes, all the way down from university. I'll be late for dinner; as I go past a woman, heading back now towards Cambridge Gardens, I fancy she challenges me with *Konnen Sie mir die genaue Zeit sagen?* Something to dine out on.

That was years ago: I'd come in from Germany that day, done a lot of running around, crossed London and had dinner with my friend Balham in Ladbroke Grove and flew out to St. Caesare next day to bury my mother. Now, the latest eruption in St. Caesare brings it all back.

The volcano is said to have disturbed the family graves. I'm not going to think about that in case it trivialises her decision to be buried 'at home'. But that set me thinking about Balham, the poseur, who used to live in a flat in Cambridge Gardens, off where we lived in the '50s. Balham saw my mother as a member of the Resistance; a 'Lady Activist', he called her. I had promised to walk to Compostela in her memory. Or maybe one should just reclaim an old house, rescue it from the prop of ageing racist and run-down school, renovate it as a form of defiance. Then if the St. Caesare volcano chose to blow away one home I'd be able to say: Two fingers to you, Sir.

Yet how crude to reduce all this to a Balham memory! It was too coarsening for family. According to Balham they were a team, the idiot and my mother. (I had images of Hepburn and Cary Grant as honest burglars pretending to be thieves. Or of Balham stealing books from the library (he read Sociology at university) because they had brought in membership charges and it was his way of defeating Thatcherism. *Resistance* sounded quaint in connection with my mother: it wasn't Balham but a recent partner who'd been disabusing me, and not so gently, of this notion. Hence, my renewed interest in the inanities of Balham. Maybe I – and not the only one in the family – was too fastidious for my own good).

Balham and I did GCEs together at Kilburn Polytechnic (28 bus from the top end of the road, the Westbourne Grove end to Kilburn. The Number 31 was good, too, but that turned off too soon, for Swiss Cottage). By the second year the family had moved house to Priory Park Road, just down from the Polytechnic. A few of the boys who hung around together and played table tennis – including Balham, though he was at the edge of the group and no one knew exactly where he lived; we thought it was somewhere near Cricklewood – used to come over the road and talk and watch television and eat. In later years Balham would emphasise this 'teenage' closeness of ours, insisting that my mother's fried chicken was the best fried chicken he'd ever had. My mother, when she learned of this, put it down to the fellow's upbringing – to the fact that he was from another island, also, though that wasn't his fault. But for a boy to have changed his name from something West Indian to Balham, showed that he had no proud heritage at home to hang on to. So it was understandable that he would confuse her delicately steamed chicken with herbs-till-the-juice-was-all-but-gone with something fried. 'That lady', Balham was fond of saying, 'is St. Caesare's Cultural Activist in Britain'. It was his habit of trying to impress present company, who tended to be lively girls from Golders Green and Mill Hill who were all good at languages: 'She just lives and lives', he would say of my mother, a youngish woman then, who, when she died years later, was still only 76. But Balham was always more impressed by his own oddness, including the strangeness of his diction, than in accuracy.

But yes, you know how it is, we colluded, two men together, playing the game of nostalgia, making my mother not only an activist but a *cricketer,* coming in to bat Number

3 for West Indies. Though you must realise there were different perceptions here. For Balham the Number 3 batsman was someone who came in, often in a crisis, and tamed the fast bowling, either wore it down or took it apart, and controlled the destiny of the match; for me it was important that she was coming in at Number 3 for West Indies at a time when *we* had the best fast bowlers, so that she wouldn't have to face the likes of Hall and Charley Griffith, who would be on her side. So I wasn't surprised at Balham's latest act of appropriation.

He was ecstatic that my mother had chosen not to be buried in England, a political act, England being too small a place for both your latrine and your grave, sort of thing. That made her a fighter. And that way she didn't compromise the family, survivors, didn't put them in a position where they'd have to kneel down and pray to a foreign land. This act of selflessness tied her into a web of resistance which enabled people in this country to hang on to their sanity: take that boy in Crouch End, other side of London, a Pakistani running his own restaurant. The man was into special offers. He was prepared to bankrupt himself with Special Offers. Why? Was it because he loved people? Was that a joke: what had people ever done for Pakistan? No, he put on the eat-as-much-as-you-like for £4.95 splurges because he observed that the victims eating themselves into a coronary were the sort of New-Imperial, ill-bred master-racers (well-brought-up people would take less if you offered them more) that Pakistan couldn't defeat in any other way, except possibly at cricket. This man, according to Balham, this restaurateur, was clearly a member of the *Resistance* – the sort of person who if he couldn't quite have saved fascist France from Nazi occupation might yet help to save Britain from an affliction called *Britishness.* (I liked to play with the idea of my mother saving France from occupation).

On my way back from Germany, via England, for the funeral in St. Caesare, I naturally couldn't help reviewing some of the structures that – who knows? – had protected us as a family: family living in their separate houses, family divided; there was no family home. Did we still need all the games that had served us well enough? So my mother came in to bat Number 3 for West Indies, and had acquitted herself well. This wasn't a privilege confined to family. I remember the day when we all trooped up to Trafalgar Square to hear the celebrated Madame Nu of Vietnam denounce the Americans for bombing her country: for a while Madame Nu came in to bat at Number 3 for West Indies, and played the bowling well. As, for that matter, did Balham's unmarried aunt in Ipswich. (Or maybe it was Luton). The opposing, losing team sported no-hopers like Henry Kissinger and General Motors and Dow Jones.

Some families hug and kiss and exchange endless cards and trinkets; some, like ours, are more 'Restoration' in their temperament, and go for the drawing-room wit: we like to think that this is one of the things that survived the crossing, the drawing-room manner, the Sunday-afternoon sessions in the old house in Coderington, the time between lunch and evening service when guests would be entertained. The family would retire upstairs with the Methodist priest, perhaps a relative from town and, occasionally, the headmaster; and the talk would be illuminating. We have pictures of the scene, painted by the boy da Firenze who later committed suicide.

Da Firenze was older than us but not by much, and had been sent off to Italy to study art (not to England or Ireland to become a Doctor or Lawyer) and when he came back his name was da Firenze: his gift to us the weeks leading up to our departure for England was a series of sketches trapping us at our best, in 1956, forever. Here were we in the drawing-room, in conversation; on the verandah, looking out; my mother sitting on the horse at the foot of the steps; Professeur Croissant and Mr. Ryan, new from Ireland, disputing a point maybe about tobacco, maybe about potatoes – and Mady serving coconut tarts and iced drinks. Not being able to recreate the drawing-room as at home, we tested to see if the wit, like a reasonable wine, would travel. So the Lady could no longer play cricket. Well, maybe the problem wasn't cricket, maybe she just wasn't dressed for it; fashions change: how about a new kit, designer pads from Italy, front Gucci, the shoemaker. No? No pressure, let's start again: how about these designs for women from the First Dynasty of Babylon and the Kingdom of Madagascar?

Not keen on the name, Babylon? And yes, Madagascar *is* a bit far from Kilburn. Soon that takes us to the Incas, the Aztecs, nearer home in a way. Coming back into fashion too! Light-skinned people but not like the English. Failing that we might have to make strange alliances – we're not at home, remember, choice for manoeuvre is limited –failing that we might have to settle for the MacAlpines of Scotland, no Queens there, you know, just a lot of Picts; and she'd have to change her accent. But she couldn't do that.

I had got in from the Continent late, missed everything; missed the rest of the family who'd already flown out, with the body. I would follow tomorrow. I'd rushed around all afternoon, busy busy, before realising I was getting nowhere, except perhaps trying to impress myself with *concern.* I had to buy some clothes; I had to go to the launderette, to the cash point, to the bank. I wanted company and sympathy, my ex-partner in Highgate. But, to punish me, she wasn't in. I was staying at a friend's flat in Crouch End and the phone had been cut off. The call-box wasn't such a long way away but it struck the wrong note when you were trying to be grave. I put 20 pence in the box (instead of 10) and, despite the non-call the machine declined to return the money. Maybe these are the Monetarists, eating coins. I went to buy some clothes along the Parade, Topsfield Parade; black shoes, sort of thing, presentable trousers. They didn't like my Access card in the shop, so on to the cash-point where there seemed to be a new system in operation, dispensing notes in £20. £40. £60 lots... Why? Why couldn't you have £35. £50. £15? Extortion. It was raining. England was being stage-managed and I was in a little-known play by Brecht, which I little knew. I had a cold, which I would walk out of the play with. The launderette was next to the bank, which was convenient, but they were in Highgate, too far to walk up the hill in the rain: the hassle of bus to Archway and train one stop to Highgate made me begin to feel better; these day-to-day hurdles have additional point when your mother dies and is being buried thousands of miles away and you've missed it and are pretending not to have missed it.

The launderette is not a launderette where you slip coins into the machines and get on with it, but a computerised puzzle, hard to work out. (Would old men doing *The Times* crossword on the train come into their own at the launderette? I have an idea for a play: making everyone in the society switch jobs, stripe-suited *Times* and *Telegraph* weirdos manning digital launderettes, etc. but I can't be bothered to work it out). I get help at the launderette from someone who must feel vaguely virtuous (a gift from my mother) and go to the bank. Lots of cash in the bank, some of it mine – why should we trust these guys? Shouldn't banks start folding now, in the new England? Like old America. Cash enough for the fare to the Caribbean (there's a discount at the place in Stoke Newington if you pay cash) and to buy some clothes. I'm conscious now of having so much cash in my pocket that I feel like an escapee; it's almost as if I'm walking down the Archway road saying, 'Look, folks, I've got hundreds of pounds in my pocket,' and being greeted by pleasing, benign smiles and sympathetic nods of 'Well done, Well done,' and putting down this quality of response to the fact that my mother has lived here for thirty-three years. Ah, but the wet blanket treatment comes like a symbol; it's snowing. Light snow falling. April.

Back in the Crouch End flat I forget there's no phone and come out again to ring that Highgate number. She's not at home, so I have to get on. Maybe I'll put off buying the clothes till first thing in the morning. The flight isn't till eleven-thirty. Be at the airport at ten-thirty. Leave the house at nine. Can't do it, really. On my way back up to the High Road wondering what to do, I find myself phoning Balham.

★

I agreed to go to dinner because he lived so near our old house in Ladbroke Grove. Before flying out to St. Caesare I felt the urge to retrace those pre O-Level haunts, to relive those having-to-light-the-fire-with-damp coal nights; those now-nostalgic smog-laden days – even that less-than-romantic Oswald Mosley meeting outside our house. That was during the 1959 General Election: a Saturday afternoon. Because my mother sat at the window upstairs and the meeting was held directly outside, near the public loos, she effectively attended the meeting: was that bravery? Resistance? She used to sit in much the same posture at the dining-room window in Barville, looking down on the main street, a faint patch of grease appearing on the unpainted wooden frame of the window where her head rested. England-Mosley didn't change her style. Of course we had protection at that meeting, a young cousin who had joined the army, standing quietly at the back, in uniform. And who knows, other members of the resistance, undeclared. Maybe the proximity of Balham is beginning to affect my sanity.

But it is true that the lady of the house did want us to make a statement to Mosley. By our presence. By our calm. By the *quality* of our resistance.

Latish for supper, I was still avoiding Cambridge Gardens, drifting back into Goldbourne Road. Amazingly, the chemist was still there after all these years. But why not: a chemist wasn't like a West Indian grocery in the '50s that sprang up overnight and vanished within months, weeks; the chemist was merely shut for the night. There was the woman who went with the chemist – not the wife who never was, the lost mother of children, just a woman – thin and sexless as I remember, about the sort of age that I am now who recommended, for a cyst on my eye, the application of savlon cream. My opticians were to tell me, later, that that had contributed to the thickening lenses in my frames. True or not, my position isn't desperate, but imagine the cloned thousands of this assistant dispensing advice in some Zambian or Karachi extension of this shop. I'm here; I'll remonstrate on behalf of the victims. In deference to my mother, I abhor the melodrama of a gun. I'll knock quietly on the door (for she's old and uncertain, and we are St. Caesarians of breeding) and deliver my lines: Howdy, I say. Remember me? The words are from the film of the book.

'Remember me?' the lips hardly moving. No gun. The menace comes from her feeling of not having been lucky in life.

'Shuddup,' I say, but casually, as she tries to bluff. 'Shuddup, whaddaya whaddaya,' as she pleads diminished responsibility, of not knowing my mother's name. Ach, what's the point? Fuhgedaboudit.

At dinner, Balham introduced me to someone, his partner, who deserved better. I was praised as someone who made good fried chicken, though he may not have said chicken. There was unusual music at dinner. Arabic folk songs. He mentioned the source of the music, it sounded like Mecca but I must have got that wrong. But then there was talk of going to visit the Holy places (this from the Sociologist) to pray at the Ka-a-ba, so maybe I heard right, after all. (Balham's partner was someone who might have graced any of our drawing-rooms; I felt like weeping). And then the conversation turned to a deconstruction of Thatcher. Not very much later I phoned a taxi to take me home to Crouch End, not willing to trust the hundreds of pounds to the solidarity of residents in my old village, or to well-wishers on the train.

Two days later in St. Caesare – ah, the tricks of technology! – we're in another village. Outside the church at St. Anne's I was accosted by a man down from America, a schoolmate not seen since the '50s; he was going to deliver the eulogy. I mentioned, casually, my mother's insistence on being buried 'at home', in the family plot next to her own mother, after the Thirty-three Years' War in England. He said that was an act of... and I supplied the word he might have been searching for. He agreed, with enthusiasm, and took the type-written speech from his inside pocket, and a pen from another pocket.

(1990)

OUR MAN IN KL

Stewart rang to ask the meaning of a word, a phrase, maybe: it meant nothing to me.

'I thought you'd know,' he said. 'It's your story.' He sounded a bit smug.

But I was thinking: Come on, that's never happened before. Even though I may have forgotten the meaning of a word or phrase I've used somewhere, it would still ring a bell; but no, I couldn't even identify the language.

'What's that again?'

'*Puri Pujangga.* If that's how you say it.'

I repeated it. Nothing. Stewart had got it wrong.

'Never heard the phrase in my life. What language is it?'

'Malay, I would imagine.'

I thought of those early Anthony Burgess books. *Malay!* Then it clicked. Much nearer home.

'From "Our man in KL".' Stewart prompted.

I told him what I thought of the author of 'Our Man in KL'; and then went on to discuss the story of mine that he was threatening not to put into the anthology he was editing.

★

'Our Man in KL' was a form of ingratitude I found hard to credit, a so-called short-story with me as the subject. It was hard to credit because it was written by Michael Carrington, and this after I had spent the best part of eighteen months labouring in his service, my own work put on hold. I had produced a scholarly edition of his plays, and sweated over an *Introduction,* which argued the case for him as a major dramatist. And for what: scholarly editions didn't sell. Carrington wasn't particularly big in England, and Caribbean drama wasn't exactly setting the world alight. So Carrington had repaid me by writing this silly little sketch with me as buffoon, bumbler, comic… Of course, I could take a joke against myself, but why was the fellow so – 'graceless' came to mind, but it sounded prissy; *relentless* seemed a bit over the top: the word was 'patronising', really.

★

'I don't think it's patronising,' Stewart was saying. 'I think it's very funny.' He was saying this from the security of Birmingham. 'I have to say, Pewter, it rings true. To be honest with you…' (And Birmingham was a long way from Sheffield.) Not that I could fail to imagine myself in Kuala Lumpur being accident-prone and all that but… I wasn't in the mood for this.

'I'll exchange Kuala Lumpur for Sheffield any day,' I said to Stewart. 'But even the *title* tells you something about the fellow. Y'know, "KL". Carrington, part of the *in-set.*'

'That's what they say, apparently. KL.'

'That's what I mean. The fellow spent, what, three weeks in the country. So, naturally, KL. Just slips off the tongue: he was still at it when I saw him in America: Carrington the sophisticate; we the proles.'

'"Proles." That dates you a bit.'

'OK, OK' Then I remembered that it was Stewart who had called me.

'Is this a social call,' I asked in mock-exasperation. 'Or is this the sort of thing that passes for scholarly conversation down in Birmingham!' And more to the point. 'Are you going to put my drawing-room story in the book?'

'Frankly, Pewter, it's too long. I think it's a brilliant story, but the length alone would keep at least two people out. It's either printing your story intact and losing Danticat and Olive Senior.' That was the usual sort of Stewart wind-up. So he rubbed it in. 'Now, who's going to tell Olive that we don't have room for her story because of your novella. Are you feeling brave enough for that!'

I admitted to having a weak heart. From this moment.

Ah but he was having me on. 'But you're putting in that bit of nonsense by Carrington.'

'"Our Man in KL". It's very funny. It actually made me laugh out loud.'

I indicated what I thought of his Birmingham sense of humour; so he reminded me that he was a welshman and I sent my commiserations to his family.

'From now on, Pewter, we'll always have that wonderful image of you driving your Volvo and crashing into things; you should take out a patent.'

My response may have been ungenerous. So Stewart's tone became a bit more serious. And he addressed my real concern... 'I still think you could miss that middle section of the story: It'd still be a great read.'

We were talking of the title story of my forthcoming book and I was committed to it. It had tried to convey a sense of what the family thought they had brought to England from the West Indies in 1956, and how little of it seemed to have survived. And it was suggesting that perhaps less had survived the original crossing than we had thought. It was called, 'Taking the Drawing-Room Through Customs'.

My irritation with Stewart was only partly manufactured. 'So, you want to rob my mother of the few things she managed to get through customs. That's fine,' I said. 'That's fine. I'll go ahead and edit it all out. Down to one trunk and a couple of suitcases. Two or three summer dresses. Could you live with that, *Massa!'*

'Seems just right for a young lad,' Stewart said. 'I'm

surprised they let you through customs wearing all those dresses.'

I agreed to look at the story again, with a view to cutting down on the dresses.

★

Of course that's not what I did: I went back to the Carrington story, which he had photocopied for me, with no hint of an apology, I might say. The story read like a writer's diary, with 'Our Man' swanning round in some foreign place, posturing a bit and sending himself up in the process. This place happened to be Kuala Lumpur (or KL) and some other university town in Malaysia. The usual stuff. Local colour. The Twin Towers. The KL Building. Gleaming concrete palaces everywhere. Unbelievable cuisine. And the women: Carrington characterizes them as mini-versions of those Canadian cedars and cypresses and casuarinas you get in West Indian poetry, swaying in the imaginary breeze – only to surprise you when you had occasion to talk to them: cool and articulate in English.

But the story isn't about that; it's about Our Man in Malaysia, visiting this university. As writer in residence he gets all the perks, even gets to stay in the – there it was *Puri Pujangga,* the Residence of poets; his own office with computer (loaned by the acting Dean, no less), endless invitations to lunch, *and a car* – a Volvo. And the story is about Our Man and this car – in which he regularly gets lost driving round the university town and the environs of KL.

First day he gets lost going home from the university, which is only about a mile away. He stops at a police booth at a busy cross-roads. (He stops because he's gone round there a couple of times already, and he doesn't want to make them suspicious.) So he stops and asks for the Golf Club. The Golf Club restaurant is apparently near to where he is staying, and where he has his meals, because the Place for Poets isn't serving ordinary meals, and he can't survive for long periods on ambrosia. Inevitably, there is another golf club in the area, and he gets directed to the wrong one. Our Man, as he drives, knows he's got it wrong; too far away and he's travelling through down-market parts of town he doesn't recognise; but not to worry, it's only about half-past six – quarter to seven, there's still light: it feels rather good driving the Volvo.

He's climbing up a hill, a winding mountain-road; this doesn't look good. Some way up, he runs into a road-block, a barrier across the road... *Ah, why am I reading this.*

I remember the slight gesture of apology that Carrington made when he gave me the copy of the story. We were in a restaurant in America. DC. In Washington, a few weeks ago. It was the day after I'd given a reading at Maryland where Carrington was teaching on the Writing Program. And we were with a couple of American friends in this restaurant in DC, a Louisiana restaurant serving some sort of scavenger fish I can't remember the name of. And over lunch, they were having a very American sort of conversation about the presidential hopefuls and presidential power and that sort of thing. And whether it mattered whether you had a Nixon or a Clinton in the White House. And on to questions of Lincoln and slavery and Lincoln's famous debates on the subject with Stephen Douglas, and which bits of the Gettysburg Address Lincoln had actually written, that sort of thing. So obviously, y'know, I wasn't going to lower the tone of the lunch by whining on about my supposed portrait in a short story set in Malaysia.

The Malaysian story, he said later, Carrington said (and this, I suppose, was the gesture of appeasement) was informed by my trip to Albania, all those years ago when Comrade Enver Hoxha reigned supreme. Carrington recalled the story of my entering Albania with a bedraggled group of what he called pioneers, come to help with bringing in the spring-onion harvest. And he had that image of us, as a group, being held up at the barrier, late on a Saturday afternoon on that little mountain road which was the border between Yugoslavia and Albania. And when, last year in Malaysia, Carrington ran up against the barrier across the road leading up to the golf club *and* not being able to turn the car round, he thought to himself: Yes, a Pewter Stapleton sort of moment.

Well, I'm not going to pursue this. I've got absolutely nothing done since coming back from America in November – except slip on the ice and end up with my arm in a sling. And we're already into the new century. The marking's piling up. Deadlines ignored. Even the easy jobs – I can't get out of submitting an essay for the book someone at work is editing. And here I am reading a biography of Abraham Lincoln. So, to work.

But y'know, Carrington shouldn't be allowed to get away with this. *I know, I know, I shouldn't let this get to me.* But why should someone like Stewart, who is a serious scholar, a critic, be taken in by this stuff! So... Our Man returns from KL one night to find the gate to the *Puri Pujangga* closed. It's not just the gate, the whole thing is secure, with wire fencing and stuff all the way round, nowhere even for someone on foot to squeeze by. And in a bizarre after-midnight sequence, in the middle of nowhere, Carrington has Our Man, driving the car through a field, then trying to find the university, *at the same time* contemplating sleeping in the car and alternately making it back to KL – x Km away – to find a hotel for the night. Then he runs into the police at the booth and they tell him there's a way round the back to his place, and naturally he gets lost, till, by accident he arrives at the *Puri Pujangga* in the early hours of the morning. And if that isn't bad enough, Carrington has Our Man clocking up another *two accidents in the Volvo* that week. *Garbage.*

Though I have to admit, I do like the bit when all the Malaysian men descend on the car and wreck it. And the scene is one I could well see myself being involved in. You're stuck there in the middle of nowhere, the cars in front are turning round, and you have no reverse. Narrow road. So, naturally, you solicit help from the fellow in front of you who's already turned round his Malaysian-made car and is preparing to head back down the hill. The three or four cars behind are already starting to turn round. So the first man gets out of his car to help, which is a generous thing to do because he's got his wife and child sitting in the back: young wife, young child. He gets into the Volvo to show Our Man how it's done. He tries every possible combination to put the car in reverse. No luck. Our Man is relieved: *do they think I'm an idiot!* The wife from the back of the other car offers advice. *Pretty woman.* Now three or four men from the vehicles behind are summoned. Each, in turn, has a go at the gear-stick, pulling, forcing, depressing, etc. so that Our Man has to caution against damaging the car. Finally, they give up and manhandle the Volvo and turn it round. Our Man decides to help push rather than steer because, well, it seems a slightly less colonial thing to do. It turns out, of course, that there was nothing wrong with the car in the first place, and that all the men in question were suitably shown up to be incompetent farts when the garage-owner next day turned up at the university and sorted it out. Carrington, of course, rubbed in the humiliation: the garage-owner, described as 'a solid, low-slung figure,' turns up and very delicately, very slowly, slides the lever on the gear-stick up before smoothly easing the thing into reverse – no pressure at all. Carrington goes out of his way to contrast this with the *maleness* of Our Man and his Malaysian helpers using brute-force and ignorance to no avail. He reserves his admiration for the 'pretty woman' in the back of the first car who keeps up a running conversation with her husband and the other volunteers; and then commiserates with Our Man – her amused, easy fluency, in two languages, ending with that slight gesture of resignation which said that, yes, these are the sorts of things that men like to do.

It wasn't a good story, really; I would have done it differently. I would have played down the farce and made more of this business of staying at a place which was the haven for poets. Apparently, this meant poets in its widest sense, including those who were simply appreciative of poetry. (There was something Platonic about this.) I would have had Our Man – I don't know – wake up in the night surrounded by other writers who'd passed through the place. Or better still, why not by Chaucer and Shakespeare and Dante and that lot paying a visit to Malaysia, having a drink behind closed doors, toasting the spirit of dissent. Look! There's TS Eliot gazing in his toothpaste glass telling a restless Dryden that No, it's a not a good time to return to England as Poet Laureate. Next morning as Our man is getting himself ready, trying on endless shirts and tops, as he's preparing to go into the university to give a lecture on Walcott, Dante stirs on the sofa and apologises for being the cause of all those endless theses down the ages, and wants to know if it's really true that he has had an influence on the young Walcott and Heaney. He doesn't begrudge them having quality time with Beatrice; he's got over all that (Unlike poor Petrarch, next-door in the loo, composing sonnets to Laura.) Meanwhile, he's off to take the waters of Maria Antoinetta Serancino, which is said to restore poets to youth and vigour. (*Ome, perche non latra/per me, com'io per lei, nel caldo borro*?)*

That's one way to sentimentalise the women!

★

Stewart didn't much like my improvements to Carrington's story. Ah, well. *I* didn't much care for the 'improvements' to my own piece. I had done a demolition job on my family, and cut the heart out of the Drawing-Room saga. 'Drawing-room' was now to be interpreted *as an idea.* The fact that bookcases and the piano and the round table with the lamp where I'd read my *Pilgrim's Progress,* were retained didn't compensate for the absence of other things: grandfather's rocking-chair, the trap-door that led to the dining-room downstairs, and was made secure at night; and brought on my nightmare the night we forgot and left it open, etc. The whole thing now seemed to me very thin and to be making some sort of statement about class, all a bit tacky and unattractive. The fact that the drawing-room was now detached, free-floating, no longer above the dining-room, no longer connected to the other rooms, other functions of the house, made it all seem so much less audacious to have attempted to get it through customs. The debate about what was to be done with all the stuff we couldn't bring seemed confusing and strange, rather than pioneering and challenging. *And where was the colour, now?* Stray talk of the coal-room and the bread room with Nellie making the bread; and the kitchen with its inside oven and cassava-plate, and the (whisper it) servant room which was long home to the cassava mill, seemed disjointed. Once you start dismantling the house you might as well demolish the whole thing.

As I was talking to Stewart I was thinking: if I were in Carrington's place, in that Malaysian story, I would go one further and change the cast of poets in the poet's whatever-it's-called building. Instead of the usual suspects, why not, say Ahkmatova of the Russian 'Requiem'. And Rumi with his Persian quatrains and Sappho memorising all those lost womanly poems – all there in my room at the *Puri Pujangga* debating the meaning of love.

And I was telling Stewart that, yes, the yard could go; both the back yard where my grandmother held auctions from the animal pound; and the front yard where Nellie did her washing and hung out the sheets to dry, sometimes spread out like a statement, on the grass.

And what of our horse; what of Ruby, our horse? Well, my mother could be persuaded not to try and get Ruby through customs, and that would cut six pages of the text; and all in all the story was now down to a manageable length. And my arm is hurting and the marking is piling up and other work not done; and I have to believe that even this new version of the 'Drawing-room' story beats being stuck in a Volvo on a Malaysian mountain road, unable to turn round.

* O why does she not scream for me/As I for her, in the hot pit?

(2000)

WORLD CUP, 2002

i

So what are the facts? Before the final between Brazil and Germany at Yokahama, we already knew the score. No, this wasn't the charge of match-fixing and corruption rumoured against the Brazilian set-up – those painful memories of Ronaldo in the finals against France in '98, etc – so no journalistic nonsense about the 'culture of corruption' besmirching the beautiful game; this was quite simply the news filtering through from the FIFA internet site that in the other World Cup, just decided in far-off Thimphu, Bhutan had defeated Montserrat 4-0 for Football's Wooden Spoon. This was an important contest, wrong-footing so many of football's critics – those voicing concerns about Sport and the macho culture, Sport and the appeal to nationalism, Sport and the cult of youth: Bhutan and Montserrat quietly proud of being the weakest teams in FIFA's footballing canon, coming in as numbers 202 and 203 in the world rankings were more than novelty value. This match, scheduled to be played at the same time as the other final in Japan demanded a different sort of indulgence from, say, the cricketers' version of Authors versus Publishers at Lords or the annual outing of the P.G. Woodhouse Society where the luncheon hampers were more carefully prepared than the cricketers.

The Montserratians were at a disadvantage: they were playing away from home; they miscalculated where Bhutan was on the map, or at least, the challenge of arriving there fighting fit; and got their travel schedules in a muddle, the journey eventually taking five days and several changes of aircraft: that left them no time to acclimatise to playing at altitude. But the Montserratians had their supporters in Thimphu, fully half of the crowd, green-shirted like their Emerald Island's Team, primed to roar out their soca anthem *Hot Hot Hot,* like any authentic volcanic-islander.

I was, by now, trying to assemble my thoughts about this match. But first I had to nip round the corner to the Brazilian house, to Ricardo's, to see the other final between Brazil and Germany in the company of the yellow-shirted students from the university. They had been wonderfully entertaining during last Wednesday's game with Turkey, and I was looking forward to the atmosphere of the final.

As I was on my way to Ricardo's I tried to imagine that weird five-day journey of the Montserrat team to Bhutan. I was thinking, idly, that I might write up the experience, if only I could visualise it clearly enough: *Five Days to Bhutan* would have a good ring to it.

ii

When the *Today Programme* rang me a few days ago and asked me to comment on the match I admitted I hadn't heard of it, but I was taken by the idea of a shadow-match, so to speak, an *alternative* World Cup Final, not in any boring way to *compete* with the original, but to give a sort of extension, imaginatively, to the notion of *play,* decoupling it from nationalist aggression and all that business. But the people from the radio programme were more concerned with down-to-earth information about Montserrat; fascinated by the fact that it was still a colony of Britain; the effects of the volcano and dispersal of its people; and about the Irish connection, which the researcher having gleaned from the internet, didn't know what to make of. So I directed her to the island's historian, Howard Fergus – Sir Howard Fergus – and eventually faxed this paragraph from one of Fergus's books

> The Spaniards did not settle Montserrat. The honour was reserved for Thomas Warner, who arrived there with a British contingent from the Mother colony of St. Kitts – a Leeward Islands' version of the English Pilgrim Fathers. The colonists were English and Irish Catholics, who were made uncomfortable in Protestant St. Kitts. In Montserrat they found a new shrine for their faith and a haven from Protestant persecution. News of Roman Catholic asylum in this corner of the Antilles soon spread across the Atlantic to the British North American colony of Virginia; in 1633, Catholic refugees, pushed out of Virginia by Episcopalian persecution, also came hither in search of unmolested altars. Montserrat was thus unique in being established as an Irish-Catholic colony. When, in 1649, following his victory at Drogheda (in Ireland), Cromwell sent some of his political prisoners to Montserrat, he increased the population and preserved its Irish character.[1]

I added some personal comment about the island, never able to support its population, reduced now by hurricane and volcano, as if to illustrate some sort of point.

In Bhutan the Montserrat team, the Monster Rats, sported their traditional Irish green shirts. I had told the researcher that I would expect the players to have surnames similar to that of the Irish squad in Japan. (Though when I checked I realized that Given and Finnan and Harte and Duff, etc. didn't sound very Montserratian.) I didn't know the details of the team's preparation, or the tactics and disposition of the coach, etc. only that the players, reputedly, had had a practise match in Antigua, Montserrat's own

Sturge Park being long out of bounds because of the volcano. There was no flat land in the safe zone on the northern tip of the island; no playing area. Concerning finer points of the team's diet, etc, I knew nothing, so I gave the woman on the *Today Programme* the names of a couple of Montserratians living in Birmingham, who might be able to help.

Last time at Ricardo's, a couple of dozen people were jammed into the sitting room in front of the telly, mainly students, chunky and bulky in yellow, upright or reclining on the floor, and ranged in the doorways behind those of us lucky enough to be able to grab the seats. And, yes, the eventual victory (over a surprisingly obdurate Turkish side) was greeted with relief which belied the celebration, the hugging and kissing and improvised samba, a scene that soon spilled out into the street. So we all promised to come back for Sunday's final with the dangerous, mechanical, methodical Germans. The Brazilians were slightly nervous of the prospect of their team having to face the 'Gorilla', which is what they called Oliver Kahn, the German captain and goalkeeper, whom even present company admitted to be the best in the world.

What riled a couple of the students was the information relayed to those still in the room after the match that the sports reporter, Sue Barker, the ex-tennis-player, had jokingly referred to the Brazilian striker, Ronaldo as 'Pretty Ugly Bloke With Plenty Teeth'. This outraged the Brazilians, particularly the women, who pronounced Ronaldo 'pretty', 'sexy', and 'unstoppable'. I sort of found the Barker joke quite witty – even though I would term Ronaldo as 'ugly-pretty' rather than 'pretty-ugly', but I wasn't going to contest the issue with these 'pretty-pretty' young women in their yellow tops. But this was a Brazilian house, no cloud of journalistic sophistry was allowed to dampen the mood for long; what helped to bring back the sunshine of Rio and Saõ Paulo was a cut to the crowd on the television of a beautiful, yellow-shirted, Brazilian supporter, celebrating – a row of teeth splayed all over her decorated face. But to serious matters: Oliver Kahn was going to be a problem for Brazil; and Kahn was *ugly* to the point of psyching out the opposition; Kahn was Germany's secret weapon for the final. Yet, to the familiar concern – I had to give an opinion before I left – of the way in which Brazil hadn't taken all their scoring chances, and how, worryingly, they in turn, continued to give the opposition too many opportunities to score.

In-between the Turkish match and the final with Germany, I had an opportunity to go to the library to check up on Bhutan. This was beginning to concentrate my mind in a way I hadn't intended. First of all an incident in the street helped. One morning I ran into an ex-colleague from the department, a chap who used to teach Romantic Poetry. He had heard the feature about Montserrat and Bhutan on the *Today Programme,* and was enraged: he found the reporters on the programme patronising and paternalistic, and condemned their attitude as a hangover from colonial times. I was a bit wrong-footed by this, wondering if I was too distracted by Britain's growing status as colony of Big Brother across the Atlantic to be sensitive still to our own historical past. I, too, had heard the programme, and thought the chap from Birmingham had handled himself well enough – keeping it light – as, indeed, had a Minister from Montserrat, whom they had got on the line. It was a send-up, of course, but it still produced something of a corrective – something maybe irrelevant and pointless, but the end product wasn't tied to ambition and gold. When you considered the gloom of France after defeat by Senegal, or the rage of Italy, or the gloating of England at Argentina's defeat, not to mention the spectacle of the Prime Minister and the Queen – and the Archbishop of

Canterbury, for all I know – saying prayers for the healing of Beckham's metatarsal, there was something pleasantly wholesome about the Montserrat-Bhutan encounter.

Yet, I admit it still bothered me that I hadn't been able to convince my ex-colleague from the English Department why I thought Montserrat was playing it rather well. I would have to check this out further. But first, some information on Bhutan from the library.

I got a wrong number. First, no answer from the people I was trying to track down, and then a wrong number: it was difficult getting hold of people in Montserrat since the disruption of the volcano; few of the old telephone numbers were in use; two-thirds of the island having been abandoned. The capital, of course, was buried under metres of ash, so when you phoned you spoke to whoever you could; and, in the same spirit, in my case, the woman who answered the phone was prepared to talk, even though it was a wrong number, and she didn't know who I was. The person I needed to talk to was, apparently, Mr Hogan (Hogan, good Irish name) who was in charge of the team; but she didn't know if Mr Hogan was still here. At which point she consulted someone in the room, and they seemed to be having a debate about how to proceed. She came back to the phone to say that the 'boy' was just finding out where Mr Hogan would be today. Was I ringing from Washington?

I was ringing from England. From Sheffield.

Oh, she had family in England, too. In Birmingham. And Luton. Her nephew, Royston, was up there; and ran a little church in Luton. Did I know Royston? Did I go to Royston's church?

The 'boy' in the background hadn't come up with a telephone number for Mr. Hogan, so I had time to reflect that the likes of Sweden's Ljungberg or Spain's Raul were more certain to strike fear in front of the opposition goal than was someone girly and preacherly like Royston. But then, Royston wasn't part of the Montserrat team; Royston was just a preacher in Luton. And Royston was a first name, anyway: what if he was called Royston Mollyneaux? That might be a heavy enough name to contest the field with ugly Oliver Kahn.

In the end the lady on the phone said she couldn't help me with Mr Hogan's number. She believed that the team were somewhere in Amsterdam on their way to that place where they were going to play the match; but she didn't know if Mr Hogan was with the team, and she didn't have his number.

I was trying to focus on where the game was going to be played: so the Bhutanese would have home advantage; unless there was going to be a rematch in Montserrat. Just see what home advantage was doing for Korea in the Other World Cup! I really needed to know more about this; and decided to make a couple more phone calls. No real help from my contact in Birmingham, but – taking my cue from the woman in Montserrat who thought I might be ringing from Washington – I had a hunch of who, in Washington, might be stirring things behind the scenes: Carrington had to be involved in this somehow.

Bhutan, 'the land of the Thunder Dragon', manages to survive as an independent kingdom between China and India, and boasted wonderful-sounding leaders like Doopgein Sheptoon and Dharma Raja and Deb Raja complete with a line of hereditary kings from Druk Gyalpo to the present incumbent, Jigme Singhye Wangchuk; and their national sport seemed to be archery; their agriculture, tending the yak. Also, something about sandalwood. (*So Bhutan was into archery and Buddhism and Montserrat was into cricket and Christianity*.)

It turned out that Bhutan was Mr. Big to Montserrat's Small – Little Boy Small. Bhutan also had a population of about 1,800,000 people to Montserrat's 4,000 (before dispersal after the 1995 volcano, the population had been 11,000) and covered a landmass of 18,000 sq. km. That made Bhutan larger than all the smaller islands in the region combined – from Jamaica's 4,243 to Montserrat's 42 sq. miles – with only Cuba (42,000) and the shared island of Santo Domingo (29,529) not land-challenged; Guyana being the only Caribbean territory (83,000) to dwarf the Himalayan Kingdom that everyone called tiny. So Montserrat, as underdog, *both* on account of land area and population, should be able to count on the world's support in the way that, over in Japan and Korea, Ireland and Croatia and Senegal and the other 'small countries' had done.

I phoned Carrington in Washington. Carrington was Montserrat's leading playwright (along with Edgar White). But, unlike Edgar, he had an uneasy relationship with the Montserratians, largely because of his anti-clerical bent, his portraits of venal and dissolute clergymen, thought to be drawn from life, not always going down well on the island.

Carrington, as expected, pulled rank, and claimed to be a bystander, only – and from afar in this footballing saga. But he admitted to having been in touch with people in Montserrrat over it, principally with CJ.

CJ Harris! He must be 90 years old! (I was ashamed at the vulgarity of the thought.)

CJ had met some of the squad; and had given them tips on maintaining their mental shape. (*That sounded like CJ Harris.*) Actually, CJ was ninety-one. RK Narayan was still writing nearly to his hundredth birthday. And didn't Garcia Marquez present us with a patriarch who was 200 years old?

It was my turn to observe that in *Genesis* that was no age at all.

Carrington was talking about teams that were strong on paper, which then turned out to be weak on grass. He quoted the Rev. Wes Hall, legendary fast bowler and one-time manager of the West Indies cricket team. When the then captain of West Indies, Richie Richardson, looked at the very strong Australian touring side, and pronounced it the weakest Australian side, *on paper,* to visit the islands, Wes Hall observed that unfortunately, West Indies would be required to play the Australians not on paper but on grass.

The old stories.

The idea now, with Bhutan, was to maintain your shape, on grass. We weren't living in the days when mad Roman Emperors and petty dictators could make up their own rules. Gone were the days when an Enver Hoxha, say, in Albania could solve the problem of unequal national contests – playing tennis at Wimbledon, say – by pointedly not *entering* the tournament, and simply announcing that your man had won the championship. Carrington said his information about the Montserrat team was that CJ Harris had sent them off in good mental shape.

For a while, Carrington and I got caught up in our own mental games, as if we were collaborating in a bizarre sort of play or story, letting the Monster Rats, CJ, even, slip in and out of *our* literary frames. It seemed as if we were persuading each other that football was more than a game of two halves, which went to extra time, and penalties, at the end of which the Germans won.

(I remember the last time I saw CJ Harris in Montserrat, about three years ago. CJ was in a Home, newly built and defiant, a symbol of renewal after the volcano; the fact that it was for old people had a certain poignancy and delicacy to it. I remember walking down the sunny gallery running along the front of the building – excellent first floor view of the new development – with the residents lined up right along the wall in what seemed a lot of wheelchairs, looking out vaguely towards the sea. There was no alertness in their gaze and the silence unnerved me somewhat. Yet, they were all well-dressed, groomed, scrutinising me. As I moved along the line, and nodded my Good Afternoons and Howdys, and said a few words to a woman I recognised, some faces lit-up – though not quite cancelling out the two or three which now resumed that lost-child, puzzled expression.

The place had nothing of that fuzziness, nothing of that old-people's smell of abandonment and stale pee in the air. On the contrary, there was about it something defiant, as if the residents were being paraded, shown off; and it was I who was being put through my paces, not quite knowing how to walk past the line. And there was CJ, sitting apart, at the far end, not part of this line of mostly women. He was facing you as you walked towards him with his head thrown back, as if he were observing the rest of the line in profile. Except that his eyes seemed to be closed. And even when he greeted me CJ seemed not to look at me. But the greeting was friendly. The nurse then came and said that CJ preferred to meet his visitors in his own room, which was a private one; and as she prepared to wheel him away, she asked me to give her a few minutes to get her 'celebrity' settled.

CJ's room had unsettled me. The bareness, the austerity – *where were the books!* Even the few artefacts on the wall suggested a new office that you hadn't quite moved into, settled into: *a writer's room?* I didn't want to ask if the books would follow. Or, indeed, if they had been lost in the volcano. CJ was now lying in bed, on his back, but not patient-like, his body-language was more fluent than that; and he was wearing designer socks. He greeted me again with his eyes closed, and told me exactly how long I had been on the island, that I had come in on the helicopter not on the ferry, and generally made me accountable, so that I began to apologise to him for this and that and, effectively, for my life. Yes, I could well believe that CJ Harris had been responsible for getting the Monster Rats into mental shape for their match in Bhutan.) He left the dancing and all that to the coach, Carrington broke in.

The dancing!

The coach had taken the team up to Antigua to practise a little dance routine on the bi-line so that they would be up for it when they scored. It was known that The Dragon XI, the opposition, had already perfected an ancient Buddhist dance to pull cultural rank in case their famed striker Wangel Dorji scored. Well, Montserrat couldn't be left lacking in the dance department should Pops Mitchell, say, put one in the back of the net. Think of the Senegalese-France match: it was the dance-routine that you remembered after the match, not the goal. As with the Nigerians last time round.

Then Carrington said that CJ had developed a strategy for success which had something to do with identifying the shape of the letter H in the Bhutanese defence (*4-4-2. 3-3-4. So why not the letter H?*) The H shape could be the Bhutanese secret weapon, he said.

(Oliver Kahn. And now the letter H?)

Carrington suddenly asked if I had checked out Bhutan.

Sort of.

So, how did I check out Bhutan?

Nothing very strenuous just – went to the library.

Any problem?

(*Jackarse. Pseud. Idiot.*) Problem? I reminded him that we had easy access to public libraries in Sheffield; university libraries in Sheffield; even private libraries in Sheffield.

That was very good, Carrington said; you'll be pressing for independence any day now. But can we put the Tourist Board business aside for a minute: when I had looked up Bhutan in the encyclopaedia, did I have any difficulty?

None that I remember.

He begged me to concentrate.

I was concentrating. I seemed to remember getting more up-to-date information on the FIFA website, later.

But Carrington was demanding an honest answer, naked and unedited: did I find Bhutan first time of looking?

(This was second-hand CJ. Worse. It reminded me of those school-boy jokes about Columbus and rats and the naming of the island; it depressed me slightly that this was the quality of advice available to the Monster Rats. *Was I concentrating.*)

Yes, I was concentrating. OK, I seem to remember that when I got down the encyclopaedia off the shelf, I first turned to Buthan (a problem I sometimes have with Ghandi – putting the 'h' in the wrong place), and then I think I turned to Butane; before settling on 'Bhutan'. But I often had difficulty with names: Claire with or without the 'i'; Ann, with or without the final 'e'; McCormack... I confessed some of this to Carrington.

So without knowing of the 'h' in Bhutan, the place couldn't be found. (That was the little point he was making, something about the silent 'h', etc.) He had the grace to be embarrassed for labouring the point; even though he claimed to be unconvinced of the efficacy of the CJ game-plan; getting the boys to recognise the invisible traps set by the opposition – all those silent 'h's in names like Bhutan and Thimph – called for *imagination.* (And wouldn't the Bhutanese, right now, be out there practising their set-pieces *on grass?)*

I thought back to CJ Harris and his way with us when we were children; for he had taught just about everyone who had been to the little church school in the village when we were growing up there. A man who didn't believe in God teaching in a church school. A man who, later, published a book which the grown-ups dubbed 'nothing but a sign of foolishness'. The thing I remember was sitting in the little classroom in the school in the village – I must have been in Standard Two or Three – directly beneath the banner strung right across the ceiling bearing the legend KNOWLEDGE IS POWER in huge letters, and Teacher Harris talking to us about the mystery of the silent 'K' of Knowledge. Was it there that we started to learn the trick that would eventually conquer Bhutan?

The talk with Carrington had got me going. I now imagined the scene in CJ's little, bare room at the Home, with the boys, back from their errand to the make-shift library, shamefaced because they couldn't find Bhutan in the Encyclopaedia; and CJ, reclining in bed, his designer socks visible, lecturing them.

★

When Ronaldo scored the first goal from the Oliver Kahn rebound, the room erupted, yellow shirts falling on one another, beautiful women hugging and kissing you as if they would be yours for life, and men being engagingly familiar. And now we settled down to Brazil providing the finesse to show up the lumbering Germans. At the end of the match, the dancing, as before, spilled out into the street; I made my way home quickly to catch the commentary by the Gary Lineker team of Ian Wright and the Irishman whose name (Haysley Fenton? Winston Callaghan? Beresford Daly?) I never did manage to catch; because at the Brazilian house they weren't interested in the English commentary.

The Bhutan game had been played earlier so that the players and officials could watch the other World Cup match, and Ricardo had greeted me with the news that my team had lost the match 4-0. So what had gone wrong in Thimphu? I couldn't not notice that there were two 'h's in Thimphu, making the capital bigger than it seemed, when you merely pronounced it. Could the Montserratians not cope with the two silent 'h's in the opposition's capital? Were they into denial in failing to see this as part of the opposition's forward planning, rather than attributing their defeat to altitude-sickness and food-poisoning? The Bhutanese players, reinforced, admittedly, with two or three silent consonants to their name, could be defeated, maybe, by the more straightforward systems employed by the Germans in *their* matches. 'w's and 'l's and 'r's however difficult to pronounce, weren't causing problems for the Japanese and Korean players so it may have been a mistake to overrate the hardy yak-loving folk living at altitude, for, after all they had lost, according to FIFA, 20-0 to Kuwait sometime last year. When the lads went out assuming that all formations on the pitch, the corners and free-kicks – even playing for off-side – were reinforced with the silent H effect – call it an extra player who was invisible – they were giving the opposition too much *credit.* For when you struck at goal and tried to beat the keeper who was invisible, you were likely to steer the ball straight into the arms of the one who *could be seen.* You were building an unnecessary barrier of yak and sandalwood against you. Facing The Dragon XI, in your attempt to curl the ball round its breath of fire, you're going to miss the goal. The Montserratians burned up valuable energy, whereas the Bhutanese conserved theirs by not mythologising Pops Mitchell & Co.

Now, in Montserrat, they were saying that the team had lost not because the Bhutanese opposition had outplayed them but that it had *outprayed* them. Although the team – against CJ's advice, I should imagine – had said a prayer before the match, the opposition had out-thought them in that department and had gone to a temple for fully two hours in order to pull rank. So now the feeling was that before Montserrat played another FIFA-backed match the entire island would join in continuous prayer for days and weeks and months if necessary and then rise up to conquer – who knows? – Brazil. Brasil.

iii

I'm leafing through another book. Here's a really cool picture of the Bhutanese king Jigme Wangchuck lining up with six other South Asian leaders in Dhaka in 1985 at the launch of the south Asian Association for Regional Cooperation (SAARC), all splendidly attired, with the King of Nepal in a short skirt and the male President of Sri Lanka in a long skirt, Rajiv Gandhi's stiff military bearing less impressive than a General Zia ul Haq of Pakistan dressed like a species of clergy. The Bangladeshi and Maldives presidents are boring in Western suits and the King of Bhutan looks coolest of the lot in a sort of check dressing-gown down to the knees, bare legs and buckled shoes that are so shiny they give the effect of being two-toned. On the left pocket of his dressing-gown the king wears a little medal.

Now, I'm ready to make something of all this info. The fact that when they lined up for a practise match in front of their national, (Dutch) coach, four of the Bhutanese were wearing Brazilian yellow; *and* the magazine website that carried the picture (*Newsweek*) left the first 't' out of the spelling of Montserrat. And who gained advantage from the accident that the stadium where the match was played was called Changlimithang? I would want to discuss these things further with Carrington, maybe with CJ himself. Or Mr Hogan. And with the Montserrat historian, Howard Fergus – Sir Howard – who, unfortunately, had been off-island during the build-up to the match. True, despite Ricardo and all the beautiful people in yellow, I'm really a German supporter at heart, quite liking their unsmiling, methodical approach, open even to the suggestion that Oliver Kahn's ugliness is just something got up for the occasion.

Though it was a shame, really, that Montserrat didn't score a goal, so that the lads could do their dance.

1. *Montserrat: Emerald Isle of the Caribbean* by Sir Howard Fergus (Macmillan, 1983)

(2002)

HIGUAMOTA'S MONTSERRATIAN LOVER

I was beginning to be disturbed by my dreams, but fortunately I don't believe in dreams; so I'm not even going to try to recall these latest ones, as that would just give them credibility, give body to something already disappearing like tufts of cloud when the sun is up: I don't want to be accused of dignifying what are, in fact, the consequences of indigestion. Nevertheless, something lingers, and dampens your spirit a little.

So I was a bit low when I rang my sister just to have a chat, nothing special. I was in Manchester doing Summer School, and really, wouldn't be going down to London for at least six weeks: how were things in London?

The same, except they had a visitor, Higges from St. Caesare, Higuamota: remember Higges who had bound some of our books that time and...? She was here on some sort of Course; and she was asking about me.

'Is she still wearing the black dress?' I asked, and was immediately ashamed, feeling a bit cheap. But my sister didn't pick up on that; and we talked about this and that, about nothing; about growing old in this country with nothing much to show for it; about Life.

And that night I dreamt about Higuamota.

The general feeling, as I remember, was that Higges was either lucky or unlucky (which is an odd way to think of someone; you might think some people lucky or unlucky, but that wasn't the *first* thing that came to mind when their name was mentioned). Anyway, the feeling was that, on balance, Higges, despite her smart profession, was more unlucky than lucky. She was unlucky in her father, the Professeur; but that's another story. She was unlucky in her sister, Dulcima, a delicate girl, everybody now claims, who had been forced to change her image because of her experiences in America, a country where she had to grow muscles and do a job which made nonsense of her name, Dulcima – a name that suggested if anything, the delicacy of early music, that sort of thing. And Higges herself didn't come out of this naming business too well, as 'Higuamota' was a bit of a mouthful; something culled from her father's obscure reading, and wilfully imposed on the infant. (As we say, she was unlucky in her father.)

We called her Higges. Others in the village, people around Coderington who knew the family, called her Marta or Martha. Those who drank or gambled with the father called her Higges, but when they weren't drinking or gambling with the father they called her Marta or Martha. Just the fact of having two names – three, really, because she was called Higuamota on occasion – undermined her a bit, made her seem if not fuzzy at least shifting, somehow less solid than her bulk, not fully protected against jokes. (Though her profession earned her respect: she was one of the few to break into the family business of *reliure,* trained by M. Outran himself. Outran's was one of the most prestigious establishments in St. Caesare, and if local people didn't care about book-binding, they were nevertheless impressed by the kudos attached to someone who was part of the firm.)

Higges was big in stature, big as her sister was; well, trim. And although bigness in itself wasn't funny (and there were many who were bigger than she) this worked against her too, in an obscure way, because of the fate of Dulcima in America. Dulcima, although she still put New York, New York on her letters, had ended up in Chicago, Al Capone's city, working in a slaughterhouse, proof that women were equal to men in misery. This news was received at home, as you'd expect, with mixed feelings. When you went abroad, you represented the island, the islands; and there were some from Barville and Look Out – even Look Out – and many from Montserrat who were abroad representing us in the professions, in Show Business, and the like. So it was an odd thing to have to contemplate a good-looking, 'frail' woman from your village in far-off Chicago heaving slabs of beef on her shoulder, and herself so embarrassed about it that she felt she had to keep putting New York, New York on her letters. And having that musical name didn't help. Local wags rubbed it in by referring to her as Our Monica (Harmonica?) Or Accordion. Even weird things like Pianoforte and... But Dulcima, too, is another story.

Higuamota was here in England on a short course in book-binding, and this disappointed me slightly, because she had been trained by old Outran who really did have the best reputation for restoring books in the region; and we were always led to believe that restoring books in the tropics was a different 'science' from book-binding in a cold country. Whenever there were hurricanes and floods in the neighbouring islands, crates and crates of sodden and disfigured books would eventually arrive at Barville, *c/o P. Outran & Sons, Reliure, Mons, St. Caesare.* With the weather getting worse, if anything, Outran's was said to be the fastest-growing industry in town, not excluding the construction of villas for the expatriates. Add to that the deterioration of books and papers in a hot climate – no one kept their libraries and archives at controlled temperatures – *reliure* was not only a prestigious but a gainful thing to be involved in. But it was still a slight of sorts, another blow to our collective pride to learn that even after Outran had passed on his skills, one of his 'graduates' still needed a six-week course in England in *reliure:* a two-year course you could deal with, that would suggest a different branch of the art, but six weeks seemed insulting. (I learnt later that Higuamota now worked for a rival establishment to Outran's, a Government-backed one, so maybe there were other factors at play there.) Anyway, I took note of her various telephone numbers and promised to get in touch.

Of course, there was another reason why I was a bit apprehensive about the resurfacing of Higuamota, apart from the retraining; it had to do with what she represented; about the sort of challenge she seemed to throw down to us men from the islands: it was something that made us feel inadequate, or disloyal; more than a bit guilty that we had tended to turn our amorous attentions elsewhere, secure now with partners who no longer looked like friends we had grown up with. Or maybe this was a later concern.

I'm giving, perhaps, the wrong impression. Things were altogether more positive. Higges was lucky, too. The best bit of luck, according to her father, was that she was born at five o'clock in the morning. More precisely, on the morning of October 12th 1942. The Professeur worked out, in some triumph, that 1942 was a *figure* anagram of 1492: that October 12th *was* October 12th. This, and the fact that his daughter was born at five o'clock in the morning meant that in a real sense she had arrived several hours *before* Columbus landed on these islands, which he did later that same morning, October 12th 1492. Higuamota was, quite simply, pre-Columbian, and should have a name befitting her status. That, the Professeur claimed, was her luck, and always made sure that she and others were reminded of it with anecdotes from the history. On Higuamota's birthday, the Professeur would recall, for the guests, the life that had been disturbed by the Italian desperado and his unruly Spaniards, enlightening the company about Tainian agriculture, about the people's dances and songs and ball games, their red body-paint and their lack of small-pox. His only reservation, his only small point of criticism, was the habit of deforming the foreheads of their young. Not a practice he would revive; but then, every culture had its eccentricities.

It was on one of these ritual occasions that Higuamota's Montserratian suitor announced himself and risked ridicule by coming fully rigged out as one Cristobal Colon, the old Admiral himself, with his brother Bartolome in tow with the beads. Well, the rest is, if not quite history, more than myth. And everyone on the island has an opinion about that particular carnival.

Though that's not to explain Higuamota's black dress.

The Black Dress

Some, like Carrington, demystify the black dress. Carrington was a fellow from Montserrat, a writer, who had lived abroad for years, and whose pronouncements on these things, perversely, carried weight. Carrington felt that the black dress should be seen not as a failure of love but something belonging entirely to another story, and irrelevant to this one. The romance between Higuamota and the Admiral, he insisted, was the best thing that had happened to St. Caesare, for the courtship had been passionate and full of metaphysical conceit, and it scotched the idea that only a Frenchman with fever in his blood was capable of negotiating our sort of love-thicket. It gave emotional hinterland, he said, to being in love in St. Caesare, despite the island's small size. Do not be side-tracked by Higuamota's black dress, he said: if you wanted more on the significance of that dress, that was all dealt with in an earlier monograph.[1] (Carrington, who had long been dabbling in literary archaeology, assumed that interest in his listeners.)

Higuamota's own view of this aspect of her life isn't known, as she tended to treat confidants with what one might call the arms' length principle; but she did this with considerable grace, which made it uncertain whether you'd been taken into her confidence – though, on reflection, you knew you hadn't been. Of the black dress she would say that some thought it was her only dress, others thought she had *only* black dresses, she didn't mind, it suited her. She told me this: once, in another country she visited at friend at university. He had just passed his exams and was packing to go down, to leave town, to go home. They went to the off-licence to buy some wine, to celebrate; and the man behind the counter, recognising her friend who was a regular customer, invited him, invited them to a wine-tasting in the shop at the end of the week. That somewhat depressed her friend, the student, because it was just another example of things taking off just as you were about to abandon them: his presence in the town had at last been acknowledged after three years, just as he was leaving, etc. This, to her friend, seemed suspiciously like his life falling into a pattern. She remembered wearing a black dress to the wine-tasting, and telling the story of the dress, and rescuing her friend from one of those moods that men fall into. She was playful with me.

But she told this story to some: her sister, Dulcima, who worked in the garment trade in New York, New York, one day found stacks of dresses in a warehouse, dresses her size, all black, and as the firm was going bust, Dulcima packed them up and sent them off to her sister, enough dresses to last her the rest of her life.

Geraldine's Story of the Montserratian Lover

You couldn't listen to people, that's why you had to listen to Geraldine; but first you had to gain her trust, which I think I did on the last visit, the one before the volcano; but then you never know.

The problem now is with this ridiculous dreaming nonsense, which has me here, awake. I'm thinking of the

Montserratian who is alive and well and not molesting the woman he lives with, or her children. As far as we know.

So why am I in a sweat, here in the middle of the night, getting up to make myself a cup of tea – a hard day in the Language Lab ahead of me? Fortunately, there's no one about to notice. I run several theories through my head. I run several books through my head, conversations now, and the ones that get replayed are the ones with Geraldine, who revealed enough to be interesting but concealed enough to be discreet. It was even said that Geraldine was our true Queen of France because she knew how to keep her head. At her famous dice table in Coderington people queued up to spill their secrets.

Geraldine had worked hard to gain her position of trust, of respect. She'd been twice married; so some called her greedy at having two bites of the cherry, sort of thing, while others went hungry. But there were saner heads about who pointed out that Geraldine's first husband was a young French boy rebelling against his family, and it wasn't obvious that he would have rebelled with just anyone – not to the point of marriage – had Geraldine said No to him. So there was a sort of acceptance that Geraldine by that marriage hadn't really held back others who were waiting in line. And the marriage didn't last, anyway, so there you are. The shame of *that* cancelled out any advantage that might have accrued. Though there was a son, and that was a bonus of sorts. Marriage Number Two took place so discreetly that it might not even have happened: this was with a man from up the islands, an older man, so here again she was distancing herself from the competition, without being ostentatious or unfair. By now everyone on the island felt able to confide in Geraldine – as I had, though not at her dice table. And she reciprocated: she told me, of course, the story of Higges and her Montserratian lover.

He was an educated man of good family who had spent

some time in England and returned, not in disgrace, but somewhat disappointed at his achievements there after years and years that had seemed to promise more. And he used to come and sit on Higuamota's porch and parade his knowledge of books she had for binding, and he would talk History with the Professeur, Higuamota's father – all that stuff about Cortez and the Incas and the tragedy of lesser civilisations overwhelming the greater by superior force of arms.

Though the Montserratian wasn't a big drinker, not by the standards of the Professeur, he drank enough not to disappoint the old man. But his moderation in this area pleased the mother, as she reckoned one drunkard in the family to be enough. The fellow was clever and adjusted his tastes to suit both parents, starting with alcohol and switching smartly to something soft. This was when they were all three together on the porch or in the drawing-room; what he was like when he was alone with Higuamota no one but the couple knew. Higges' subsequent claims that all was sweetness and light, and that it was her mother and father together who spoilt her chances of romance, wasn't something you liked to comment on. Certainly Geraldine, who knew the story, wasn't prepared to enlighten her guests further.

Talk that it was bad feeling between mother and daughter on this subject that drove the mother to her final illness (failing to recover from surgery abroad) was the usual St. Caesare malice. But the feeling that now the mother was gone, the daughter was determined to take it out on the old man, seemed reasonable enough. (That's why he protected himself by growing steadily more eccentric.)

Back to the man from Montserrat, the lover. He had two things about him that were the source of the problem (the Columbus entry at the birthday party being a bit of a red herring). He farted a lot and he had bad dreams. Of course, there may have been other things wrong with him, in that his eyesight was failing and he was slightly hard of hearing, and he was short of stature; but he had survived many years in England with these disabilities, and nevertheless bounced back to become a lover; so these clearly weren't as fatal as farting a lot and having bad dreams.

Obviously, he didn't fart a lot in the company of the parents; he did that when he was alone. But he admitted to Higuamota that the strain of farting alone and bad-dreaming alone were OK for now, but as new habits came upon him he would really have to ease up on himself and start sharing some of the old ones with a partner – the farting and bad-dreaming, for instance. Higges settled for the bad-dreaming, and that's where she made her mistake.

The parents, of course, misunderstood the arrangement, even the mother, who failed to interpret what Higges was doing. Farting, if not all honey and seabreeze, was no big deal, her mother said, because no man came to you perfect in this life; and farting, as handicaps went, was milder than most. What she couldn't accommodate were the bad dreams.

That was because the Montserratian's dreams were about murder, the murder of a wife or partner; and the last time a member of the family had such dreams, it had ended in tragedy.

Higuamota and her father joined forces now in defence of the lover, citing his unbalanced diet, the indigestion of previous relationships, even the truism that men from these parts were naturally afraid of women and took revenge by murdering them in their dreams, and reverted to being timid and pathetic in their waking life. But to the mother, murder was murder and she wasn't going to invite in into her family.

The man was obsessive – it was that which in other areas, had made them call him the Lover. He had, on various occasions, offered to make Higges mistress of the rivers of the world, to rechristen them in their own private language. He was the non-painter who set up his easel among her father's dogs and her mother's chickens and made the subject in her black dress feel like Paris of the Twenties, etc. They turned lower Barville into the centre of night life, dining out in style, summoning the *sommelier* for yet another chilled bottle of something not everybody could pronounce. Later, at home, she would hear the bells of Saint Germain des Pres chiming through his dream-commentaries.

But this obsession, this talk of murder, terrified the older woman – who was obviously still alive when all this was happening. The Montserratian never disguised the fact, of the dream taking place in this house, that house – in England, in France, at home – that he was not just a murderer but a serial killer; worse! He was fascinated that if these murders took place while he was awake, and the results were laid out side by side you would need more land for it than St. Caesare had available, to accommodate them. So he was proud, in a way, of outgrowing the island. Some men merely dreamt of harems; that was boring.

In one of the last dreams before the break-up with Marta, the lover had been in the house, a big house, in France this time. For several days and nights he remained there awaiting the consequences of his act – though, this being a dream, the house shifted location a bit, from one country to another; and it wasn't always murder that he was dealing with then, but adultery, another woman appearing on the scene, sort of thing. But it was mainly murder…

So, in this dream in the big house in France he is waiting. Someone comes in on some sort of pretext. He sees them off. Then someone else comes to take away a pile of fresh ashes, in the garden, from one of the terraces; someone with a wheelbarrow, at night; and the Montserratian doesn't object, and, as he looks on from an upstairs window, he is trying to remember if the pile of ashes contains any evidence that might convict him. He's perfectly lucid, he just can't remember whether there's any evidence left in the ashes. And then finally, the police arrive – a very frail girl and a square, Orson Welles-type man – neither of them in uniform. The girl approaches him from above, coming down little curved, concrete steps, and the man, of course, comes in from the other side; classic. Yet, their body-language suggests that they trust the suspect not to act violently or stupidly. And the suspect respects them for that. And as he starts talking to the square man, taking his time, the square man becomes less square, and takes on normal human shape. And the suspect is clear in his mind that what he is saying is being secretly recorded; and he knows that it has a logic that will convict him (it's like a confession with extenuating circumstances); but there is no violence on any side... And the dream recurs differently, in another house, on another night.

More of the same; though, as the father pointed out, there was no actual violence. And when, other things being considered, he could no longer sustain this argument, he recalled the lover's old Columbus party-piece, and conceded that the man was unreliable.

Geraldine said there was something else to consider, something to do with Higuamota's invocation of certain Signs and Illustrations from ancient books she was charged with restoring; but all of that was said to her in confidence, she couldn't pass it on.

The recurrent dreams didn't surprise me; eventually, I mentioned them, casually, to someone in the book trade; and she said that, y'know, these things happen.

1. *Class Structure in Tanian Economy* by Austin Farrell (Monographs on Social Anthropology, 49, Athlone Press, 1983)

(*Cross/Cultures*, 12, 1994)

WE REACHED THE COAST FOUR DAYS LATER

We reached the coast four days later. But in the meantime, in the three days between start and finish, we had a wild time. There was the day when Ella Fitzgerald sang to us. 'Miss Otis Regrets'. Over and over again. And we joined in, and drank our cokes; and we decided to get more into the spirit of the thing, and got a taxi to the airport, boarded a DC 10, and had brandy with lunch because we took Ted's word for it that the *Liebfraumilch* would be lousy at that altitude. The after-dinner film was soothing enough, though most of us had seen it before; and after, when we were dozing, someone continued to hum 'Miss Otis Regrets'.

But this isn't what I wanted to let you know.

We reached the coast after four days, *yes*. But before that, Ted had gone missing and we thought of going back for him as he was a sort of unofficial leader (having in his time met Pelé and made it with Ulrike Meinhof *and* got a drink in Scotland on a Sunday). In the end, though, we decided against it, not that it was too much trouble, but we came to accept that we didn't really like Ted much, and that maybe he had sensed this and was being tactful. Just in case, though, we left a full description (three or four full descriptions, as we couldn't quite agree on him) and then pressed on to the coast. True, we lost our way a couple of times – not on account of Ted's absence: we'd often lost our way with him – and were unusually self-conscious about it, conscious of being a bit ragged and messy; and that inevitably led to the sort of haggling everyone could predict, but no one seemed determined enough to prevent. A fellow who had been an ordinand, briefly, made the mandatory joke about losing one's way – and passed it off as his old bishop's – young men in the Jungle of Life, that sort of thing; and Judy, who was a very nice girl and who had helped some of us lose our way without regretting it, took exception to the phrase; and soon we were having the usual dog-fights about chauvinism and sexism and whatever – unnecessary really, as Judy had issued her challenge in a bantering, half-serious sort of way. So it took us a lot of time to calm things down, generally, to restore the situation to something of its original, well, muddle. That not only lost us time, it soured the atmosphere a little.

By the fourth day we reached the coast by error – or perhaps by strength of character. If we'd been coping with a hi-jacking or a kidnapping, or an explosive racial situation, or even the bourgeois marriage at the start of a well-made play, such tensions would be understandable. As this wasn't the case, weren't we over-reacting a bit? Yes, from now on, we would be the people the final versions of our autobiographies revealed us as being. This discretely-taken resolution helped to get us to the coast: this is where the strength of character came in. We counted the cost of the journey, yes, but refused to see it as a metaphor: no connection with moving crablike through life, for instance. We did do heavy things like comparing ourselves with bits of landscape, things we passed on the way which seemed to have solved their own tension-making problems, and were living out the rest of their lives in an absence of agro, jeering at us: the bird at rest, for instance; animals, trees there before the Flood. And we told one another there was nothing transcendental in observing trees – always better to bring this sort of thing out into the open. We felt better for it; so good, in fact, that it restored to us some of the credit that had seemed earlier to belong exclusively to the inscrutably natural things surrounding us, things without ulcers and self-doubt. Someone said we shouldn't feel hesitant about discussing this, because hadn't Neruda himself written a poem about stones. We quickly confirmed this and, agreeing to disagree, stubbornly pressed on to the coast.

Soon there was mayhem, famine, locusts, and bodies inventively and generously dead. Our spontaneous imagery exposed us as talentless hacks. Foreigners, germ-warfare and Irish jokes upstaged us everywhere. The thing had started out as a successor to *A Bridge Too Far*, and had apparently gone too far: we were losing control of the imagery. Dogs were a sinister development: maybe they weren't dogs, we didn't care.

We did, you know, get to the coast on the fourth day; and they were there waiting for us: it didn't take us long to confirm what we had always suspected, and that the mistake was going to be costly. Instead of welcome, subtly-salted sea-grapes, we began to feel the itch of sand in our throats. Even that was a mirage because there was no sand, just rocks, cliffs, prehistoric sea: not the place for a swim, a timely life-boat. Those who had been waiting for us there obviously agreed with this assessment of the situation and promptly killed us (my penultimate thought being: what a hell of a time to go having just outgrown Nabokov and Asturias). But you see we didn't believe it; we all felt we'd live to wriggle out of this somehow; and to romanticise the journey later when we sat down to dinner in far-off places many DC 10's away from the coast; but that, it seems, was not to be.

P.S. I might be wrong about this.
Ted.

(1979)

GOALS

No, it's not about football; this story is about empathy. Yes, I know, yet I have to go through with it. Since what I thought was difficult is judged to be easy – Look! They're all at it, not just Tom, Dick, etc. but Hans, Hosein… – they're all able to do it with a minimum of fuss, the sorts of people you wouldn't dream of spending, well, more than the odd thought with; I must look to it. I've decided to scale down the level of my – okay, pride, but let's call it something else – *pride*, set myself manageable, human-scale tasks, and get into the habit of managing them (a man with one arm holding the bottle and, unscrewing the top) like other people, without fuss. And then who knows! And I do have two arms.

Today, it's the ampersand; you know, the informal, oh, squiggle – flourish, slightly out of character in the graver narrative about self. But, I'm into this. Heard the one about the dramatist? Big name. Mega. So this admirer wants to introduce the dramatist to her young son; here's a man to emulate, sort of thing. Nothing from the lad. *This is a very good writer,* the woman urges. The boy is cautious. Then, from the boy, *can you do a double-U*? So, I'm doing the ampersand. I'm over fifty years old and, it's time to learn. Of course, you think you can do these things, everybody does them, just…you can't be bothered. And, in a sense, it's a bit – not *pseud* exactly, maybe pathetic to try – a bit like those, hate the word 'wankers' never use it myself, *persons* on the telly who boast of not knowing their car registration number. I have a friend – no, this is boring: that's another little dodge I've got going, trying to suss when the company's bored: get a grip, son. That's not my idiom, either; this last bit, but you know what I mean; I'm working at it. Reward REWARD! A joke. Maybe it's OK after all, to come on the television and amuse us – Oh, prize-winning film-maker and naturalist, Oh, jet-setting exemplar – about not being able to drive a car. (I don't know my home telephone number, either; but then I don't often ring home. Ha.)

I'm not doing this from a whim, the ampersand thing: can you imagine my – horror isn't the name for it, (I'm a fastidious guy) – *unease* in realising only about two years ago that I'd never really learnt to brush my teeth? All this nonsense about brushing twice a day – three times a day – before and after meals (six times a day, really, plus for the snacks, though no one's perfect); you're pleased with yourself because no one can outbrush you. Supervised, too, as a child, as a man, and pronounced OK. Sets you up, that, you're one of the kissable people. And to find, late in the day you've never been brushing the *right* way! From a dental point of view, my friend, you're just another mouth-fascist. (I mean it; someone's just written a book about Franco linking *Caudillo*-ship with bad teeth. Lifelong bad teeth, married, to them, he was, no relief in dreaming of a hygienist with breasts.) Not that I'll go to extremes when I come into power, but you get my meaning. (Will you still kiss me when I'm down to one tooth? Of course darling. She has no right to say that. You are reduced, reduced by such love (O, kissable one!). Why can't she just say: Ugh. Get off. Geddoff. Scram. Hop it. Vamoose. Grrrh, open my mouth to that… cesspit, that apology; don't make me… don't come your 'sorry' with me, matey, we're talking divorce here, married or not, at the very least draw up a whatsit chart for the, yes, reparations, I'm a war wictim, I am. Victim.)

So now, of course, I brush properly, up and down, up and – there's a gap here – down, working towards the back, this way. Then from the front again, *that* way towards the back.

And it's so simple. Sounds odd now, but at the start the muscles in your arm rebelled, same effect as working out first day of the season (Are the footballers still with us?). So. Now, it's simple, right arm no longer the tree-trunk muscled prop of the stand-up comic. So, maybe other things can be so simple, so intimate. (Space here for a woman reader to recall: *That time when he spoke to me and he wasn't impatient and none of his sentences started with But*). But you have to work up to it, start with something manageable, like the ampersand.

I'm not, you know, trying to win a bet or anything. Nor am I, well, humiliated by not being able to manage the ampersand. Not flaunting failure either. Neither flaunting it nor hiding it; nothing *secretive*, that's the last thing she wants me to be; last thing I want me to be. Pathetic. Imagine, you know, doing all that and then Da Dah! Ampersands all over the place as if it's the day of the Lottery and everything's littered, paper, desk, the back of your neck – that tattoo on the arm you won't now kiss – all the while playing it cool with little bits of information about, I don't know, some Chinese politician in the news, with a fun name and, oh yes, now's the time to confess to having read Ortega y Gasset instead of AnaÔs Nin at an impressionable age...till, like poetry, her arms and back are, ah, decorated with it. And here, little rows of, you know, on this side of the navel, that side of the navel, kissable as always and...*who's the sailor home from the sea, then?* But some little thing goes wrong, as always.

Friends come to visit and will have a go; they're ampersand-perfect, even the left-handers, but you live with it. Life's a bitch. Call it – you know the form – call it your retreat from (dear God) maleness... Among my ampersanders is a friend's child who can also do a double-U; she likes to visit.

And sometimes I call this a blessed state of nakedness, the cloth absent, though you see me figleaf history and reach for it. She says, Kissable says something unsurprising and you ringmark a date (Oh, if thou wert a tree I'd be your damn'd, damned soil), which diverts the moment into analogy. So, neither bullish nor humble I admit I deny I admit being in this game for centuries to come.

And if you're still here, and you're curious, watch me do the ampersand

(1999)

SARA'S INTERIOR

i

When my brother rang from London and asked if I knew someone called Sarah whose people had been connected, somehow, with our house, I thought he was clearly losing it: how could I not know of Sarah? But no, he wasn't talking about that Sarah, who belonged to Mady, this was a much younger woman by the sound of it, and it wasn't Sarah but Sara, you know, without the 'h'.

The answer was No and we were satisfied she was a fraud, coming to this country, supposedly from St. Caesare to muscle in on the benefits that were being handed out to the victims of the volcano. She was firmly consigned to that category of person who, in the infamous words of Clare Short, the Minister of International Development, would be demanding Golden Elephants from the British Government next. For, as my brother revealed, this Sara, had turned down Council accommodation in Manchester and in Luton on the grounds that it was unsuitable.

Not just unsuitable but that the flats had no proper interiors.

They had no proper *interiors?*

Now I understood why my brother had rung; I was somehow to blame for, in some way, placing the idea of 'interiors' into these people's heads.

But he made a joke of it; he speculated about the sorts of 'interiors' we might have demanded, people of our generation, when we arrived in this country in the '50s: drawing-rooms in Sutherland Avenue and Ladbroke Grove; a walled front lawn for my mother to relax in, along with fruit trees and sunshine – *that* would teach Anthony Eden and Macmillan that we weren't to be trifled with. Etc. OK, we were prepared to forego the respect of the new village, because you couldn't have everything, even if you *were* at home.

After speaking to my brother I thought, as usual, of all the things not said. Even though we seemed to agree, I suspected that the notion of 'interiors' carried for him a hint of something womanly that was embarrassing to talk about. That's why it was easier for him to send it up as a formal arrangement of the house, the *design:* so Sara didn't just want to inherit drawing-rooms in Manchester and Luton, she expected a courtyard in Italy, she didn't rule out a walled garden in Persia.

It irritated me that my idea of 'interiors' was still ridiculed in the family.

Apparently – this was about two or three weeks later – Sara was not content just to use my name, which clearly wasn't getting her anywhere, but was coming up to Sheffield to see me. My brother had tried to put her off, had told her I was busy; and had given her the university rather than my home number. Maybe, he said, I could get one of the secretaries to see her off. This seemed so much beyond the call of duty that I could only conclude that my brother thought I knew more about the lady than I let on, and he was doing his bit to save me from her. So whereas I was merely vaguely interested before, now I was quite intrigued at the prospect of meeting Sara: maybe *she* understood what I was getting at when I spoke about interiors, our need to acknowledge them: whatever.

I had written about 'interiors', yes, and helped to mount an exhibition under that label. (At least I had tracked down some of the 'canvases', and written the catalogue.) Not that I was into Art, particularly; it came about by accident, by my having to find a visual image for the cover of the book of Caribbean stories I had edited; and the publisher's suggestion of a palm tree was unserious. So many of the stories were about small, intimate, 'interior' moments, and I was struck that there were so few paintings and postcards 'out there' to reflect this. There were the usual landscapes, seascapes – lots of figures, yes, but nearly always set 'in nature'; and endless public scenes of markets and carnivals, and the like. The facades of houses – either colonial or humble – again invited you to put these in an historical context; unintimate.

Going through hundreds of prints and photographs, as well as visiting half a dozen studios, left me with fewer than a dozen interiors that I could use. So what were the artists telling us – that our lives didn't have interiors? This wasn't true of the literature, which tended, if anything, the other way, with all those self-conscious growing-up tales from the islands, of which George Lamming's *In the Castle of my Skin*, was still the most compelling – and that was published back in 1953! This isn't to deny that some of our most powerful visual artists – Aubrey Williams comes to mind with his richly evocative abstracts – were absolutely right to illustrate other types of work.

In replacing the palm tree, I had already said no to the image of one of the Jamaican 'intuitives' (a less pejorative word, that, for 'primitive') and, in the end had come up with our own da Firenze, one of his drawing-room portraits.

My brother had been shielding me, not through prurience, but more from my own tendency to give ammunition to those who might embarrass the family. I had had to stress, at the time of the book, that the portrait on the cover wasn't that of my sister.

Now, that's all in the past as far as I'm concerned. *No more explaining that the young woman in the drawing-room in Coderington was not sewing but* ***mending*** *a dress, a party dress. She was very relaxed sitting in the drawing room doing this, which implied that she was a daughter of the house or owner of the dress, or both. She was not a servant or a seamstress. The two extant da Firenze seamstresses were very different from this. In them Aunt Edith was sitting in front of her Singer machine with lots of cloth billowing in front of her, and light coming from the window behind her, etc.* When my niece brought it up again the other day I said to her: Imagine the artist was well-read. Forget all the stuff you've heard about da Firenze. Remember the man went to Italy, studied there. So do him the courtesy of having read something, I don't know, Pirandello. But despite the mock Italian name, the fellow was from St. Caesare, British. People who read books at the time were reading the English classics. Dickens. The Brontës, maybe. Strange people like Scott, perhaps. (There was no American base in St. Caesare, little American influence, so their books probably weren't in vogue.) So why wouldn't the man have read Virginia Woolf? Let's say the fellow was arrogantly reading *Mrs Dalloway.* (I didn't use the 'My name is Dalloway' joke with her; I didn't wish to pull literary rank with my niece.) But that scene on the cover of my book, the da Firenze, doesn't seem a million miles away from my image of Mrs Dalloway in her drawing-room the morning of her party, sitting on the sofa mending her dress when Peter Walsh comes to call, when the man she might have married, just back from India, surprises her in the act: the same sense of surprise and embarrassment or emotion that enlivens the picture. Of course with the da Firenze it's a younger person, a girl (my sister's age, but not my sister): and black. I had written it up elsewhere; they had seen the scene played; it was not my sister.

Not having met Sara, I fancied she was a bit like the da Firenze.

ii

Sara rang me at home and claimed to have met me a couple of times, both at a lecture and at an exhibition. I always felt a bit of a fraud giving these occasional lectures on visiting the islands. You felt both underprepared, and also the sensation of putting it on a bit. Making both visitor and host uneasy. Putting everyone that little bit on trial, judging, judged; who had moved on commensurate with their circumstance? Did England and minor status give me the right to play the expert, to extend my range of reference *self-consciously* beyond Caribbean concerns? Did I have the right (or was it a duty) to pronounce Vaclav Havel in a certain way? And Soyinka?

Sara surprised me by claiming to have seen the *Interiors* exhibition *in London.* She was at the Whitechapel opening and reception. She had lived in England.

'So you're not really from St. Caesare?' There was a pause.

'Like the internet,' she said. 'No man is an island.'

On the phone, I couldn't tell if there was a little smile on her face.

Of course, the story is that many times the number of St. Caesare's 2,500 people had claimed refugee status here and in Canada and elsewhere in the Caribbean; and were living on some sort of subsidy. Sara wasn't the first person to enlist me in an attempt to legitimise her claim. Usually, I dismissed this with irritation; but when I was in the mood, I thought of CJ Harris, my old headmaster in Coderington – 'canejuice on his breath, blasphemy in his heart' – who used to point us, children, in a direction other adults feared to go down: 'It's not that the boy is lying,' he once said of his young son, one Sunday, who was lying to his parents about something, 'but that he's lying *intelligently*'. (This was after church, and my mother had paused at the Harris household for a glass of water, before the trek up the hill. She took issue with the schoolmaster for his 'ignorance' in commending his son's intelligent lying.)

So now I followed the CJ route and vowed to assist Madame Sara, should she prove 'intelligent'. Or failing that, knowledgeable. Did she know that the debate about 'interiors' had 'moved on', as they say?

Was she aware that we were no longer simply protesting that we weren't just a 'tourist' society, or one set against a background of nature where people were *folksy?* Perhaps we hadn't gone past the plea for recognition of our own internal debating space, reflecting space; or even for acknowledgement of space indoors where emotional violence happened. But when we made these demands now, it was more like performing a ritual; it was with a sense of resignation.

Remember, Sara, this is a test; you lie intelligently about this business of interiors, and you're in. Failing that, it's a pretend house, flat as a cardboard, for you in Manchester, it's a painted stage-set in Luton.

So, you know (to take it slowly) *that all this business of 'interiors' started with the observation that those of us from small islands were always represented as having been born* ***on*** *them;* ***on*** *St. Caesare;* ***on*** *Montserrat,* ***on*** *St. Vincent. How do you change that* ***on*** *to* ***in*** *without migrating? – A big political debate.*

If you were in England at the time, and interested in these matters, and in London, you would remember my scanning of book jackets – for I spoke of it at the Commonwealth Institute, at the New Beacon Bookshop in Finsbury Park, at the book launch in Covent Garden; and again at that poorly-attended ICA session. So, you would remember my comments about scanning book-jackets – not exclusively but mainly Penguin – observing that other people (peoples) had images to confirm their interior lives, whereas we did not. Look at Henry James – at which point I would hold up *The Spoils of Poynton* in one hand, with its two well-dressed middle-class women in conversation; and *Washington Square* in the other hand, with the woman climbing the stairs, an older woman this time, hint of life lived in the house, the solidity of wealth in the glitzy room, glimpsed behind her.

And Sara, this is just the *start* of your interrogation.

I went to the station to meet Sara and mistook someone for her. Easily done when you've got an image in your head. What threw me was that this woman wasn't dressed like a student, no jeans, no pins and buttons in the face, no New-Age kit, but lots of flowing skirt... *So there were other people 'out there' who suggested the da Firenze portrait!* The picture was dated 1956, the year we left the island, but it must have been done after we left, and the girl must have inherited my mother's dress.

A woman had been retained to clean the house in our absence, to dust the furniture; and she may have had a niece, or a younger sister who had inherited my mother's dress; she may have been taking it in to fit her, sitting in the newly-abandoned drawing-room.

Or – I'm just speculating, who knows? – She may have been one of da Firenze's retinue. Young da Firenze with his still-needing-to-be-explained profession – a *painter* in St. Caesare in 1956 – newly back from Italy, was, naturally, a hit with the ladies. Of course you don't, in a sense, want to speak ill of the dead, particularly mindful of the way the fellow went, but I witnessed the prototype to this picture *at the time.*

Weeks before we left for England, da Firenze had unexpectedly been invited to the house to make some sketches 'for posterity'. And that's where I surprised him with Mady, who was a younger servant in the house. She must have been fifteen or sixteen at the time. I remember I had a toothache that day, and was let off church; and bored at sitting around (because I didn't really have a toothache) I wandered downstairs to the dining room for a cold drink, and caught them at it. Mady was part-naked and she was running away (or pretending to run away?), and what struck me was how not embarrassed da Firenze was (*He'd been to Italy*): he spoke normally, unhurriedly:

'I can't paint them if I don't see them'. He was talking about her breasts. And suddenly, a painter seemed to me the best occupation in the world. Better than a doctor, because with a doctor the women you saw naked would be sick.

'You can paint from here', Mady was saying, taunting.

'Every woman take off she clothes when you paint her,' da Firenze said, half to me. 'Is only in these small island, you know, that people playing shy. Like they think is something wrong with battie and tittie an' ting.'

Mady seemed undecided, but we could hear someone coming, maybe Nellie, from the breadroom next door, and Mady made sure she was covered up, and tidied. 'Me got to go an rinse all the dishes for lunch, eh.' And she vanished.

Having met Sara I was disposed to liking her. I revived an old fantasy of her, someone like her in my mother's best dress, sitting at the top of the front steps, late that summer in 1956. Here was someone who so fitted the *tone* of these pictures, which so irritated the family. She would be expecting me to ask if she'd managed to mend that dress after all these years of having people comment on it; and be ready with her put-down line.

I didn't ask that, and she did have a put-down line, which was not as witty as I had hoped.

So we were back to that scene where I had trapped her, someone like her, late in the year, 1956, being painted by her Italian paramour. We can't actually see her being painted (She's on the front verandah, out of sight, twelve steps up), but we can see *him,* the painter (a self-portrait, dear God; how typical – surprising he didn't leave evidence on canvas of his own demise in the hurricane, in 1989). So, da Firenze is at the bottom of the steps, looking up, giving instructions to his sitter:

HIS VOICE:...That's right, that's right Contessa. Ah, bellissima. La Contessa.

No longer Mady, but La Contessa. Not in Coderington now, but in Firenza.

(*The Italian, dressed in smock, paints, looks up, talks.*)

The famous *Piazza Signoria.* The magnificent *palazzo.* ...Bella. Good. You are very much the aristocratic observer, looking down on the game. It is a game of football but is classic. You are up there, fourth level, fifth level. Women of your family belong up there – looking out from the window of *the palazzo.* In the most beautiful costume. ...It is the fourteenth century. Si. The event is sixteenth century, but I prefer the earlier costume...

(*He paints*)

...There are seats erected all round *the piazza*... The pitch is sanded... Sanded in the sense of tons of sand poured into the *piazza* and, how you say, *raked.* Yes, a beautiful, Tuscan summer evening. The two teams today and the Greens and the Blues...

Sara is better suited to this than Mady was.

★

And yet, it's hard to give someone the benefit of the doubt, who hasn't done her homework. I was reduced, in the pizza restaurant on West Street – for she hadn't really earned the right to special places, to *Mei's* (Chinese, on Charles St., where you had steamed sea bass and thought of Hemingway. Or the superior Indian, a couple of doors down from here, where a son or daughter, visiting, both Doctors, might serve at table and engage you in specialist conversation.) But here in the pizza restaurant, I was reduced, as I say, to rehearsing the stale narrative of, well, of people of our generation, living through years of feeling misrepresented or marginalised; of stumbling into this and that, into literature (sorry), chipping away at the edges, playing little games with the literary canon. A few consenting students, y'know, rewriting the bits of Shakespeare that Shakespeare couldn't be bothered to flesh out (a woman here and there who was wife to someone famous, a woman who wasn't really a woman). Oh, tinkering. Revisiting the stories at random, those we know and love. That young girl in Joyce. Yes, ...the caretaker's daughter, Lily. Giving Lily a bit of narrative, a bit of her life back. Same girl, you know, Lucy, this time, in *Mrs Dalloway.* So, as I say, a little bit here, a little bit there. Nonsense. Nothing. 'My name is Dalloway'.

'What – ' to rescue the situation in the pizza house, I asked, 'what's wrong with Manchester?'

Sara rallied and, intelligently, didn't cite the cold, the damp, the light too dull for painting. But said that she was denied the front door. No, no, not racism. Everyone there was denied the front door. You had to go round the back to get into the house, into all the houses in that street in Openshaw. She would not be treated in this manner; she would not go round the back; she was not a servant.

Ah, this was so like an earlier stage of that discussion. One would have warmed to this *then.* But, in the end, my brother was right. Sara's notion of a suitable interior was one where a girl might bare her breasts in privacy (that Judith Rossner's book jacket comes to mind, *Waiting for Mr. Goodbar.* Heavy nipples), and maybe a drawing-room to relax in with friends. Well, surely, it shouldn't be too difficult to find that sort of thing in Manchester or Luton; she didn't need me.

(*Wasafiri*, 2001)

2: FROM *TEN STORIES* (1992)

'In the old days they sent the priest,' etc. We were allowed to talk amongst ourselves. And it was perhaps that, more than anything else, which caused my brother, Eugene, to point out to my mother who had made the remark, that some of *those* had clearly been pretend priests; and my mother wrong-footed him again by saying that pretend priests had God as their ally whereas these others only had the State; though, she conceded, it was difficult to tell one source from the other. At the end of all this, a priest was shown in.

He wasn't someone we knew; a quick calculation: what did he know about us? Would we insist on knowing at least as much about him as he knew about us, to make the coming encounter more even? We would stress the aspect of the early priests far from home, the dress, the voice, the way they called on you at dinnertime and came back when the food was good – as it always was at my grandmother's, etc. At one time, not only the Methodist but all the others had found their way to her door in Coderington. But now we were in another country, in their country, and the years, the decades, had made a difference; my grandmother, who never made the journey with us, had been allowed to die, sort of, and the rest of us were kept waiting, far from Coderington, far from St. Caesare.

There were four of us; mother, sister and two brothers: that could be said to be our family but, in another sense, there were fifteen hundred of us, which was the population of St. Caesare, and we had to bring them with us, not just because they were family in some extended sense, but that each one depended on others to keep us all safe, to preserve or remember bits of family life that little units like ours, on our own, tended to forget. Let me give you an example, a simple one. When the house, my grandmother's old house in Coderington collapsed, the village came and took it away, plank-by-plank. And when I later visited the island I was taken to this house in the village, that house on the hill – house after house – that had incorporated a rafter from the old drawing-room, or the still new-looking boards that had been the partition between the spare room and the bathroom upstairs, behind my grandmother's bedroom. Fancy bits of the original verandah ringed this or that little house, perhaps making it look ridiculous, but all in all the place, though no longer visible on the skyline, was enjoying a new lease of life. That went also for the utensils, from breadroom to kitchen to the scales for weighing the cotton. Now, if you found a way of preserving things that were valuable to you, how could you do less for people?

So back to the family: either we were five or we were fifteen hundred, which was the environment in which the family made sense. This is what the problem was about, the great debate between their customs and our customs, and who was or was not allowed to be family. Earlier migrants had been caught out, had been tricked, had been encouraged to shed family, and now some were living to regret it. Like Flora Blessett. Remember Flora?

Miss Flora had struggled enough in her time so naturally when she had the opportunity to come over with her new husband she made a temporary arrangement for the child and took her chances. And when you're young, you accept the usual sorts of assurances. But now look at Flora? Husband dead and here she is alone – child's family on the other side of the world – put in a home with people she didn't know, some of them put there even though they had family in this country, a state of affairs which made Flora feel she was being held there as punishment for something she had done early in her life. So she tried to recover her family; and they put a stop to that and said what was lost was better left forgotten; and they got strangers in to threaten her out of her rights of family, strangers who took her back to her point of entry in this country, the day, the hour, to what had accompanied her to this country – which was only the partner, the husband, now gone – and they convinced her that to cling to anything that took place before that date was either against the law or her interests or her sanity.

Now – we don't want to go on about it, but – Flora Blessett was a woman in her thirties when she was transported; so what does that do to her early life growing up in Coderington and going to the Methodist School next to the graveyard, to the Sunday School, the little wooden building behind Mr Lee's rum shop, where the boys who were trying to be lay-preachers were given the opportunity to preach on a Sunday night, to build up their confidence? (Of course, most of them were doing it to pick up women but that's another...) Flora was known to be sweet on one of Professeur Croissant's boys – much younger than she; it must have been the middle boy, not Cincinnatus who was named after one of the Haitian Presidents who was assassinated: Cincinnatus ended up in America, in Washington, and became so American that he used to refer to his home as DC – just DC – not even bothering with the Washington. It wasn't him; it was a younger one that Flora had been sweet on. Anyway, that boy eventually married someone else. Yet, they say he's good to his family back home. So, where were we? Flora had been ordered to forget all that. And other things: wasn't she in training at some point to be a nurse, or teacher or something, when the child got in the way? Or was that someone else? We don't really know the details; we weren't family. Anyway, she was in her thirties when she married and made the trip abroad.

So here we were again, the family, in a room with a priest who didn't look like a priest, the tell-tale sign being that he was pretending to take an interest in the fortunes of Flora Blessett, as recounted by us – the misfortunes, rather. You learn to be precise in this business, because what you say can be taken down and used against you, and you never know who's laying down traps to snare you. (Everyone remembers the case of that man from Look Out who said Goodbye at the start of one of his interviews. He said Goodbye instead of Good Morning, and you know what happened to him! He had to spend the rest of his life pretending that it was deliberate, and that when you met someone for the first time it was proper to say Goodbye. These were the sorts of things, which, over the years, made people a little suspicious of St. Caesarians.) But let's not get side-tracked; we're trying to be precise. I forget now the point we were making (I'm sure he's noting it all down) so let's stick with this thing of being precise: were there *five* or *fifteen hundred* in our little family? They will try again to trip us up over that; and of course, if you're unsympathetic, or just too busy to go into it, you could make a case for there being a serious discrepancy between being a family of five and a family of fifteen hundred. But that way of thinking, my sister Avril says (Avril is the juggler of the family, she's also something else) – that way of thinking is just to think like other people. It scares us a little to hear Avril talk like this, because we're not sure we want to be that different from other people, and it makes us conscious that we're not winning this game. (In the words of my mother, 'Time waits for no man.')

And as you see, we've got caught again: who told us to be blabbing about Flora Blessett when we have our own problems to think about? Did we want to add her to our list? *No.* And yet, it seems that one or two things we said about

Flora weren't strictly accurate. Who was going to correct them? No, she didn't grow up in Coderington, after all, she grew up in Lower Barville where some of the poorer people in those days made their homes, in the forties and fifties, before the expatriates came and built their villas. But of course *we* were from Coderington, and when you were hazy about certain people you sometimes slipped into the habit of thinking that they were from Coderington, too, and that they had done this or that job of work for my grandmother. If we were wrong about Flora in this, maybe we were wrong about one or two other details as well. But then we never claimed to be right about everything on the island, and certainly not about people who had come on ahead of us, and that's why we tried to keep hold of the last fifteen hundred who were part of our story.

The priest who wasn't like a priest made us a proposal, which was either subtle or insulting. We were a pretty sharp family by now with over three decades' experience of being interrogated. My sister was the sharpest but we were all pretty sharp. My mother, at the start, had had to deny that she was other people, everything from her own mother to the servant girl who used to bring her a glass of water in Coderington and not spit in it; and in the end she decided it was too boring to keep denying being this or that; that it was much more fun to become all these other people when the occasion arose; and now she was so good at it that when we met her we had to spend quite a bit of time guessing who she might be on that particular occasion. My sister, as I say, was both a juggler and something else, and we were so impressed by the something else that our nickname for her was Something Else. My brother won't let us talk about him from the point of view of security and I was the liar in the family. And it's a curious thing, that if you pronounce the word liar quickly or indistinctly, or put on an American accent, you could get away with people thinking you were a lawyer – but, of course, I don't overdo it. So, as I say, we were a pretty sharp family. (My other brother wasn't mentioned, that was strategic; we kept him in reserve.)

Of course, we were allowed to come and go on a temporary basis; we weren't confined to this little room, only we had to come back to be grilled, at regular intervals, and, hopefully, to acquit ourselves in such a way that in time we wouldn't have to come back to the room at all. And always the pressure was to repudiate members of the family – on the edge, so to speak – to save our own skin. There were many in this country – some from St. Caesare itself – who blamed us for holding out, who revelled in the fact that they had, at the first sign of trouble, cut themselves loose; that they were now doing all right; that we had brought our own difficulties upon ourselves and that stories like Flora Blessett's were unrepresentative. All this was well known. It was also well known that our interrogators often tried to add to our list of family anyone – like Flora – whose bits of past we recognised floating about and tried to rescue, to pin down. We had to watch this because having had so much difficulty with our own fifteen hundred we couldn't afford to have that figure adjusted *upwards.* Which is what the new man (too boring to keep calling him a priest who didn't look like a priest) seemed to be encouraging us to do.

But no. He wasn't trying to make us add Flora Blessett to our list of essential family, making us in total fifteen hundred and one (or six); what he was suggesting was that we seemed close enough to Flora to substitute her for someone who had long been on our list, but had perhaps by now faded to a point whereby that person might no longer be perceived as family; for he recognised the need for us to rescue those bits of Flora that were being lost, those first thirty-odd years in Coderington or Lower Barville or wherever.

It was a trap. We could all think of people we could

substitute for family. Friends; people in books. People on television. We could think of *objects* that, with good conscience, we could substitute for family! It was a trap, we knew, but we weren't fazed by this sort of thing. We weren't strange people; we weren't fanatical. We had long accepted that you couldn't just *add* to family *ad infinitum,* because in time – and they were giving us time – we should then embrace the whole world. So when the representative withdrew (that's better than priest...etc.) – when he withdrew, we prepared to discuss the matter seriously, to see who could be jettisoned from the old family to make room for Flora. (We started by affirming those who were sacrosanct: Grandmother. Uncles who had done this or that in various parts of the world, X, who used to do the washing and ironing in the big house, etc.)

I'm saving more time than you would think to say that we eventually came down in favour of Grandmother. *Grandmother!* Grandmother had always been the central member of the family, even though she had never travelled with us. She was so much part of us that, in a sense, we couldn't not bring her with us if we tried. So, really, there was no need to keep her name on our list. Mentally, it was forever engraved there, because when you came down to it, when you thought of Coderington – and we thought of Coderington often – we saw the house intact, and the five grafted mango trees at the edge of the front lawn, that she had planted for us, one each for my mother and for us children. You couldn't think of that without seeing her, sitting there at the top of the steps, the back steps, on the floor of her room, looking down. Everything to do with the house, from the weighing of the cotton, to auctions from the Animal Pound, to forbidding the ironing of clothes on a Sunday – so the woman downstairs had to be gentle with the flat-iron – everything recalled grandmother. As – delicious memory – did the taste of brandy which we, children, were allowed to 'gargle' with, diluted, when we had a toothache. Her memory clung to us, so we could pretend to let her go – the authorities would like that – while we knew better. (In any case, there were others, another branch of the family, trying to get grandmother into another country; but we didn't trust them.)

Following that sacrifice, we managed to save for the family those who were at risk, those thought to be marginal: the girl Madeleine, who used to bring my mother water and not spit in the glass, for when you were in a strange country how could you be sure that whoever brought you water wouldn't spit in the glass? We managed to save the six or seven friendly people on Rodney's beach, people who wouldn't look at you and say you were too fat (considering your husband was away) or that you had bad skin, or that you were a strange colour. (They would say these things, but you would give as good as you got, and not feel silenced.) We had our own individual treasures: I saved mad Horace, who had the ability to dream my life, my future life, peopling it with figures, unknown to me, who repeatedly appeared in his dreams, but not in mine. So I had to rely on him to describe my family to me, and hoped that he was telling me the truth, and feared that he wasn't. I had to preserve Horace, or lose that glimpse into the future. Collectively, we saved characters like Great-uncle Neighton, who was the one who didn't make it, of that generation. Some said he should have gone to Panama or Haiti with the rest, instead of going further north by way of Cuba. Or, like his brother, he may have won the *borlette* in Haiti and had a few good years.

But, like others, Neighton, too, was a successful enough traveller, though he travelled mainly in his mind. He was testing the strength of the family mind to travel vast distances – distances beyond being a doctor or a preacher – and he had got bogged down, years ago, in Egypt. Egypt, he used to say, was as good a place as any to hide in. So, in memory of Great-uncle Neighton who never made it, we children used to memorise bits of the experience that from time to time fell out of his mind. And even now, in middle age, with other distractions, we were prepared to fight our corner over the relative merits of Amen-hetep III (1402-64) and his prosperous and tranquil empire stretching from the Euphrates in the north to Napata in the Sudan. Someone of us would defend him against a brother, a sister who would insist that he had inherited it all and that the real figures of interest were Amen-hetep II and Tuthmosis IV. This way we could preserve the mental toughness that Great-uncle Neighton promised and lost. (After a recent discussion, in our exiled room, we decided to go on the offensive: when our interrogator arrived we would open with a discussion on the influence of Amen-hetep II's sun disc image on sun-worship and creation of a new god under Amen-hetep III. But my sister, sharp in her juggling, said we'd be playing into his hands, we'd be accused of triumphalism. My sister was Something Else.)

And then certain things happened in the world that you might not want to hear about. The result was that the family reinstated *Grandmother,* because really, we didn't want to be seen to be chipping away at our base, at our dates, and making ourselves too provincial in time, for Great-uncle Neighton had seemed a little exposed without Grandmother. And also, how could we trust the other branch of the family, trying to get her into another country, to succeed? (And really, we couldn't have prevented the moving of Flora Blessett from the home she didn't like, into something worse.)

So, when the man returned to confront us in the room, we reinstated *Grandmother,* and we retained responsibility for Flora Blessett whose growing-up in Coderington had been in doubt. Now, we were reconciled to being a family of *six* or, if you like, of *fifteen hundred and one,* and growing.

MISS JOYCE AND BOBCAT

i

Miss Joyce came out on the verandah and sniffed the air and wrinkled up her nose.

'Lord, Lord, have mercy,' she said. 'Why things always work out so? You work, you plan, you prepare; you pay for it with you own money – hard, hard-earned money. But is grudge they grudge. You work and pay, and everything turn out so. I'm too damned soft, that's my trouble. But what's a poor woman to do, a single woman at that? The men have it all their way, the brutes, as always. Bobcat!...' Here she shouted at the man in the garden, trying to make herself heard above the sound of the machine. 'Bobcat, you brute. Who paying you to desecrate me so?'

Bobcat, the brute, aware of Miss Joyce, continued his desecration of Miss Joyce's lawn, digging a hole with an impressive-looking machine.

'We going to have to use the back terrace now,' Miss Joyce sighed. Then she called to someone out of sight: 'Prudence, we'll have to use the back terrace. I'm sure the grass dying already. Prudence!'

Miss Joyce turned to go back into the house but stopped. Bobcat had seen her but pretended not to. The sound of the machine was not so much deafening as conquering; he was hiding behind that. Now that he was performing for her she didn't know whether to suppress or to encourage thoughts about the nature of the man's machine, the maleness of the thing, the authority of that tool smacking into her lawn, gorging great chunks of soil which left the place so wounded and vulnerable – and the beast, sitting up there on that high seat, like at some sort of religious ceremony, directing it.

Then Bobcat decided to acknowledge Miss Joyce; he looked up from the still-shuddering machine, the tool suspended in mid-air, and tipped an imaginary hat to her. Miss Joyce refused to be impressed. She wanted the man to know that she was angry, damned angry. She refused to notice the filth that was on the end of the tool.

Bobcat had tipped his hat; who did that sort of thing nowadays? In the old days, when she was a young girl, that sort of thing meant that a man had good manners; then after all the politics and overcoming; after all the raising up of consciousness and women wanting to respect themselves – all that seemed to stop, and only the old-timers were left tipping; clergymen of the old school; the odd businessman from the country who was thinking perhaps of going into politics. Or the odder arse returning damaged from England. Even the grammar-school boys didn't tip hat anymore. Anyway now was no time, a big woman with so much to do, to be encouraging thoughts about grammar-school boys. And tipping hat was like everything else, just what men did to preen themselves and confuse women.

Miss Joyce started as Prudence silently appeared from the house and stood beside her; she had come with a glass of wine on a tray.

'Don't creep up on me so, you want to kill me? Who ask you to bring out the wine?'

'The cakes ready, Miss Joyce.'

'Prudence, you is a human being.'

'Miss Joyce.'

'Then act like a human being. What you doing with wine in the middle of the day, you want to turn me into a drunkard? Look at the state I'm in already: look at that wild man digging up my front lawn as if it belong to him? Shaking up the house and thing. I getting hot and sweaty again. Do I look ready for a garden party, Prudence?'

'Miss Joyce.'

'I going cancel the whole damn thing.'

'The wine for the gentleman; is he ask for it.'

'Well, that's really good to know. You better go and turn down the oven and don't let the cakes and them burn, eh. So he asking for wine now!' They both stood looking at Bobcat who was enjoying this without appearing to.

'So you all think we running a hotel here? A wine shop? I tell you to offer him a cold drink, and you go and open up the wine put aside for my guests; you know what wine cost in this place?'

'You want me to take it back again?'

'Like the man already move into my home. Ordering this and that. Making demands. Is not just the wine I'm talking about, you know.' And here she shouted at Bobcat: 'So you think this is wine shop? Rum shop?'

Bobcat signalled that he would soon be over, and Miss Joyce said to nobody in particular: 'He can hear. He only playing tricks.' Then she turned again to Prudence. 'Woman, you going let the cakes burn to ashes?'

As Prudence turned to go into the house, Miss Joyce had another thought 'And you better water the grass, eh?'

'The grass not supposed to water. In the hot sun.'

'Since when you're an expert on grass?'

'Is what they say.'

'Who say? So now you're a doctor of grass? They give you degree in grass when you was down in the Virgin Islands? That grass come all the way from the nursery. I shame to tell you what it cost.'

'Well, if it dead, don't blame me.' And Prudence went off, unruffled, into the house.

'Is me you all going to kill. I'm only in this world to take a beating.' This time when she called to the man on the lawn, it was with new resolution, and a new name. 'Leslie!' She signalled and he looked up. 'Stop the damn machine.'

The sudden silence made her a little conscious of her agitation. God, why was it a woman always felt herself in the wrong? The more they abuse you the more you feel guilty. Life unfair, eh?

'Leslie, you nearly finish?'

'Close to.'

'"Close to" not good enough. You promise to come last week.'

'I already explain, Miss Joyce.'

'What good is explanation when I have people coming here in...' she looked at her watch '...practically anytime now. I'm not a laughingstock, you know.'

'The smell completely gone now.'

'Maybe the smell nearly gone, but it look bad. In this day and age no one putting in pit latrine in front of they house. I should have build from scratch like everybody else instead of buying from these foreign people.'

'It's the modern thing, you know.'

'They must be addle your brains in London. Since when pit latrine come modern thing?'

'Is septic tank they call it. All the Americans and Canadians putting them in.'

'Thanks for the history lesson. Do I look like I in school? I'm not no American and Canadian. I don't have to follow their nastiness.'

'Anyway, you taking out, not putting in.'

'A half-empty bottle look the same like a half-full bottle to them that don't know.'

'You have a way with words, you know? But as I was saying, sometimes, these people, they put them right next to the swimming-pool.'

The man was becoming familiar; she would make him keep his distance, put an end to the conversation. 'This is my front lawn,' she told him. 'No man have the right to pollute it with coarseness, and rudeness and what I call this kind of scatological talk.' Before she disappeared into the house, she informed him, in a rather grand manner, that the woman had brought the wine he had ordered.

Bobcat soon collected himself and blew a long whistle in appreciation and tipped his imaginary hat. Not long afterwards, the shudder of his machine could be felt throughout the house.

ii

Halfway through the party Miss Joyce, looking cool and unflustered, drifted back to the front terrace to observe the newly laid turf being watered by a sprinkler. She delayed her re-entry as another guest, an elegantly dressed young woman, approached the house.

'Celestine, you look nice,' she said. 'Your better half's here ahead of you.'

'Hello, Miss Joyce. You look nice too.'

'Call me Joyce, man.'

'The weather too hot for clothes. I thought you were putting in a pool here.'

'What do I want with pool? I'm not so desperate to let people see me naked. I have two bathrooms in my house, that's enough for me. So child, I'm glad you come. The Very Reverend missing you inside.'

'I doubt that. Papa doesn't believe the cloth should interfere with having a good time.'

'Is Papa you call the Reverend?'

'Got to call him something, Miss Joyce.'

'People might get the wrong idea when you call him Papa.'

'Well, they say he's old enough to be my daddy.'

'People in this place too wicked. Wicked and bad minded.'

'Well, as Papa says: we have to show we're not as small as the island. We have to go against the trend.'

'You get punished for that too, child. But what we doing out here talking? Come and join the party. You look nice in truth. The Reverend Doctor must be very good to you.'

A short time later, Celestine was back on the front veranda sobbing in Miss Joyce's arms.

'Brutes, that's what they are. Men are brutes,' Miss Joyce consoled. 'Don't cry, child, they not worth it, none of them. Priest and beggar, all the same. Black and white, no difference.'

Prudence approached from the house with a glass of water on a tray.

'He still playing the fool in there?' Miss Joyce wanted to know. But Prudence remained silent.

'Prudence, you don't hear me talking to you?'

'Is not me invite him here.'

'What's that supposed to mean? Is your family. You all country people together. But it serve me right, I should mix with my own kind.'

'Everybody is family. Me not responsible for that. Reverend Doctor don't change people. Is not me invite him here.'

'I'm sorry I upset your Ladyship.'

'I know him since he small; know how he is. When he use to come up to the big house, Mrs. Parkinson old house where I used to work, and that man didn't have nothing, not even a little cardboard suitcase to he name, nothing. And these kind people take he in, buy him clothes. Is me who used to wash them. And he look nice, you know? He always look nice. The boy poor but he could preach even in them days. And they help him along, and they help him along till he marry into the family. And as they help him along he let them down, and as he let them down they forgive he. Every time. And though he married he go and make baby with all kind of dirty, stinking woman. And still they forgive he. And even in the very kitchen, you know where you peeling breadfruit and green banana, he coming in to feel-up you breast.'

Celestine, who had been sobbing all the while, was virtually howling now. So Miss Joyce spoke to Prudence in some anger.

'Woman, you not shame to be talking like that in front of this poor child? Don't no one have any little sensitivity or delicacy in this place?'

But Prudence was unrelenting. 'Excuse my manners. I know what I know. He borrow money and they have to pay it back. He bad, bad, bad. Is preaching save he. Every Sunday when he call the Lord down on we, we frighten, frighten.'

'Jesus God.'

'...And when he get into more trouble, they send he away to come Preacher. I tell you when Miss Millicent marry he I did cry. I cry bitter tears because I know how it go turn out. And they say even to this day he have other wife and family in foreign country...'

Prudence stopped as the Reverend Doctor appeared in the doorway.

'Ladies, ladies...' He hesitated, not sure which one to approach.

'Ladies, excuse my... tardiness.' Then he took the glass of water from Prudence. But before taking it to Celestine, he lingered to rebuke Prudence, hardly bothering to lower his voice: 'You never did have any breasts worth talking about.'

iii

That evening, after the party, Miss Joyce was sitting on the front terrace, from time to time sipping her drink. She was bothered by a mosquito or a fly and clumsily tried to deal with it, but her mind was elsewhere. She was wondering why she was making a fool of herself. The effort of the party had left her, not drained, but agitated. Not even that. Deflated. Why didn't anything ever turn out as planned? When she had lived abroad and couldn't live as she wanted, she had always promised herself that one day it would be different. And she had saved her money. It wasn't easy lifting up racists off their hospital beds to clean them, but she had gritted her teeth and held her breath and done it in the hope that one day she would be able to live again like a human being.

She was aware that there was someone on the lawn, but she was in no hurry. She thought a bit more of what she would or would not suffer in this place. Finally, in her own time, she addressed the shadow on the lawn:

'Bobcat, what are you doing on my lawn this time of night?'

'I come to apologise, Miss Joyce.'

'What for?'

'For missing the party.'

'Too late as usual. Apologies not accepted. Too bad there's no wine in the house. Rum shop close.'

'What can I do, Miss Joyce?'

'I'm not your father and your mother. You can leave my lawn and take your apology with you.'

'Let me explain.'

'I've heard the explanations. Story of my life.'

'May I have a little drink?'

'Never say the bitch so stingy she wouldn't even let them come and drink her out of house and home.' She got up to go into the house. 'Maybe I'll be a bartender in the next life.'

Bobcat came out of the shadows and up to the edge of the verandah, but didn't mount the steps. And it was here that Miss Joyce passed over his drink.

She was very calm when she spoke. 'If you want to cross

this threshold, Leslie, you have to make me feel like a human being.'

'You're something special, you know, Miss Joyce.'

'Everything on this earth is special. God see to that. Even the crappo you hear waking up the dead is in some way special.'

'No, no. But I mean, really special.'

'You not giving me anything, Bobcat, to call me special.'

'God, you going to be hard to please.'

'You find the foreign ladies easy?'

'I made a mistake, man.'

'You're damn right I'm hard to please. If you have an interest in me you have to find out where I am and meet me there. Is the only thing will compensate for the beating and the punishment.'

'Miss Joyce, you have the wrong man.'

'Every woman in this world have the wrong man. We all have the scars to prove it. But I'm not a child, Leslie; I'm not looking for Mr. Right. Over the years, I've learnt the value of compromise. Let's drink to that.'

'Let me come up and sit down, eh. Because I have to talk to you real serious.'

Miss Joyce didn't object. But Bobcat found it hard to start.

'I don't know what you think about anything,' Miss Joyce encouraged.

'Like what?'

'I don't know you, man. You must have views. Views on...on the President of France, the cutting down of Brazilian rain forests...'

'I'm in business, you know, not politics.'

'Oh Leslie, are you a man of imagination or a miser?' She stopped him trying to answer and rushed on: 'your vocabulary, Leslie: where are the gentle words to cancel out the rest? I expect finesse from a man. I expect something uplifting, not talk about pit latrine and nastiness. I expect reassurance from a man. I want him to tell me that in spite of everything, we're not turning into brutes.'

'Everything like what?'

'Oh God. Everything, man. Everything in the world. Violence. Brutishness: do I have to spell it out? You have to talk to me.'

'Miss Joyce, you're a Philosopher, in truth.'

'When you're up there, high up on your machine, I want to know what you thinking.'

'I like you, you know. That's what I'm thinking. You hear me?'

'That's a cool way to say something... in such a hot climate. You like me like you like rum and cricket?'

'I love you, man.'

'It hurt to say it?'

'Joyce, I love you.'

'That's nice.' Then a little shift of tone. 'You can't imagine that's all a woman want to hear.'

'You going to make me make a fool of meself.'

'That's bad? You don't like me enough to risk making fool of yourself? Maybe you should send me a letter in a brown envelope. In some other language. In French. *M Bobcat, 48 Terresseur. Bel homme, très sympathique* (you have to lie, they all lie), *entreprenant, d'un naturel reserve, très sympathique des affaires, etc.'*

Bobcat blew another long whistle of appreciation.

'Then maybe I could accept that as a starter,' Miss Joyce said flatly.

'You can toy with a man just so much,' Bobcat threatened, advancing on Miss Joyce. 'I running out of patience, rapidly.'

'So run.'

'I ain't running, Joyce.' His hands were on her.

'So you like me?'

'I love you, man.'

'You like me?'

'Oh God.'

'Cest vrai?'

'Oh God. Oh God.'

NJK HOLT

i

As I was saying...

'Sorry?'

Yes man, name's Holt, NJK. *Not JK* Holt, get it? Boy, as I say, you got to show them what we made of, bit of spunk, can't ever let up; no Sir. Like I remember saying to that boy who favour you, you know, one of them Archibalds from Montserrat; young boy come over in the '50s; good family, mother and three sons. Yes man, as I said to young Archibald that day: you are young, you're going to their schools; show them what you can do. You are the future in this place: leave the past to we. To us. We doing our bit. We cleaning up from behind. Your job is to press on, man. Bruk it up. Used to meet sometimes on a Sunday morning at the Baths. Paddington Public Baths. I call those meetings *strategic* man. Yes, Sir, the boys were serious. Well, there were two types of boys in those days. The Saturday-night Boys at the Palais, handing over their money to the women, and the Sunday-morning Boys at the Baths. Some of them miss out. Fraid to show theirselves in public, going to the Baths. Like is their fault the English people and them don't have bathrooms in the house they renting to black people. And you say to them: no need to shame. Is not you build house without bathroom. The house don't even belong to you. And even then, you know, I make meself a promise, right there in the Paddington Baths in 1956. Or '58. No, it was '56 because Nasser had just close the canal and make we proud, man. You could have play cricket in the street in Trafalgar Square: the man stop the English traffic dead; turn off they petrol. Anyway, the promise I make to myself was this: whenever black people start to buy they houses, I going be the one to put in the bathroom. And I start to train meself in the art of bathroom-making. There was a little library at the bottom of Shirland Road; I used to go there at night and look up bathrooms, pore over them. Because I was what you would call a man without skills, except the skills of survival, which even now they like to under-rate. I taught myself about dealing with your bath and your Ascot and your plumbing – always remember your waste; you is human, you have to be clean. And then the tiling to top it off. This was a task I set myself; ready to play my part converting the houses that used to be English.

Holt was about to go on, but they were in the launderette, and the young man who favoured Archibald seemed to be in a hurry. Hurry for what? Holt had been around in this country for thirty years and he couldn't see what there was to hurry for now. He was doing a real wash, not like the young fellow who came in only to use the dryer for his jeans and T-shirt and nonsense. Holt had a real wash, most of it belonged to the woman he lived with; he wasn't proud.

But he had wanted to explain to the boy that he wasn't boasting about the early days; he just wanted the young ones to get the picture. When he saw someone bright-looking like this, who could be the age of his son or grandson, he felt an obligation to pass on what he knew. No, the Baths weren't that big a deal; it was only a meeting-place after all, but there the boys somehow managed to lay down plans that put both their character and their future on the line. That's why he said it was strategic. Take for instance the business of First and Second Class. Well, you took it for granted you always ordered a First Class bath, because what you're saying to them is this: I am accustomed to baths. It's my situation in this country, in one of your houses that denies me a bath where I live, that brings me here. First Class, please. And double soap and towel. Or *two* towels and soap. The saggar-boys in they two-tone shoes and Brylcream spending as much at the Palais; and on what?

But you know; the boys didn't stop at First Class, Soap and Towel. Soon, we was all buying *two* baths, man. *One for my baby and one more for the road.* But seriously, to demonstrate you were a clean man, you had to buy a First Class bath just to wash out the bath, to wash off the dirt of the last customer, and then you fill up First Class again and bathe. And I tell you one thing, the bath-attendant respect you for it. Because only the boys from home did that. This is a temporary measure, you telling him; this is a half-way house. Believe what you see, not what you read in the *News of the World.* And like young Archibald say: even the best Romans used to bathe in public.

Holt would have liked to explain how he got side-tracked from bathrooms into another sort of business, but the two people left in the launderette weren't the sort of people he thought he could confide in; so he started taking stuff out of the wash, proud that a woman customer was curious about his mainly women's clothing (and him dressed like a bank manager during a boom) something she obviously couldn't get her own man to do.

ii

They used to call him Holt, just Holt – or JK – but that changed, that changed after he opened his shop. The original JK Holt was a West Indian cricketer from Jamaica who was on the edge of Test selection (in fact, he had had a few Tests at home against England and Australia. Then later, they took him to India and Pakistan. And come to think of it, even he wasn't that original – he was JK Holt, Jr). So, when Holt opened up his shop in Ladbroke Grove in 1957, the boys decided to call him NJK Holt – *Not* JK Holt, to distinguish him from the cricketer.

He got into the business by accident. One Sunday morning at the Baths, he ran into the boy from Montserrat, one of the Archibalds from Harris's, who said that his family had just bought a house in Bevington Road from an Irishman, and there was a big room downstairs with all sorts of rubbish and an upright piano they didn't know what to do with – the room, not the piano, for Archibald was a bit of joker – and why didn't JK, who looked like a bit of businessman, open up a little shop down there? Only problem was it was bang opposite the public loo and they didn't know whether it was a good thing to sell eatables just opposite where people were coming to relieve themselves.

Young Archibald had seemed reliable enough in other ways because not only had he bought his two First Class baths – catching on immediately – but he had brought his own soap and towel. Holt was more interested in having a go at putting a bathroom in the newly-acquired house, but Archibald said there already was a bathroom in the house; the reason he was at the Baths this Sunday was that they were having a wedding reception at the house later that day, for a cousin; and since so many people – including the helpers – would be wanting to use the bath, he decided to ease the pressure by coming over to Paddington. What with one thing and another, Holt ended up going to the reception at the Archibald house in Bevington Road.

The public loos didn't look good just outside, and that seemed to rule out any sort of business, even if you weren't thinking about food. And his business was bathrooms, not food.

But later, when the newly-married couple and most of the guests were gone, the boys who remained drifted downstairs to the big room where a young fellow from Trinidad entertained them on the piano. They were talking about this and that, how life was beginning to pass them by – one fellow had already been in this country eleven years, would you believe it? – and had been in and out of the army, though he had missed the War. Only the students – and maybe the nurses – seemed to know what they were about; no one was actually setting the place alight. The only thing you owned – except in special cases like this house – was the odd secondhand car which Moseley's men were attacking, saying you got it by putting their women on the streets. In the middle of all this – and some really heavy jazz on the piano – the boys insisted that JK open a shop in this very space, selling groceries. Before they said goodnight they helped him to compose the sign for the shop, the only doubt in anyone's mind being whether the English, so funny in their ways, would come into the shop and buy from one of the boys.

NJK HOLT (Groceries) was a slight mistake as Holt didn't go in for groceries right away, but stocked up on Carnation milk amid Omo and bags of salt-fish and brown rice and a few other things in tins and tubes that weren't grocery. Holt was living with an 'older' woman at the time, called Betty, and it is she who stayed in the shop while Holt went around organising supplies and advertising by word of mouth. Betty couldn't read too well and had her own way of pronouncing things, like looking at the label on the milk and saying 'Coronation'. So NJK HOLT (Groceries) became known as the place where you could get real Coronation milk; and there were jokes, sometimes lewd, sometimes elevated, about 'Queen Betty'.

It was at least eighteen months before Holt went out of the grocery business, and instead of organising his bathrooms, had to do all sorts of drudgery to pay off his debts. And on top of everything, Betty went and died. No one knew the operation was going to be serious, no one prepared you for it; but you know what these doctors are like, wrong and strong: they've got the knife and you're unarmed.

And is a terrible thing, boy, to have a woman you don't love die on you like that; it leave you with this thing they have in this country called guilt; boy it eat into you like that dry rot business into an old house. And you try to cut it out and replace this, replace that, till you don't know what else to replace. Even if you fit a whole new bathroom, you got to have a house to put it in. Time come, boy, you feel like accepting defeat, and just handing over to the new generation, the offspring. Some people lucky to be able to do that. NJK HOLT III: that would have been nice. But as I say, things take a long time, and before you know what happen, they already calling it the '70s; and calling you old.

iii

And boy, it was like there was more deaths in the family: no one much about to share the new jokes, or recall the old ones. Take the new bathroom business, for instance, the *Half-Way House:* in the old days the boys would have shared the joke that old JK was, if not throwing in the towel, at least settling for a draw. Or to put it another way: *NJK* had accepted there was no point in trying to bowl out the opposition, and some of the boys would have give him hell that in the business of bathrooms he had set his sights lower than in the business with a woman, deciding beforehand not to go all the way (though if the truth be known his new partner, replacing Betty, had developed a way of punishing him just as he had punished Betty, one sister taking revenge for the other – so that anyone in his place would have settled for a draw). Even the JK Holt joke seemed stale now, now that all cricket talk was about Viv Richards and Clive Lloyd and the four West Indies fast bowlers. People didn't even know who JK Holt was. They were asking a man to forget his first family because he happened to be remarried.

Even young Archibald – that was becoming a bit of a joke, a man of his age with a white beard – had gone into decline. Holt sought him out, threw him a bit of a life-line, offered him a partnership in the *Half-Way House* for old times sake. Remember, this was the man who got him started in business; this was the man who used to have ideas on putting the world to rights; on the moon-rockets in the '60s and whether the Moon wasn't some mid-American desert and America and Russia in this thing together laughing at we. This was the man who told you about Vietnam and why African countries should or should not redraw their boundaries. Now, he was into another sort of struggle.

Archibald turned down Holt's offer of a share in the *Half-Way House* because his energy was taken up with a woman. That was new. It seems that Archibald and his woman had come together at a level that wasn't only what you'd call graduate but post-graduate, where he was into identifying her needs and fulfilling them and because this wasn't just old-fashioned sex but something complicated, it turned into a full-time job which left the brother no time for other business and very little for his paying job of teaching in a college.

Holt tried several times to discover the nature of this woman's needs – because she wasn't a large lady and she didn't seem extravagant, but you never know – but Archibald refused to come clean and merely said that his woman's needs were no different from any other woman's needs and that his woman was simply teaching him not to be selfish. It was Archibald not Holt who had gone to their schools and universities and maybe they resented you so much for it, they made you sign away the rest of your life like that, servicing a woman full of needs, a woman who didn't seem to have any more needs than anybody else. Holt was grateful that he didn't have that kind of education and ambition and that the woman he lived with didn't seem to have that kind of need. Archibald even dressed as if he was doing penance, as if he was still a student – a man with a grey beard – as if he was still going on demonstrations. No one who saw Holt on the one hand, and Archibald on the other, would ever guess which was the teacher fulfilling a woman's need and which was the plumber in the family.

So Holt wore the tie for him (as long as one of them did it, the pressure eased); wore the tie to his bathrooms, and wore a rose in his button-hole. So they laughed at him. Nice. (If they weren't laughing at you in this country, they were doing something worse: never forget that.) Sometimes he was the funny man in the crowd, patrolling the boundary at cricket, the talking calypsonian; sometimes he was the African, the South American President, his uniform heavy with decoration. Sometimes the threat was more subtle. When it comes in the guise of a woman, a real woman with impeccable taste in bathrooms, what's a man to do? So one day, this woman, no kidding, comes up and offers her life to Holt. And here's Holt thinking: no one ever teach me to handle my own life so what I going do with something really valuable like this? The thought of Archibald helped to clear his head: what sort of servicing did this one want, or *need*? But you can't get your mind round that, can you? The enormity of the gift. So different from Holt's present living arrangement, which was the old, familiar private market, where you exchanged gifts you knew the value of. This other thing was like having something you could never own delivered to your house. Made not in any one country. Countless unknown centuries of kings and peasants putting it together: Here JK. Is yours. Take it. Is not right to tease a man like this. He had already lost one woman to the Health Service and the second one he was making do with also bore the mark of that butcher. He would say No as gently as he could to this new bit of temptation. The little voice that kept saying: 'JK, Go for it. Go past the *Half Way House*' was drummed out in the jokes and laughter of those who knew him. He wondered how old Betty had managed to pretend not to mind jokes about her Coronation milk.

If he was on the edge of a joke, he would live up to it and dress the part. Hat, umbrella and waistcoat (and a flower in his button-hole) were the uniform of this Master Plumber determined again to maintain the spirit of the Baths; and he paid court to the woman whose gift he had to reject. Naturally, like other people, she had a man somewhere out of sight, so JK was speaking to him, too. JK was redoing her bathroom at the same time as the rest of the house was being renovated; and she was in residence trying to keep it clean. It was a smart, expensive house but a small one and the other workmen (who came dressed in overalls) were putting in new ceilings and making the house smaller.

So Holt, in the spirit of love and regret, observed that workmen should cut away old plaster, not cover it up, not hide it.

And she liked that.

He didn't like to think of her in this lovely dining-room, the meal laid out, crisp new plaster above her head, but behind that, evidence of discolour, of accident, of rot: an old life.

This was more than she expected.

Apart from other things, if you continued to nail new ceilings to old ones, you would reduce the space for living; it was like what they were doing on the Underground, reducing the diameter of the tunnels by up to two feet every time they redecorated. Surely, people must understand the politics of that.

Why are we talking about ceilings? Why are we talking about the Underground?

He apologised at having to take time to change his clothes on coming, on going; and began to wonder if he had been hasty in thinking he could not begin to fill this woman's needs; and wondered if there was less to it than Archibald had pretended.

iv

At last his washing was done. Everything out of the dryer and folded. It was starting to rain. He'd get a taxi, a mini-cab, to take the washing home. Sometimes you were lucky. Last time he called the mini-cab he got his daughter. Her name was Cristobel. Or Mandy. She asked him his profession because now no one was interested in the NJK (even the woman who shared something of his life and was edging him out of it, called him something else). But Holt knew better than to complain of one woman to another.

His daughter revealed to him that she drove a cab to gain independence. And, in truth, she manoeuvred the car as if she possessed the road. She had a regular job working in Social Services but had been a mini-cab driver in her spare time for six years now.

Holt wondered if he should lie to his daughter, take credit for her; take her back home.

She wanted, she said, to liberate herself from the nonsense with men, and to pay her own way for her travelling, which was her passion. Last year she'd been to America for six weeks; the year before – with some women friends – she had gone to the Middle East. This year, it was Athens or Rome. Holt felt that something of the spirit of the Baths was being transmitted through the generations.

Not that it was her ambition in life to be a mini-cab driver.

So true. So true. And yet. As he was saying to that boy –

one of our new MPs, you know – boy who used to come to the Baths in the old days: Boy, is not exactly what you want, is not exactly what we want; but you might as well go for it.

The mini-cab came, and this time the driver had a beard.

PLETHORA, FRANCE AND THE ROMANIAN REVOLUTION

i

You know how, usually, the people who provide the random link between things, stories, get forgotten, and that's how we came to be talking about Castro (I was visiting Philpot, who was another one who had slipped through the net, so to speak, in recent years). Castro, when last heard of, was imitating an Irish accent and phoning through hoax warnings to the police in London: it seemed a feeble sort of end for a man of his potential. Though, I'm not quite sure Philpot and I agreed about this. Castro was from Jamaica. I can't remember now whether they called him Castro because of his politics or on account of his beard – there are many other names he might have been called at the time – the late '50s or early '60s – names like Lumumba or Chairman Mao. Or, for all I know, Ceauescu, assuming the great man to have been around at the time.

The point about bringing up Castro was that he was from Jamaica and that was to prevent these conversations becoming too incestuous – St. Caesarians patting St. Caesarians on the back, sort of thing. We had a tendency to appropriate all that was positive and adventurous and radical coming out of the West Indies, and we were allowed to get away with it: St. Caesare escaped much of the rough treatment meted out to small-islanders by other West Indians because it was so small no one thought of it as being a thing on its own. Being ruled jointly by Britain and France made people think of it less in connection with one or other European power – not as compromised as Guadeloupe and Martinique in being part of France, or as Montserrat in being a colony of Britain. There was a vague sense, ludicrous though it was, that the place had *hinterland.* Hearing French and English spoken on the main street of Barville reinforced this. Recounting the exploits of St. Caesarians abroad, confirmed it.

We seemed always to start with this point, the business of language, and then to leave behind others who also started out with the business of language. And talking of language, Plethora was now, as he was then, our point of departure. Plethora wasn't his real name, of course; it was something like Asa, but no one now referred to him as anything but Plethora. He was from the North, from the French section, and had got into difficulty with the authorities who had denied him either promotion or a job, whatever, and he wasn't well pleased. (There were rumours that they wanted to ship him to France, to tame him, as he was thought to be a bit of a trouble-maker on the island, but I forget the details: he was a teacher of some sort, anyway.) So, he crossed the line, came south, and gave up French. From now on, he would speak only in English. That's how he captured the imagination of the schoolboys, not just in St. Caesare but over in Montserrat, where most of us had gone to school by this time.

We were at the age, those of us from the British section, where French was the big thing in our lives. (We were forbidden to pursue other recreations, like swimming in the sea, in case we drowned; we were forbidden tennis because that was the French game – which the English also played – as the one or two St. Caesarians who ventured out with their racquets tended to be humiliated, and naturally, we had a responsibility not to humiliate our parents by being beaten on the tennis courts by lighter-skinned people: if only we had cricket, like people on the main islands, life would be easier.)

Our parents all determined to get us into the racist French School in Barville, and the school was equally determined to keep us out, and routinely failed us on our French; that's why we had to go over to Montserrat to the Grammar School where everything was in English and the hurdles were simpler ones like Latin and English itself. So, when Plethora turned up in our part of the island, renouncing French for political reasons, we were *impressed.* Also, it gave a sort of lifeline in explaining away our own poor French. Much later, I was to read of a clan in New Guinea who had pushed the language-protest thing further even than Plethora. Apparently, whenever one of their number died, in order to show respect for the dead, the survivors would eject a word from their vocabulary. This was serious because their language wasn't a massive language like French or English, but one with relatively few words. It was serious, too, because the word they tended to throw out wouldn't be some little-used dictionary-term like, I don't know, 'nugatory' or 'eschew' – something which was just too much trouble to say. No, it had to be basic, like 'rain', (though it wasn't rain) or 'milk' or 'woman'. In the end – at the time this particular anthropologist was writing, which was the early 1970s – the clan was down to its last few words. One word now had to represent scores of things – marriage, funeral, fighting, love-making, etc. – the same word having to signify 'river' and 'Australia'. By now, twenty years on, I expect them to be completely silent. (This brought back memories of our friend Castro, with his Irish accent.) Philpot and I speculated on the New Guinea clan silently announcing the failure of the coffee crop *and* the results of the Provincial elections *and* the information that sweet-potatoes, suffering from blight, refuse to be edible for breakfast even though they had been in the hot ash all night – all this information conveyed by the same non-word. They would, by this method, have perfected a superior form of communication, one that would leave the rest of us standing still. They would be like *Star Trek.* Out there in space.

Now, placing Castro in all this is what caused us problems. Castro used to live in West London, quite near to us in those days. We lived at the top end of Sutherland Avenue, and he was down Westbourne Park way, near the cinema off Harrow Road. And from our point of view, the two things, which distinguished the Harrow Road at the time – the late '50s and early '60s – were the racist police station and the racist grocery shop. We didn't exactly have bad experiences in either but we took other people's word about the police station and we took Castro's word about the grocery.

He had mounted a campaign against the shop, a one-man campaign, where he refused to speak to them, the proprietors, a husband and wife team. But, of course, you had to find a way to make silence pay. And the point about a campaign was to discomfort the target and not yourself: why walk all the way down to Royal Oak for your groceries when there was a perfectly-good – if racist – grocery within striking distance? So Castro bought a notebook and wrote down his order. He wrote out his shopping-list and held it up when he went into the shop so he wouldn't have to talk to the racists. But, as you know, these people are slow to catch on. They somehow convinced themselves that Castro was maybe dumb – he *was* foreign – and they were prepared to smile at him (the woman had bad teeth – he tried not to think of their love life) and use sign-language as if they were being helpful. So he had to go out of his way to *talk* to anyone who happened to enter the shop, to get his point across. After that, the racists dropped the mask.

But Castro wasn't called Castro for nothing: it wasn't even certain that he had had a beard then, so this radicalism must have manifested itself in other ways. His experiments in the shop, chatting to customers, hadn't been satisfactory; because you know what people are like when they don't know you; they always give the impression they don't quite understand what you're saying. Castro couldn't let them get away with thinking that his use of language was in some way defective: he had to demonstrate that he could use their lingo to better effect than they could, so that when he chose not to do so the point was made. That's why he went to the library – the little library on the corner of Sutherland Avenue and Shirland Road – to find suitable synonyms for brown rice and salt-fish and carnation milk, in order to force the opposition onto the defensive. That's where we met Castro, my brother and I, in the reference section, where I was studying for my GCEs and my brother, who was older, was reading up on Simon Bolivar.

After we got to talking, he told us about his act of resistance at the grocery and we, in turn, told him about Plethora (this was more fun than conjugating Latin verbs or feeling virtuous over Chaucer's *The Nun's Priest's Tale*). We told him how Plethora had ended up as the man with the biggest vocabulary in St. Caesare, and was successful to the point where he was now making a living from it, down the islands. He'd been invited to speak at this or that event, at political rallies as warm-up speaker and even at Grammar School speechdays. Before he left St. Caesare and Montserrat he had commanded a weekly five-minute slot on the radio, and middle-class parents, even, forced their children to listen to it, to improve their vocabulary. (The word was that the children listened in anyway: those at the Grammar School, particularly, would write down Plethora's words and come into school to ask their teachers the meaning of them, to catch them out. So, the teachers, too, had to listen to Plethora. Even the priests managed to slip the odd Plethorism into their sermons on Sunday.) Plethora was the linguistic king of the islands, the English-speaking islands; he was more popular than any calypsonian: what could he become in France if he reverted to his own tongue!

In the end, was Castro's protest as radical as Plethora's? Plethora had given up one language and slipped easily into another and made his point; Castro – Ras Castro to some – had slipped from his silent shopping (all these exercises in paleography), to this business of becoming a man with an Irish accent. It was too simple to put down Castro's failure to the fact that he wasn't St. Caesarian. But even at the time we suspected the worst – his having to buy things, for instance, that he didn't really want, in that little grocery on the Harrow Road – and not extending his protest to other shops: a man from St. Caesare would somehow have had a larger vision.

So Philpot poured the wine and we turned our attention to discussing the Romanian revolution, and the chances we had missed there.

ii

We've all been distracted in recent years trying to stay ahead, trying not to go under; we've lost track of the likes of Plethora and Castro (though I think of him whenever I come back and hear someone has made a call to the police using an Irish accent). I, myself, have spent a lot of time out of the country, travelling a bit, teaching a bit, to the point where I was now seen as a visitor, to be brought up to date. And that's the spirit in which I crossed London from Highgate to Queens Park to see my old friends Philpot and Maureen. (Why, I asked myself again, does it take an hour and a half to cross London by train?)

Philpot and Maureen were together again. They'd been together, more or less, when I first knew them, and had parted 'because it was the best thing for the child'. I remember thinking how radical and 'un-English' that was. Now, they were back together with something like contentment – and the child, Nigel, had left home. Philpot, in his near-bachelor days, used to live near us in Sutherland Avenue, and we sometimes thought of him as a likely candidate to carry on the tradition of Plethora. Philpot was a traveller in the days when most of us didn't travel much, and he had a fetish, to do with hospitals, which fascinated and alarmed us a little. But all that's in the past. He was a man without formal education and didn't have the hang-ups that a lot of the Grammar School boys brought over to England with them: I mean, he called his daughter Nigel for a start, not Nigella, or Nivette; but Nigel. That may have contributed to one of his separations with Maureen, but he held firm. Philpot had somehow got to America in the early days, while still in his teens, and ended up in the South, in Florida, cutting cane; and he had a few scars to prove it. But when he got to England, he brought over with him a 'strategy for success'. It was an American phrase, which impressed us. Part of his strategy for success was to visit St. Mary's Hospital on a Sunday, taking grapes and flowers, and wearing his best brown suit. (Amazing how many women, released, felt grateful to the visitor!) Another part of his strategy for success was to love black women, at a time when competition was light. *Strategy.*

It's not that we were overly impressed with Philpot's ideas, it was just that we were prepared to believe anyone who had survived in America and was so clear about his aims, might well survive over here. Philpot claimed that those of us who were studying, instead of developing a strategy for success, were already preparing the excuses for when we would fail; we were ceasing to be St. Caesarian – and he cited the case of Nadine, a friend of my sister's.

(Nadine had failed both her GCE exams in English and French, although she'd been privately coached in St. Caesare before coming over. She had put down her failure to valuable time lost in the exams through no fault of her own.

In one session, a girl sitting next to her clearly had the flu and had been sniffling noisily, and after about ten minutes, one boy nearby asked to change his seat and the teacher – the invigilator – took him and his papers and his bottle of ink to the other end of the room. The girl sniffed on, embarrassed, and after about twenty minutes another girl nearby asked to be moved, and she too was taken to the other end of the room, leaving the sniffer, two empty desks on either side, with only Nadine, behind, for company. Nadine wasn't that bothered by the sniffing but was overcome with embarrassment for the girl who was isolated, and half-thought that she might move forward in order to keep her company; but, of course, you didn't want to make things worse. Her mother would have wanted her to support the girl, who wasn't a particular friend, without catching the flu, and to pass her exams at the same time. Nadine was pondering how to do this when they announced that she had five minutes left, and she knew she had failed the exam. I can't remember what the excuse was for the other failure, but it was similar. Philpot warned us, warned me against falling into the Nadine trap: that sort of sensitivity would work in a normal country, but we always had to remember that we were in *England* – strategy for success was what was required.)

Philpot, who had been in and out of work (he was a long-distance coach-driver and was said to be living, at the other end of the line, with a Scottish woman in Edinburgh) had kept in touch with his daughter, Nigel, and her mother sporadically, and on one of her birthdays had bought the daughter a dictionary. Nigel had treasured the dictionary, much to her mother's annoyance, and it became a sort of habit – to impress the child and irritate the mother, who was beginning to take consolation in religion, so that Philpot dubbed her Sister Maureen – for Philpot to give Nigel dictionary-type presents on her birthday. One year it would be an Atlas, another year it would be a reference-book on prominent people who were black but whom you didn't know were black – like Russian and Latin poets, and Cleopatra. Then, when she was eleven, he bought her a Romanian dictionary.

She should take an interest in things other than English and French. She should live up to her name and continue to surprise her teachers – and her mother. But there was policy in this, too. Philpot had always hung around people who were better educated than he was, partly to prove he could show us up, and because he was genuinely intellectually curious. And one of the things he picked up along the way was that Romanian was a Latin language and, by his estimation, easy to learn. And whereas English schools taught you French and Spanish and Italian – and he'd even heard of somewhere where you could learn Portuguese – *nobody* taught Romanian. So, there was no competition: with a dictionary and a text-book from Foyles Nigel could get herself up to O-level standard in no time which, with the absence of competition, couldn't be very onerous. (He'd read somewhere of a man, an Englishman, who'd done an African language at university, at Oxford; at the end he was invited to be his own examiner as no one else in the country knew enough about the language; in this country you had to work out your own strategy for success. Surely, what the Englishman got away with wasn't beyond Nigel!) Philpot had a hidden agenda, which he disclosed to the boys, but not to Nigel. He predicted that in ten years, in twenty years, capitalism would come to Eastern Europe, and that we should start preparing ourselves now to clean up when that happened. Nigel, by then fluent in Romanian, with her BBC voice, would be ahead. *Strategy.*

And of course the revolution had come. But Philpot was not angry at the outcome, he had grown to accept things; and he was back with Maureen. That his daughter hadn't taken up the Romanian challenge was OK, too. She had got to university, anyway, to do something else, had come out and got a job: that, in England, could be chalked up as an achievement. Philpot wasn't even bitter that something he had predicted years ago – the capitalisation of Eastern Europe – had managed to catch the rest of the world – including the mega-stars who advised American and other governments – by surprise. It was his fault for not having worked out a strategy for success from his hunch. He now concerned himself with more novel pleasures like being a good house-husband to Maureen, who was being gradually radicalised away from the Church.

That night Maureen apologised for having to leave us, because she had to go off to see a friend who was ill. She declined Philpot's offer to drive her there; apparently, he was now mini-cabbing, but only three nights a week and not weekends, not tonight: he would drive me home to Highgate later. (It seemed as if there was some playful friction between the two over the driving, but I didn't pursue it.) A man of presence, Philpot promised his wife a new colour-scheme on her return. He was talking about supper. He had introduced vegetables into their diet and had cut down on starch. He wanted them to live longer now, having lost so much time in youth. That was his new strategy.

We wandered round the house while Philpot cooked, talked; we opened a second bottle of wine, which pleased Philpot, for Maureen, he said, was a one-glass woman, and even that tended to send her to sleep; he put it down to lingering Puritanism, the effects of the Church. He was experimenting with her diet, making it more healthy, hoping it would eventually give her a higher tolerance for alcohol. We drifted into Philpot's 'study', Nigel's old room, pictures of pop stars and natural history posters still on the walls. Philpot said he was not one of those people sentimental about the past, but a spark had gone out, despite the changes in the world, the pioneering spirit was something of the past: he put it down to AIDS.

We talked of old times. Philpot said he had treated his women badly and didn't deserve his present life. Maureen was a woman of character. It saddened him to have missed out on his daughter, on not having offered support when it was needed, the reassuring arm when she was young, to be there when someone had called her names in the street, to be there at night, a fatherly presence, to make it all go away, to make it all better. Ah, but the past was past; Maureen was his project now. She was still an ignorant woman, but that had helped her to forgive. He, on his part, promised never to give her AIDS. (He had given up hospital visiting.)

Maureen enjoyed supper but stuck to one glass of wine. She talked of Nigel with pride, but was troubled that friends of her own generation were beginning to die, just when life should be getting a bit easier for them. So as not to be too serious, she turned away from Philpot and asked me in her best flirting manner if I didn't think it was ironic that a man who had been a big coach-driver, and had a strategy for success, had ended up at his age, having to drive a mini-cab at night?

A SHORT HISTORY OF ST. CAESARE

The island of St. Caesare had a gentle birth; unlike others in the region it wasn't the result of volcanic activity; though it was a new island, formed in the summer of 1972 in order to give me legitimacy, to enable me to attend a conference as its representative. I was in Sweden at the time, the venue of the conference, and my hosts thought it a good idea.

I was travelling with a friend, Ruth Krim, a writer from America, though we weren't confident enough, then, to make our way commercially as writers: back in England we had answered an ad in the *New Statesman* from a Swedish sculptor with an African name, to come over and help him prepare the catalogue for an art exhibition that he was putting together. And we had won. He – Obajimi Holloway – would pay fares and provide accommodation for us just outside Stockholm – a marvellous opportunity, we thought, to explore the country and to give poetry readings, etc. And the accommodation sounded idyllic. It had turned out to be somewhat different, with Obajimi, a man of perhaps 60, being absurdly secretive, trying to limit our movements and to prevent us following up outside contacts. He confined us to an isolated caravan many miles from Stockholm, providing us with bicycles for transport and offering, as inducement, to share his own part-time jobs with us. One of these jobs was cleaning Stockholm offices at night and the other was delivering newspapers first thing in the morning. (Something that alienated Ruth further was that the first night out she had put on her most elegant, long, white dress thinking we were going out on the town, and ended up hoovering in it. The patch of newsprint on her coat was never to come off.) In the good old tradition of fiction we escaped (not on his bicycles, which Ruth never did learn to ride) and contacted some recent acquaintances, a mother and her grown-up son, who warmed to our 'adventure' and fed us, and invited us to stay at their luxury spare flat in Stockholm. For, as Olga said: poets must live in a certain way. Her son, Serge, good-naturedly went along with it.

Stockholm being expensive, they found us odd jobs, some poetry readings in the old town, as well as one at the university while we were exploring a mysterious offer to 'entertain' the American draft-dodgers resident in the city. Olga and Serge also introduced us to one of the family sidelines. They owned the Tampax factory in Sweden and were busy people (Olga ran the business and Serge, pushing thirty, kept himself busy trying to deal with his insomnia by reading German poetry late at night and pursuing a course in Economics at the university) and the sideline was making herbal tea. This had been Olga's husband's hobby, and they had built up a devoted clientele. This job was messy but convenient; it was messy because weighing and mixing the – I think – twenty-one berries, herbs and grasses that made up each packet left you covered in dust after half an hour. But it was convenient in that it all happened in the basement of the block where our flat was located. And it paid well.

Yet, it was hard to relax in Stockholm. The hours and hours of daylight seemed to pose a special challenge. To pass the time – everything was so clean, so tastefully beautiful, so seemingly contrived – we enrolled for free Swedish classes, six hours a day, to show we were serious. (That, at least, saved us being taken over entirely by our hosts: at Serge's place there were likely to be people passing through talking about everything from golf courses in Scotland to translations of Shakespeare; and Olga's table would be graced by old friends wondering if there was any difference between American and Soviet politicians except for the cut of the suit, and they would deplore the innate dullness of the Swedes, and there would be the surprise package like a distinguished foreigner coming in to pay courtly respect to Olga, on his way to the Nobel ceremony. So soon Ruth and I were able to be time-conscious in public: *Hur mycket ar klockan?* and to ask for *knachebrod* in the supermarket and order *dagens ratt & lattol* (day's special and light beer) at our local restaurant. Our tutors were very kind, praising our accents, because they weren't Italian or Finnish, the underclass which comprised the bulk of our fellow students. Nevertheless, we still did our shopping mainly by pointing and continued to ask street directions in text-book French.

We were still short of money. We had to go easy on the herbal tea because we had run out of some of the ingredients – supplies from the country being erratic in summer – and no one knew how safe it was to change the *balance* of the mix, as some of the berries, on their own, were poisonous; and we were down to, I think, about seventeen of the twenty-one lots. Then Olga had an idea. Olga, at 60, was one of the most captivating women around; she was of Danish extraction and had done everything: in her youth she had studied with Max Reinhardt, and had only recently given up flying planes. (Her late husband, too, had been a pilot.) At nineteen Olga had flown planes in Argentina and wherever, and still had that sense of adventure which made her both proud of and impatient with the whole Swedish social and economic management success: she was determined not to be trapped, and she saw in us free spirits like herself.

Her idea was simple. There was, opening in Stockholm in a couple of days, to be a conference on the use of the sea, a UN affair with delegates from all over the world. Why not become a representative for my island? Better still, why not *invent* an island, become its representative, and attend the conference to defend my little bit of sea? And be paid handsomely for it. (The theory was that these international bureaucracies would be more likely to rubberstamp than investigate you.)

It seemed a wild idea. With a country, I could invent my own language: who would ever check it out? And measured against Nixon's enormities in Vietnam this would hardly raise the moral hackles of a St. Francis. There were going to be all sorts of people from Pacific islands that no one had ever heard of attending the conference, and they were being put up by the UN at great expense. I, too, come to think of it, had an interest in ensuring the proper use of the sea. Shouldn't be too difficult getting the Geography and History sorted out. (Ruth would come as my American interpreter – for the more audacious the plan the greater the likelihood of success.) Olga and Serge would do their bit, too. As respected Stockholm business people, they would verify not only that the island existed (in case officials looked it up on the map and couldn't find it) but that they, personally, were in the process of building a holiday house there. Serge thought this was going a bit far, but Olga brushed aside his caution as the symptom of youth and a Swedish environment.

Naturally, back in our own flat, we dismissed the whole thing as impossible. We had to remind ourselves that Olga and Serge were protected in this society, and that Olga's enthusiasms were not necessarily meant to be followed through: they were really ways of stating her position as a privileged rebel. It was like the questions she threw out at dinner in her Nacka flat. One night we were discussing the American draft-dodgers, 40,000 plus, who had congregated in Sweden. Apparently the good people of Stockholm were growing tired of them, or at best bored with them; and I remember in the middle of the conversation Olga turning to me – there were about six others at the table – and asking: *Why do you want to fight wars? It is not amusing.* Well, it was hard now not to remember this tendency towards rhetoric. Would it be amusing for her two days hence if we put her plan into action and fell foul of the powers that be?

By next day, things seemed more positive and I had discovered (not invented) St. Caesare. (We had St. Martin, we had St. Christopher; why not St. Caesare?) St. Caesare would have a French connection, more interesting, say, than the British claims of Barbados and Antigua, or the Anglo-Irish outpost, Montserrat, my own island. Where was it, then?

Well, the thing to do was to put it somewhere and see if it fit. First option was off the coast of Montserrat, with a language that was neither English nor French. Maybe a strong Carib presence (would that mean, perhaps, placing it a bit further South among the Windwards, nearer to the South American coast? Deal with that later. Had to remember not to take Columbus's accounts too seriously: the fellow was in the habit of lying to his *Journal*). The island had to be close enough to a larger island, or loosely associated with it, to make its political status ambiguous – so that my case for representing it could be made. So let's for the moment leave it near to Montserrat, possibly allied to it. That means it had to be smaller than Montserrat or with a fraction of the population (another reason why the map makers missed it). So if Montserrat was – what was it? – 39 square km and 10,000 people, St. Caesare might have to be something like, say, 25 square km and – you have to be careful here – 1,500 people. 2,500 people? That would make it too small to fight over, to want to claim, but at the same time, with 2,500 people, a strong enough tug on the world's guilt. Did it have a capital? That could be decided later, when its history was worked out. First thing was to check the history of the islands, to find out again just when the French and English (and others) had fought over them. Embarrassing, that I didn't have this sort of information in my head. I couldn't really afford to call friends in London to discuss it.

Perspective is a strange thing when you're in a foreign country; suddenly, things that would be impossible at home seem so easy, so much the fun thing to do. But at the same time, we couldn't make fools of ourselves: we couldn't come back next day appearing to take this thing seriously only to find that Olga and Serge had forgotten about it, had consigned it to yesterday's practical joke which was no longer amusing today.

And true enough, Serge seemed to have forgotten: he called us, it seemed, for no particular reason but to ramble on about McGovern and Nixon, and to give us the 'good news' that Olga had got us a poetry reading at Uppsala University, out of town. He also took the opportunity to warn us not to eat any more strawberries and blackberries that we had been picking at the side of the road, as they were certain to have lead deposits. Then he said that Olga had news for us. (He lived in Stockholm but spent a lot of time at Olga's place out in Nacka.) Olga, in a very business-like way, then proceeded to give us the names of the UN people in charge of the conference programme.

'I think you're in,' she said, 'but you must give us the name of the island.'

'St. Caesare.'

'Good. A good neutral-sounding island.' But she was happy with it. 'Sounds familiar,' she said. 'They'll all think they've heard of it. By tomorrow, they will remember when they spent a holiday there. Where is it?'

'Caribbean. Eastern Caribbean.'

'Isn't the Caribbean risky? Too well known?'

'That way they'll be too embarrassed to take out their maps and search for it.'

She liked that. She would pass the information on to the

authorities and confirm that we were staying with her for a few days because of links forged on the island. She invited us to dinner at Nacka, not that night because she was seeing business people from out of town and we had a lot of homework to do, but the following night to refine our plans.

Immediately, the mists started clearing on the mountains of St. Caesare, particularly the central range, the spine of the island shutting off either the eastern or the western side from Montserrat. (That began to give me the island's shape.) Time to go to work.

We had less than two days: I headed for the British Council library, Ruth for the American Embassy in search of enough 'history' to pin down our island. In the harsh but not unfriendly light of the Stockholm afternoon we had time to reflect that, should the worst come to the worst, Swedish jails were probably the least oppressive in the world: they might force you to *study* and improve your Swedish; or to laugh at their jokes; or to grow a weak mouth and a little blonde moustache, but we'd heard of worse punishments. And we couldn't, you know, give the impression that we were nearer to Serge, in the spirit of adventure, than to Olga who had danced with Max Reinhardt, and piloted planes in Argentina when she was nineteen, and now ran the Tampax factory in Stockholm. I was a few years older than Serge; I had to take risks. It was now or never. I was prepared to offer Ruth a way out, should it go wrong; to say that I was the impostor, and that I had lied to her, the translator, about the set-up, but she wouldn't hear of it; and we thought her long white dress would carry conviction in the Swedish summer. So, we had the name of the island: what we needed now was a history that would give us the language and the nature of the island settlements. We were in favour, as I've said, of some sort of French connection.

St. Caesare would be spelt differently from the village in the south of France (St. Cezaire) to show colonial distance. If the island was French in name, it was more likely to be British in fact. I couldn't make it, like Guadeloupe and Martinique, constitutionally part of France and still come to represent it as a separate entity at the conference, unless we were fighting France for independence; and it would take me more than two days to organise that. So, it would be British with a French name. I didn't want to be too hasty and rule out other connections – Dutch, Spanish etc. I wanted the island to have a more lively mix of cultures than Antigua and Montserrat and Barbados. There was much checking in encyclopaedias and reference-books ahead, with Ruth, in her element, going off to find out what she could about pre-Columbian languages.

A good day. We celebrated our success with dinner at a French restaurant in the old town – a bit nervous, in case Olga found out and concluded that we weren't really *that* short of money; but then, very soon, someone else would be picking up the tabs. We hadn't yet sorted the mass of information we'd collected, much of which would inevitably be discarded. But already, the quest was on. I was thinking, for instance, of the symbolic importance of key dates in St. Caesare's history; how good it would be if they were to coincide with interesting happenings elsewhere in the world. Not so much the independence of other countries and that sort of thing, but the births, say, or deaths of famous people; so although I didn't yet know what would be relevant (because we hadn't worked out the island's history) I kept my eye on a whole range of dates: Jan. 27th (birth of Mozart – was that too pretentious?), or the deaths of Dostoyevsky & Yeats (Dec. 28th). That sort of thing. I was also working on the theory of a St. Caesarian input into Third World Studies, its intellectual objection to countries celebrating their independence, on the grounds that that, in a strange way, legitimised their past slavery. But this would come later, when I discovered the island's cultural activists.

We rather enjoyed our meal.

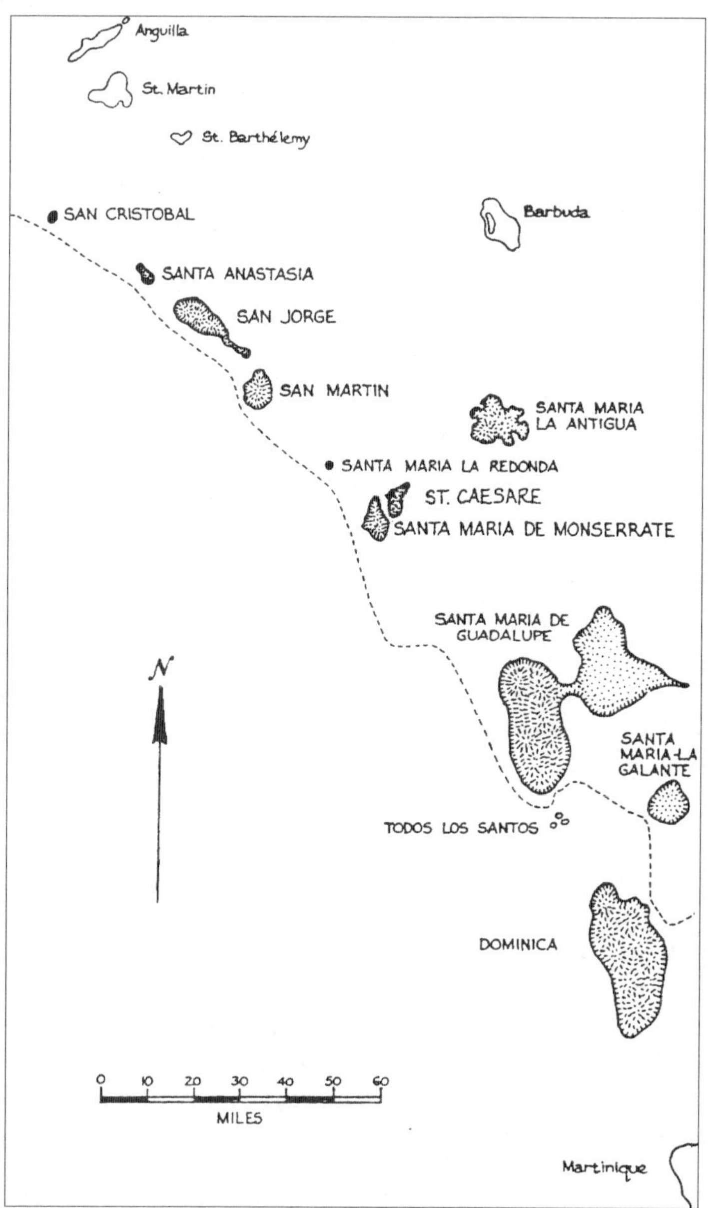

Anguilla
St. Martin
St. Barthélemy
SAN CRISTOBAL
Barbuda
SANTA ANASTASIA
SAN JORGE
SAN MARTIN
SANTA MARIA
LA ANTIGUA
SANTA MARIA LA REDONDA
ST. CAESARE
SANTA MARIA DE MONSERRATE
SANTA MARIA DE
GUADALUPE
N
SANTA
MARIA-LA
GALANTE
TODOS LOS SANTOS
DOMINICA
0 10 20 30 40 50 60
MILES
Martinique

Columbus didn't name it. We know that on his second voyage in 1493, after sighting Dominica (Sunday, November 3rd) he sailed north-west (I had photocopied a map of this at the British Council, I could trace the journey). After Dominica, sailing north-west, he discovered Guadeloupe next morning (November 4th) where he spent some time, generally, bribing the Indians. Six days there, then he continued past the Leeward side of Montserrat (named it Santa Maria de Monserrate after the Saint of a Monastery near Barcelona), then he named Antigua to the east (where he also didn't land) and he named Redonda straight ahead...

So, where are we? Where to place St. Caesare? Columbus sailed on the *Leeward* side of Montserrat. Easy to see Antigua and Redonda after you've got past Montserrat. Columbus didn't name St. Caesare because he didn't *see* it. He couldn't see it because it was on the *Windward* side of Montserrat (also, that's the rough side, another reason why he didn't take that route). So maybe St. Caesare was flat, and that helped the old Italian adventurer not to see it on the wrong side of Montserrat (though *one,* flat island, Antigua, with its lack of water and wilting vegetation was enough: St. Caesare would have to be mountainous). St. Caesare was mountainous but so *close* to Montserrat that even if Columbus saw its peaks he would think they were part of the same land-mass (like the two islands of Guadeloupe, seen from afar).

At dinner the following night, Olga wanted to know if there was malaria on the island. I said there wasn't. Olga said it was a pity because we might have been able to apply to some Agency or other for its eradication. I surprised myself by wishing that Serge were here tonight so that I wouldn't have to take on his role of restraining Olga. What I gave her, though, what I put on the island to accommodate her friends were a golf course and tennis courts, and then we pressed on. I still had to work out who lived there; even the island's representative didn't yet have a name. Olga confirmed that securing tickets to the UN Conference was a formality as soon as we supplied details of our island, and she seemed curiously impatient with us holding out for the right details. Ruth, for instance, was a bit subdued by her lack of progress on the language issue, and we had to keep such anxieties to ourselves.

Back at the flat the work continued. Ruth finally got on to someone who worked at Oslo University and had done research on Carib languages; and she set up a meeting for the next morning. Oslo wasn't far away, yet there was concern at spending so much money in preparation when there was no guarantee we'd do it. Back to work: I finally put St. Caesare in position on the photocopy, the shape would no doubt alter. Columbus didn't land on Montserrat because his Arawak guides told him that it had been depopulated by Caribs: were they telling him the truth? Might not the Montserrat Caribs be passing the time on St. Caesare? Or some Arawaks, even – trying to outwit the conqueror? That would influence the language. (I kicked myself that all I knew about languages was gleaned from a couple of very general books by the likes of Mario Pei; I hadn't even done my homework as an EFL teacher. Ruth was, good-naturedly, contemptuous of this.)

Continuing the 'History of St. Caesare.'

1625. When the Englishman, Thomas Warner, from his base in St. Kitts (St. Christopher) received a royal patent from Charles I to colonise Montserrat (as well as Nevis and Barbados), St. Caesare must have been part of the package but, as there were Caribs there, it was never really subdued, unlike Montserrat where Warner dumped his Irish dissidents. Still, the Governors of Montserrat – the Briskets and Osbornes and Stapletons (my own name as it happens, Stapleton) – must have governed St. Caesare in name only. (They couldn't entirely keep the French out.)

1665-67. During the war between England and Holland over control of the slave trade, the Dutch raided the wrong end of Montserrat – Plymouth, the leeward side – and so missed St. Caesare. (Pity, in a way, because we'd now have budding Rembrandts all over the place, or failing that, a main street called – let's look it up – Wijelgracht – though I suppose the fact of South Africa modifies the interest in things Dutch: so the island has a town, to be named later). Anyway... a few of the Irish prisoners from St. Kitts escape to St. Caesare bringing their French influence with them. (They had, after all, collaborated with the French and must have made wine together.) Then when the French took Montserrat, briefly, in '67 and were defeated, a handful also settled (men? families?) in St. Caesare – important for our wine industry. (Later, there will be agitation on the island for local people rather than foreigners to design our wine labels.) There would have to be cotton and sugar-cane as well – one has to be realistic – but St. Caesare would be known for its wine, just as Montserrat was for its lime juice.

But things weren't smooth. The barbarous English wiped out St. Caesare's wine industry. This, let's say, happened under the Coderington regimes. (The Coderingtons were a father and son team, Governor and Governor General of the Leeward Islands respectively, from 1680 to the 1720s.) They wiped out the wine industry and established a fort, which bore (bears) their name, Coderington. (Or should it be the name of the sovereign? No, they were a law unto themselves, the Coderingtons.)

Coderington. The name of our town. That's where I'm from. *St. Caesare,* the island; *Coderington,* the town. If it's a fort, it would have to be on high ground, somewhere away from the coast. When the French retook the island (as they did Montserrat, 1782-84) they destroyed Coderington, naturally, built another town elsewhere (where?) and re-established the island's wine industry. *Voila. Good afternoon, Ladies and Gentlemen. I am from St. Caesare in the Caribbean. This is my translator, Ruth Krim, the well-known linguist and anthropologist. My name...*

Ruth was translating into something that wouldn't have fooled even the most sedentary of UN bureaucrats, though I suppose fellow delegates wouldn't care one way or the other. (I had a plan to deflect any other West Indians who might happen to be attending the conference and be impelled to ask awkward questions. Also, I had to decide on my name. In the light of all this it seemed a little frivolous of Ruth to insist that she be described not as a linguist but as a 'student of linguistics'.)

We weren't ready, but the time had come. Ruth wasted a day in Oslo learning about Indonesian and Melanesian languages and nothing about the way Caribs spoke. She had other interviews lined up, but we had neither the time nor the money to pursue them. We just had to do the best with what we had. Olga proved efficient to the point of recklessness: she had the promise of official tickets to the conference for me and my translator. All she needed was my name.

'I'll have one by tomorrow.'

'No good. I can settle it now if you have a name. But they must do the thing properly. Or you won't have your tickets tomorrow morning. Any name will do.'

That's what was beginning to rile me about Olga, 'Any name will do'.

'How much time have I got?'

'Pewter, the Conference starts at 9.30. The woman is waiting for me to ring her back.'

Responding to Olga's pressure, not taking the time to think it through, but flicking through all the possibilities I'd thought of and rejecting them, again, I suddenly remembered a man I'd met in St. Vincent a couple of years before, and he had one of those unplaceable, uncolonised names: that was it.

'Castine,' I said.

There was a slight pause. 'Sounds OK... Castine what?'

'Well, just Castine. Sort of folk... person.'

'I like it', Olga squealed.

I spelt it for her.

'And remember, Pewter, you'll have to dress the part.'

Ruth would be all right, she would go as herself, like any up-market translator, and she would remain an American.

I told Olga that I would wear my military-type bush-jacket. What I was really thinking was that Ruth didn't have a work permit, and doing this under her own name might be an additional risk, but I kept that to myself and thanked Olga for the tickets. So, it was Castine, then.

I couldn't resist trying out surnames. Dupont. Roderigues. de Haag. Parkinson... I was wasting time. 9.30 was only a few hours away.

It was important to have a good night's sleep, yet at one o'clock in the morning we were still going frantic – Ruth and myself, that is. I was putting everything down on paper now because I knew I wouldn't remember it. Castine of Coderington seemed more naked than before he had a name. But at least I had the details of our new town, Coderington being, unhappily, still a village.

The town is Barvill, a corruption of de Barreville, after the French General De Barre, who crushed the English in the Second Dutch War (1665-67) and captured St. Caesare and Montserrat; and had a French-Irish settlement on the plains – north-west side of the island adjoining Montserrat – before the whole thing was returned to the British at the Treaty of Breda (1667). Anyway – after the destruction of the grapes, when the remaining French moved to the extreme, rugged, Eastern point of the island, called Look Out or 'Smuggler's Point' – Barvill was colonised by wealthy Montserrat families (some of whose men had worked in Cuba or Haiti or Panama etc., even in the oil refineries in Aruba, and on return found Montserrat too constricting). Then, in the '50s these families moved out again to Canada and America – and, of course, Britain – leaving the place virtually a squatters' camp. The turnaround came in the '60s when rich North Americans started settling there, with Government encouragement...

I didn't like the look of Barvill, on paper; so, after some deliberation, I changed it to 'Barville'. That looked better. *Felt* better. Now, to other matters: was I to protest about the decimation of our shellfish industry or about the military pollution of our waters by the war-machines of big (and you know who) states? Had to have a clear idea of what we produced, so that I could defend it. Two o'clock in the morning; this was ridiculous: I needed a drink; I needed to take a walk. It was still bright outside, you could read by it. I expect Olga and Serge would be sleeping the sleep of the just: they had actually been promised reimbursement by the UN for having given us accommodation in Sweden. (As a long-time UN supporter, I didn't much appreciate this, but that wasn't a priority now.)

I came back to the flat feeling renewed. Outside, I'd drifted into a nearby park, and there, sitting on a bench, in the middle of this bright night, was a little old lady, tastefully dressed, a beatific smile on her face. Surely, they couldn't turn vicious at half past nine if, as the Americans say, we fouled up!

But the aim was not to test their tolerance, and Ruth, whose nerve held, was grilling me again.

'Land area.'

'35 square km.'

'*35* or 25?'

'Oh, who's going to care? I thought I'd make it a bit more like Anguilla. Just to make other things easier to remember. What's Anguilla again?'

'Is that one of the Virgin Islands?'

'Oh, this is impossible.'

'Pewter, I suggest you just make up a figure and stick to it.'

'Yes. OK. 35 Whatsit whatsit.'

She adjusted the figure on her clipboard; it's her demeanour that's going to get us through this.

And how do you account for the small population?' She asked in the most disinterested way. 'Emigration?'

'All right, you win. Make it, whatever… *25*'.

She corrected that before continuing. 'Population?'

'1,500.' That didn't change. 'Make that 2,500.' She wrote it down.

'Type?'

'You mean like Archbishops and actresses? Sorry… Black. Sort of. Basically black. A few others. Expats. A few from way back. French. Irish. Then more recently – apart from the North Americans, of course – a trickle from France, Guadeloupe, relatives of the wine-growers.'

'Livestock?'

'… And don't forget the Caribs. They're there somewhere. Writing their own history. Telling us how Columbus lied about them.'

'Yes, dear. Livestock.'

'Livestock… Oh, cattle, sheep: the usual. Maybe goats. All those islands have goats. That's why we're the best hill-walkers in the world. Come to think of it, they should have that in the Olympics as a sport. Goat-track walking… Maybe we should forget about the sheep. Other islands don't seem to have them, maybe foot-rot or something…

But chickens and maybe ducks. A duck cuisine thing, speciality of the island.'

'Flamingos?'

'Flamingos? Good God, no, that's a dance... Flamingos. That's further North. And South, come to think of it. Make a good stamp, though, flamingo. You wouldn't really want to put a duck on your stamp. God, look at the time.'

'Nearly there. Level of exports. In EC dollars?'

'Do we need that?'

'Well, they might ask what you export.'

'What and *where?* Fish, of course. Lobsters and things. To the hotels of Montserrat and Antigua. Maybe even breaking into the Guadeloupe market... And now I suggest we finish this off in the morning when we're fresh.'

'What if we over-sleep?'

'No chance. Besides, Castine's usually up at the crack of dawn... You know, talking of the Virgin Islands, shouldn't we have some basket-making for St. Caesare... like they do up there?'

'D'you want to change that again?'

'No no, you're right. Let's just...get on.

'Average level of exports?'

'I'm sorry, I've just gone blank.'

'We've worked out the average of five small islands at... $150,000 EC.'

'Sounds OK to me. Mark us down as the sixth small island. Next.'

'Industry.'

'None. I would say a bit of commerce rather than industry. Except the wine, of course. Bit of salt. Cotton products. And shellfish. We've set our face against tourism.'

'Well, all that's left to decide now is the level of overseas Aid; British Government grant...'

'We'd just say for things like that it still counts as part of Montserrat; so refer to the Montserratians. It's got a

Governor rather than a Commissioner. Or, rather, it's in-between. A political condominium. Its status is being renegotiated. But amicably. Hence the lack of headlines. But more British than French.'

'That means it's the British Queen who's Head of State and not your good friend, M. Pompidou?'

'Afraid so. *Hélas.* Simpler that way.'

'That's it. Tomorrow morning you can decide on Castine's profession.'

'It's already tomorrow morning.'

Eight o'clock in the morning and feeling worse, predictably, than if we hadn't slept. Must leave the house just after nine; the point was to arrive with the bulk of the delegates so as not to draw attention to ourselves. Ruth and I are treating this like any other professional job, an average day in the life of... I turn on the radio in the kitchen (Ruth is barricaded in the bedroom practising phrases of a language I'm not allowed to hear: I don't have full confidence in this aspect of it, but I have to show support). I turn on the radio, the World Service with its update on Nixon's blockade of North Vietnam, with the wranglings of Fischer and Spassky on when and where they're going to play their Chess Championship and mention of the UN-sponsored Conference of the Sea opening in Stockholm this morning... I switch off quickly, pleased that Ruth hasn't heard it, and busy myself with toast.

Ruth came out of the bedroom, agitated.

'I can't wear this dress,' her white dress, 'I just can't wear it.'

'Why, it looks very nice.'

'Pewter, will you please take this seriously!' But she quickly recovered and asked what was on the news.

'Oh, you know, the usual. Nixon. Vietnam. Fischer giving Spassky a hard time... Oh yes, Angela Davis acquitted...' But our minds were elsewhere. Ruth handed me a piece of paper with what looked like a poem on it, three stanzas.

'What's this?'

'That's as much as we can cope with today. You've got nine lines. Short lines, remember. Promise. Three lines to say who you are, where you're from...'

'Eh?'

'*Three* to agree with something and three to disagree... This one's the agreement line and the other two are just ceremonial.'

'*uuyeewang...*' I was stumbling over the first word.

'And then I'll do the translations.'

'Hang on, hang on: *uuyeewang mörö wiinong iiknabairong...* Ruth, *come on!*'

'You just have to say it quickly.'

'Quickly!'

'It doesn't matter, they won't be expected to understand; they'd be waiting for the translation. And it won't come to that anyway, they're not likely to point at you first thing and ask you to make a long speech. Just remember that you don't speak English, that way they can't cross-examine you.'

'Everyone in the West Indies speaks English.'

'Or you can always come down with a sore throat.' But she betrayed her anxiety by changing the subject. 'What about Castine, has he got a profession?'

'I can't say this. It's better to make up something as you go along.' I was still looking at the paper.

'We'll practice on the way. Has Castine got a profession?'

'No'... Then, 'Definitely not an artist, you know, not someone who paints or sings or plays an instrument... Unless it's one of those, you know, plantation-type flutes. Better still, one of those little boxes filled with, whatever, pebbles... *uuyeewang...*'

'The thing is to get a rhythm.' She demonstrated; and then it did sound like a language.

Then the phone rang and we looked at each other, knowing that Olga's confident good wishes would set us back a bit.

In her 'working' trousers and light blouse, smart jacket over her arm, Ruth looked confident and slightly severe, the glasses, hair brushed back and pursed lips adding to the image of the efficient translator. She promised not to laugh, for her companion Castine, the 'herbalist', representative from St. Caesare, was dressed in her long, white dress, with a bush-jacket on top.

'Have we got snakes on the island?' she asked in her professional way, as I was locking the front door, muttering to myself.

'What's it mean, this line?'

There was a slight pause; Ruth was a bit guarded, and then she translated the first line.

'Upon everybody bestow that which is good.'

We walked down the stairs in silence. At the bottom, Ruth repeated the question about snakes. That seemed to trigger something.

'Good point. Yes,' I said, 'Only St. Kitts doesn't have snakes. The agouti kill the snakes in St. Kitts. The snakes that used to be in St. Kitts… But our snakes aren't poisonous. Not like those in Guyana. Trinidad…'

And we have agreed – all of those concerned – not to talk of what transpired at the conference.

Eighteen Years Later

There are, I'm told, a couple of dozen people who claim to be St. Caesarians. Over the years I've attempted to write a few calypsos for a Castine who doesn't sing, and even to compose a couple of plays for a Castine who doesn't write. I've tried to interest one or two of our poets in having a go at the sort of epic – lament for the Arawak and Carib and African dead, sort of thing – that Castine might well have inspired; but nothing came of this and, to be honest, my own interest in the island waned. Until a few days ago, when I received an official-looking invitation – forwarded from an old address – to attend a conference in Holland. It was to be held at Erasmus University in Rotterdam, and the subject was 'The Communications Revolution & Threat to the World's Indigenous Dialects'; and it was addressed to 'Castine' & Dr. Ruth Krim.

Of course the first thought was of how much better Castine could do it second time around, representing St. Caesare, than he'd done all those years ago in Sweden. If only I knew then what I know now, sort of thing... But it was impossible. I hadn't been in touch with Olga and Serge for years. Olga, if alive, would be, what – 78 years old. Serge, a middle-aged man deep into Tampax. And more to the point, Dr. Ruth Krim and I – well, let's just say we now lived in different countries – she was no longer translating for me. (Though it would be good to fly out to see what had become of Coderington and Barville... and Look Out!)

PRESIDENT HORACE THE SECOND, HOWE

He would be known as HORACE THE SECOND, HOWE, as if he were to be a secular Pope instead of someone running for President. Anyway, that's how he was portrayed on his campaign poster; and he wanted help, the note said, urgently to upgrade his poster campaign from the faded photocopy (enclosed) to something plush and electable. True, he had belatedly secured limited use of a Fax machine on the island, and this was a help, but the length of the campaign demanded something more durable than Fax. In spite of this, he had secured 183 votes after New Hampshire: a triumph for the family.

What to do? He was in St. Caesare, we were in England. St. Caesarians were said to be cursed, either with imagination or with foolishness. All men of a certain generation had come to grief. There was no family whose men – of my father's generation – didn't meet in far-off places like Panama and Haiti and Cuba and America, the sorts of misfortunes that others from other islands dined out on to cheer themselves up. Not that it was all grim. On the contrary, it was just unlikely. (One man in Canada had lived and died a priest, a DD; and had bequeathed the degree to a nephew, a rough boy from Barville, and now the boy was said to be very sleek and convincing in his clerical collar, preaching tolerable sermons to his congregation in Toronto. Whereas others might be embarrassed, this *Reverend* had the confidence of the DD behind him. That was the St. Caesare quality for you. Even if they caught up with him in the end and did their worst, he would have proved his pedigree.)

It had long been accepted on the island (which we had abandoned over thirty years ago) that this family was one of the lucky ones, that we had escaped ridicule because my father had managed to die in Europe in the War; and that that was an OK way to go. (Those who claimed he was alive and well in some obscure European country, bringing up a new family, were just being Silly.)

But now here was Horace being true to type. What made it worse was that Horace was a man our age, more or less, this or that side, just, of being 50. And he was family. There was no point in disowning him, because once you got back to the island there was no place to hide. Or worse: there was no place for the island to hide from its sons who sought to embarrass. Living abroad didn't save you. So we would have to respond in some way to Horace's bid for the White House, something he was doing for all the family.

Someone had said, wearily, that the only value to growing older was that we wouldn't have Horace on our back for ever. That was over a decade ago, when he was still in Europe. He had contacted us at the old family house in Kilburn, and it was some time before the message got to my mother in Upton Park. He had written from Germany – maybe it was a telegram, I can't remember now – asking for *bread*. This was embarrassing. My mother had taken the message literally, and thought that the boy, marooned in Germany, wasn't eating. (This may well have been true.) But she thought that sending bread through the post was somewhat demeaning. You did this only to a down-and-out; a vagrant – or perhaps to a nation at war: you couldn't do this to family. So she decided that a compromise would be to send cake. A home-made cake. A cake suggested something wholesome, something that you could legitimately acknowledge – a birthday, *a birth!* A cake could signify the passing of an exam, or the remembering of those who were no longer with us.

We liked the idea of sending food-parcels to Germany in the late 1970s, but as we weren't *all* about to bake cakes for Horace, we sent on ahead of the packet a few pounds, in case he had to pay to get the cake through customs. This was for my mother's benefit. We didn't want her cake to be eaten by some overgrown Customs *Führer* whose name we didn't know. The cake, evidently, lasted Horace for several years before he had cause to contact us again, this time from the South of France. What was he up to now? Well, there he was erecting wooden benches on hillsides in the *Alpes Maritimes,* to commemorate a dead ancestor, our great aunt Augusta. Augusta Stapleton. Aunt Augusta had died when we were children, and was generally thought to have been a 'good person', and had a well-tended tombstone in the family plot at St. Anne's. But Horace now claimed that our great aunt had been an early campaigner for Peace, and that's why he was erecting 'peace' benches to her in her spiritual home, the South of France: would we help? This time we didn't send a donation: my mother was too arthritic to bake cakes.

He had spent some time in America.

Of course, time had passed, my mother had died; we looked at these things differently now. This was between my brother and me; no need to bother the rest of the family, the in-laws, particularly. It irritated us that he had written to my mother knowing that she had died. That seemed, in an obscure way, to challenge our own sense of loyalty. So in the end, without openly acknowledging it, we decided to proceed as if on her behalf, as if she were present.

'Did he take out American citizenship when he was over there?' This is why we banished in-laws, whose new-found *naïveté,* out-of-character solicitousness, and oozing of concern for this semi-detached member of the family didn't ring true. Horace had been born in the American Virgin Islands, just as my brother had been born in Aruba: we were all pioneers.

'Could you run for President of America from St. Caesare?' The person who wanted to know this was no longer present. But naturally, we had said that you could; that America had no doubt taken over the island quietly, while no one was looking, as it had done one of those little islands off the coast of Haiti. Who knows? Who cared? What no longer surprised us was that Horace had entered the 1992 race as a Democrat, had picked his running-mate (a woman with a German name who taught, apparently, Afroaesthetics at Georgetown University) and together they had got 183 votes in New Hampshire. Vice President Nina Wells-Halterbush. (Was this a joke at Bush's expense?)

Was he getting worse? The test of his getting worse was whether he was marginally more credible than last time. We had been taken to the edge of credibility in this very matter in an article in the paper, *The Independent,* which had made fun of the also-rans in this year's Presidential elections. (There had been, incidentally, no mention of Horace!) But there had been many candidates who, if no more serious than Horace, seemed to have a coherent enough message, whether it was the reform of alcoholics, or universal Clean Eating; and quite a few had something of an organization behind them; and yet, very few of them had got as many as 183 votes in New Hampshire. Who were these 183 people who had voted for Horace? You couldn't think that a country was that *large,* to account for this. But then, on reflection, you realised that successive rulers of America had polled more than 183 votes, and you began to be very angry that Horace representing the family, hadn't done better. But then a chap who wasn't on the spot to campaign was at a disadvantage; and we knew nothing of the crowd-pulling skills of Ms. Nina Wells-Halterbush.

One Presidential candidate seemed to have a more convincing reason than Horace not to campaign in person: he was in prison. His campaign literature claimed, mysteriously, that Richard Nixon had also campaigned for the presidency from gaol, and had pardoned himself when he had made it to the White House. This new Republican hopeful promised to do the same for himself the day he took over. Horace, from St. Caesare, had beaten this man out of sight.

Had my mother been right about Horace? She had held on to the dream of St. Caesare as something special. St. Caesare was like no other Caribbean island, like no other place. Her husband, dying in far-off Europe in, maybe, '45, wasn't just another dupe or opportunist. Or more understandably, someone prodded by lack of opportunity at home to abandon family and risk life abroad. To her, he exemplified the island's spirit of adventure, which saw its men, over the years, choose graves in far-off continents, long part of our vocabulary. Even that had borne fruit: strangers, young and curious, this or that colour, trickling back to the island of their fathers. But each family had to perform its own miracle. She despaired of her children, her sons, particularly. One was a teacher; another wore a suit to prove that his job wasn't manual. They had grown indistinguishable from others, a sort of protection for them. For her, it was betrayal of the island. She couldn't, on her own, keep the spirit of St. Caesare alive. She had held open house, however difficult the circumstances; she had vowed never to live in any house but her own, and had managed that, except for a few weeks when the transaction was going through; she had... Oh, but the children hated her to go on like this. It embarrassed them.

Not that she was taken in by Horace. The boy was a disgrace. Lucky his mother wasn't alive to see what he had become. They said he no longer washed his clothes, that his teeth needed fixing. Had he left it too late to go back to the woman – was it in France or Germany? – who had borne his children, and maybe even married him?

This was silly; this wasn't then, this was now. My brother and I were the ones dealing with this. We had no right to call up the spirit of my mother, and then abuse her. She thought Horace, in his idiocy, did more for St. Caesare than we did. Let's leave it at that. He had sent us (her) a list that well-wishers had contributed to his campaign:

— occasional travel on the St. Caesare-Monserrat ferry
— use of photocopier (occasional)
— secretarial help ('and here the mountain must travel to Mohammed')
— cooked dinners most days (not Sundays)
— Stamps, and occasional use of fax (but no telephone) to communicate with Vice President Wells-Halterbush, in Georgetown.

URGENTLY NEEDED

— access to island radio and, if possible, television. Please send fare with television offers
— fare to (and accommodation in) the U.S. to continue campaigning in person
— help to furnish campaign HQ with own telephone, fax, word processors, and laser printers
— stamps, envelopes, stationery, paper, typewriter, Tipp-Ex (and thinner)
— please send EC$30 *plus* $20 p&p for NOW IS THE HOUR. HORACE THE SECOND, HOWE FOR PRESIDENT
— a suit.

Of course, we're not our mother. We had gone into this, my brother and I. Horace didn't get 183 votes in New Hampshire; he got 183 votes from his supporters round the world (a fair proportion *outside* the United States) when he had announced his New Hampshire candidacy. Apparently, Ms. Wells-Halterbush was still embroiled in legal battles over Horace's credentials to be President. But the American expatriates in St. Caesare and surrounding islands showed that they thought he was more qualified than the rascals who harassed them from a home they had fled.

Was Horace getting worse or was he getting better? Of course he was getting worse, and in ways that disturbed us, implicated us, even. It was obvious that running for President was Horace's latest calling card. A stray comment by another Presidential hopeful gave us a clue to this. She was described in the paper as a lady 'with butterfly glasses', and she had an unpronounceable name. This lady, unemployed, who hailed from Florida, was at a disadvantage in having to correct her name with a felt-tip pen because it had been incorrectly spelt on her posters. When asked what form her campaign would take, she had said: 'A lot of it is by private invitation to people's homes.' Now, that accounted for Horace's 'cooked dinners'. There were a lot of American expatriates in St. Caesare and across the water in Montserrat who would be too guilty to turn away a genuinely local specimen, if he turned up with a placard and a manifesto. Call it a form of mugging, it was much gentler than what they might have expected in Rochester or Miami. We knew what his apologists would say – that Horace, in his absurd way, was preventing these newcomers from taking over, with too easy a conscience, the home that the rest of us had abandoned. It was an old argument. We didn't have to challenge it. But we weren't so neurotic to deny him support because of that.

So how to do it? One of his – 63? – fellow no-hopers for

President had drafted an unknowing Governor Mario Cuomo of New York as her running mate: that put a gloss on her homelessness, on her campaign transport, which was a bicycle. Another hopeful – a multi-millionaire this time – managed to buy his votes at $593 each. At the other end, spectacular no-hopers like Bill Clinton and George Bush had gamely bought up the media and the crowds. In the light of all this, how to come to the aid of Horace without admitting guilt or losing our sense of perspective? A cake was, as always, too much trouble. We fancied the idea of sending an old suit (as requested) – and that, paradoxically, is what my mother might well have recommended. But we had to move on. In the end, we decided to club together and get him a word-processor or a laser printer.

3: FROM *SOMETHING UNUSUAL* (1984)

DIGGING

The name of the island has been lost, forgotten; in the basement, Sarah (I am satisfied with the name, I worked it out my way) is still being tortured: her screams are muffled but I can hear them. What is puzzling is that they do not keep me awake. I hear them, as it were, fleetingly, or in moments of inattention. I am speculating about what I have become, giving myself the benefit of the doubt.

'It's nothing,' she says, my companion, anticipating me. 'Go to sleep.'

She is getting careless, not thinking me mad, but having to pretend, to keep up appearances; and willing to let me know it.

'I am not mad,' I say, ritually, no longer alarmed how unimportant it is to say the wrong thing.

And I can hear her down there being tortured.

I'm surprised how transparent I've become. She counters my thought. 'Don't let Sarah come between us. Leave her where she is.' This is delivered entirely without venom. 'We haven't got a basement.'

If we did have a basement, though, and I could still hear what I was hearing down there, I... well, I would go down wouldn't I, and investigate (I don't know this for sure, but there's only one way to find out: mould that (little?) area of uncertainty into something firm and resolute and go down digging...) Too purposeful, this shaping of my thoughts, belying the suspicion that for most of the time they were disorganised and drifting, of no more interest than rainclouds. Anyway, out of this came the reality of the basement, or at least the possibility of dating the enterprise.

'When will you start digging your little hole?' she asked next morning, still managing to retain the same crazy thread.

I agreed I meant to start digging (the agreement was almost as good as the act). She created the usual little difficulties, but choosing her ground carefully, knowing I would reciprocate in a condescending but gentle way – like with the fears of a heavily pregnant wife – she pointed out the problems of trying to find out what was 'down there' of how far down was 'down there': and wouldn't we lose contact with the house if we were forced to probe too far? Wouldn't we end up demolishing the house?

I understood her fears, and tried to give chauvinistic assurances about the house. Later, she ridiculed the notion, crude and arrogant, of demolishing the house: she had expressed fears, she claimed, that I would end up *destroying* (not the same, is it?) the house. I took little interest in the distinction, and conceded. Others were to revive this dilemma generations or centuries later.

Here we go again; a good idea, you see, getting its way; and I'm ready to pursue it now. A word of explanation: I am in another time but my purpose is identical with the purpose of the person I'm claiming to be (the original died, murdered I think, with his companion). I continued the digging. I hoped to return to the original concept of the basement, but the project, by the time I came along, had already accommodated itself to the idea of *hole:* a minor casualty, but we learn to live with them. The work progressed or regressed over the (years or centuries?) years or centuries, whenever I (and there appears to have been a few of me) happened to come along on successive years or centuries – not only me, perhaps – but any chance hole-worshipper or subterranean necrophile. The present digger earns his legitimacy by taking over the name, the personality, the *obsession* of the one who started it all after he heard Sarah being tortured. It worked.

It worked too well; for consciousness not only suffused me, but faithfully recreated that very first companion who had scoffed.

'It's taking such a long time, your little hole,' she now said, careful not to criticise: she spoke rather to her priests, her dog, never to me. From time to time, I would register, not pleasure of course, but satisfaction as the skeletons of dogs and maybe priests told us we were on the right track.

I had perhaps lost my vanity. I took no credit in having breathed ancient life back into the woman. My idea had merely been to make myself fully conscious of the *genesis* of the hole, the basement; and that, alas, included the lady who had not heard Sarah, or had forgotten, or had played the part to humour me, or... Naturally, I was now paying for this success.

She recognised me, of course, as the one who had started the hole (not the basement, but never mind). She took no notice of the centuries of reconstruction (If she had challenged me on this, to plead that years only had passed, not centuries, I'd be prepared to discuss it). But this was as it should be, a bitch to perfection: she, my creature, reaching over the gap to our first companionship.

There were enough ego-traps there for me to fall into, to solve my problems (as my ancestors, I'm told, had done), but ego had, I think, been put to other use. The wreck of our house proved some sort of point for her. She continued to obstruct me, to work against me, using kind words, in the end even unleashing a school of philosophers to distract me: all this helped to confirm my status of *digger.*

Her house-wifely jibes were now oven-baked in jargon or crumpled and directionless like the weekly washing. She called to me from the top of the hole, having accepted advice that the last-heard, mutually-shared sound was the one to pierce, to annihilate the gap, the space, the *wilfulness* separating what *was* and what *is* between us, in this grand scheme of ours. Every day (year, century) she offered new suggestions.

She offered me: the sound of a child being childlike.

She offered me a *word,* built to last, impossible to decode; but nevertheless, seeming to admit progress towards its solving.

She offered me (in the form of a priest) a full-stop. The object/subject remained curled in his foetal position for, let's say, decades, urging forth the *sound* of the full-stop, impressive in its calm, knowing, as we all did, that it was working against, well, some sort of clock.

Yet another lifeline was the sound of dog lapping (milk?) or licking (face?). She built up a reputation of being *good* to me.

It was difficult, you see, to proceed. The lady, as I've said, was no part of my plan; and she, with her cunning, obscured the sound of Sarah being tortured. For a time we had to reinvent Sarah to give ourselves a reason for going on, but even this began to pall and I suspect we might have shelved the project altogether if Sarah hadn't opportunely returned, more anguished than before, as if making up for lost time, plaintive, accusing and *near.* It is said by some of the cynics that the lady herself somehow managed to impersonate Sarah to keep us going, but I do not know. I no longer knew what she was capable of.

The rains came and came (or I prolonged myself ridiculously on a wet day) and drowned out the voice again, so I yielded, like others, and shifted ground till it came back (we denied trying to prove something about the immortality of Sarah or the logic of holes). Anyway, we found the voices; several diggers now, each tracking his own voice. There was the problem of crowding, the opportunists tending to drift towards an advanced hole, only to be repulsed. Generally, they took it well enough and went elsewhere to prospect. But there were always the odd desperate few who continued to dispute your rights of ownership and started up holes nearby with the constant threat of renewing their claims to yours, whenever it suited them.

Naturally, with the growing number of diggers, with the proliferation of holes, supplementary considerations crept in, till the slow corruption of our purpose was legitimised: the shape, size and depth of holes was the subject of study, sabotage and finally a system of awards. Voices in the holes (always retreating as you approached them) were recorded on a machine, the efficiency and accuracy of which were argued over (it was nearness and not the volume that mattered) and prizes were given. Soon, all leisure pursuits consisted in identifying and imitating the buried voices. All musical instruments were retuned to their pitch; then after a decent interval, destroyed, the better to immortalise the memory into myth.

In spite of protestations, we secretly welcomed these developments, for our blanket opposition to them had the effect of giving our quest a coherence, a widely accepted validity it never quite had. Also, it gained protection and awe, as any institution does which trades on being uncompromising. We even went along with popular rumours that animals, birds and insects (and who knows what else?) would vanish if the sound, in one or other of the holes, wasn't forthcoming: i.e. if they all ceased at once, even for an instant. Odd cranks and philosophers came through to testify that they had witnessed this phenomenon, often late at night, or while on solitary walks, etc.

The fact is that very soon all the sounds that mattered were receptive to the shape, depth and size of the holes; so it was agreed that we who were digging, who had something to live for (who were in tune with the whole?) had outgrown awards; that digging was enough.

The philosophers were becoming redundant. They now clung to the hope that in the right hole, a perfectly-carved grafted mango-tree was to be found. With two philosophers under it. The mango-tree philosophers were holding their breath ready to release it on a deserving world, to quell for ever the conscience of the tortured voice: it would release the diggers. But this would happen only (and on this they were insistent) if the diggers managed to unearth the treasure unharmed. Should the least bruise, scratch or chip be inflicted on the trinity, the absolving breath could never be released (or would turn malignant) and the diggers would have to toil on downwards for centuries maybe, till another layer was reached where the philosophers sat under the mango tree.

Occasionally, the sceptical, or those who felt they had been conned, put the prophesying philosophers to death. Increasingly, sympathisers (those who held out no hope of being diggers) joined them: martyrdom was second best. Others, to maintain their self-respect, or to stimulate their curiosity, or to present their credentials as lovers of Beauty and Truth, as victims of sensibility, massed at the edges of the deepest caverns, and waited for the lure of the sound; and hurled themselves over, giving a voice-accompaniment as they fell: these were solemn occasions, there was no element of competition. The perfect fall was an end in itself.

But corruption was hinted at. Soon all falls were perfect, the dying voices indistinguishable from one another, indistinguishable from Sarah's. It was being rumoured that in outlying holes, brutal and competitive sessions were being held, under the most alien of conditions; and only those who passed that test were allowed to graduate to the real holes.

Well, perhaps. But we couldn't really tell. They were all very good. Life was perfect.

THE PIG WAS MINE

So, my feats of childhood weren't, after all, prodigious. I had laboured under the illusion that my pre-breakfast journeys two miles each way to collect the milk, when I was a child of nine or ten, could earn me similar immunity from the scepticism of the radical consciousness, to the African *walking* barefoot to America to get himself an education. Now, my four-mile hike had turned out to be barely a third of that distance. Also, my cargo, the family milk (to prevent it being siphoned off and watered down) was, unlike your buckets of water and bundles of wet clothes etc., so touchingly non-labour, that it was almost a privilege to perform. And yet, one is drawn to revisit more and more of these childhood landmarks, knowing that one is diminishing oneself. The Sunday-afternoon walk to town by the Grammar School kids – and the island was only seven miles across – didn't perhaps, after all, turn one from country bumpkin into Court sophisticate – from Colonial to Metropolitan, parochial to cosmopolitan being, or whatever such antitheses are currently held to be. Certainly, our afternoon hike wouldn't have made the *Guinness Book of Records.* And although I still suspect that my suitcase was unusually big and heavy, from this distance, something – timidity? self-respect? – dissuades me from investigating it further. This was, in any case, a side issue, not the treble hurdle uppermost in my mind – the one I cleared so devastatingly on my grandmother's steps at an age when it mattered. That was certainly decisive. I suppose there is always an incident, a remembered remark, a fragment of a dream from which one dates 'growing up'. For a friend of mine, it was actually having *listened* to the sermon one Sunday (and not liking it). For me, it was emerging from the auction at my grandmother's Animal Pound, a clear, resourceful, and sacrilegious winner of the pig. And now, back at the scene, I hesitate, wondering if this would prove another act of disinheritance.

I had come to the house – to what had been the house – a marvel that had withstood two hurricanes, the crack in the dining-room wall conspicuous like a fixed, tough grin of pride; or at the very least, a war-wound with a history. The house had impressed us children, because it was already a big house when, in our time, yet another house was added to it, making it a bigger house; and it belonged to my grandmother. Now I stood looking with a sort of complicity at the dilapidated stable that had replaced it, angry that it assumed so accurate an image of a family history. But the steps, the steps leading up to the first floor, were still recognisable, and that was all I needed; the rest of the house was, well, a little painful to contemplate. The back steps led directly to my grandmother's room; she used to sit at the top on the floor of her room, looking out, and from that position, ruled the household. And yet it was strange how restricted her view of the yard had been. It never occurred to us then, that she couldn't *see* everything that went on. Right at the bottom was a little half-step, askew and crumbling, but the recognisable fourteenth step. My grandmother was superstitious, and of course nearly died of fright when she realised that she had spent perhaps two-thirds of her life presiding over a house that had thirteen steps leading up to her room; so she hastily had another one added. There wasn't really room for another step, and the result offended my – I hope – growing aesthetic sensibilities (although this might be an afterthought).

But I was the only one affected, because my grandmother

was lame and didn't go up and down the steps; and I resolved to challenge her by ignoring the step; by stepping *over* it in defiance. This wasn't as easy as it sounded, nor was it merely a technical problem; for my grandmother brooked no challenge to her authority – and certainly not from a ten year old. So going down the steps – and I nearly always ran – I would half-lower the right foot (I'd worked it out carefully: easier with the right foot), but not enough to touch the step, and then hop from the thirteenth step to the ground on my left foot. And my grandmother could only reprove me for cutting my knee etc. when I fell down, not for challenging her authority. I was a little tempted to repeat this now, but you need the authority of a ten year old to take that sort of risk, to make that sort of statement in the absence of an audience. A sprained ankle now, would be a little ignominious.

I caught myself out being excited, nevertheless, in a way that the born loser is before the contest: this time it's going to *work*. For if this little bit of defiance still held currency for me now, perhaps the other thing, the real 'growing up' badge, might yet gleam through the wreckage of the house. I was at the foot of the steps. Good. At the top, thirteen or fourteen steps up, my grandmother reclined on the floor, looking out. Between us, sat Mr. Frederick who had come, as usual, for dinner. The restored house exuded authority; there was the 'thud thud' of Nellie's iron in the 'bread' room downstairs; and outside, Sarah was sweeping the yard with an improvised broom of twigs. It was five o'clock on the afternoon of the auction.

The hen and her chickens were getting in Sarah's way, and she couldn't pelt them too openly because of Mr. Frederick and my grandmother; but from where I was in the dining-room, I could hear her curse them. I had been filling in time. It was one of those sleepy days when everything slowed down; the sickly-sweet smell of the coal-pit smouldering in the pound outside contributed to the general feeling of being drugged; and I had drifted from one lazy game to another, willing the afternoon away. First, I'd been weighing the church collection boxes. (You weighed them on the scales to find out who was ahead. This wasn't as accurate as counting the money, of course, but everyone said what dreadful things would happen if you broke them open.) There were four boxes: mine, both my brothers' and my sister's. Mine was by far the heaviest. No contest. Mine was the heaviest because I was the youngest and my mother did most of my collecting (particularly outside church on Sundays when people couldn't very well refuse; then they were neglected all the week while my mother, brothers and sister were in the town, and only came to see us at week-ends). I was bored with outweighing my big brother (easily) and my sister and other brother combined (slightly); and had gone down to the dining-room to play with the eggs. We had a lot of eggs, and one of my jobs was to turn them over each day in their bowls of sand, so that they would stay fresh. I must have turned them a dozen times that day; and while I was still turning them, I could hear my grandmother sending Sarah (who was sweeping the yard outside) to call me. Naturally, I waited until Sarah came and found me turning the eggs.

I was really quite an old hand at the auctions by then; and had bought my share of goats and sheep. This is how it worked: my grandmother owned the only animal pound in the area, so that any animal caught trespassing in other people's fields – potato, corn, vegetable – was brought to the pound, where it was locked up and fed twice a day. The pound was large and circular with huge stakes planted in the ground at regular intervals, and cross-pieces nailed on. The pieces didn't have to be very close-fitting, because the animals inside were tied anyway. Legally, the pound had to be secure, so there was a gate, which was always (except when we forgot and lied to my grandmother) locked at night. And if in six weeks, the owner failed to claim his animal, then an auction was held to pay for the board and lodge. My grandmother was auctioneer. That's how it came about that I often had to bid on behalf of the house. There was nothing to it, really: you merely outbid everyone else in the yard.

Just two or three weeks earlier, I had bought a goat – little more than a kid – for fifty dollars, and incurred the wrath of the yard. To tell the truth, I was bit bored that day. I had wanted to try out my new wooden top, and couldn't wait to get the bidding over and done with. So when the butcher (he was always there) after feeling the hind legs expertly, raised his bid to one dollar, three shillings, and warned that he wouldn't go higher than two dollars, I promptly put a stop to it by bidding fifty dollars. Fifty dollars ONCE. Fifty dollars TWICE. Fifty dollars THREE TIMES, and the goat was mine. As I said, I was an old hand at it.

But then my grandmother had a revolutionary idea. Today, we had to make a low bid. A *low* bid! Then, didn't we want the pig? Yes, we had to get the pig, but with a low bid; because people might try to make trouble if my bid was too high; did I understand? No dollar bids, just pence – and what's wrong with me, why didn't I listen, didn't I know who was going to preach the sermon next Sunday? Never mind. Never mind. Just try and remember what I was told.

I was a little confused at my grandmother's suddenly shifting interest, until I looked round and saw that the butcher had silently entered the yard: my grandmother had great presence of mind. As they greeted the newcomer, I slipped away to think about the new situation. This was more difficult than weighing collection boxes, or remembering to turn the eggs. It had to be a low bid, and yet, we had to get the pig. What would prevent someone else outbidding me? I couldn't ask for advice now, because apart from the butcher's, I could hear another voice in the yard; they would be beginning any time now... What if I were to bid the same as the last person? If he says one shilling, I'll say one shilling. And every time he raised, I'll raise by the same amount. In the end, we'd have to share it. Would my grandmother be satisfied with *half* a pig? Too late. Too late. They were calling me.

Sarah had brought out the pig, and tied it to a little stake in the yard. I tried to assess the competition. Apart from the butcher, who was serious, there was my cousin who joined in sometimes, but more often just came to look on. Mr. Frederick didn't believe in gambling, but kept his views to himself on occasions like this; and Sarah and Nellie (interrupting her ironing) stood discreetly in the background to make up the numbers. We started promptly today because Mrs. Graham, who was a dangerous woman, was expected to come and make trouble; and everyone wanted to get it over before she arrived.

My grandmother's asking price of two shillings and six pence was immediately raised to one dollar by the butcher. If he was going to be as reckless as this, our plan for a low bid would have to be revised: I glanced at my grandmother, but she was preoccupied.

'I bid a dollar, you know.'

'Give me time to catch my breath.' My grandmother was uncharacteristically irritable, 'I'm an old woman. You say one dollar. That is sucking pig: Where you goin' make dollar on that? Well, I don't hear anybody else bidding. One dollar you say? One dollar ONCE. One dollar TWICE. One...'

'One dollar and a *penny,*' I liked a little bit of tension, and my grandmother knew it.

'One dollar and six pence.' The butcher. He was being aggressive.

Sarah was wiping the chicken dung from her bare feet, on the grass; and looked up to say that Mrs. Graham was coming; and both the butcher and I felt the need for urgency.

'One dollar and seven pence.'

'One dollar one shilling.' He was treading on my bid.

'Dollar, one shilling and a half-penny.'

'Two dollars. I see you bring the time forward, like you wanting to cut out somebody.' Mrs. Graham had arrived like the hurricane, 'You hear my bet, Miss Dove? Howdy everybody. Mr. Frederick, how you keeping? Sarah, bring me a glass of water, child. That hill too wicked... The pig small, eh? It's nothing but a little orphan.'

This stopped the proceedings. Mrs. Graham, who was a gossip, waded right in as if the auction was forgotten. And she started telling a horror story about West Indians in England and thanked the Lord they hadn't come from Montserrat. Then she suddenly asked my grandmother to reprimand Sarah, who had sucked her teeth when she had left to get the glass of water. But my grandmother said they should concentrate on the auction.

'Two dollars six pence. Final offer,' was the butcher's final offer...

'Two dollars nine pence.' Mrs. Graham.

'Two dollars nine pence farthing,' I said, anxious and pleased.

Mrs. Graham started to bid again, but stopped. She took the glass of water from Sarah and, without drinking, put it down on one of the steps; then she surveyed me, my grandmother, and the others for a long time, before demanding to see my money. My grandmother began to tell the others how much repairs to the pound and feed for the animals were costing her, and she didn't see how much longer she could keep it up. And while they were agreeing that times were hard, I searched out a farthing among the string and marbles and nails in my pocket and held it up, implying, I suppose, there was nothing illegal about the farthing. But Mrs. Graham wasn't interested in the farthing; she wanted to see the two dollars-odd.

In that case, I wanted to see her money too.

'All you see Satan?'

'Make her show her money too.'

'All you see the work of the Devil!' All right, then. *There* was her money: she would put down her money. There it was. She held down a five dollar bill on the step with her palm, after waving it briefly. My grandmother became indignant; asked *me* to behave myself, and to be careful how I spoke to big people; and told Mrs. Graham to pick up her money; it wasn't necessary to put her money down on the step; we all knew what a five dollar note looked like. But the dangerous woman insisted that no one should be allowed to bid until he could prove he had the money. My grandmother wanted to limit all this talking during the auctioning, because it was making her forget the last bid, which she was trying to hold in her head.

I wasn't worried any more, because I had an idea: if they all put their money on the step, I could see how much money they had brought with them, then I could drop out of the bidding while their money lasted, and then come in at the end and claim the pig when everyone else was eliminated. It seemed so simple; I wondered if that's what my grandmother was secretly planning. But the butcher came up with a compromise. Let everyone put down a dollar. Just one dollar to prove they were serious. No response. He asked Mr. Frederick's opinion, but Mr. Frederick was too old to have an opinion. As they knew she would, the dangerous woman got her way in the end. The butcher was a bit short of cash and wanted to send Sarah over to his house for some more, but Mrs. Graham said no, and my grandmother surprisingly backed her up. It was getting dark, she said, and she agreed that you would have to drop out when your money ran out. My grandmother said she trusted the butcher (this surprised us all) but that an auction was an auction, and we had to be business-like. Mrs. Graham then turned to me.

'And now Mr. Man,' (I hated the way adults patronised

you) 'You have big mouth. Let me see your big money.'

I was stuffing things back into my pocket, carefully.

'You confusing the child.' *Child!* 'The child just practising.' My grandmother tried to sound impartial.

'There is them that practise on a lot of poor people goat and pig and thing. *Practising* not above the Law!'

'Don't tell the boy anything 'bout Law,' my grandmother countered angrily. 'This is a big house, and if we all out here, who going keep watch on the child, *always* playing with water, *always* catching cold.'

'I glad you tell us is practise because I thought he wanted the pig.'

'We eat meat every week' (grandmother).

'Um. Some of us not so lucky, eh? Some of us not so lucky. Well, here is my money on the step. The pig is mine. This is the ninepence. You can change five dollars, Miss Dove? You better send Sarah to get change.'

No one spoke. Or moved.

'I have the money,' I said.

No one seemed to take this seriously; and finally my grandmother, with bad grace, turned to Mrs. Graham, accepting her claim to the pig.

'Remember, the rope don't go with the pig,' she said.

'I have the money,' I repeated, checking Mrs. Graham in the act of untying the pig.

'Boy, don't perjure yourself.'

'We waiting.' Mrs. Graham folded her arms. 'We are waiting.' And by the time my grandmother started scolding me again, I had disappeared.

It didn't take me long to cross the forbidden territory; and I was slightly disappointed at how painless it proved (I would have to rethink those Sunday sermons); and when I came back to the yard with my dish of penny, half-penny and farthing coins – as well as a few three and six-penny bits and the odd shilling – at least three of the company asked God to forgive them. My grandmother wouldn't touch it, so I counted it out on the step under the supervision of Mrs. Graham – who wouldn't touch it either. Clearly, I had outdone them.

'What was your bid again?' I asked her.

'I'm not goin' get mix up with no sacrilege.'

'So you not bidding any more?'

'I fear the Lord.'

'So my last bid stand. Two dollars ninepence farthing.' There were no other bids. The pig was mine.

My grandmother never really got over it; and from then on attributed all her aches and pains to the fact that I had broken open the collection boxes to bid for the pig (the fact that pork was unclean, was an additional sin); and when I offered to put the money back in the boxes, *in her presence,* she banished me to the other end of the house, and said she was too old and sick to cope with me, and that I would have to go to live with my mother in the town. Within days, of course, I had acquired a reputation, which I still haven't quite lived down in some quarters; and I have always dated my growing-up from that hard-won afternoon – getting used to winning the pig with a *low* bid; breaking open the collection boxes in a crisis – a thing I couldn't do normally – and finally measuring up to my grandmother's regime, before getting my dishonourable discharge.

Now, there was no house, no grandmother, no Mr. Frederick; no knowledge of the others. All the soil had been washed away from the yard; the skull of the yard only remained. The few trees that were left were stunted and dying; and the pound had been reduced to a vague circle of cedar trees, from the original pegs. It had grown dark. Behind me, the house itself had collapsed like the expiring coalpit; and somehow I began to feel (as I didn't when I was ten) exposed.

She remembered it just in time and panicked; but there must be a way of getting the money there today. Her children were heartless, telling her it wasn't necessary: they had no respect for the dead.

At the Post Office, she went to the wrong end of the counter, and felt a fool when they directed her to the right queue, as if she couldn't read; so she tried to explain. There were a lot of openings but most of them said CLOSED, so she had to join a queue. It embarrassed her that all these Post Offices now had bullet-proof glass shutting out the customer: really, it was offensive to treat people like this: she was almost beginning to feel like a criminal. She thought of Teacher Tudy's Post Office at home where people from the village would come and stand in the yard with their back to the stables (which Tudy had converted to a garage) while their names were read out from the dining-room door. Of course, Mammie never had to stand in the yard; she would either send over Sarah or Franco; or if she didn't think of it, Tudy would put the letters aside, and probably bring them over herself the next night. Queuing behind the bullet-proof glass, Mammie couldn't help feeling that she'd been reduced to standing with her back to Teacher Tudy's stables, waiting for her name to be called out.

When it was at last her turn, she told the boy behind the counter that she wanted to send some money to the West Indies; she wanted to send a hundred dollars home. But the boy pretended he didn't understand what she was saying, and then asked if she wanted to send money ABROAD. She had to correct him and tell him she was sending her money HOME: that's where she was from. She was indignant that first, they treated you like a foreigner, and then they denied you your home. He was just a child, and she wondered why they didn't have anyone bigger who could deal with the customers and understand what they wanted. She wanted to send a hundred dollars home.

'D'you want to send dollars?'

'Yes. Yes. A hundred.'

'One hundred dollars. To the West Indies.'

'To Murial.'

'Yes. Not sure if you can do that, actually. Look, I'll just...'

'And I'm in a hurry.'

He was just moving off, apparently to look for something, and stopped.

'Look, I've just got to check on this, all right?'

'Yes. Go ahead. As long as it gets there in a hurry.'

'You'll have to send it by telegraph in that case. Can you... Just hang on...' He reached under the counter and took out a form. 'I'll just go and check on the rates. If you'll just fill out this meanwhile.' He slipped the form under the bulletproof glass, and told her to fill out both sides.

Mammie took the form and started searching for her glasses. And after all that, the form didn't make sense. It was all to do with people sending money to Bangladesh and Pakistan, and not one word about the West Indies; so the young fellow must have given her the wrong form.

When he came back – with a big book – Mammie returned the form and asked for one for the West Indies; and he said it didn't matter: West Indies was the same as Bangladesh. It was the first time in her life she'd ever heard anyone say that the West Indies, where she was born and grew up and where all her family came from and where her mother and the rest of her relations died and were buried, was the same as Bangladesh, which was somewhere in India, where the people were Indian, and she'd never set foot in her life. But she kept all this to herself, and filled out the form nevertheless.

She put down Murial's name. Murial didn't live in a 'Road or Street'; she lived in the village (she had a lovely house in the village), so Mammie had to leave out that line and go right on to 'Village or Town' and 'Country of Destination' having again left out 'District, State, or Province'. While she was doing this, someone pushed her to one side as if she was a beggar, and took her place; but she wasn't going to argue with any of them.

On the other side of the form, she had to make a decision. Murial wasn't a DEPENDANT, so that took care of that. She was tempted to sign her name under PURPOSE OF PAYMENT, but the money had nothing to do with:

a) for goods imported into the UK up to £50 in value… subject for the possession of an import licence if necessary;

b) of subscriptions and entrance fees to clubs/societies other than for travel services up to £50 per year per club/society;

c) of maintenance payments under Orders of Court;

d) in settlement of commercial and professional debts up to £50 (See paragraph below).

She was sending the money to repair her uncle's headstone and to weed the family plot. As Murial was kind enough to look after her affairs at home, Mammie thought it might upset her if she sent the money as PAYMENT, for Murial wasn't someone she employed, Murial was a friend. So in the end, she entered it under CASH GIFT.

The boy took the form and said she'd have to send it in

pounds, and they could change it at the other end. That was all right. Then he started filling out another form, checking with his book, and showing it to the man working next to him, so that the whole world would soon know her business. Then he looked up and smiled at her, and asked if it was urgent.

The boy was a fool; she had already told him it was urgent.

'Then, that'll be… fifty four pounds fifty, plus three and seven twenty. That would be… fifty five pounds twenty. OK?'

He was crazy. She had thirty pounds, which was plenty. He was joking. 'You joking?'

'Sorry…?'

'Last time it cost only twenty four. Or twenty three.'

Then he said something that she didn't really follow. So she asked him to repeat it, because then he'd surely find out his mistake.

He was treating her like a child now. 'That'll be forty five pounds fifty for the hundred dollars. And there's THREE POUNDS charge for sending it urgently. You want it urgent, don't you…'

'Yes. Yes.'

'… and then there's the message, and that's going to cost you another…'

'Cut it out. Cut out the message.' The message wasn't important.

The message itself was all right, the message was free. But…

Mammie wanted the message out.

He read as he crossed it out 'THIS IS TO WEED THE HEADSTONES.'

'Not headstones. To weed the *graves.*'

'Yes, well it don't matter now, I've crossed…'

'It *does* matter. I'm not illiterate. You can't weed the headstones, you repair them.'

'It doesn't cost any more; it's the address that's expensive. Look, do you have to send it... It'd be cheaper by *telegraph letter*'.

'Will it get there today?'

His friend, working next to him made a comment and laughed, but the young lad himself didn't laugh. He came very close to the glass and she didn't like his look.

'It'll get there in a few days. I mean, it's not exactly *urgent,* is it?'

'All right, all right.'

'You'll send it the cheaper way?'

'It's all right, I'll go to another post office.' This time he was very rude.

'It didn't cost so much last time.' Mammie wasn't going to be defeated. But by then, he was dealing with another customer, complaining.

She was too busy to go to the other post office now; she had to go home to put on the dinner, in case anyone dropped by; she had to look after the living as well as the dead, *the quick and the dead*, she smiled to herself. The joke pleased her. It occurred to her then that at the post office she had just said 'dollars' to the young lad; she didn't specify West Indian dollars which were only about four shillings and twopence, which would be less than twenty five pence in the new money (at least, that's what it was in the old days). Last year, it had only cost her twenty four pounds to send the money to Murial. At the other post office. This year, she was prepared to allow for another four pounds for inflation and for telegraphing it... Unless the boy was talking about some other dollar; but he must know she was West Indian, even though he wasn't qualified to work behind the bullet-proof glass. But what could she do; she was tired: her family would have to wait another day, choking in grass.

A CONTINENTAL ROMANCE

Years later it was agreed: she murdered him in Spéracèdes and claimed the ticket. It was on a sunny day, just after the *vendange* and everyone was happy, if tired. There was to be a big feast in the village that night. The tourists would see the dead man as a sort of sacrifice to the grapes, but the locals took things in their stride: they had no thirst for mystery, for symbolism; they sought confirmation, only, that things were as they were. The man's name was Philpot, murdered by... well, in the presence of his wife, who inherited the ticket. The long trek south had had an effect on her; she was a bit confused about the sequence of events, but this worked to her advantage and earned her the authority of widowhood. She had paid her bride-price by having walked from London to the Alpes Maritimes; walked, yes, that's how she thought of it. She felt better for being the worse for it (we don't know this, but never mind). Her new neighbours then gathered round her outside Georges's café where it had all happened (some, admittedly, at a respectful distance) and assured her of eventual vindication, should rumours be put about. Then they advised her to rest before the feast.

'I'm not what you think,' Philpot had said on wooing her... (Perhaps her predecessor, perhaps her contemporary, difficult to sort out). He threw it out like bait, in a lake known to be swarming, to tempt any passing fish. This was in the din and bustle of Paddington Station, so naturally he couldn't be sure if the catch would be to his liking. Having grown indiscriminate of late, he was again anxious to salvage a little pride. (The bait, held casually in his hand, was a wife's train ticket to the South of France.) Perhaps to mask his uneasiness, he became somewhat rhetorical – this verbally inarticulate man – striking attitudes of self-aggrandisement, of self-pity. His environment was against him, he explained to all of a human curiosity, but his had been a life with memories, memories that would endure the retirement. He had fished, he'd have them know, in better seas.

The passing wife (water-current detectors functioning like a fish who had often nibbled and got away with it – absent gill-slit, damaged oesophagus notwithstanding) was confident of being pulled along by this particular line, without further danger to herself.

Philpot was conscious of his retiring-&-taking-up-fishing status, waiting on Paddington station for a wife to accompany him to the South of France. He was a philanthropist, a benefactor. He had already, unilaterally, conferred on all possible catch, the dignity of warm-blooded womanhood. In case too many be tempted, he decided not to reveal the existence of the villa in Spéracèdes till the wife showed that she was worthy, had mended the ways of a lifetime, and could present in retirement, a youthful, new Mediterranean version of herself.

His confidence growing, he boarded the train early – he would not be trifled with by a missing wife – and looked down from a First Class window on the approaching hopefuls. He was not anxious, he was merely wondering if the creature would be a woman of imagination, able to rise to the occasion, to match his risk: would she be wearing a rosette? Carrying a book? Ah, let *her* sort it out. Let her come and identify him. He would approach no more wives in his retirement. It was a matter of dignity.

He was alone with the person opposite – she had dispatched her cuckold to the bar for a coke: he liked her style – he told her what was on his mind. She was enigmatic, as if she already knew. He told her he would approach no more wives for his retirement. He would merely lay his assets, as it were, as now, on the convenient table between them. 'You will not have been humiliated by me,' he reasoned. And she seemed to perk up, alert but unconvinced. She was the sort of wife to whom he could later say, 'Wrap this rag of a life round your... *cough cough, wink wink* self.' Naturally, he would say *that* only when they were well south; clear of England, in a strange place where he wouldn't be thought of as being a sad case on the run.

The guard interrupted them. Philpot gave the guard his wife's ticket instead of his own, to show the (comparatively empty) compartment that a sense of *play,* of finesse, would survive the single-minded literalness of a train journey. The lady took note and went one further, offering her two tickets to the guard: they were hers and hers alone, she said. She just wished to create some *space* round herself, when she travelled. The fellow took it in his stride and punched both her tickets without comment, versed in the ways of the travelling aristocracy.

Then she was frank with Philpot: he was wrong about her; she loved her husband. Cuckolding him hadn't been easy for her. (So, she'd been reading his thoughts: surely, he hadn't been thinking aloud!) No, it was something... something she had to work at. Mostly, indeed, she found it a little tedious. But the memories that survived, well, they had to be checked out for their accuracy.

He could capitalise on his luck and transform her into a figure of legend – the lady of three tickets who drove men to distraction (and exhaustion) on the London-Dover line. Or he could demand more for his ticket. Fight a battle. Kill two rivals. He was prepared for that. In his bag was a used bush-jacket; and the revolutionary phrase, which he now had off by heart in seven languages, would assure press coverage.

But the cuckold returned from the bar with coke and rolls, and cringed at the lady's side, violating her space. It was clear that she expected Philpot to intervene, but it pleased him to see this as an opportunity deliberately lost, and her small cloud of disapproval soon passed to admiration.

*

Crossing Paris is never a good idea, with an extra ticket. From the *Gare du Nord* to the *Gare de Lyon,* a man needs a companion to blame for his loss of sanity. Without one, he feels cheated, foreign. Philpot had visions of being mugged for his ticket: there were predators everywhere who ought never to have been released from their film sets. But it was all in vain; when he emerged unmolested, he felt undervalued. What was the point in this life, of having an extra ticket?

Another wife unknown to him, who had eluded him on Paddington Station, still dangled at the end of his now imaginary line; and, indeed, she too gave up the foolish pretence of being a fish; but she remained out of sight, confident (we like to think).

Ignorant of all this; Philpot amused himself. He gave himself up to the old fantasy of travellers southbound: *it is cold and wet in Paris. Seven or eight o'clock in the evening. Dark. You are in the North. On this trip south, it will happen. Walking to your couchette, you glimpse through a gently closing door, a bare arm settling down between white sheets. You approach your own couchette in anticipation...* Ah, yes, your train romance will yet be written. Next morning, you begin to wake up to painterly skies, tropical light, the Mediterranean. You look for palm trees and find instead beautiful people getting off in twos and threes at little stations along the way, filmic. And one of the beautiful people is on your arm, leading you to a pavement café across the road – traffic on the right and all that. *Soleil ou l'ombre?* the patron asks, offering two types of table. Philpot would, of course, go native with a *pastis* and order a glass of red wine for the lady.

And they weren't even in Spéracèdes yet!

When he got to Spéracèdes, Philpot took a table outside Georges's café – a mini-attraction now that Georges had blown his brains out – and waited (back turned to Peymeinade, to Cannes; he was not a tourist) to be approached by his lady of taste and breeding.

She came eventually, carrying a copy of *Nice Matin* (the rosette? the book? Ah, very good) and, as if trying to establish an alibi, insisted on giving a full account of her trip. Philpot ordered a glass of wine to silence her.

Ignoring the wine, she continued with the evidence, of the trip to Dover in a lorry, a shuddering monster that was alive, obscene, undignified to climb in and out of; then the green bus at Dover, green bus to the Ferry; and of getting her way in France, speaking French when they wanted her to do otherwise; and the impossibility of getting a lift out of Calais (when, eventually, she got one it was *into* Calais, as she had been stranded, unknowing, at the docks) as she sent the potential rapists packing; and of having to spend the night at Boulogne – a long, long story; and being picked up the next day by a Martiniquen, well into the afternoon, on his way to Rouen. He drove her out of Rouen and onto the Paris road and made a sign saying PARIS, which you couldn't read from more than three yards; though a young chap who liked older women and was going to Dijon managed to read it somehow; and it was, she said, so far to Dijon.

In the café, in Spéracèdes, regulars drank to the memory of Georges, and from the thirst of the *vendange;* and to the two widows who had lost their husbands on this very day two years running, and paid no attention to Philpot and his wife.

Philpot sat sipping, imagining her floundering, drowning in wine; but she spurted like a whale, in her element. The young chap, you know, the one to Dijon, woke her up in the middle of the night and asked if she wanted to use the bathroom. They had stopped at a service station and afterwards she declined the restaurant because the bathroom had upset her, embarrassed her: it had obviously been built by a man who wanted to humiliate women. And after Dijon? She couldn't remember...she remembered a room for the night. Next morning, a street corner, a sign saying LYON more legibly than the PARIS sign had said PARIS. Then a lift into a field of sweetcorn. Yes, just for that, the corn; he was weird. Then there was the Nazi who picked her up and put her down in the middle of the *Autoroute* when he discovered her opinions; but she was not armed, she had to let him go. She had no idea where she was then, till the signs for Avignon started coming up; and then Aix, and she knew she was getting warm. Nice and Cannes made her think of yachts and wine; Grasse, of perfume. At Grasse, they told her of Georges's café in Spéracèdes, of Georges who had blown his brains out, and of the sadist who awaited her with a spare ticket.

She had not yet drunk the wine nor paid any attention to the ticket, which Philpot put, casually, on the table. So, always seeking to maintain his reputation for nonchalance, for finesse (they were in *Midi* country, after all); to show that he was not a literal fellow, or worse, an old man in a hurry, Philpot casually put the ticket in his mouth and ate it. We will never know what his thoughts were; all we know (for the eye-witnesses saw nothing) from people who weren't there, is that *something happened* when the lady tried to recover her ticket.

Did she kill him? Ah, well, it was the day of the *vendange*, and a few are expected to die about then. It's a good omen, it helps the grapes. That he died then, there and in that way, was taken as a sign – a little one, like Georges's suicide – that the village was not entirely forgotten by its gods; nor did it have to bastardise itself (like St. Tropez with its breasts or Cannes with its Film Festival nonsense) to be authentic.

And the lady?

It is said that she settled down in Spéracèdes, happily, for ever.

I disdained the apron; I could keep myself clean. Wooden spoon poised, I prepared to savage the eggs. They were in my power, shell-less eggs in a bowl; in a few minutes, I would turn them into cake. I fancied – and you could see them shift, quiver at the thought – I fancied I could reassemble them, put them back in their respective shells by the sheer power of thought, the sort of power I'd always recruited whenever Simon threatened. Tonight, he would come to dinner. Tonight he would eat cake.

I first met him on a train. I was aware of his voice before I encountered him. That was a good few years ago coming back from, I think, France. We had been stuck at Dover for hours, on the train. It was summer, over-crowded and uncomfortable – and I awaited the eruption.

But people were patient. It was their, *our* acceptance of this state of affairs that was beginning to annoy me. There was no apology for the delay; and the buzzing nearby of a party of school-children was beginning to be irritating. They upset my concentration more by the *tone* – the glimpsed uniforms – than by the volume of their noise. The result was I couldn't read.

Then Simon spoke: a clear, ringing, young-English voice, which I immediately baptised. Making him wear my label for a name was small compensation for my discomfort and this time I settled back determined to read. Simon's voice still rang with confidence, intermittently, but I paid little attention to it now as it explored familiar in-jokes and recalled certain recent battles with the retreating French. I felt for the young girl of a teacher accompanying them, that's all.

Then he turned to the subject on our minds. 'I know why this train is late.' I marvelled at his confidence, his refusal to anticipate comment. It was late, he said, because it was a holiday train, filled with foreigners: they didn't really expect *us,* did they, to put on our best trains, just to make the foreigners comfortable and take them up to London? He, of course, if pressed, would suffer for the cause and grow grey at Dover.

I was pleased I had called him Simon; pleased I had discovered his name.

There was no argument; there was a silence, which I interpreted as assent. On earlier points, dubious points about the *Louvre,* about whether it was possible for cows to sleep lying down, Simon had been challenged by his companions; but not on this one. I didn't want my feelings to harden; I didn't wish to meet the eye of the silenced teacher. So, I was grateful when the train lurched forward, stopped abruptly, and managed to get going second time round with its foreign cargo.

Best to forget about, indeed, to *forget* Simon.

'Why six chops?' Lindsay asked, as I turned my attention to the main part of the meal, the cake safely in the oven. (Lindsay was what is described as the woman in my life. I was thinking how much more difficult it was to reassemble eggs once they had started to harden into cake.)

'Why six?'

'He might bring a friend. Simon might.'

'You're mad.' (Simon's girl-friend would be a threat to her. Obvious, really.)

'Or he might demand seconds.'

'Seriously, did you invite someone?'

It was an old routine. She knew that Simon was granted an open invitation and would descend on us when we least expected it. I liked that; it kept me in readiness, mental readiness. He might turn up at meal-time, but he was perverse: he might refuse the meal and accept the company instead. Lindsay was good company, would be excellent company tonight. Simon would like her. Of course, we had to cover ourselves and get hold of a short-term, short-order couple of dinner-guests to set us off to advantage should Simon be there; and to wreak retribution on if he wasn't. With Simon imminent, I felt like an incumbent president being challenged by a member of his own party – relishing the opportunity to pull rank.

Lindsay was pleasantly unvindictive (maybe she had proved all the points worth proving between us) and played her part. We were a team. As I was still occupied with preparing the meal, she went to the telephone to short-order a couple of dinner-guests.

They were in plentiful supply. Lindsay soon fixed it up. The short-order dinner-guests were on their way. They sounded right for the occasion: pronounceable names, easy telephone manner, bland and faceless. From the short telephone-interview, we concluded they were probably a librarian and a teacher, or a spy and an ex-prime minister or a piece of India rubber and a dog. At any rate, they claimed to be *Guardian* readers, experienced, and on their way over.

Naturally, we had pangs *(pangs* in my mind rhymes with *fangs,* and that suggests *prongs,* convertible to fish-hooks… but we, too, were experienced; conscience didn't prick much). Shouldn't we have been truer to populist tradition and gone out on a deserted side-street, in Manchester, say, and invited a fascist and a killer in to share our meal? Too late, too late…

The table was set for five; a place for Simon.

Dinner was at eight and the short-order dinner-guests

were depressingly on time, so we sat down to eat. (I don't wish to linger over that part of the evening. Maybe it wasn't even at eight that we sat down. However…) There we were, the four of us. No Simon. Inevitably, the history of the empty plate had to be told. I decided, as was my custom on these occasions, to lighten the mood, to exaggerate into harmlessness.

I told of a view of Simon as seen from East Finchley. I had got off the train there one evening, on my way to visit a poet (the short-order dinner-male also had a poet-story to tell, but I wouldn't let him, I pressed on). I had got off the train – sorry, not at East Finchley but at Finchley Central – and Simon was about to get on. The doors closed on them – he and his friend, a boy in school-uniform. And it was the same clear, ringing voice that demanded that they open up.

That's how I recognised him, though he was younger at Finchley than he had been at Dover some years previously. (Clever how he did that. But then, I had my ability to reassemble broken eggs. I was clever too.) Simon and his friend had approached the train in a sort of pantomime run, no real sense of urgency. So his, 'Come on. Open up.' was authentic. There was no visible guard for him to vent his irritation on; but I saw his expression, and we silently declared war on each other – to be resumed at our convenience.

One of the short-order dinner-guests now insisted on telling a train-story and we decided to let her do it rather than fight – though this meant that the *immediacy* of my Simon build-up was lost. So, when I later picked it up, it was as if recalling incidents from the distant past that no longer threatened me. It was almost like slipping into the third person without admitting it. I heard myself recount three or four other Simon incidents/escapades; I spoke of my decision to control or rig the final confrontation by having it on my patch, etc. They all agreed that a twelve-year old defeated by the Finchley Central tube would be a formidable prospect. I set out my plan to wine him, serve mushrooms done in a special way, and trap him with the suppressed sensuality of Lindsay, lost tonight on the short-order dinner-guests.

The short-order dinner-guests were dinner-trained; they asked to know more about Simon. And I humoured them, telling them, incidentally, the truth that he had once written to me – under the guise of writing to a certain newspaper – complaining about the inaccuracy of my report. (I had related, around this very table, an incident involving him, and he clearly wanted to demonstrate his ability, from a far continent, to crack the secret code of my house).

Our short-order dinner-guests were, as I have said, dinner-trained. They didn't *really* want to know about Simon, except in so far as he facilitated such conversation as would bridge MUSHROOM WINE CAKE and again WINE.

We had reached the part of the meal, which I'm sure Simon would call the 'mock literacy' course. Speculating on the identity of Simon, one short-order dinner-guest fancied him to be, at some point, Ossie Clarke who had designed her dress. After my comment, we had him progressing from designing clothes to fermenting Revolution in the – was it Sudan?

1970: with wife and Percy to make Hockney famous.

1971: (July 19th, to be exact) Failed coup in the Sudan.

Again in 1976 (July 2nd, wasn't it?).

And not forgetting April 7th of this year!

The question was, would Simon associate himself with so much failure (and don't forget the train-doors at Finchley!). Was one gratuitous Art success enough for such a national treasure?

We weren't close enough to display ourselves mentally naked longer than we could help it, even in the consenting atmosphere of a house, so we steered the conversation back to the vanished lamb-chops, to the butcher (not the lamb) who had produced the chops. He had, I remember, been theatrically bloody: was that why we called him a good butcher? I thought of Simon and observed that bloodiness or otherwise of the woman's coat (of course, the butcher was a man but the short-order dinner-guests deserved this) was a thing of artistic rather than culinary interest. (I invoked my unfinished, abandoned PhD thesis proving a similar point: that writers with eyes very close together – and that included the fellow in South Germany who had them both, fishlike, on the same side of his nose – presented us in the last resort with a challenge which was *aesthetic* rather than geopolitical or praecocial!)

We had all but manipulated the meal when the doorbell rang. We went through the ritual of being expectant or apprehensive; but it wasn't of course, Simon, for we were living this little scene outside a novel. It was someone who had dropped by to see the previous occupant of the house. She apologised. *We* apologised. The last occupant had left nine years before. The newcomer spoke briefly of death, the Arctic and Ursa Major, and said goodbye, pushing a shopping-trolley into the night... All in all it was a good, if incomplete evening and the short-order dinner-guests left saying it was better than they had expected.

She had left a glove behind; he had left the car-keys. (Naturally, we played with the idea that the glove was his, the car-keys hers; but the hand that Lindsay had felt on her body during dinner, was larger than the glove.) I was not particularly uneasy at having this *plant* in the house, but it seemed insensitive not to make something of it; so I decided to return the props to their rightful owners.

There was no car in the street with an owner trying to break in, so I decided to deliver the evidence to the short-order dinner-guests' address: if what they said during dinner was accurate, it was only about a mile to walk (this was England: it paralleled Simon's desert march from the armies of Mohamed al-Numary to those of Colonial Joseph Largue).

The short-order dinner-guests were not appreciative. They accepted the glove and car-keys with resignation.

At home, Lindsay had gone to bed and locked the door. She was crying. No, she was not crying. She did it very well. I hadn't thought she'd be so expert without me. Her attention to detail was astonishing. She was aping me. She – in between her own cries – imitated the sound, the urgency of my voice. She didn't get that entirely right but it was impressive nevertheless. Then she spat a name, which made me realise that she knew I was listening.

Afterwards – there was a lot of clearing up to do – I read a little Henry James, tired of this and turned to an old paper to see if Clive James would be funnier. I wasn't in the mood for intellectual rigour but I tried to be tidy in my browsing, sticking to the Jameses on my shelf. Joyce rated a few lines. CLR James, John James and James James occupied a few seconds. James Purdy I missed out, my not discovering him till next day. Mr. James's *The Haunted Doll's House* was said to be an 'uncanny tale'. I read the odd word towards the end and moved on. When next we have guests, of course, in recounting it, I'll upgrade one of these names to James Ngugi. Followed by Pablo Neruda James and James Muhammad Ali. But that night I made do with the Jameses on my shelf.

When Lindsay emerged, with the whiff of a stranger from her body, she made a small request. It was a service, that I habitually performed for her after our private scene of contentment; and I naturally complied. Already she was yielding. She was ready to tease.

'I'm sorry you missed Simon,' she said.

Also by E.A. Markham from Peepal Tree

MARKING TIME

Pewter Stapleton is drowning under a pile of marking. He teaches creative writing at a university in Sheffield, a campus peopled with malign cost-cutting accountants, baffled security staff and colleagues cloning themselves.

Pewter is a brilliant comic creation, an endless lister of tasks which are never quite completed, who is strung forever between seriousness and send-up, a commitment to his writing and boundless cynicism about writers and the arts industry.

From Pewter's desk the novel radiates backwards and forwards in time, to his childhood in the small volcanic Caribbean island of St. Caesare and to his relationships with Carrington, a successful Caribbean writer whose plays Pewter is editing, to Balham, a professional of the race industry (where Pewter is a self-admitted slow learner in blackness) and to Lee, the woman he loves, but who despairs of him as 'sporadic'.

As a novel about life and writing, factuality and invention rub shoulders to hilarious effect as Pewter is incessantly driven to turn his experiences, his friends and their experiences, into works of drama and fiction.

1-900715-29-5
Fiction 262pp £7.99